bamboo ridge

No. 118

JOURNAL OF HAWAI'I LITERATURE AND ARTS

ISBN 978-1-943756-04-9
This is issue #118 of *Bamboo Ridge, Journal of Hawai'i Literature and Arts*
(ISSN 0733-0308)

Copyright ©2020 by Bamboo Ridge Press
All rights reserved. This book, or parts thereof, may not be reproduced in any form without permission.

Published by Bamboo Ridge Press
Printed in the United States of America

Bamboo Ridge Press is a member of the Community of Literary Magazines and Presses (CLMP).

Founding Editors: Eric Chock and Darrell H. Y. Lum
Guest Editors: Juliet S. Kono and Jean Yamasaki Toyama
Managing Editor: Joy Kobayashi-Cintrón
Copyeditors: Normie Salvador and Gail N. Harada
Business Manager: Wing Tek Lum

Typesetting and design: Jui-Lien Sanderson
Cover art: *Memories of Oscar* by Jui-Lien Sanderson, oil on canvas, 20" x 16"
All photos courtesy of artist

Bamboo Ridge Press is a nonprofit, tax-exempt corporation formed in 1978 to foster the appreciation, understanding, and creation of literary, visual, and performing arts by, for, or about Hawai'i's people. The organization is funded by book sales and individual donors and supplemented in part by support from the National Endowment for the Arts (NEA); the Hawai'i State Foundation on Culture and the Arts (through appropriations from the Legislature of the State of Hawai'i and grants from the NEA); the Hawai'i Council for the Humanities; and the Hawai'i Community Foundation. This publication was made possible with direct support from the National Endowment for the Arts and the Hawai'i Literary Arts Council.

Bamboo Ridge is published twice a year. For subscription information, back issues, or to purchase books, please contact:

Bamboo Ridge Press
P.O. Box 61781
Honolulu, Hawai'i 96839-1781
808.626.1481
www.bambooridge.org

Bamboo Ridge Press gratefully acknowledges generous donations from the following individuals and organizations in 2019:

Carol Abe
Nancy Aleck
Robert Alm
Amazon Smile
Anonymous (13)
Alakaʻi Antonio
Esther Arinaga
Ann Asakura
Kathryn Au
Cristina Bacchilega
Doreen E. Beyer
Richard Bibeau
Marlene Booth
Cliff Burigsay
The Cades Foundation
Karleen Chinen
Jodie Chiemi Ching
Eric Chock
Ghislaine Chock
Marytina Choy
Jayson Chun
Sandra Chun
Renee Chung
Xander Cintrón-Chai
Rhoda Cleek
Sara L. Collins
E. Shan Correa
Rebecca L. Covert
Sue Cowing
Cathy Song Davenport
Kay Emocling
Deanna Espinas
Foodland Super Market, Limited
Carol A. Fukunaga
Claire Gearen
John Hara
Marie M. Hara
Mavis Hara
Gail N. Harada
Jennifer Hasegawa
Hawaiʻi Community Foundation
Hawaiʻi Council for the Humanities
Hawaiʻi State Foundation on Culture and the Arts
Leonore Higa
Ann Higashi
Peter Ho
Victoria Ho

Craig Howes
Ann Inoshita
Island Insurance Foundation
Maureen Izon
Lisa Linn Kanae
Nora Keller
Scott K. Kikkawa
Nelli Kim
Milton B. Kimura
Joy Kobayashi-Cintrón
Brenda Kwon
Terry Lau
Elsa Lee
Juliet Kono Lee
Lanning C. Lee
Spencer Lee
Denis Leong
Diantha Leong
Jeffrey T. Leong
Peter C.T. Li
Iris Lim
Rinehardt Z. Linmark
Jan Luke Loo
Jackson Luckett
Anna T. Lum
Chee Ping Lum
Darrell H. Y. Lum
Eric Lum
Eydie Lum
Mae Lum
Tan Tek Lum
Wing Tek Lum
Marion Lyman-Mersereau
Jere Masumoto
Gordon Mau
Deborah Morikawa
Lillian Nakamura
Marc Nakamura
Liela Nitta
Ethel Aiko Oda
Carol Ohta
Claire Onizuka
Marcus Oshiro
Benjamin Padua
Louise Pagotto
Elaine Pahio
Harry Palmer
Anne Parkinson
Christy Passion
Patrick Patterson

John Reider
Mylene Reyes
Judy Sadoyama
Lei Ann Saito
Russell Saito
Kent Sakoda
Electa Sam
Marc Sanabre
Jui-lien Sanderson
Kathleen Sato
Suzanne Sato
June Shimoda
Stanley Shimoda
John Simonds
Davis Siu
Lara Siu
Michelle Cruz Skinner
Smithsonian Institution
Aviam Soifer
John Soong, Jr.
Susan Soong
Sidney Stern Memorial Trust
Monica Sullivan
Gary Tachiyama
Hazel H. Takumi Foundation
Bob Tam
Liane Tam
Noe Tanigawa
Virginia Tanji
Ken Tokuno
Lee Tonouchi
Dennis Toyama
Jean Yamasaki Toyama
Scott Turn
Keith Usher
Amy L. Uyematsu
Ruth Watabayashi
Chiye R. Wenkam
Western Union
Sylvia Wilmeth
Mark K. Wilson III
Beverly Wong
Eileen Wong
Liane Yajima
Loretta Yajima
Tiffany Yajima
Tyler Yajima
Lois-Ann Yamanaka
Charlie Yamamoto

CONTENTS

IN MEMORIAM
Marion Lyman-Mersereau
    11   Joe Tsujimoto
Joe Tsujimoto
    14   Reading by Window Light, February 14
Wing Tek Lum
    15   Marie Hara
Nora Okja Keller
    17   Reflections on Marie, shared at her memorial
Marie Hara
    18   When I Am a Ghost

EDITORS' CHOICE AWARDS
Poetry – **Christy Passion**
    20   A Letter to My Father
    21   Fires
    22   It's My Fault
    23   A Kind of Sacrament
    24   Storyteller
    25   Rorschach Test (upon viewing a photo of a vine)

Prose – **Michael Puleloa**
    26   Man Underwater

New to Bamboo Ridge – **Cavan Reed Scanlan**
    37   Custard
    42   (h)improvi(d)sing
    44   Kukui Gardens
    46   Speaking in Tongues

ARTIST PROFILE AND PORTFOLIO – Jui-Lien Sanderson
Jean Yamasaki Toyama
    49   Floating in the Ocean

Dana Anderson
    59   Ahupuaʻa
Sally-Jo Keala-o-Ānuenue Bowman
    60   Namings
Carol Catanzariti
    62   Make the Night Sleep
Jacey Choy
    63   Winter
    64   What You Won't Remember
Brian Chun-Ming
    65   Hidden History
    66   We Sat Quietly
April Melia Coloretti
    67   Ice
Earl Cooper
    68   Fruit Brothers Aria
Sue Cowing
    69   Our Plumeria
    69   Time in Cahokia, A Circle of Cedar
    70   The Tao of Forgetting
    71   Allspice
Brian Cronwall
    72   Hiking Above Kahana Bay
Diane DeCillis
    74   The Art of Kintsugi
Kathleen DeSaye
    76   The Nightmare
Elena Savaiinaea Farden
    84   The Ocean Is Medicine
Tom Gammarino
    85   Futures Studies
Caroline A. Garrett
    97   Magnitude
Bora Hah
    98   A Free Life
William Hanson
    103   Hawaiian Hall, Bishop Museum, Honolulu
    104   Draft Board Number 2, Downtown Honolulu, Anno 1971
    105   Temple of Puʻukoholā
Jeffrey Hantover
    106   Goethe in Honokaʻa

Mavis Hara
    107   A Fish Story
Gail N. Harada
    112   At Keahualaka
    113   Gaman Trilogy
Joseph Hardy
    119   Tinnitus
Jennifer Hasegawa
    121   Ode to Pepeʻekeo Mill Camp
    122   Two-Minute Memoir
Ann Inoshita
    124   Famolare
    124   Stickers and Happy Face Stamp
    126   Waipahu Rain
Scott Kikkawa
    127   Excerpt from *Red Dirt*
Maya Kikuchi
    139   Pacific
Brenda Kwon
    140   Refuge
Kapena M. Landgraf
    142   Maka
Lanning C. Lee
    143   False Wiliwili
Lenny Levine
    155   Autocorrect
Virginia Loo
    161   Women's Work
    164   The Argument
    165   Pavarti Picks Her Battles
    166   What Goes Around
Darrell H. Y. Lum
    168   Comfort Chicken
Aʻala Lyman
    169   Death
    169   Fear
    170   Grief
Marion Lyman-Mersereau
    171   Lei Conservation
    172   For a Good While
    173   Just Clouds

Jennifer Santos Madriaga
    175   Obscuring
    176   Banished/Vanished

Marcia Zina Mager
    177   Epitaph
    178   Entrance

Carrie Frances Martin
    179   Hāmākua Coast

Rick McKenzie
    181   1967

Tyler Miranda
    182   The Wretch of Makakilo: On Family
    183   The Wretch of Makakilo: On Diversity
    185   Flip the Bird

Tamara Leiokanoe Moan
    187   Ka'ena

Dawn Morais
    189   Shenandoah

Susan Miho Nunes
    191   The Walking Lady

Claire Oasa
    204   Najuma
    209   Wild Pigs at Night
    210   Walk Always

Derek N. Otsuji
    212   A Pair of White Terns

Kathy J. Phillips
    214   By Lantern Light

Anthony Russo
    216   Kid Ross

Mia Sara
    224   Vocabulary

Stuart Jay Silverman
    225   The Channel at Mā'alaea
    226   Crossing The Caldera

John E. Simonds
    228   The Looking Glass

Cathy Song
    230   The Short Sweet Flight
    232   The Tree of Life

Eric Stinton
    234   The Weight of Departure

Shelley Stocksdale
    238   Six Ways of Catching Fish in China
Coralyn Sunico
    239   Kumon
Samantha Tetangco
    241   Rice Street Haibun
    242   Portrait of a Filipina on Her 37th Birthday
Delaina Thomas
    243   Day Before Obon
Ken Tokuno
    247   Pianissimo Finale
Julie Ushio
    257   Cross Words
Amy Uyematsu
    264   Little Tokyo Haiku, 2019
    265   Dazzling
J. Fumiko Wong
    266   The Passage
Lois-Ann Yamanaka
    268   Cat Hater, Cat Lover

BAMBOO SHOOTS

Doreen E. Beyer
    271   Memories of Home
    272   Newell's Shearwater
    273   Whisper
Lanning C. Lee
    274   Midwest Aloha
Vanessa Lee-Miller
    275   Kāloa Pau: Notes From a Fisherman's Diary
Darrell H. Y. Lum
    276   Boy and Uncle: Valentine's Day
    276   Silence

AFTERWORD – A Bamboo Ridge Press Legacy
Wing Tek Lum
    277   Preserving *Bamboo Ridge*

    280   CONTRIBUTORS

FROM THE EDITORS

Reading through over two hundred fifty submissions for *Bamboo Ridge* Issue #118 was a near-Sisyphean task. We read many pieces several times over, discussing the pros and cons before making our final selections. To be sure, our choices are not the result of some exact science, but often guided by our own personal likes or dislikes, our own understanding of language and its usage. However, we tried to be judicious through the give-and-take of our dialogue in our consideration of the material that came from Hawai'i, across the states, and as far away as Norway. We believe to have done a fair job with results that you will enjoy.

This anthology celebrates the forty-second year of Bamboo Ridge Press publications with writing from almost seventy diverse contributors, about a third of them new to our pages. We are pleased to feature artwork by Jui-Lien Sanderson and Editors' Choice Award Winners Christy Passion for poetry, Michael Puleloa for prose, and Cavan Reed Scanlan, who is new to *Bamboo Ridge*—all chosen for their interesting characters and portrayal of the redeeming qualities of love despite the hardships found in life.

On a sad note, last year recorded the deaths of two of Bamboo Ridge's greatest friends and supporters. While mourning the deaths of Marie Hara and Joe Tsujimoto, we are inspired by their creativity and their vision of a thriving literary culture in Hawai'i. Both were extraordinary writers whose work will continue to inform, inspire, and entertain readers. This legacy has been assured by the creation of the Bamboo Ridge Press digital archive that includes their work and those of other writers who have endeavored to keep Hawai'i, past and present, alive in their writing. (For further information on public access to digital files of our publications, turn to Wing Tek Lum's essay "Preserving *Bamboo Ridge*", the final piece of this issue.)

As a tribute to the work and lives of Marie and Joe, we wish to share the following eulogies and poems in their memory.

—Juliet S. Kono and Jean Yamasaki Toyama, Editors

IN MEMORIAM

Marion Lyman-Mersereau
JOE TSUJIMOTO

Joe was my working husband for several years—our classrooms were adjacent to each other and we collaborated on a few units. He had a class read the play and watch the film *Twelve Angry Men* when I taught the judicial branch. He taught *Inherit the Wind* when I taught the world religion unit, and *Romeo and Juliet* during the sexuality unit. We worked together seamlessly.

Joe was a writing mentor of mine and taught me how to not procrastinate with grading. He was always the first teacher in the middle school to finish his report card comments and we teased him saying it was because all he had to read were two-word poems where the writer juxtaposes two nouns making an original connection . . . his favorite being *bra – hammock*.

Joe had countless poems and short stories published in Bamboo Ridge anthologies. Bamboo Ridge also published his last book—*Morningside Heights: New York Stories*. Joe's second book was *Lighting Fires: How the Passionate Teacher Engages Adolescent Writers*. In the introduction to his first and widely used book, *Teaching Poetry Writing to Adolescents*, published by the National Council for Teachers of English in 1988, Joe recalls his adolescent years that informed him as a teacher. He writes:

More than twenty years later, I relived my hopes, sentiments, and anxieties through my students' eyes, and realized what I have been doing with them is right.

And what have I done? Nothing very much. Nor anything very new. As artists do to themselves, I merely encouraged them to transform their "handicaps"—their feelings of being odd—into virtues. Of course, I didn't mention handicaps or feelings of being odd. Instead I talked about originality. I said that in writing or painting or dance, originality is the one thing that distinguishes a work from another and determines its worth; that originality is the one thing that sets them off as the individual human beings that they are. As I think back, nothing appealed to me more than the teacher challenging my creativity. Boy, I was going to do something that no one had ever done and make buildings tremble. That kind of confidence is assumed by youth, when their imaginations are fired. Nothing is beyond their reach. Few truly important things are.

Joe also taught me to be brief so now I shall share the poem I wrote for his retirement.

Marion Lyman-Mersereau

Your first piece of advice to young writers
was "to remember and invent"
and all who sat in your class
every student
remembers your constant comment
or was it a question?
It seems it was always said with aggression
"Capisce!" was an imperative from you
and each class would respond
not knowing
It's what you most wanted them to do
Capisce! Understand!
Understand the power of words
the influence of utterance
that has depth and substance
Understand the power of words to explore
to underscore meaning with sound
Understand the power of words
that incline the mind
so it can communicate—
You told them to create
then be bold enough to share their work
since you were never one to shirk
your own devotion to the Muse
You would cajole, sometimes abuse them
without mercy, with vicious
yet never malicious tenacity
knowing each one had the capacity
within them to be original
You commanded,
"Emphasize your lip movement!"
yet it would be an improvement
to simply state
"Enunciate!"
but you always liked to do
things your own way
You lit fires inspired by your own passion
and many have become published—
have won, like you, writing accolades

Marion Lyman-Mersereau

Your influence has broken down barricades
that block adolescent expression
Most teens have no clue
but you made sure yours do
They learned they have the ability
they have the facility
to dive deeply into the ocean
of complex emotions
that surround their stormy lives
One of your mentors
Joseph Heller
gave you a Catch-22 view of life
and your tough-guy exterior
gave you that superior
New York City attitude
where seeming rude
wasn't because you were in a mood–
it's just the way you were
Your rough, abrupt manner
always fooled kids and adults alike
until they saw your interior—more like Jell-O
no sweeter, softer—like marshmallow
You said we teach who we are
That means many students have come far
because they were blessed
with a tough-love poet
who taught them to reflect
to connect
their minds to their hearts
weave words and make sense
to realize
they are Infinitely Immense
Joe, your reach went far and you were, truly, an original.

JOE TSUJIMOTO
READING BY WINDOW LIGHT, FEBRUARY 14

There's something about the soft, graceful movement of slowly sliding the thumb and forefinger, on either side, to the top, right-hand corner of the page, about to turn it, to catch the other half of the last sentence, to complete the thought on the next page, where the fingers, the thumbs, really, secure the pages on either side of the open spine, all this while rarely missing the sound, the inflection, the rhythm and momentum of the allusive words, as the image and the meaning, as one, come to fruition, like a blossoming rose, joining a host of other roses, past and soon to come, creating an eloquent bouquet, here, smell it, just for you.

Wing Tek Lum
MARIE HARA

I first met Marie Hara about 42 years ago when she came to my office to speak about the Talk Story Conference which she was organizing (along with Arnold Hiura and Stephen Sumida). We had an initial connection in that her brother-in-law Mickey was my best friend in 3rd grade. Her invitation changed my life.

The Talk Story Conference in 1978 was indeed a watershed event for many writers. Its goals were to consolidate, celebrate, and encourage the creation of literature by and about Hawai'i's peoples, the many distinct ethnic groups that make up our cultural pluralism. One hundred-fifty authors and lovers of literature, locals here and some Asian Americans from the mainland, gathered together to begin conversations which continue to this day.

And Marie, then a mere instructor in the University of Hawai'i English Department, had to deal with the resultant negative fallout from long-tenured senior professors. She later likened her situation then to being a rebel in the Empire (I suspect a *Star Wars* allusion). Nevertheless she persevered, and in fact taught the very first university-level Asian American literature courses in the state. All told, she went on to teach at the UH for 38 years, nurturing her students with her own unique, homegrown perspectives on literature and creative writing.

In this same literary groundswell, Eric Chock and Darrell Lum started publishing the journal *Bamboo Ridge*. Marie was a staunch supporter of their efforts to foster this new wave of local literature—as a contributing writer, as a copy editor, as a volunteer for numerous readings and fundraisers, as a member of the board, and for these last 13 years as our president. In my mind, she was an elder sister whom all of us could brainstorm with, bounce off new ideas, or ask for help. Her usual response was to "go for it"—although on a few occasions, I also recall there were some keen words of caution or admonition.

In 1980, a few of us also started a writing group to share and critique each other's early drafts. We have tried to meet once a month continuously for these nearly 40 years. Over time many writers have come and gone. But Marie was one of the remaining four from the original group. With her passing, there are now only three left, and we old-timers and our younger peers will all miss her singular, sometimes quirky, but always invaluable aesthetic.

As fellow writers, we were privileged to read Marie's creative works, primarily her short stories. Many of these were eventually published in her collection *Bananaheart* in 1994, which earned for her the Elliot Cades Award for an emerging writer. Early on, she used a pen name Mary Wakayama—until some of us successfully prevailed on her to publish under her true name. In the last several years she began writing poetry as well (notably about being a doting grandmother). Everyone has their favorite Marie pieces. If I were to choose, I would recommend her understated description of a picture bride meeting her husband for the first time, a classic piece entitled "Fourth Grade Ukus" (the title says it all), a recent poem about a dangling button, and the heart-rending story about a stevedore racing home to see his dying wife.

Marie though did not stop at writing for herself. She shared her talent for the sake of other people's projects. At one point she wrote articles for the weekly newspaper, *The Hawaii Herald*, and then wrote grants for the Academy of Arts. She helped interview and then edited a project on elderly picture brides in plantation towns. She wrote the script and served as producer for the feature film entitled *Kenji*, to celebrate the 100th anniversary of Japanese immigration to Hawai'i. With Nora Okja Keller, she co-edited *Intersecting Circles*, an anthology of poetry and prose by hapa or mixed race women. And she served as editor for a book on the Kula Sanatorium.

One of the interesting qualities about Marie was that she felt hard work and talent should be recognized, how we as writers were often overlooked. I remember on several occasions she discussed with me about who she felt deserved awards. I always encouraged her, though usually begged off doing any of the work myself. But Marie took this task seriously, and regularly wrote letters of nomination for local authors whom she cared about. Indeed many of us would not have been so honored had not Marie taken the initiative.

Marie was someone who knew so many people—both town and gown for instance, small potatoes and some big ones, our forbearers and our younger generations, writers and just regular folk. She served as our liaison with the university for our mutual benefit. There was one time we were thinking of approaching a downtown executive for a contribution. Marie volunteered, but her connection was not because of some business relationship through her husband's practice; rather Marie had been his high school teacher decades previous.

One last thing. Marie often had an opinion about some issue and was no shrinking violet about sharing it with others. Yet she was in fact also a very good listener. She had a knack for asking the right questions, or getting people comfortable enough to share their own thoughts and experiences with her. Maybe it had something to do with her reporter's inquisitiveness or some well-honed techniques in interviewing. Or, maybe it was because her interest in us was genuine; she took the time because she was really concerned about us.

The Talk Story Conference had a wonderful motto: "Words bind, and words set free." In a sense this was true for her as well. Marie bound us together; Marie set us free.

Nora Okja Keller
REFLECTIONS ON MARIE, SHARED AT HER MEMORIAL

I consider Marie both a dear friend and a role model who showed me by her gracious example how it was possible to balance motherhood and writing, teaching and friendships, while being an all-around-good person living a good life.

Marie was hapa, but not just in terms of being Japanese and Caucasian. She was also spiritually hapa, considering herself both Christian and Buddhist, mixed with a sprinkling of various other belief systems. One of the most open minded and open-hearted people I've ever known, Marie loved hearing about people's experiences and beliefs, and if she heard something new that made sense to her, she'd say something like "Well I don't know, but . . . okaaay! . . . sounds good to me!" And that'd become a part of her, too. In Marie's heart and mindset there was always space for everyone and their viewpoints, no matter where they were coming from, without conflict or judgement.

Those of us who have gathered here today to honor and remember Marie Hara do so because she had a positive impact on our lives. There were times when she helped us, healed us, laughed with us. As a family member, friend, teacher, writer and artist, Marie contributed so much to our happiness and to our well-being. We loved her and she loved each one of us. Although we are sad that she has gone from this life, we can still foster a deep gratitude for her, and rejoice in all that she was and all that she brought into our lives.

By reflecting with joy and gratitude on all the positivity Marie brought to this world, we create more love and more positive energy to both honor Marie and to benefit all living beings.

Marie Hara

WHEN I AM A GHOST

I want to walk through air up Makiki Street back towards the past.
I want to wander around the Pumping Station staying dry in the stream,
    Gliding up through the wet jungle to misty Tantalus.
I'll jump over to Mānoa Falls, then appear suddenly up and down the pop-up streets,
    Visiting in the windows of someone's family at dinner, someone's funeral at church.
I'll flit back near Queen's Hospital to be seen briefly in the long, dark basement corridors.
Maybe I'll join the Queen at the Palace sitting formally next to her window, her back to me,
    Watching the crowds, the soldiers, the tourists making a bustle of air and movement
    Mauka toward the water of Honolulu Harbor.
At 3 a.m. there will be lots of my old pals, friends, and faces I should, but can't remember,
    Trying to see them working or shopping or lingering as before.
Like rustling leaves blown around in wet, windy weather, we will float upward to the big boats,
    Aloha Tower, schools of fish.
We will skip over the noisy streets, join in the milling crowds, the energizing dusty smoke
    Maunakea markets, red firecracker paper scattering.
We will stream forward, directly through the coastline road with marathon runners sweating wetness
    Nimitz Highway, scent of May Day lei flung into the ocean.
Carefully watching all things night shadowed at the airport that changes shape from John Rodgers to HNL
    We identify the living ones.
They continually arrive and depart, intent on their destination, domestic or international.
I do not smile or frown, but I gaze all around with full attention
    When I am a ghost.
Nearing the moment of the dawn we may choose to rest at ease, the welcome
    Stillness in the mortuaries, crematoria, or cemeteries
    Dotted into silent places or flush flat against bubbles of sunshine,

Places quiet and still magnetic.
Or
We may continue to stay afloat in the raft of floating cloud particles,
    Runaway flower petals and other such debris.
For a while longer we stay a part of others' memory, weightless enough to hold onto.
Until the bothersome questions occur:
    Where am I?
    What is this?
    Why wait?
When am I not a ghost?
Forget the who.

Note: From reading Hilary Mantel's *Wolf Hall*, I got interested in the first person singular present tense as a historical device that has one big positive attribute: the speaker cannot know what will happen next even if the culture, the history books, and *everyone* know.

EDITORS' CHOICE AWARDS – POETRY

Christy Passion
A LETTER TO MY FATHER

Your first great-grandchild was born a couple of weeks ago
screaming in this world at a tiny but determined four pounds
eleven ounces. Tyler hasn't adjusted to not sleeping yet, he's anxious
about being a new dad. If you were here, I'd imagine you'd put your arm
around his shoulder and tell him about how it was when Drake was
born, or maybe a funny story about dating one of the nurses.
You always knew what to say to make it better.

Mom's decided to finally let go of your car and I'm dreading placing it
on Craigslist. I thought to call your mechanic George who always
admired the car and offer it to him, but learned he passed away, almost a
year ago now.

Juli's got a new job as nurse's aide for a care home which you would
think wouldn't be such a great match, considering she has the patience
and volume of a mynah bird, but who knows? Maybe she'll light a few
fires and get them old people up and dancing.

I haven't heard from Drake in awhile, but we both know that no news is
good news. I wonder if you see him different now, and you want me to
look at him different too. With Drake not really here and you gone, and
learning George is gone now too, it made me think about how we all start off as
a whole, then piece by piece we drift apart. But then, there's Tyler's
baby and Juli's new job and I think the whole is not separating but it's
shifting and moving so it's becoming a new kind of complete, even while
being undone. You're looking down on us and I bet you see us all,
tethered together by that stem of family, not just petals falling away
from the center. I bet you see the mosaic of us, a flower in full bloom,
both good and bad, want and need, all the birthdays, funerals, weddings
and heartaches. I bet you see us now as you always have, as family,
coming up short but everlastingly, and mostly, ever lovingly tied
together.

FIRES

Sometimes it isn't all burning to the ground. Sometimes we
get lucky in the early hours and the ER waiting room empties,

the nurses get caught up with their charting, and the intern
is able to finish her takeout from Bangkok Chef. In the breakroom

the talk's usually about high school football or which departments
are hiring. One of these times, not feeling particularly chatty,

I went up to the helipad and looked out at sleepy Honolulu,
just a few red taillights trailing on the roads, cold buildings.

The cars hurrying to Club Femme Nu with doors and girls
open all night. That light, in that apartment, a fretting father,

a feverish baby. The homeless that we know by name asleep
behind dumpsters or in abandoned Corollas smoking meth.

Looking out, a whole city of matches and kerosene. My view,
like my hands, accustomed to being immersed in ache. Relieved

when I see the flashing siren, the white wheeled box pull into
the driveway, the small men fumbling the rig's doors open

I wonder who I would be without these fires, my hands trained only
in catastrophe, to care for you and you and you. What would my city

look like if I taught kindergarteners the alphabet or farmed tilapia
in tanks? If I treated cancer and infection with rightful fear versus

the casualness of a stapler, would the words have come out
more easily the night you came to me wrecked over the affair

did you want me to shake with our world falling apart?

I move with steadiness to the elevator.

IT'S MY FAULT

Even though it's sunny,
the world is still falling apart.
I should be at a rally for migrant children
for birth control, for turtles—definitely the turtles.
I want to tell you it's the damn heat,
It's July after all, that keeps me inside
but it's not. It's my back that I tweaked
after my workout, the cat's got a bad cough
and the fridge is empty. That fearless Amazonian
that resides in me, needs to get to a bar to
order a stiff drink. She's creative when she's
80 proofed and there's world problems to solve,
but I'm counting calories for bikini days ahead,
did I mention it's July? And that's why
Jesus H Christ, that is why

A KIND OF SACRAMENT

I could argue
that this is sacred

the wiping away of blood
matted in his hair

how we turn him, his body, perfect
in all its twenty-three years, to wipe away gravel

clinging to his scapula and thighs
skin still warm in the places we touch

removing the IV tubing
disconnecting the ventilator

the sheets we smooth, not a crease
to disturb his image should a mother arrive

before the medical examiner does. How we
don't cover his head with the same sheet

covering his body, but place a towel instead
over his forehead and eyes to imitate someone

just asleep; a makeshift cap shielding the sun—
so this might, for a moment, diminish

the shock of death coupled openly with youth.
Our defeated slow hands lingering on an ankle, a wrist—

without knowing his name,
without having heard his song—
cared.

STORYTELLER

We are all called to bear witness
half-blessing half-curse the words that must come
as stories unfold around us. Most of us
will stand tongue-tied, barbed by what we see.
Sit next to me, start from the beginning
tell of the sunlit spaces: the skinny kid making the basket
at the buzzer, grandma's glazed guava chicken for Sunday dinner,
the majestic Pacific. Call out the shadows: another lump after
the final round of chemo, sewage spill off Sand Island, war.
Speak their names as they come bright into this world,
sons, daughters, nephews, nieces. Remember their names as
we bury them on ordinary days, Father, Mother.
Our accomplishments, our children, our honorable
mention science fair project in high school,
choices made over late night tamales and cheap bourbon.
Confess it and be reborn, shiny as a new star for
what are we if not remembrance? Bile, connective tissue,
muscle driven by chemical reaction: is this the sum of us?
Light a candle to Mnemosyne that she be merciful and
keep the flicker of memories alive as we tell them to our grandchildren.
The desert that stretches for miles on end
are the crumbs of stories from eons of forgotten Gods
withering without our eyes watching
without our mouths forming their names.
Tell your tale, be an oasis in the desert
with each breath—fertile lands of life
the Nile cresting in the summer rains
the light and dark of the dunes.

RORSCHACH TEST
(upon viewing a photo of a vine)

To a nurse it's IV tubing,
to a five-year-old, a cherry Twizzler
it's the exact shape, the missing molecule, the quadratic
equation the youngest in the think tank
needs to grasp, as she solves the problem of plastic.
Others may see Wonder Woman's lasso, a cat toy,
femur fracture, dental floss, spider spit, Jacob's Ladder,
Mary's crown or Buddha's path to paradise.
But I am a woman
and this could only be one thing,
this, this is sex.
This is how it comes on to you,
innocuous, a tendril putting out feelers
The cocktail sent over from across the bar
a swipe-right-sexy text, the clumsy chatter
so you can be close to those lips. It's the finger
brushing away strands of hair across a vulnerable collar bone
and the swollen jugular vein just above is carrying
Gabriel's message down
that curve is a shoulder, a hip, a backside
that looks great in jeans but better
in a shower with the water rolling over that crest
onto strong thighs, mesmerized, oh my—
I would ride that into the sunset, Cowboy. See it,
I know you see it too, the flickering tongue
ready to do more than just slip salacious secrets
into an all too willing all too ready . . . ear. Can you hear
it twist in the shade reaching around, full and erect
in the holy light of the moon penetrating
night's briny air lapping your cold skin, a thousand tiny
needle pricks breasting the surface then subsiding, lifting again
and dipping slick like a sinner, certain as a riptide.
It's not reaching out for redemption,
it's seeking release and like a drunk at the bar
charged and fearless I'll drink to that, drink it down,
the stem, the leaves . . . sweet salty air and all.

EDITORS' CHOICE AWARDS – PROSE

Michael Puleloa
MAN UNDERWATER

In the morning rain Henry Kaikilani stood on the Kawela shoreline and looked beyond Molokaʻi and the wide, quiet of the Kalohi channel—to Lānaʻi and the sliver that was Kahoʻolawe, and then the place of his own ancestors, Maui. An orange brilliance spread out above the mountainside at Puʻu Kukui; it pushed away cloudbanks, opening up the sky.

Inside Kānoa Fishpond and over the mudflats, finger-sized mullet rippled in the murky shallow water around him until the dorsal fin of a pāpio cut through the surface and carved through the school. He stepped slowly toward the distant reef as streams of sunrays on the surface of the water inside the fishpond spilled toward him from Maui. He walked like a man with conviction, his back to his home, his eyes toward the reef and then into the Kalohi Channel. He had made up his mind to pull out the giant heʻe from its winter home and finally bring it ashore, even if it killed him. The ocean was, he now believed, at least an honorable place to die.

Against all odds, his doctor once said, Henry had outlived his wife and the friends he had made as a child growing up in Kawela. Those who still knew him said the ocean kept his body and mind younger than what they really were. His friends also said that inside his old wiry frame rested a spirit so connected to the sea he could breathe in and out like the giant pulses in the shifting tides on the Kawela shoreline.

The children of Kawela, who spent afternoons looking for sand crabs and shrimp and baby mullet, or rummaging across the sandbars at low tide, believed Old Man Henry would remain a fixture of the shoreline after they were gone. He was a man who so embodied the shoreline that the children suspected he was simply a permanent part of it, a piece of its living history. And now, more than ever before, since they knew his wife had died and he was all that was left in his own home, the children were convinced he would become part of the place where the Kawela shoreline met the sea. *Perhaps a stone,* they thought.

The children had come to call him Papa Henry and they knew he had seen the giant octopus, the heʻe, many times. "I've watched it glide in," he told them, "from the blue depths of the Kalohi Channel. The end of each summer for two years, I've seen the heʻe spread its arms against the current and surge forward nearly fifteen feet. He crawls across the seafloor until fastened to coral and braced against the current. He's big, like a man underwater."

MICHAEL PULELOA

Although he was a skilled fisherman, Henry still felt anxious the first time the heʻe approached, when it eased itself up from beyond the opaque depths of the ocean and onto the reef. Each of its arms could have easily wrapped around Henry's legs and his waist, his torso, his throat. They could have easily wrapped around Henry's body and anchored him underwater. The heʻe had pulled itself onto the ledge of the green reef, sprawled itself over a massive coral head, and turned to face Henry, its body shape-shifting like a piece of the sea and the earth, the pigment under its translucent skin pulsing in brown and red waves.

While thinking of the heʻe, Henry let his feet sink inches into the muddy shallows as he made his way past the school of mullet and toward the stone remnants that marked the deepest part of the pond. The fish swarmed behind him until he turned around and waved his spear over the surface and the school broke apart and disappeared into the calm brown water. He rested his gear—a mask and snorkel, fins, a three-pronged spear, and a stainless-steel tee—upon the stones of the fishpond before stopping to quietly pray for safe passage in and out of the ocean.

He was almost seventy, but because he dove the reef outside Kawela, the people who lived on the shoreline assumed he was younger, sometimes by more than ten to fifteen years. "No man near seventy," they said, "could hold his breath underwater for three minutes. No man near seventy," they said, "could see beyond the distant reef from the shoreline."

But the children knew otherwise. They followed the old man in the afternoon, begging for stories of the things he'd seen on the reef. Fishes. Turtles. Sharks. Whales. They followed him on the shoreline until he'd finally turn around and tell them the story of the heʻe, which he knew was all they wanted to hear.

In the early afternoons, he sat them on the sand at the shoreline and then stretched out his arms while describing the fluidity with which the octopus moved toward him underwater. "Intense speed and silent strength," he told them. "He builds his stone home each winter under a massive coral head. Then he waits for prey . . . ." And this was the moment the children loved the most since it was then that he'd wrap one of them in his own arms, pull one of them close, and imitate the sound of the heʻe's beak breaking shell or bone by popping out the top row of teeth in his mouth. The children were delighted when he did this—finally letting them into a part of his secret life, and to them, a still somewhat unrecognizable world. When Henry placed the child in his arms back on the ground, he exposed the top row of dentures on his tongue and the children would cringe and laugh and then turn and run down the shoreline toward their homes.

MICHAEL PULELOA

When he was well beyond the broken wall of the fishpond, Henry cleaned out the lens of his mask using a mixture of naupaka and spit before wiping away the hair from his face with seawater. He pulled on the mask and slipped the snorkel inside the rubber strap near his ear. Slowly, he leaned forward into the water with his fins in one hand and his spear and the steel tee in the other until his head was immersed and the only sounds were his breath moving back and forth through the snorkel and the cool water rushing into his ears and over his back.

He pushed off with his feet, sliding across the surface of the water, just a few feet from the sandy bottom and he drifted slowly until the depth of the water reached chest-high. He then dropped his spear and the tee and put on his fins. He scanned the space around him for specific coral formations and stones he had set at the beginning of the winter season, then began to follow them out to a depth where he knew the water visibility would be perfectly clear.

He didn't see much beyond fifteen feet, but he knew exactly where he was heading, even imagined the island now behind him and the way its shallow southern valleys might appear to widen, and then almost shut as he shifted directions, making his way toward the reef and then over its ledge toward the open sea. He felt the water temperature change from warm to cold and then back to warm again, as he swam through small currents toward the reef. Soon, small schools of weke and manini and kole began to appear—the weke skirting across the seafloor in search of tiny crustaceans, the manini and kole in cloud-like formations falling over coral with their tails toward the sky as they pecked at limu and sometimes each other like birds underwater.

The heʻe, Henry knew, was waiting for him. And he knew to settle on a plan before he reached the reef, then its ledge, then the heʻe. He had given up on the idea of luring it out from the hole with a cowry or fresh bait—weke or manini or kole. He was going to use his spear and tee. That was right.

The reef and the ocean outside Kawela were sanctuary. And when there, he somehow felt at peace, even amid the loss of his wife and the fact he was old and alone, and the world outside Molokaʻi was changing at a pace he didn't much care for. In the ocean, he forgot about things on the shoreline that did little good for a man his age—that in his small part of Kawela, he was only one of a handful of people left who had lived there all their lives, that outsiders now complained about how and where he chose to fish. Not long after the death of his wife, he began to question the meaning of his existence and his usefulness to anything related to Kawela. He had gone too far. He didn't like that.

In the ocean, Henry felt in control and complete. There was a world for him just outside the Kānoa Fishpond where almost daily he would watch the heʻe he now imagined devour lobsters and crabs and fully grown fish, and, as he swam past more of the stone mounds he had built at the beginning of the winter season, he kept his focus beyond the tiny underwater particles shifting in the current and forgot all the troubles on the shoreline.

Winter in Kawela meant rains and storms. There were days when mud ran down the southern shoreline and no one left home. Days when howling, heavy winds from the east drove ripping white caps across the blue depths of the Kalohi Channel toward Oʻahu.

And then there were days after the rain and the storms, when the weather completely turned, when the last of the winds and currents sent the murky water beyond the shoreline and the reef, leaving Kawela almost in silence and its air with an eerie chill. This was when the surface of the ocean was completely motionless and when, if he pleased, Henry Kaikilani would spend entire mornings presiding over the distant reef outside Kawela. Days when the ocean was a mirror to heaven, he thought.

He knew the ridges and crevices and the caves of this reef as one might know the rooms of a house well enough to walk through in darkness. He liked to think he knew the fish on this reef by their generation. He marked time by the ever-changing size of their schools.

Some of the children in Kawela found Old Man Henry's stories even more intriguing than the things they were learning in school. They'd hurry off the bus in the afternoon and make their way to the shoreline without saying a word to their parents or even changing out of their school clothes. They searched for him on the shoreline, and if they didn't see him, they wandered down the beach with their eyes fixed toward the ocean and out at the reef. At first, Old Man Henry said little to them, even when they prompted him with questions. And because he said nothing except for what he might teach them of the shoreline, to them, he seemed like someone from a different world, an old man without a connection to anything except for the ocean outside Kawela. But the children understood Old Man Henry this way: He taught them about the ocean since it brought life to him.

It took nearly ten minutes before Henry swam out far enough to reach the small waves breaking over the inside of the reef. He felt a surge of water move across his back and over his calves, then slip toward his feet. He held the spear in one hand and the steel tee in the other, keeping them both close to his body and from dragging over the coral and sand until he passed the breaking waves. Beyond the shallow inside section of the reef, where the depth fell enough so he could no longer stand and raise his head above the surface of the water, he paused to take a clear and panoramic view of the way the reef sloped away from him and the ocean water became an opaque blue. He hovered just beneath the surface of the water with his back to the shoreline as he watched a pair of blue and yellow uhu beneath him join a school of skittish palani, then a two-foot kala gliding near one of the cracks of the reef.

The heʻe he sought was the largest he had ever seen in the water off Kawela. He steadied himself beneath the surface of the water just beyond the reef and made a vigilant inspection of the coral formations and two underwater stone structures on the ocean floor beneath him. He had stacked these stones himself into pyramid-like piles with rocks large enough so they withstood the shifting currents of the winter months, so that together they marked two points that when aligned led him in the direction of the massive coral head where the heʻe had made his home in winter. When he was over the first stone structure, he became more aware of his breath. He listened to the hollow sound of air slowly move in and out of his snorkel and he was instantly reminded of two things: the first, that he was the only person in the water for miles; and the second, that in his life, he had only remembered holding one heʻe that came close to the size of the one now somewhere in the labyrinth of seascape beneath him.

Henry remembered he was standing on a wooden crate one afternoon in the yard of his small childhood home. He had his arms raised in front of him with both his hands slipped into the gill slit and the mantle of a heʻe. Although he held its head above his own, he couldn't keep its tentacles from sweeping across the grass.

His father was there, and there were others from Kawela who had come to see the heʻe, as he held it up and tried to get the last few inches of its arms off of the ground. He was still wet and cold from the dive, but also excited since seeing his father wrestle the heʻe out from its hole and the open water before flipping it into the cooler on their flat-bottom boat. It was probably adrenaline that had saved him when, after his father pulled up the anchor and the outboard engine began sputtering along toward the shore, the heʻe, with Henry sitting on the cooler, snapped open the cooler and began to slip itself around his legs, attach itself to the floor of the boat, then sprawl toward the gunnel. It had taken all of his father's help to keep the heʻe from completely crawling out of the boat with Henry in its grasp. His father grabbed the ends of four of the arms and ripped them upward toward the sky while Henry pulled the arms stuck on his own legs away from his body. They stood there for an instant when he was finally free, the octopus squirming and spread out between them before his father pulled the head to his mouth and bit into an area near its eyes.

The struggle had left Henry with circular marks the size of coins around his thighs and arms, even as he held up the dead animal on the wooden crate in his yard over an hour later. It was an overcast day, just after a storm had passed, and every minute or so, he heard someone gasp at its size or the dull thuds of small swells as they crashed upon the shoreline. He was wet and cold and getting tired. He knew he could've died that day, that even though his father had speared and wrestled the heʻe into the cooler, that without his father there, the heʻe would've simply pulled him overboard and dragged him into its underwater home; the images of that possibility seared themselves into his consciousness, and he was suddenly standing there on the wooden crate in exhilaration.

Henry had grown up the youngest of four boys, so he was always trying to prove himself. They were a tight-knit group, a real brotherhood, but if there was one of them who took most to their father, it was Henry, so it seemed natural that Henry was the one Dad took to the ocean to teach about life underwater. And by the time his older brothers had graduated from high school and were moving away, Henry was already the fisherman in the family. He could lay net, throw net, bottom fish, and troll, all before graduating from high school.

He was also proud of the fact that he delivered fish to some of the elders in Kawela. It was something he had done with his dad when he was younger, but something he did now just on his own. The uncles and aunties were always happy whenever they saw him, but he made it a point to learn which fish they wanted most, then to try, as best he could, to deliver those fish to them. Some wanted fish they could fry, like āholehole or manini or kole; some liked to bake uhu or small mahimahi; others mentioned poke or sashimi, so he'd bring enenue or ulua. In the elders' faces he saw true aloha, and he kept this with him, even if he didn't always know it, long after they were gone.

After high school, he stayed on Molokaʻi. There was more than enough for him on the island, and in some sense, he felt committed there, a kuleana, the right to enjoy life in a place where he had grown up witnessing so many wonders in the natural world, and the responsibility to help maintain that lifestyle for those who would search for it in the future. Even though his parents and some of the aunties and uncles in Kawela still disagreed with his decision, he had in fact made the right choice if only because he had continued, during this time, to perpetuate the wisdom and customs he found in Kawela as a child.

Henry had mixed feelings about his father's death. After his mother had died, Henry was certain that a part of his father had died, too. He found his father a completely different man. At first, his father stopped making trips into town and spent most of his time on the shoreline or in the yard. He then began spending days in the house, watching television, getting up only to eat or to use the bathroom or to return to his bed. Henry tried to get him back on the flat bottom and into the ocean or at least back to the shore. Once, Henry didn't bring home fish for his father for a week. But his dad didn't seem to notice or to mind. He kept so quiet he left a void in their small home. And in the end, Henry thought, he died of a broken heart.

Michael Puleloa

At the cemetery, after his brothers and all the uncles and aunties from Kawela had paid their final respects, Henry dropped a picture of himself onto the coffin. It was a black-and-white his father had taken of him in the yard, holding up the he'e, on the day he almost died in the ocean.

It was still morning, but there was already enough underwater current just off the reef's ledge so Henry had to paddle constantly with his fins to stay in one place. From the stone mounds beneath him, he slowly made his way toward the massive coral head where he expected to find the he'e. He was looking in the distance for a round formation he had come to describe to the children as a giant head of purple cabbage, something with a deep-ocean color and almost perfectly round except for its flattened, greenish top. He knew it reached over four feet off the ocean floor but was also a piece of the underwater landscape that might go completely unnoticed if he weren't specifically looking for it, and if he didn't approach it from the direction of his stone guides. He knew the reef well, probably better than anyone else in the world, but he still took time, even if he didn't really need it, to get an initial bearing during this transition to life underwater.

While he was sure he would come across the coral head if he stayed on the line he had set with his stones, he also felt as though he was seeing the things before him for the first time. The sunrays were just beginning to reach the ocean floor, and the light piercing through the clear water split a school of ta'ape and to'au. Their yellow and red bodies burst outward the way water does when spilled on concrete, and then just as quickly, they re-converged into a swarming ball as if in a complex orbital dance. The school of ta'ape and to'au moved up and down in the water column like this until the fish broke apart and Henry was finally left with a clear view of the greenish round top of coral beneath them.

He took time to circle the area and to assess the rich seafloor before making his first dive. Between the green and blue coral formations, he looked for stones that seemed out of place, overturned stones. Whitish or gray. They would look like algae had been growing up around them. He kept his spear and the steel tee in his right hand and he used his left to gently pull himself through the water. When he saw upturned stones circling the base of the coral head, he drew in a little closer, to ten or twelve feet, and then he began to look through the spaces between the stones for the he'e itself. He tried to move as little and as calmly as possible, using the current for propulsion and his arms and the blades of his fins to steer himself into position.

Normally, when he came across a he'e's hole on the shallow sections of the reef, he would swim right up and begin moving away the stones with the tip of his spear until he saw the thin tips of arms. He would tickle the legs with his spear and lure the animal out a little before thrusting the spear and then maybe the tee into the thicker flesh near its head. If it fought, he would work around the hole with the spear and the tee until he saw its body and was able to secure it in his hands. He liked to pull the octopus from its hole with one hand and with his other, pierce the tee though the gill slit and out the mantle. Then he would surface with his arms at his side, his spear in one hand and the tee with the heʻe in the other. But Henry knew that with a larger heʻe, like the one now beneath him, he would need to make more than one dive. He would begin the same way, teasing it from its hole with his spear until it wrapped its arms along the shaft and exposed the meatier flesh of its body. He would strike first with the spear, then the tee, trying to pin it down so that he could calmly resurface for air. If he were lucky, the heʻe would struggle with the spear and the tee until he was down again, and he could use his second dive to wrestle it from the hole. This would be ideal.

The colorful school of toʻau and taʻape converged one last time over the coral head and then shot away down the reef. He took one last look around, slowly scanning the area for the best angle to approach the heʻe, then he set his breathing, three complete breaths, before he leaned forward and pushed himself to the seafloor.

He immediately sensed the heʻe was there even though he didn't see it. It had pinned stones from the seafloor to the bottom of the coral head, making a wall around its base, so with the spear Henry carefully began removing the stones. He saw arms slipping against the coral, so he stopped for a moment to determine the direction of their movement and to assess how the heʻe might be positioned behind the wall. He felt the rays of the sun on his back and a cold emanating from beneath him. He had plenty of time left underwater, so he backed away just a bit and circled the coral head one more time. Nothing had changed, so he rose to the surface and towards the warmth of the sun. Then, as if on cue, a tiny tip of an arm began waving at him just outside the little hole in the wall.

He'd rarely seen a heʻe, once threatened, return to a position in its hole as if waiting for prey. He thought perhaps he was lucky and that it had mistaken the disturbance as the result of shifting current, so he watched and waited, hoping the arm would slip out further from the hole and begin to restore the fallen stones. He waited for a few minutes, hovering just beneath the surface of the water with the sun on his back, but nothing changed. The thin tip of the arm swayed in the current just outside the hole.

There was only one thought that crept into his mind as he readied himself to make a second dive, and that was of the children on the Kawela shoreline. He imagined them circling around him, plying him with questions after he brought the heʻe to the beach. Aside from what was about to happen in the next few minutes, that moment was the only thing he could remember looking forward to. And he caught himself there, nearly a half-mile from the shoreline and alone in water twice as deep as he was tall, smiling just enough so that salt water seeped between the snorkel and his lips into his mouth.

He was ready now. He returned his full attention to the ocean floor and the coral head and the little hole with the arm still waving in the current. Then he calmed himself, filled his lungs with air, and dove headfirst with his spear and tee pointing toward the hole. When he was deep enough, he braced himself against the coral head in the oncoming current, using his left hand to attach himself there and the other to gently place the tips of the spear and the tee against the arm and into the hole. He was upside down, pushing with his fins, trying to get an angle with a view into the hole when the slithering arm quickly swirled up and around both the spear and tee, just as he'd expected, but it took a tremendous amount of restraint to leave his hand there, holding on, when another arm shot out through the wall and began to wrap itself around the first one. The spear and the tee banged against each other and made an underwater sound like a long, thin strip of metal siding that had fallen off a roof and was bouncing on the sidewalk. It took just about all his might to keep the ends of the spear and the tee in his hand from suddenly cutting through the water like blades.

When a third arm appeared, he let go of the tee and took hold of the spear with both of his hands, moving his left onto an open spot on the shaft of the spear. He was floating now, fins just beneath the surface, his body inches away from the coral head. The end of the tee had disappeared behind the red, pulsing arms of the heʻe, so he worked for leverage, trying to find a place on his body that he could press against the coral head and use to help thrust the spear into where he expected to find the heʻe's head. When the third arm wrapped around the spear and moved him into a position where he had his left shoulder against the coral head, he kicked with his fins and in one swift motion rolled his torso toward the ocean floor to drive his spear into the hole. There was a crunching he felt in his hands, and when there was no longer tension in the spear and he saw the arms suddenly expose the steel tee and sink to the ocean floor, he let go of the spear and took hold of the coral head again with his left hand. All that was left now was to retrieve the tee and secure it to the octopus before he surfaced for air.

At times like these, Henry didn't think much about life outside the ocean. But it was hard for him just then not to wonder about the heʻe. *Why the outer edge of the reef all these winters (without a mate)? He was certainly large enough, strong enough. Able.* Henry wondered for a moment about the fact that somehow it had lived more winters near the reef than all the others he had seen or caught, and then he wondered whether or not he had done the right thing. He began to resent the thrill and the relief he felt when there was no longer any tension in the spear when suddenly he felt a surge of sticky flesh wrap around his ankle and slide up his leg. He was shocked, but he knew instantly that what he felt was an arm—like the one he had just seen go limp—coiling around him. Instinctively, he reached back to grab the arm, and he panicked just a bit when instead of freeing his leg, he found himself held by the wrist. He looked up to the shimmering surface of the water and then back down to something that made him panic just a little more.

The he'e had revealed himself and was now completely wrapped around the coral head. He was looking directly into Henry's eyes, sizing Henry up. He had anchored himself using the rest of his arms, three around the underside of the coral head and three around the top. There was no hint of fear. He was there underwater, entirely poised.

The he'e then began to pull Henry toward him.

An arm suddenly shot up Henry's back and around his neck. Another arm slid further up Henry's leg. The grip tightened around his wrist.

Henry ripped at the arms sliding up and around his body, but there were too many, and they were too strong. He'd get away from one to have another take its place. The arm cinched around his right wrist was now pulling itself up his forearm, but he ignored it. The arm around his throat was now up the back of his neck and moving into his ear. Suddenly, there were flashes of memories. Days on the flat-bottom outside Kawela. Afternoons cleaning reef fish on the shoreline. He was sitting beside his mother at her bed. There was a black-and-white picture falling onto his father's coffin. He tried not to panic. He was on his back, at the top of the coral head. There was a blood-red arm now moving itself across his mask, blocking out the sunlight. An intense burning starting to move down his throat. He felt the tip of an arm twist into his eardrum, and then another arm prying into an orifice of his body that nothing else had ever entered. He tensed up and squeezed himself shut. He closed his eyes and imagined becoming part of the reef. He felt like a stone.

After Henry had stopped fighting, the he'e finally let go of the spear and began to slide to the top of the coral head. There, he held Henry for nearly a minute in what appeared more like an embrace than a struggle before he finally pushed Henry upward and out of the water.

From the sky, it might look as if Henry was on a pedestal floating just above the surface of the ocean. He would be more than half a mile from shore. The only man on the southern shoreline for miles. The sun would be warming his chest and his face. He'd be slowly opening his eyes.

In that moment, everything would be perfectly clear—he'd be thinking about his wife, his father and his mother, the aunties and the uncles. And he'd be longing for the children on the Kawela shoreline.

NEW TO BAMBOO RIDGE

Cavan Reed Scanlan

CUSTARD

Damn. Mary's birthday today. I got nothing. Ah, guess I'll do her chores for the week. Just like last year. Patrick shrugged as he trudged home, still sore from football practice. He felt ashamed for his lack of mindfulness for his baby sister. He had no excuse; she was an angel. For her fourth birthday, he had carved four honu out of mango wood and had hung them from an old wooden coat hanger. He had painted the sea turtles Board-of-Water-Supply green. "Twer-dohs wub gween!" she had squealed. They had hung from a nail on the wall near the bathroom in the narrow hallway, and Mary had named each one—Shelly, Splashy, Slow Poke, and Jake—saying good morning and good night to each of them religiously.

Patrick smiled briefly at the memory before guilt settled back in. His worn Keds took turns kicking a dried monkey pod up the sidewalk, its seeds rattling in the pod as it finally skittered off the path. That type of effort was not typical of him; none of the other siblings received gifts from him. He loved and cared for his siblings deeply yet found comfort in the detachment that came with being the eldest male, and surrendered to the ease of it.

But Mary was different. Her flu scare at three, her trachoma at five, her getting clipped a year later by the Lincoln Capri on Lincoln Avenue—each challenged his resolve. Not being able to protect her was bad enough without also forgetting her birthday, which her short life had shown was not a guarantee. Lips pursed, he looked up, took a deep breath and exhaled quickly before crossing Kaimukī Avenue, regret dragging behind him.

The sun had not yet dropped below the canopy of massive banyans in Crane Park before the bookies and gamblers started to arrive. It was Thursday night, and Alice's Drive In was the place to be (Chunky's, across the street from the stadium, was the spot on game days). They came to throw around malts and burgers to the high school players who might have a nugget or two that could give the sharps an edge in the weekend games. The local carhop had a distinctive pink and seafoam-green neon-piped sign that blinked "Alice's" in script above the corner of the lot, and it rotated lazily on its axis throughout the night, matching the rhythms of the traffic below. It anchored the mauka end of Kapahulu Avenue, which ended a mile or so down the road makai at Walls and the zoo.

Inside, high schoolers postured and chatted and laughed a little too loudly. They pecked at fries and looked everywhere else but at the person talking to them. "Mack the Knife" blared from the jukebox. The girls in the nearest booth giggled while the boys at the counter silently wished they were Bobby Darin so they could make girls in a booth giggle. Patrick grabbed a stool at the bend in the counter near the door opposite the jukebox, propped himself up on the counter over both his thick brown forearms, and half-listened to his teammate Winston Mau lie about a girl. Patrick's thick eyebrows framed safe cognac-brown eyes, and his flared nostrils saddled a squashed Polynesian nose. He felt he was handsome enough like how a base hit isn't a homerun but nonetheless has value—but relied on his charisma more than his looks to carry him.

    The star center and linebacker could often be found at Alice's after practice, killing time before walking two more blocks home. The music and chatter were a welcome respite from the austere and cramped two-bedroom on 2nd Avenue, where his very Catholic folks and six younger siblings barely got by. Mostly, he hung out at Alice's for a burger or fries dropped his way by friends who couldn't (or wouldn't) finish their own. He and they both knew he tried not to eat at home so there was more for his younger brothers and sisters, their friends, the revolving door of relatives, or anyone else from the neighborhood who dropped in. In this he felt no shame, remembering one of his father's sayings: "You shame, you starve."

    One of his younger brothers, Raymond, hopped out from the kitchen with his hands behind his back, untying his apron. Patrick flinched at the image, knowing Raymond was the most likely of the brothers to end up in that pose as his head is pushed down to avoid the roof of the squad car. Raymond washed dishes here most afternoons. It was the only job he'd been able to keep for more than a month. He bounced from booth to booth cracking jokes and stealing fries. He danced up the aisle toward Patrick wearing a smug look.

    "What, forgot again, uh?" he snickered, stopping a stool away. Over the years Raymond had learned the reach of his brother's left jab and knew to keep his distance. "No worry, I never get her nuttin' too. But whoa, nuttin' from the big boss braddah numbah one?" Raymond tsk'd. "I t'ink so Mary might cry."

    Patrick felt the embarrassment well up, only to be tamped back down by pride. His eyes leveled solidly toward Raymond. "I tell you one thing I won't forget: this right here." Patrick's index finger wagged back and forth between the two of them. Raymond leaned back, wiggling his fingers and feigning fear, but as soon as Patrick looked away his smirk faded and he sidestepped his way around his brother and out the door, staying clear of the right hand he knew too well. "Eh, Taks." Raymond called over his shoulder as he held the door open for a short Japanese man who hobbled in. Taks shot two quick nods upward with squinted eyes through his cigarette smoke toward Raymond, stepped in, and approached Patrick.

"Eh, Pachrick, how you?" Taks greeted him with a friendly fake punch to the ribs. "You hungry? Tirsty?" Taks leaned over the counter, "Myrtle, honey! Get dis boy one freeze. Tank you, sweethaht." Milton "Taks" Takayama was a well-known character around town. A WWII veteran and member of the famous 442nd, he had worked his way back home from the war after some years running numbers in Philadelphia. He walked with a pronounced limp—German bullet to the hip—giving him an authoritative gait that didn't fit his slim frame. He got a lot of mileage out of the battle wound, jabbing himself hard in the chest with two crooked fingers and proclaiming at the first chance he got, "Dose krauts no moa nottin' on dis musubi!"

"Eh, Taks," Patrick said with nervous courtesy.

"Eh, so what, how's da Komida boy doing?" "Did Russell Komida just get dumped by that crazy Pake girl whose father ran the mom-and-pop on Harding Ave?" "Was Bobby Mahoe hobbling after practice?" "Was Charlie Ah Sam's drunk dad at it again?" The questions wound through the place like Cokes through swirly straws. Some angles were easy enough to pick up without insider help: if the waves were up, Sonny Malama's legs would be dead; if it was the end of the month, the Lum brothers would be exhausted from hauling and stacking crates at their grandpa's nursery. Games in September meant Renny Tabayan and the Gomes boys would be wrecked from picking mango all week. These more nuanced pieces of gossip had to be gathered the old-fashioned way—a hearty slap on the back, an orange freeze or chocolate malted slid down the counter, a couple bucks slipped into pockets. Mr. Lee, the owner, was a notorious gambler, his fingers in almost every sporting event in town. The old saying was "Alice's is where odds are made, bets are laid, and debts are paid." Patrick and the other boys didn't much care about the blurry ethics of it all—free food and adoration went a long way in bending a high school kid's moral axis.

"Uh, yeah, um, he's doing good," Patrick replied. *How the hell am I supposed to know how Russ is doing?* he thought. *It's not like us guys sit around and talk about our feelings.* But he knew the game and liked the perks, and by now he knew how to appear to be giving guys inside info while not really saying anything.

"So what, he good den? Okay, okay, das wot I t'ought." Guys like Taks were constantly reaffirming whatever rationalizations they had for their bets, so they'd often take whatever a kid said and rearrange it in their heads to match their hopes for the outcome. Taks laughed again: "I guess das what you get for t'inking wit' da boto instead of da brain!" They both cracked up. Though he didn't hold Taks and the others in high regard, he did respect their rawness, and he knew one-liners like that from a classic like Taks would stand the test of time.

After declining multiple offerings of a bite to eat from Mr. Pang, his teammate Glenn's dad, Patrick gathered himself to leave. He made sure to say goodbye to Myrtle without getting in her way, remembering to thank her for helping with his sister Mary's communion the week prior.

"Aw, honey, of course. Anyt'ing fo' you guys. You give mama my love and we'll see you at Mass." She shot a furtive glance over her shoulder, slouched quickly, then pulled out a bakery-pink pie box from under the counter. The edges had started to lose their crispness, but the box was firm enough to slip across the counter, along with a brown bag. "Fo' good luck tomorrow," she mouthed with a wink, not missing a beat in clacking her gum. Myrtle worked the morning shift across the street at the bakery, so every so often she would send Patrick or one of the siblings home with something for their folks.

"Oh, nah, no need. Thank you. But, oh," Patrick stammered, but Myrtle was already halfway down the counter, clutching silverware in one hand and a coffee pot in the other. He quickly slid the box between his Pee-Chee folder and the Latin book he carried around for show. With a couple coughs into his sleeve to avoid eye contact with anyone else, he grabbed the brown bag and stepped off the red-cushioned stool and into the bustling lot.

Once across the street, he opened the brown bag – ham-and-fried-egg sandwich, white bread, still warm. No doubt Mr. Pang had bought it and had Myrtle give it to him. The first half of the sandwich, sliced diagonally, went down in two bites. He rolled the bag closed, saving the other half in case Mary or one of his brothers was still hungry. After clearing the last moist chunks of bread from back corners of his mouth with his tongue, he shook his head, then sheepishly unrolled the bag and inhaled the rest of the sandwich. It was selfish, he knew, but he reasoned away the guilt by telling himself Mr. Pang meant it for good luck the next night, and he didn't want to mess with a Chinese man and his superstition. Then he pinched back the bakery box cover to see what Myrtle had packed. Even in the half-light of dusk, he could make out the delicious brown blotches of an overcooked custard pie. His favorite. As he salivated and resisted jamming a couple fingers in for a taste, his big-family survival instincts kicked in. *How am I going to sneak this by everybody? Should I just eat the whole thing now?* His march slowed as he approached the huge mango tree that dwarfed the Ah Sing's yard. That's the spot to do it he urged himself. But his feet kept moving—past the Aiwohis and the dilapidated '41 Ford out front, past the Souzas and their permanently hanging laundry, past Mr. Muraoka cleaning fish on his front porch—and placed him at his own front steps.

It was rare to see their front lānai empty, let alone at nightfall, yet there he stood, alone with the limp, greasy pie box in hand. The orange freeze had initially checked his appetite, but now his hunger surged. The ham and fried egg had not even registered. Patrick closed his eyes and began to guess exactly what he would see upon entering: Daddy would be either reading the paper or mumbling over rosary beads, indifferent either way; Francis and Raymond would be sweeping the parlor and preparing the fala mats for bed; Lina and Leina would be helping Mama sand kukui nuts for lei she'd sell in Waikīkī that week; Mary would be busy over the sink; Rose would be taking too long in the bathroom. He smiled and shook his head, as if accepting this fate, and plodded up the steps with his hands full, easily pushing open the door with his hip. The knob hadn't turned in years, which didn't matter, because the house was never locked.

He was glad to see Mary was where he had predicted. His mother looked up from her shells. "Eh, you come home now only?" He had long gotten used to his folks' broken English, the result of the priests' English-only orders a decade earlier, and was glad for it. Scoldings in Samoan lasted a lot longer, usually involving more than words. "And Mary birfday too, uh?" None of this registered with his dad, who didn't bother to look up over the front page. Francis and Raymond shot "good for you" glances at him while he wasn't looking, and each sister gave her version of a halfhearted hello.

"Sorry, Mama," he apologized as he hopscotched his way through the tiny, crowded house and into the kitchen. Mary wheeled around just in time to plunk a ball of suds on his nose. "I guess I should have left the dishes for you, since I figured, you know . . . my birthday," she teased.

"Not this year, sis. Keep scrubbing." He swiped at the fading bubbles gathered on his nose and peeled back the top of the pie box. "Thought you might like this instead."

"Brother! Yes! My favorite!" Her shriek made everyone but their dad crane their necks toward the kitchen.

"Only for you—no taste tests," Patrick warned, pointing at both brothers, who shrugged at each other, helpless under their big brother's mandate.

"Love you, Brother! You're the best," she said, wrapping her arms around his waist and squeezing her ear into his muscular chest. Patrick turned his broad back to the living room to hide the exchange from the others. He looked out the window over the sink and saw Mrs. Chow clicking on a lamp in her parlor. The liliko'i on her fence had begun to flower.

Mary pulled back for a moment and looked up at him. She was beaming. *Another memory*, he thought. She again hugged him deeply, squeezing the guilt right out of him, then set to cutting out a healthy piece for their father.

Cavan Reed Scanlan

(H)IMPROVI(D)SING

No shirt.
Dad's standard look
around the house. His hairy gut,
taut like a water balloon
the color of baked manapua,
stood at attention, locking in the
hastily tied knot of his lavalava. I learned
early that hair can grow in such odd places—
in the outer ear canal
on the hump of the neck
on triangular slats of the lats
on the small of the back—
and that there was both a
revulsion and a beautiful
symmetry to it.

It was my kid birthday party
with no cool games laid out, just an open deck
overlooking the driveway and Kaimukī. After
I bemoaned the lameness of the set up,
I was desperate. Friends milled around
in the living room, politely searching
for some sign of a party. Dad scoffed in disbelief.
"What do you mean? Of course we have games!"
he exclaimed, and proceeded to grab a broom.
"Everybody, make a circle on the deck!" he announced,
us seven-year-olds obliging. Planting himself
regally in the middle, he stood the broom
straight up—broom side down—
and let go.

As the worn brown handle fell
toward Benny Shibuya, Dad snagged it
at the last moment. An impressive physical
feat. The quickness of step and agility of reach
belied his heavy frame.

They all erupted in cheers.
Then he did it again. Toward Jason Pacheco.
Louder cheers. Again. Toward K.J. Kwock.
More cheers.
I was in disbelief. Hopping around with his bare
bulge of belly hanging over the faded yellow lavalava,
his hardened purple nipples poking through
curly chest hair, he looked like a mix between
a weathered rhinoceros and an old sumo wrestler
to whom retirement had not been kind.

The made-up games continued, as did the laughs,
and when my friends had gone
he yawned "Last trick" at me
and stood the broom
straight up—broom side down—
and let go.

As the handle clacked at my feet
on the parlor tile
(no acrobatic save this time)
I asked
"What trick is that?"
He had already dumped himself
into his La-Z-Boy and yanked up
the synthetic wood lever like
an emergency brake.
He smirked, yawned
"How to watch your son
clean up after his own party"
and settled in
for his afternoon nap.

KUKUI GARDENS

Because Aunty worked graveyard shift
    we had to clean house early or else
        Rose would get sasa and take it out on us
            in the housing with no houses

Before playing Jacks or War
    we would check the laundr(y)mat machines for
        stray coins to buy Icees
            and lemon peel or Jolly Ranchers

When Chinese jump rope stalled because
    Jojo kicked too hard and
        broke Theresa's handle
        Oka, oka!

    it was up the government-built stairs for
        sliced white bread, pisupo
            and diluted Luau Punch

We conquered summer rain with
    dance routines on the cool
        tile and Marvin Gaye 45s

The needle surgically plucked
    then placed repeatedly
        on wax in grooves
            ensuring we nailed the lyrics

First one done with chores
    had first crack at controlling
        the brown push-button cable box

We lasted late for
    Night Flight on USA
        Escape from New York on HBO
            and rated R movies that taught u

    cussing and kissing
    violence and betrayal

We prayed our girl cousins would fall asleep first
    so we could punch channels at the end of the dial
        where we would wait, hushed
            for flesh to flash through wiggling colored lines

There we would lay
    sweaty on the parlor fala
        scattered like fallen
            I Ching sticks

with only each other for
    pillow and sheet
        our skin tapa-tan from summer in the sun
            our bones forged firm from millennia on the sea

There we awoke
    sweaty on the parlor fala
        (who wen' hog-cheese da fan?)
            limbs braided like the pandanus fibers beneath us

unaware
    we were weaving
        the basket that carries us
            still.

Cavan Reed Scanlan

SPEAKING IN TONGUES

No one was smiling. No one ever smiled
in these old photographs.
Not just Grandma and Grandpa;
in every picture relatives
from decades past had that look—
glum, flat, distant eyes
each brown face hammered into place,
a stone stare of surrender.
There were no smiles to groove laugh lines
over their temples, no comforting
creases through cheeks to reassure me
of people, kind and loving.

With a wink Grandma would sneak me
a folded dollar bill
from her smooth, firm hand
and whisper *you good boy*
in her thick Samoan accent.
Grandpa never said much;
he conveyed a peace that contradicted
our father's stories of getting sasa.
Grandpa's chuckles at our goofiness
floated between subtle approval
and muted delight. His witty
one-liners were more
cryptic decrees than loving affirmations.

A blind shark can still smell

The ulu leaf is quiet when it's alive
but loud when it's dead

The pictures did not tell us such things.
That is the problem with pictures—the silence.

Grandma had a long white hair
that fell from the mole on her cheek;

it bounced on her breath when she spoke.
That long white hair came alive
with each word,
with each *p*
and *f*
and *s*
in Samoan.
It would dance when she laughed,
a pixie tale in flight.
On hot days it would cling to her cheek,
paralyzed by sweat.
She was proud of that long white hair.
Is good luck she would say, dismissing
our pleas to play with it lest she lose
a lifetime of good fortune
with one errant yank.

As for Grandpa, he thought
professional wrestling was real.

Their superstition made them
perfect Catholics. They shipped nine kids
to Hawai'i, where the nuns and priests
from Sacred Hearts and St. Patrick's
forbade my grandparents
from speaking Samoan
at home. With blind devotion
my father's parents
promptly snipped their mother tongue
from their own—broken
English only to their children
from then on.
My father was seven.

The older siblings had Samoan
cemented in their throats,
but for my father and the younger ones
the cement was never allowed to dry.

Cavan Reed Scanlan

Hence my aversion toward priests and nuns—
they denied me the chance
to cement my own throat
with the *p*'s
and *f*'s
and *s*'s of my ancestors.
Perhaps no one was smiling
in these old photographs because
they feared their descendants
would be looking for tongues
no longer there.

ARTIST PROFILE AND PORTFOLIO

Jean Yamasaki Toyama
FLOATING IN THE OCEAN
Jui-Lien Sanderson

Photo by Blake Abes

Jui-Lien Sanderson's route to Hawai'i was circuitous, from a farm in a remote village in the mountains of Taiwan to San Francisco and finally to Hawai'i. Along the way, Jui (pronounced "Rae") had to make a living and she did it by graphic design. She explains, "I worked in Taipei as a graphic designer and art director for an advertising agency and later for a trading company." She learned how to transform the demands of the client into artful designs but had to put her "art of the heart" on a back burner.

Jui's adventurous spirit took her to San Francisco, where she met and married an artist. After some time, they decided to move to Hawai'i. "I was ready to live in grass huts and fish for food. Little did I know hula dancers and grass huts were just tourist attractions." She was soon disabused of this image of paradise when reality hit with the birth of her daughter and the "wild papaya gathering days were over."

She needed to work. At that time, her husband was the art director at a local publishing company. When his boss learned that Jui, his art director's wife, was also a designer, he hired her too. Through the years she worked her way up from designer to creative director. At some point during this time, there was a divorce, and years later Jui found a new life with her marriage to Keith Sanderson.

We writers know how difficult it is to really write while doing a 9–5 job. It's the same for any artist. Thus, thanks to support from her husband Keith, Jui has been able to pursue her own art while still being a freelance book designer. Lucky for us.

When Jui was chosen to design *What We Must Remember*, a book of linked poems, she already had over 20 years experience. Having dealt with a variety of people who knew or were often unsure of what they wanted for a book design, she had learned to listen. Four of us—Juliet S. Kono, Ann Inoshita, Christy Passion, and I—had long email discussions. We had several false starts regarding cover image: one, a startling photo of Joseph Kahahawai; another, a picture of a gun; and yet another, the whip-lashed back of Horace Ida.

About the process, Jui says: "Without seeing the manuscript, I had initially provided several ideas for the cover with Joseph Kahahawai as the focus, but

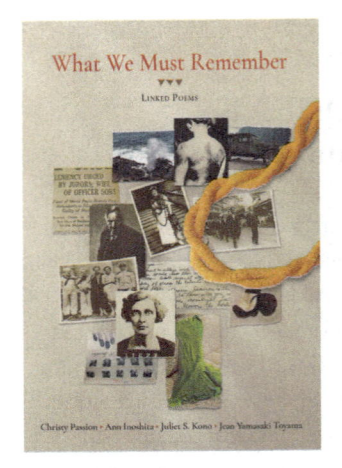

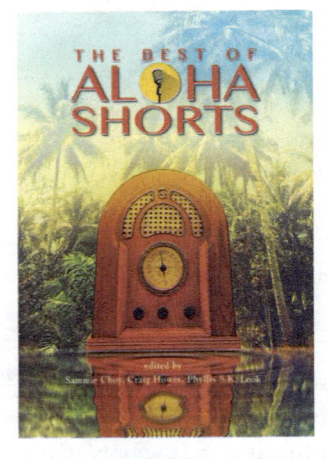

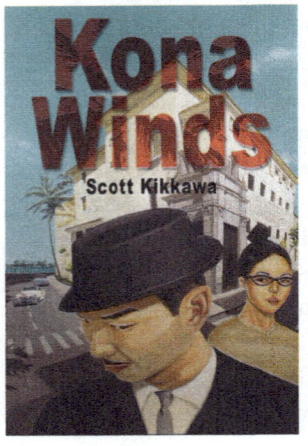

Christy had read a book with collage images on the cover. After reading the poems, I thought the collage would provide a broader perspective of the whole story. Jean and Juliet were really helpful in providing whatever images were relevant to the book. I wanted to incorporate a lei in the design to commemorate Kahahawai and also to add some color to the cover. The lei uniquely suggests a visual link just as the poems of the renshi do."

With her next Bamboo Ridge Press book project, Jui had free rein and followed both her instincts and the theme of the collection: "For *The Best of Aloha Shorts* the cover design was completely up to me, I wanted to reflect the old radio show on HPR, so I turned one of the O's into a spotlight with an old mic in it. Since HPR had just updated their logo, the old logo with palm tree design was no longer in use; in order to capture the audience who used to listen to the show, I put an old radio in the palm grove, with its reflection in the water as an attempt to tie the image to HPR."

As one of the editors of *Kona Winds*, I witnessed the back-and-forth email discussions among all involved in the production process. It was like gang table tennis. This, that, no, yes, try again, back again. Jui was more sanguine about it: "When I was working on *Kona Winds*, I had an initial meeting with the author and some of the editors. Scott Kikkawa, the author, wanted a retro look, since the background story was of the fifties. He had his friend, Tommy Hite, paint the cover image based on one of the scenes in the story. We had talked about making the car red, so it reflects the title font, but in the end, it was decided to keep it beige."

Most recently, Jui designed poet Cathy Song's début short story collection, *All the Love in the World*, using an oil painting by the author's husband, Doug Davenport, for cover art and Song's own handwriting for the title. The result is a well-

JEAN YAMASAKI TOYAMA

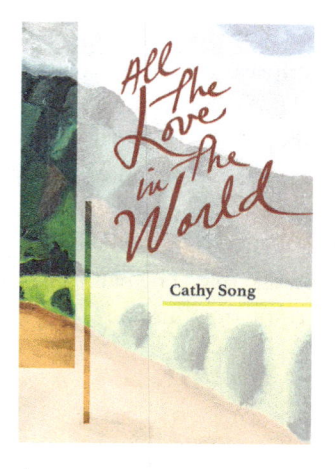

conceived wraparound image that both depicts part of the geographical setting for some of the stories and adds to the very personal content of the book.

Jui explains the difference between her two professions: "As a designer, it is important to keep our eyes and ears open. I have to remember that authors spend months or years on the book; they are closer to the subject matter more than anyone else. I am there to provide my professional input and services. Communication is the most time consuming and the most crucial part of the whole process besides the labor. Good designers gather information by listening to all parties involved, digesting everything, and coming out with the solution. Disagreement happens. Fortunately, everyone I've worked with are mature adults, so I haven't had to make a compromise that I wasn't happy with so far.

"As for my own art, most of the time, inspiration remains in my head without being materialized. Over time it evaporates. Ever since I was a child, I liked to draw and think about the world. I spent my early childhood in a rural mountain village in Taiwan, where farming lives are intimately connected to nature. Village children run around in their bare feet. That direct touch with the earth shaped my love for nature. Most of my adulthood is in the suburban area. Although surrounded by people, I often feel detached from the crowd. This detachment makes me an observer rather than a participant. I watch lives from a distance. Often even my own. Where there is truth, there is beauty. All of these, I would wish someday to be able to express with art in whichever form they may be."

"Great creativity comes from experiment and play. I try to bring that spirit into my design work as well. As with any creative activity, I need to be moved by the subject in order to be engaged and desire to express. Inspiration comes from all directions, at all times. I can be walking down the street, out shopping, reading a book, watching the news, taking a shower, listening to music . . . ."

"There is a big difference between commercial art and fine art. Commercial art involves clients and other stakeholders; its main purpose is to sell. That means the designer has to keep the target audience in mind. In fine art, there is more freedom and creative control: I only have to be true to myself. Express what touches me."

With this issue of *Bamboo Ridge*, Jui combines both her commercial art as book designer with her fine art featured in this portfolio. The cover design of this book is from her heart and she describes it this way: "The cat under the tree is personal to me. He was our family cat for 14 years. His name was Oscar. He

Jean Yamasaki Toyama

was mischievous. Any chance he got, he'd sneak out to the yard, get the brown dirt all over him. He'd come to the door pretending he wants in, then make us chase after him. He loved pouncing on the screen window for geckos and birds. After he passed away, we buried him in the back yard, under the orange tree. The painting depicts his spirit rising from his body."

JUI-LIEN SANDERSON

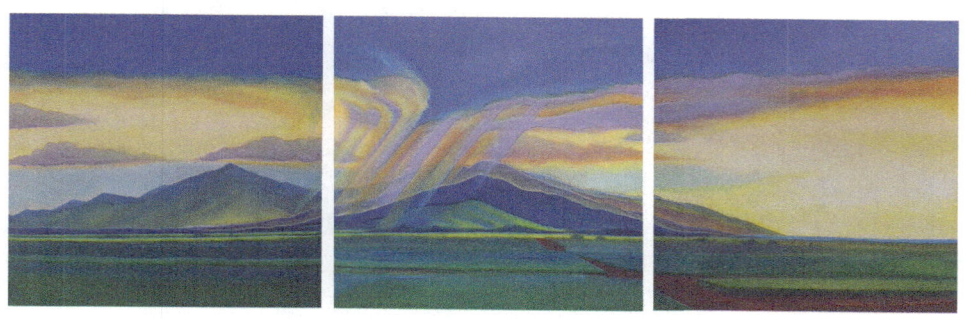

Mount Kaʻala, by Jui-Lien Sanderson, oil on canvas, 72" x 24"

Waiʻanae Coast, by Jui-Lien Sanderson, oil on wood panel, 30" x 24"

Jui-Lien Sanderson

Celebration, by Jui-Lien Sanderson, watercolor on paper, 6" x 4"

'Ohana, by Jui-Lien Sanderson, oil on canvas, 20" x 16"

JUI-LIEN SANDERSON

Hotel Street, by Jui-Lien Sanderson, oil on canvas, 30" x 24"

Mālaekahana Beach, by Jui-Lien Sanderson, oil on canvas, 24" x 18"

Jui-Lien Sanderson

Makuakāne, by Jui-Lien Sanderson, oil on canvas, 30" x 40"

JUI-LIEN SANDERSON

Gossip, by Jui-Lien Sanderson, oil on wood, 24" x 12"

Whatever, by Jui-Lien Sanderson, oil on wood, 12" x 24"

Jui-Lien Sanderson

Night Watchers, by Jui-Lien Sanderson, oil on canvas, 16" x 20"

Alligator Tree, by Jui-Lien Sanderson, oil on canvas, 16" x 20"

Dana Anderson
AHUPUA‘A

In this valley, the ahupua‘a runs
from cool Pali heights to the sea.
The path of the sun follows the ‘āina;
the moon follows the sun.
Rains nip at the moon
and all run to fathoms deep.
I dive over the lip of the world
into dream.

On a spirit mountain,
I take my grandmother's reluctant hand.
We step along the ridge of her grief.
I leave her at her son's grave.

My mother takes my other hand
and we dance,
moving to the strains of "'Alekoki,"
listening for the ‘auwai to run full again.

Our hearts fill and rise along valley walls,
skim past a Punchbowl of souls
and loft like storm birds riding thermals.

I let go.

Sally-Jo Keala-o-Ānuenue Bowman
NAMINGS

Over the decades, it has been my privilege to receive from ancestral spirits Hawaiian names for members of my family. They are now connected by these names to the ancestors, our island homeland, and to me. As years pass our names can grow in metaphorical meanings that offer life guidance. I received my own name when I was 15, Keala-o-Ānuenue, The Path of the Rainbow. Our names are nā makana a ka poʻe kahiko, gifts from the ancestors. I now honor all I have named.

Leiokanoe
    You are Wreath of Mountain Mist
    Gentle water of life touching the heavens
    Concealing, revealing the highest peaks

Kaleohanohano
    You are The Voice of Dignity
    Hands on the heavens, feet on the earth
    Thoughtful, careful, patient, calm
    Compelling all to listen

Hilinaʻi
    You are Abiding Trust
    Sacred bond of dearest friends
    Believe the power of aloha

Nāiwiponoikamalulani
    You are The Righteous Bones Protected by the Heavens
    The ancestors walk with you always
    Never shall you be alone

Kaʻimihōkū
    You are The Seeker of Stars
    Those same stars guided Kānaka Maoli, the First People
    On pathways in vast waters
    On starless nights, fold yourself in patience and trust

Kāheaikamelekai
    You are Called by the Song of the Sea
    You shall always hear the ʻaumākua
    Their wordless song binds you to the dawn of time

Keolaokeao
    You are The Life of The Dawn
    Each day the East reveals that hidden by night
    Signs and wonders waiting for you

Kāhealeʻa
    You are Joyous Call
    The ancestors will always answer
    Listen carefully before you call again

Hoʻomalu
    You Protect
    Ever mindful of earth, sea and sky, teaching
    All creatures are your kuleana

Kealakai
    You are The Pathway in the Sea
    Travel this moving road between your homes
    Linking the now and the long ago

    Take joyful heed, you whom I've named
    Eō, Yes, I am here, Keala-o-Ānuenue
    I have passed to you
    Name-gifts from homeland and ancient ones
    I am with you now and ever
    Sing our songs to the yet unborn

Carol Catanzariti
MAKE THE NIGHT SLEEP

When tiny cells metastasize in Mom
she calls them her night,
the dark time
when all sounds amplify,
all movement accelerates.

She tries to concentrate to reverse
the relentless march of those cells,
trip their invasion with the power of her will.

She flips (as she calls it) through Google
to discover tall tales of cure, ointments,
chemicals which she calls
her "fractured fairy tales."

She visualizes placing her cancer cells
in a basket which, in her mind,
she carries to a Dumpster
never to see again. But
marching sounds return
and return again
and again.

She decides to take control of her goodbyes
from the deepest love:
to her first-born daughter on sabbatical in Italy
she asks: "Bring back hazelnuts from a fertile tree."
To her middle-born son now living in the Philippines
she directs: "Watch your feet when you dance the *Tinikling*,
but dance one for me."
To her third child, a son born in Honolulu:
"Live pono for us all."

They gather with her as she makes the night sleep,
makes it awaken to the light.

Jacey Choy
WINTER

I'm not like Hina, Maui's* mother,
who worked all day beating kapa
into cloth, who asked for more
sun to finish her work. No.

I'm too selfish to think about others,
to think about work, to think about
making a world, I'm too busy day-
dreaming, listening to roaring surf at Bellows

Beach, sitting on the warm sand
with my father, my husband, my children,
my plate of grilled shoyu chicken,
potato salad, kim chee, missing

my mother who loved to swim,
her strong strokes silent in the salty sea,
who walked with me along Punalu'u
beach searching for glass floats,

imperfect green balls bobbing like bubbles
in the waves, who laughed openly at
herself, her mistakes, thirteenth child
of fourteen, one of the few who
died before the others.

I'm not like Hina, Maui's mother,
but I, too, wish for someone to capture
the sun, to slow it down, to let the filtered
light wrap around me, wrap around my
daydreams, lighting up an inky sky,
and keep the goddess, Poli'ahu*, at bay,
before she throws snow upon the soothing
sand, and my dreams freeze and shatter.

Jacey Choy

* Maui is a Hawaiian demigod who, among many things, captured the sun and slowed it down so there would be enough sun for his mother to finish making her cloth.
* Poliʻahu is a Hawaiian goddess of the snow and cold who ruled a mountain on the island of Hawaiʻi. She used her power to keep volcanic action in check, but also when she was angry or upset.

WHAT YOU WON'T REMEMBER

A woman said that when your life comes to an end,
it's not your work you're going to remember,
the work you chose because your pal convinced

you to do it, the work that others said was unskilled
women's work, the work that your dad's wife told you
was for those who can't, the work that taught you how

to observe kids, read body language, the work that
helped you understand what kids need to make sense
of the world, that your hands on them must be light,

like running them over a Ouija board, feeling
the energy but not interrupting it, the work that
unleashed wonder and spread it around, like
the balls on the pachinko board, the balls
that have a path though almost imperceptible,
yet know where they are going and unconsciously

seek to find their destination, the work that feels like
it's moving in a lighted galaxy among meteors avoidable
and unavoidable, the work that led you back to the beginning,

when all you did was read books, when all you did was write
letters & poems, when time slowed down, when you felt each
summer day pass, lying under the rainbow shower tree,

watching the blossoms rain down on you when the trade winds
shimmied the branches, when all of your work felt like play.

Brian Chun-Ming
HIDDEN HISTORY

The sight of her freezes me in place, as I step out from the stacks
of the East Asian collection, six books under my left arm
yellow legal pad in my right hand, and cheap BIC pen clamped in
my teeth.
Here on the 3rd floor of Hamilton on a Sunday afternoon
on the far side of the Asian section
where only the dedicated or mad, roam questing for the elusive.

I'd come hunting history among these old books
only to find a young woman with raven black hair sitting
at a desk, empty just minutes ago.
A leather-bound journal opened
pen in her left hand
luminous in the midmorning sunlight,
filtering through the windows
eyes closed, touching her neck with two fingers of her right hand
lingering on a point just under the corner of her jaw
smiling, wistful, mysterious and unknowable.

I am embarrassed to have found her in an intimate moment
lost in a memory known only to her and one other
and so, retreat slowly back into the musty silence
of old books, witness to a quiet human moment
not captured among these time worn accounts.

Brian Chun-Ming

WE SAT QUIETLY

On the day we buried you, we sat quietly
in the Mormon temple on Beretania and listened to the Elder.
As he pleaded with us to temper our anger
not to retaliate, because God had a plan
then he spoke of the beauty that you'd find in Heaven
now that you'd gone home to the Father.
We shifted uncomfortably on the wooden pews
grim in our sorrow,

Then that long procession of cars
up through the lush, vibrant green of Kalihi Valley.
Down towards Kāneʻohe, taking the left
onto Kahekili Highway
pushing on to Valley of the Temples Memorial Park
to watch you lowered into the red earth
while your fiancée wept quietly
held by your mother
as we stood in silence.

It been over a decade now,
all that's left is the slow burn of rage
and a bronze plaque with your name
I bring flowers to,
clear the grass from,
pour a shot of whiskey on
but it's never been enough to ease the loss
of your laughter.

April Melia Coloretti
ICE

The same word for a cold drink,
left out of the loop,
the queen of mean
or clean-cut diamonds,
glistening like sunshine
on the newly engaged.

Strong as that infatuation,
blocks are used to ride greens
of golf courses or its active
verb frosts a rich chocolate cake.

It's also the drug of choice
for my brother,
killing him to feel alive;
the glass pipe burns
while chemicals boil,
and his haunted eyes
stare out into the endless night.

EARL COOPER

FRUIT BROTHERS ARIA

Hama-Otsu, Japan

I love the sound of the greengrocer's truck
that echoes and drifts
through the apartment block
every Thursday afternoon,
playing folk songs
from a small speaker on its roof.

The twin brothers who run it
sing as they weigh and sack and sell.
And you can buy stanzas of peaches,
quartets of apples,
whole ballads of grapes
or watermelon the size of bongo drums.

Watermelon so sweet that
when you slice into them,
sugar drips off the knife,
and each ripe bite
hums to your teeth—
"Encore, encore!"

Sue Cowing
OUR PLUMERIA

The gold plumeria we planted fifty years ago
still stands by the window,
roots reaching down and drinking in,
branches dropping their blossoms
and all their leaves every November
standing bare
then coming back in March, a promise,
flowers first.

The tree grew quietly by the window
when robbers came, and floods,
when Joy died and mothers and fathers died,
when ideas came and prizes and rejections,
when realizations came and were forgotten,
when friends came to celebrate
and left with flowers.

TIME IN CAHOKIA, A CIRCLE OF CEDAR

We stood beside the center cedar pole
of Woodhenge, the ancient solar calendar,
hoping to watch the god-sun rise, align
with the pole of the autumn equinox.
Thick clouds hid the actual sun that day,
but the rising light revealed
a young man in jeans standing beside us.
He'd grown up near Cahokia, then moved away
and now was back, spending a lot of time
here and in the surrounding woods.

Sue Cowing

We'd walked those misty woods the day before,
delighted by shocks of coral and sun-gold leaves
against rain-blackened branches, wild turkey flocks
pecking breakfast from the leaf-fall,
silent ballet of a dozen white-tailed deer
vaulting through the browse line. There is more,
the young man said. I have heard children
running and laughing in those woods, and once
a man in deerskin asked me without words
what my intentions were.

THE TAO OF FORGETTING

The fear of forgetting,
it's self-fulfilling.
Suddenly every forgotten thing
becomes a sign.

The worst thing you forget
is that you have always forgotten.
Your eighth winter
you famously lost three coats
but no one thought
she's losing her mind.

How can you not forget now
when there is, always,
more and more to remember?
Maybe forgetting's a blessing,
a natural way of being sure
you remember what is important
to you alone.

ALLSPICE

It planted itself
in our Hawaiian garden,
first bold green leaves, then
a sturdy bush, and now a tree
whose leaves I like to crush
for the sharp spice smell.

Through the window the other day
I noticed actual blossoms on the end
of a single branch.
I kept meaning to go out
and smell them.

Brian Cronwall
HIKING ABOVE KAHANA BAY

Clouds shape the air above Kahana Bay morning,
    creating oceans around white continents
        in the searching sun. Keaniani Lookout Trail

begins its beckoning by the Park Center restroom, its road
    quickly changing from pavement to gravel to green-sprout.
        Breeze blows softly in the trees; the rocks

quietly emerge underfoot. Soon, the land rises,
    damp red earth under the grass, its hill wooded
        and winding, roots and fallen leaves the stairs

and carpet. Shadowed, crossing a bouldered stream
    now only moist, steps pass by the lau hala, passing
        time; by noni, whose healing stench is not

yet ready; by ʻākia's false ʻōhelo, monument guarding
    the Kapaʻeleʻele Koʻa providing berries to poison
        fish far below. These stones, the blessings

for the bay running dark with akule; there the prayers
    for the piercing black eyes, lids like lips
        opening to receive the run coming onshore:

kahuna kilo iʻa, master of fish-watching speaks:
    there, it moves, yes, signal the akule's arrival!
        But here today, only the wind, the sun,

the sound of gentle waves below, and, from the lookout,
    green mountains, a living valley, surge moving to shore,
        the springs of sweat on the forehead,

the taste of canned iced tea, and red ants crawling on white socks:
   time to begin the descent. Under kukui trees,
      switchbacks float down, land beside the road.

On the beach, I shed my clothes to my swimsuit
   and let the waves of Kahana Bay wash away sweat,
      dirt, doubt, and healingly carry me away.

Diane DeCillis
THE ART OF KINTSUGI

The Japanese art of repairing broken pottery with lacquer dusted with powdered gold celebrates the pottery's unique history by emphasizing the fractures and breaks rather than hiding them. Also known as the art of precious scars.

To make the repair
the surgeon
must fracture
the sternum
east west

he must think in halves
to spread the ribs
right left
and then consider what is right
what is left

he must palpate
the jagged edges of loneliness.

    Once I dated a guy
    it was snowing
    there was a concert
    we were to go together
    words drove us apart

    when he ran to his car
    sped off
    I ran after him
    my hands clamped
    to the bumper
    feet sliding in snow,
    the zigzag
    of tracks like an EKG,
    before letting go.

DIANE DeCILLIS

In order for the surgeon
to find the wound
he must feel
the muscle
that builds the walls
that have grown too thick
observe
how hard the muscle
has worked
lifting and lowering
the weight of love and sorrow.

To make the repair
the surgeon must admire
the beauty of wholeness,
cobble and collage,
in order to form

the gilded scar
that marries
the sides,
smooths the edges.

Kathleen DeSaye
THE NIGHTMARE

Nightmares were an unusual sight on Birdseye Island. Not that most people would notice them, even if they were as common as half-elves or gnomes. This one was particularly sneaky, clinging like a sloth to the underside of a large teenager's book bag as he trudged uphill on his way to school, yawning immensely in the crisp morning air. It shied away from the bright sunlight, seeking refuge in the shadow of the teen's bulk. He appeared none the wiser, jostling his bag to hang more comfortably on his shoulders.

Dice watched the little creature, plodding dully after the large teen and wondering if he should bother calling out a warning. At that size, a nightmare was relatively harmless. No doubt it was a practical joke played on the big guy by a friend clever in working magic. Not much point getting involved, he reasoned. Besides, the last time he had poked his nose in someone else's business, he had ended up in detention for two weeks.

Then again, he hadn't seen anything so fascinating on Birdseye Island in months. It was a small, quiet, and totally peaceful island. Dice could hardly stand it. What he desired more than anything was to find somewhere interesting, somewhere that he might have a real adventure. Somewhere like Goth's Triangle.

Of course, Birdseye was no Goth's Triangle. Try as he might, he found no one on the entire island who shared his desire for a more exciting life. The student council had lately rejected his proposal for a Thriller Club when they discovered that he had no interest in watching horror movies and instead intended to seek real thrills and hunt for danger across the island. The disappointment at the rejection was a bit more depressing than he liked to admit to himself. It turned out that the students of Golgoth High School were content living ordinary, boring high school lives. Shame. As it was, he just couldn't muster the spirit to call out to the fat teenager and warn him of the nightmare crawling up his back.

Early morning fog clung to the rolling hills of Birdseye Island's Golgoth District, dew glistening on the grass like gemstones. The morning was unusually chilly, though Dice wore no jacket, only his school sweater over a button-down, sleeves already rolled up to his elbows. Cold never bothered him. Yet he could feel the hairs on the back of his neck standing on end. He gave another glance at the nightmare. The fat teen was clearly oblivious to its presence. Guilt at the thought of doing nothing weighed heavily on Dice. He took a deep breath and opened his mouth.

"Yo, big Bones! Great game last night, eh?"

Dice let out his breath in a puff of air. Two members of the Golgoth Bats baseball team approached the fat kid, grinning stupidly and raving loudly about last night's win. The large teen joined in with their exclamations, falling into step with them as they headed up the next cobblestone street. As Dice continued to mentally debate whether or not he should say something, the trio ducked into a crowded deli halfway down the road to grab a bite to eat before school started. At that hour the avenue was bustling with students making their way toward school, and against his better judgment, Dice allowed himself to be swept up in the crowd. A glance at his watch told him that the bell would ring in less than ten minutes, and if he was late to school one more time, he risked suspension. "Sorry, chubs," he muttered under his breath and dismissed the nightmare from his mind.

He had a difficult time making his way to his locker, weaving through packs of students filling the stairwells and hallways. He spun the lock to input his combination and popped open the locker door, all the while trying to remember which class came first that morning. Just as he concluded that it must be algebra and reached for his textbook, a hand flew in his face.

"Dice Byrnes! Is this your flyer?" Lacy Tonron, junior class student council president, waved a familiar piece of paper under his nose.

"Not now," Dice snapped, brushing aside her hand and reaching for his algebra textbook.

Lacy leaned against the locker beside his, as if to say he couldn't get rid of her that easily. "You know Vice Principal Petty forbid you from any student organizations, Byrnes. So what am I supposed to think when I see this flyer?"

"It's probably old." He shrugged, growing annoyed now. What class came after algebra? History?

Cold eyes flashed behind frameless glasses. "Then why was it pinned up on the bulletin board over the girls' volleyball flyers that I hung on Monday? I am two seconds away from reporting you to the dean!"

If Lacy went to the dean of discipline, she no doubt would not rest until Dice received a write-up. He temporarily gave up trying to remember his schedule and surrendered his attention to her. Snatching the flyer that she still waved aggressively, "'Looking for adventure? Craving danger? We can help,'" Dice read the sloppy letters aloud. "'Join us, Adventures for fun.' So what? Who says it's mine?"

Her finger slapped against the bottom of the flyer. "That's your phone number!"

"So?" he bristled, snatching textbooks at random in the hopes that they would be the ones he needed. He shoved them forcefully in his book bag.

"Anyone with a vendetta against me could've made this! Maybe you made it—trying to frame me! If anyone's going to Vice Principal Petty, it'll be me!"

Dice slammed his locker shut and strode off down the hall, ignoring the indignant look on Lacy's face. He crumpled up the flyer and shoved it in his pocket. "So much for that," he said, heaving a sigh. The student council may have denied his idea for a Thriller Club, but he had reserved some hope that he could arouse interest in his fellow students via some secret advertising. In retrospect, he realized he should have perhaps spent more time on the *secret* and less on the *advertising*.

He managed to arrive at homeroom on time, with barely a minute to spare. Glancing at the clock, he reassured himself that he had been right to leave the nightmare alone. If he had stopped to talk to that kid, he most certainly would have been late. Then he forgot about the matter entirely when one of his classmates reminded him of his algebra test, and he whipped out his notes to do some last-minute cramming.

Something was wrong.

Dice sat in his literature class, halfway through second period, absently drumming his pen against his notebook. He had a bad feeling, like an itch beneath his skin or a whisper tickling at his ear. He knew the feeling very well, though it was always unpleasant to experience. Sometimes it was an unsettled stomach or pressure between his temples or against his throat, sometimes chills or shortness of breath. Today: an itch and a whisper. Whatever the sensation, it only ever meant one thing: Someone was in danger.

"Can you cut it out?" the girl next to him whispered, giving a pointed look at his fidgeting.

"Sorry," he said and popped the butt of his pen in his mouth instead. He leaned back in his desk, looking first toward the windows, then to the clock hanging on the wall above the door. Twenty minutes at least until the period ended. He scratched behind his ears to dull the itch. He'd wait it out.

The air in the classroom was warm, heated by the sunshine beating in through the windows. All evidence of the cool morning was gone, burned away by the sun fighting to conquer spring. The windows were open, though the only real breeze in the room came from the slowly oscillating fan beside the teacher's desk, clicking to a lazy tempo. With each click Dice could feel time crawling along, and with it the bad feeling behind his ears grew and grew. He found himself entirely unable to concentrate on the lecture. The buzzing in his head was too loud. With fifteen minutes until the bell, he decided fifteen minutes was too long to wait.

He raised his hand. Feigning sickness, he requested to see the nurse. "What's the matter?" his teacher asked, pursing her lips in disapproval.

"I feel nauseous—I think I'm gonna throw up. I've felt sick all morning," he lied, clutching his stomach for effect.

She looked him over skeptically. Then she waved her hand at him. "Fine. Go."

Snatching up his books and slinging his bag over his shoulder, he raced out of the room with such alacrity that his teacher became slightly more convinced of his need to vomit.

Dice flew down the flight of stairs at the end of the hall, then crossed the hallway beyond in a flash, glancing in each room as he passed for a sign of the fat teenager he had seen that morning. The whisper in his ears was so strong that he knew he must be close. Somewhere on this floor.

Sure enough, in the third classroom on the right, a familiar long, brown ponytail and round, cheerful face caught his eye from amidst a sea of upperclassmen. "Bingo," he muttered to himself. From his vantage point he couldn't see the nightmare, though he was certain it was still clinging to the teen somehow. Now all he needed was a way to talk to the kid. What was it the baseball players had called him . . . ?

A knock on the door drew the attention of everyone in the classroom. The teacher, unfamiliar to Dice, raised his eyebrows at the interruption to his lesson. "Can I help you?"

"Is there someone called Bones in this class?" he asked.

Several students looked toward the fat kid, who had an uncertain frown planted on his face. "What's this about?" the teacher said.

"Mr. Powers wants to see him in his office immediately," Dice lied.

The teacher shrugged in careless approval. A few catcalls escaped from Bones's classmates. He grinned good-naturedly and stood, snatched up his bag, apologized to his teacher for the disturbance, and met Dice at the door.

"Am I in trouble?" Bones asked lightheartedly as they strode down the hall together.

"Yes. This way," Dice said curtly, making a beeline for the stairs.

"Mr. Powers's office is that way," Bones said slowly, motioning in the opposite direction.

"We're not going to Mr. Powers's office. Hurry up."

Intrigued, Bones trailed after Dice down the next hallway, though he paused when he saw Dice open the door to the boys' bathroom at the end of the hall. "Where are you going?" the large upperclassman said through a grimace. "What'd you say your name was again?"

"Dice," he introduced himself, motioning for Bones to enter the bathroom. "Just do me a favor, okay? There's something I need you to see." Sighing somewhat, Bones stepped inside.

Kathleen DeSaye

A quick glance told Dice that the bathroom was otherwise unoccupied. As a precaution he locked the door behind them, ignoring Bones's protest. "You have a nightmare," Dice stated by means of explanation.

"What? What the Hell are you talking about?"

"A nightmare—a noxkin. I saw it on you this morning," Dice said. "I didn't get the chance to warn you at the time, and basically the guilt was killing me, so I tracked you down. Where is it now?"

Bones stared at him. "A noxkin?" he said dumbly.

"It's a creature conjured by magic, usually to play a nasty prank on someone. It attaches itself to its target and eats their energy until they become incapacitated, then returns to its master—"

"I know what it is!" Bones interjected. "I just—are you sure?"

"It was on your bag," Dice confirmed with a nod, motioning to the book bag hanging from his shoulder.

Hastily Bones dropped his bag on the floor and quickly rummaged through it in search of some sign of the creature. "Nothing," he said.

"Check your shoes. Your hair."

Bones popped off his shoes and socks, then ran his hands over the long braid tied down his back. When he ruffled his hair, Dice saw something dark on the back of his neck. "Hey, don't freak out," he began, "but lift up the back of your shirt."

Bones swore heavily. He loosened his tie and tore off his school sweater with urgency, ripping off the shirt underneath without question.

"Holy Hell," Dice breathed, holding a fist to his mouth.

"What? What?" Bones cried, spinning around and craning a look over his shoulder to see his reflection in the mirror. A scream burst from his lips at the sight.

The nightmare had sewn itself into Bones's broad back. Its jet-black body had taken over like a weed in a garden, expanding with pulsing, purple veins along Bones's spine and across his shoulder blades. It had sunk its sharp teeth into the flesh just under his neck, one spindly hand digging in for a better hold. Its legs had already fused to Bones's spine, black tendrils spreading under his skin and across his entire back. Perhaps worst of all, it had tripled in size from when Dice had seen it only two hours previously.

"Aaugh! Get it off!" Bones roared, grasping desperately and unsuccessfully at the nightmare.

"Stop yelling!" Dice snapped with an automatic glance toward the door. "The last thing we need is someone seeing that!"

"You gotta get it off! I gotta go to the nurse!"

"What's she gonna do, call your mom? Stop moving! Calm down!"

Panting somewhat, Bones obediently stilled, and Dice approached with a critical eye. "I can't believe it's gotten so big so fast," he said, frowning at the nightmare. "And you didn't notice it! You're not in any pain?"

Bones swore rapidly, eyes squeezed shut as if it might drive the image of the noxkin from his mind. "No, I can't even feel it. Just knowing it's there . . . !"

"Are you half elf?" He noted Bones's pointed ears, studded with rings, and his towering height.

"No! Now would you quit calmly analyzing and help me out or call an ambulance or something!"

"I just don't get it. Nightmares devour a person's energy—their thoughts, feelings—until their host loses consciousness. Then they return to whoever conjured them and basically throw up all that energy, revealing secrets and sometimes transferring the stolen energy to their master. They're like little leeches. Emphasis on little," he explained. "I've never heard of any human able to stay conscious hosting a noxkin any larger than a rat. You seem fine—and that thing is gigantic!"

"I am aware!" Bones roared, nearly blue in the face with terror. "Do something, would you?!"

"Right," Dice said. He stepped forward, bracing himself as he reached toward the nightmare. "Just stay still, all right? I'll get it off you."

"What are you gonna do?" Bones asked with a nervous squeal, shying away somewhat. "I meant call the police, not pet it!" The noxkin shifted its weight, sinking its teeth deeper into his shoulder.

"I'm gonna peel it off you, then destroy it so it can't return to its master. It'll release the energy it's stolen from you. It'll be fine."

Bones hardly agreed that the word "fine" applied to this situation at all. "Have you done this before?"

"Yeah, yeah," Dice assured him. "More or less."

"That doesn't sound convincing!" Bones cried, turning so the noxkin was out of Dice's reach. The redness in his face had drained. He was beginning to look pale. "It's a yes-or-no question! You either have or you haven't!"

"Fine! I haven't. But I've seen it done before, and I know I can do it," Dice explained hurriedly. The noxkin had most certainly swollen in size since Bones had removed his shirt. Dice could hardly believe that Bones was still standing, much less arguing so adamantly. "Just trust me, all right? I'm a Hearken, okay? I've done stuff like this my whole life. Now quit moving!"

Bones hesitated. Dice took the opportunity to grasp him by the shoulder and shove two of his fingers into the nightmare's mouth, yanking backward like a fishhook.

Bones yelped in pain. The nightmare let out a guttural growl. A knock sounded on the bathroom door.

"Yo, why is the door locked? Who's in there? Open up, I gotta take a piss!"

"Someone threw up," Dice shouted back the first excuse that came to mind, forcing his hand between the nightmare's teeth as it burrowed its talons deeper into Bones's flesh. "Use the one on the third floor!"

"I'm not going all the way up there! Anyway, I'm not squeamish. Open up!" The boy in the hall banged loudly on the door once again.

"C'mon," Dice muttered to himself, wiggling his hand around inside the nightmare's mouth. If he could encourage the nightmare to absorb his energy instead of Bones's, it would release him in order to transfer to a new host. Unfortunately it was already so tightly bonded to the large teen that it was reluctant to let go.

Bones swore quietly, leaning against the porcelain sink and taking deep breaths. "I don't feel so good, Dice," he said, swallowing hard.

"Hang in there," Dice urged as the kid outside the door continued to shout insults at the bathroom's occupants. The noxkin simply would not budge. There was no choice. "This might hurt," he warned Bones, then grabbed the base of the noxkin's spindly black neck.

A flash of light burst from Dice's palm. The noxkin squealed, pulling its teeth from Bones's shoulder and thrashing its head wildly. Bones shouted in pain. Acting fast, Dice shoved his wrist into the nightmare's open mouth.

Immediately it sank its sharp teeth into Dice's arm. The black veins that had grown across Bones's back retracted rapidly, shrinking and morphing into clawed feet and hands. In seconds, it had completely drawn itself away from Bones. His back was raw and red but otherwise unblemished by the nightmare's roots. As soon as it was completely cleared, he collapsed to his hands and knees, gasping for air.

Meanwhile the nightmare clung to Dice's arm like a monkey, biting him just below his elbow and grasping his bicep and wrist with its talons. Much larger and stronger than it had been when Dice had first seen it, it took only moments to begin sinking into his flesh, sucking on his energy like a vampire hungry for blood. And it began swelling in size, three times faster than when drawing from Bones, inflating like a bag of popcorn in the microwave.

"Holy—it's on you, man! It's on you!" Bones exclaimed, scurrying to his feet and backing up toward the beveled window.

Dice held out his arm, weighed down as it was by the nightmare's expanding bulk. "Close that window," he ordered. Bones obediently slammed it shut and locked it. "Now stand by the sinks and try to keep out of the way. It's going to let go of me and I'm gonna kill it."

Bones nodded, wordlessly scurrying to the place Dice had indicated. Once Bones was safely in place, Dice turned his attention to the nightmare.

The noxkin continued to swell like a balloon, now roughly the size of large cat. Its webs had spread up Dice's shoulder, and he could feel them pulsing across his chest and shoulder blade. Taking a deep breath, he concentrated his energy. And his arm began to glow.

A loud hissing sound filled the room, like cold water hitting a hot pan. The nightmare shrieked. It opened its jaws, releasing Dice's arm, and yanked away its hands, ripping its roots from Dice's body. He cried out as it tore itself away in desperation to abandon its new host. Then it fell, hitting the tiles with a loud smack. Claws sliding on the smooth surface, it managed to roll onto its four feet and arch its back, letting out a furious growl as it gazed with wild eyes up at Dice.

The kid in urgent need of a bathroom knocked again, though this time there was a change in his tone of voice. "Yo, is everything okay in there?"

"It's fine," Bones called. "Use the other bathroom, dammit!"

At the sound of Bones's voice, the noxkin turned its attention to the large teen. It crouched like a cat ready to pounce. But Dice was ready.

Flames burst forward in an angry roar. White-hot fire shot across the bathroom tiles, consuming the noxkin in a sudden inferno. The heat alone sent Bones shrinking back against the sinks, shielding his eyes from the blinding light.

Dice pulled away his arm, and the flames vanished, leaving behind nothing but a cloud of smoke rising toward the ceiling.

Elena Savaiinaea Farden
THE OCEAN IS MEDICINE

The ocean is medicine.
On the darkest nights
when the full moon has climbed to the height of a starless heaven,
young women of the village wash their hair by the sea,
in hopes some bit of moonlight will spill among their strands
in the same way kisses and whispers slip from a lover's lips, unravel
    in long ripples of
luminescence
from shore to horizon and back again.
"The moon is in love tonight," my grandmother tells me.
"She sings a rising song of rebirth, of light coming out of darkness,"
    she explains.
—Hānau ka pō.
Too old to make the nocturnal journey with the village women,
I offer to bring back moonlight water for hair in the calabash that once
    held grandfather's ashes.
In the small corner of our house,
alone like the moon,
my grandmother sings softly as she dips down to bathe in moonlight,
to dwell in pale blue glow,
to have love live in the lining of her skin.

Tom Gammarino

FUTURES STUDIES

It's five weeks into Val's first semester at the University of Hawaiʻi and he's sitting in his awesome-sounding-but-actually-kind-of-boring English class, The Rhetoric of Videogames, streaming a podcast with his cochlear implants while the teacher, this overzealous PhD candidate in a retro tweed jacket with elbow pads, gives a sermon on the seven types of ambiguity (or something). The class started out interesting enough—on the first day they staged Plato's allegory of the cave with flashlights in the darkened classroom—but then they started talking about postmodernism and reading *The Life and Times of Tristram Shandy, Gentleman*, and Val lost the thread.

But now the teacher has just written the word "remediation" on the board and asked if any of them knows what it means. No hands have shot up, and Val feels just inspired enough to pause the really interesting discussion about neuromorphic computing he's been listening to and pick the thread back up: "Isn't that like when you adapt something to a new medium?"

"Precisely. Any examples spring to mind?"

"Loads. Like how about *Star Trek* being a TV show, then a cartoon, comic books, board games, RPGs, videogames . . . ."

Some palm trees outside the window seem roused by his answer.

"Excellent," the teacher says. "Anyone else have an example?"

"*Lord of the Rings?*" this girl proffers from the far end of the seminar table. She's hapa like Val, wears tortoiseshell glasses, and participates altogether too much. In point of fact, she's sort of annoying, but she catches Val staring at her sometimes anyway, because she looks more than a little like an age-projection of his childhood friend-cum-pen-pal, Hana. She's not Hana, though. Her name is Maya.

"Great," the teacher says. "It started as a novel, of course, but how have you seen it remediated?"

"As a film," she says.

"*Three* films," the teacher corrects her.

She shrugs.

"You're not a fan, I take it?"

"It's my favorite novel of all time," she says. "I just never felt I needed to partake in the Hollywoodification of it."

Val is moved to interject. "Why not? Those movies are tours de force." More than once he'd shown up raccoon-eyed to high school because he'd stayed up way too late finishing the whole trilogy.

"I don't need to watch them," she says. "Frodo's been trekking through my head since I was ten."

"You read the novel when you were ten?" Val's sure she's lying. She has to be. He tried reading it when he was fifteen, but much as he loved the films, he couldn't really get into the books. The prose was so ponderous, and it was just so damned long.

"More than once," she says, and Val notices her lips, which could only be described as pillowy.

"De gustibus non est disputandum," the teacher says. "Any other examples? Something less obvious perhaps?"

And the class moves on. But it's clear to Val that he and Maya have some unfinished business between them.

He catches up with her on the outside stairs after class. "Maya?"

"Yeah?"

They've never spoken one-on-one before. In fact, except for a couple of professors, he's not sure he's spoken to *anyone* one-on-one since he got here.

"Look, I'm willing to make a deal with you," Val says.

"Oh? And what might that be?"

"I'll read the novel if you watch the movies."

"You've never read it?"

"No. I mean, I tried, but I didn't get very far. I generally prefer science fiction to fantasy. I like to think it's the nonfiction of the future. I do love the Peter Jackson movies though."

She pokes her tongue around the inside of her cheeks for a few moments. "And why should I care whether you read it or not?"

"Because if it's your favorite novel of all time, shouldn't you want to be like a missionary for it? Spread the good news?"

She looks skeptical. "Is that why you're pushing the films on me?"

"What other motive could I possibly have?"

Val might even believe what he just said, that this is all about art and has nothing to do with her tousled hair, her ponds-for-eyes, the chocolate chip of a beauty mark on her cheek. "I have them all on my laptop if you ever want to watch," he adds.

Her face contorts and she looks at her phone while he taps his foot and studies some birds on a wire. At length she says, "What the hell," and it's as if she just told him his biopsy came back negative.

"Awesome! How's Saturday?"

"This weekend's pretty bad, actually. My auntie's visiting from Arizona."

"Well"—he consults the time on his phone, as if he doesn't already know it—"you doing anything now?"

"What, like *now* now?"

"I live just over in the dorms. I have a single." In general, freshmen get roommates, but Val didn't want one, and his parents have enough money—and enough experience with the law—that rules look infinitely pliable to them.

She nods and smiles. "I guess I could do that."

And Val has to press his luck: "It's only 10:30. We could make it a marathon if you want and watch all three. I mean, if you're not busy. I have some Hot Pockets we could eat. The total running time is just a little over nine hours, I think."

"Let's take it slow," she says.

"Totally," Val says, and he reminds himself that while computer processing power may double every eighteen months, not everything is a computer—at least not yet.

Nevertheless, three hours later Val and Maya are lying on his bed, attaining escape velocity from Val's solitary past. Granted, Val was preoccupied with Maya's ache-inducing suchness throughout the movie, but while he could perhaps have *imagined* her leaning into him with dilating lips and beckoning eyes, he would never have predicted the actual occurrence of that event here in three-dimensional meatspace. Val has never kissed anyone before, but he has no time for terror; he needs to perform. Fortunately, having seen many thousands of kisses in his life—in movies, city streets, shameful dreams—he finds that, for the most part, his mirror neurons know how to do this. But he is learning too: he never realized, for instance, how kissing is so much more than just a mouth thing, how their eyes and, especially, their noses are involved in ways they themselves probably don't understand. Maya's hands are wrapped around his back, his are running through her hair, and after a time he feels a powerful compulsion to do *more* than just kiss her, but he doesn't know the rules of engagement and doesn't want to presume. He will content himself to follow her lead.

"I'll have to go soon," she says.

"Just a couple more minutes," he pleads.

And then, for another forty minutes, they just stare at each other, separated by a few inches at most. He doesn't believe his face has ever been so near to another one, not even his mother's. He's so close he can focus in on only one little bit at a time, and he finds all of these human frailties there—blemishes, dead skin, a stray eyelash—but somehow they only make her the lovelier to him. At irregular intervals, they change the angles of their heads, and they smile a lot, and Maya bites her bottom lip sometimes, which reliably stiffens his hard-on, but mostly they are just looking at each other, memorizing the other's face in a sort of unforced ritual that feels so natural and fulfilling that they can't have been the first humans ever to have done it. It's a wonder there isn't a name for it.

Tom Gammarino

Then Maya declares that she really does have to go.

So they hug for twenty-five more minutes, and then she ever so gently tears herself away.

But she leaves a piece of her there with Val, lodged right in the part of his brain that thought it knew anything about anything.

Falling in love is the last thing Val's first month of college has prepared him for. For that matter, it is the last thing the past twelve years of his life have prepared him for. Having gone to an exclusive private school on the Upper East Side, where his able-bodied peers treated him like a cipher at the best of times even as he got an A on every test he ever took, Val learned not to place too much stock in relationships. Early on, he found some relief in retreating to his bedroom after school and abusing the stuffed monkey with stuffed cochlear implants that his audiologist had given him. He hurled insults at it ("You're so stupid," "You never should have been born," etc.), stabbed it with scissors until the stuffing came out, used matches from the junk drawer to set fire to its face and the place where its balls would have been if it had any, until one day he came home to find the monkey was gone; presumably his mother had thrown it out, though they never talked about it.

At least he'd had Hana's letters to look forward to, but year by year her replies came more slowly, and with fewer words in them, until eventually the interval between letters grew to forever. Fortunately, by this point in his adolescence, Val had learned to take some of the edge off his loneliness with books. He especially liked the science fiction novels of Arthur C. Clarke, which he read on repeat. Compared with the precious, sentimental crap he had to read for English class, science fiction excited him with its infinitely expansive scope and its refusal to over-esteem *Homo sapiens* or flatter that species' capricious inner life. As one of Vonnegut's characters put it in a passage Val underlined twice and drew an exclamation point beside: "The hell with the talented sparrowfarts who write delicately of one small piece of one mere lifetime, when the issues are galaxies, eons, and trillions of souls yet to be born."

By high school, Val's love of science fiction was resolving to a new love of science fact, in particular where it touched on computers, which Val took to be the engines of the future, if not yet its gods. By the end of his freshman year he had taught himself three separate programming languages and read up on Boolean set theory, artificial intelligence, and machine learning. In his sophomore year, the dean, likely intimidated by Val's combination of off-the-charts intelligence and plain weirdness, allowed him to enroll in Intro to Comp Sci, an elective usually reserved for juniors and seniors. Val used the class to begin designing *TheOdicy*, a "god game" in which players governed a community of one hundred people,

Tom Gammarino

making sure to balance every member's well-being even as terrible, random accidents—dismemberment by lawnmower, sudden-onset blindness, AIDS from a toilet seat—befall them. He finished only a handful of modules that year but enjoyed every second, which cemented his feeling that comp sci might be his passion and calling in life. He was especially taken with the possibilities of virtual reality, which looked to be becoming more of a thing. Because of his implants, he was already able to have audio transmitted directly from a computer to his auditory nerve via Bluetooth—no need for speakers or headphones—and he saw no reason why someday soon he couldn't have images transmitted directly to his optic nerves as well. Eventually, he felt sure, humans would fulfill the cyberpunk dream of plugging in their nervous systems altogether, allowing for full immersion in augmented and alternate realities. No doubt that day was coming, but having chanced on an old book in the library called *The Age of Spiritual Machines* in his junior year, and then having followed the transhumanist trail through dozens of other books, Val soon came to believe that "day" would last about a nanosecond before we whooshed into whatever was next.

Unfortunately, Val appears to be the only person at the University of Hawai'i with a deep understanding of the future. In the end his parents had agreed to send him here only on condition that he do his graduate work at a "real" school (his father has a BA from Princeton, his mother from Stanford; both have JDs from Yale, which was where they met), and while he'd found the insinuation that UH *wasn't* a real school unbelievably arrogant at the time, his experience so far was making him wonder.

On the jittery first day of class, after the students had gone around the table introducing themselves, the sixty-something, washed-up hippy of a prof, Dr. Harmon, had had the naiveté and gall to say to Val, "So you'll be our resident transhumanist this semester—there's always one." Val had done his best to humor the ignoramus, but inside he was stewing in his own bitter juices. Harmon then went on to write "Futures Studies" on the board, to circle the last 's' in the first word, and to pontificate, unpersuasively and for much too long, about how the future is "open and multiple"—as if every "choice" were *not* the result of a causal concatenation of events going all the way back to the Big Bang; as if there were some possible past in which Val's parents did *not* take him out of Hawai'i when he was five or in which a recessive mutation on connexin 26 did *not* make him profoundly deaf. It was patently offensive.

And if the dinosaur of a prof wasn't bad enough, the syllabus revealed that the assigned reading was going to be almost entirely about alternatives to capitalism and the possibility of self-rule for Hawai'i. Granted the class was entitled "Introduction to Political Futures," and these might not be uninteresting topics in their own right, but Val was fairly certain they'd be moot within a couple of election cycles at most. He made a point of staying after class one day in the third week to try and convince Harmon to assign some essays by real futurists like Vernor Vinge, Ray Kurzweil, and Nick Bostrom, and though Harmon didn't do that, he did try pandering to Val by assigning an essay called "The Cyborg Manifesto," published in 1985. The essay, admittedly, led to one of the better group discussions they'd had thus far—Mike, the thirty-something anarchist with the bare, sour-smelling feet, had especially strong opinions about it—but Harmon clearly expected Val to be electrified, and he simply wasn't. Donna Haraway, the author, presents the cyborg—part biological, part mechanical—as a way to deconstruct simplistic binaries like self/other, male/female, right/wrong, God/man, culture/nature, and civilized/primitive. Val was all for that. The problem was: Haraway used the cyborg as a mere *metaphor* for what flesh-and-blood humans might become, and Val thought that was a failure of the imagination. But as usual, Val was alone.

That is, until, with a little help from J.R.R. Tolkien and Peter Jackson, he suddenly wasn't anymore.

By the time Val and Maya finish *The Lord of the Rings* trilogy a week after beginning it, they are so preoccupied with exploring each other's corporeal, mortal bodies, not to mention that most ancient of information-copying technologies, that by rights they have to start the trilogy all over again.

Is it any wonder that The Rhetoric of Videogames thereupon becomes Val's favorite class of all time? That he understands the Romantic poetry they are made to read for homework far better than he would have otherwise? That *The Lord of the Rings* becomes his favorite novel and the movies Maya's favorite movies? That he begins to see this glow around everything?

Falling in love has been a stroke of incredible luck for Val. His brain is gushing with beautiful drugs. Never mind that his grades have begun to tank and he hasn't made a lick of progress in *TheOdicy* lately; Maya is clearly the best thing that has ever happened to him.

Except that maybe she isn't. Maybe she's the *worst* thing. The fucked-up truth is: Val's not sure. In embracing his humanity, he worries that he might be betraying his *trans*humanity. After all, none of this is supposed to happen. None of it fits with any obvious extrapolation from the past. No girl ever desired him before, not in this way. He can't begin to understand what Maya sees in him. She is so *cute*. She isn't normal in the pejorative sense—she loves horror movies, plays electric bass, and has enough scars on her legs to attest to her having grown up skating in a skatepark—but she does have a generally positive outlook on the future, and, Singularity excepted, Val can't find any good reason why she shouldn't. Could it be that Harmon is right? That the future—the futures, rather—really are "open and multiple"?

Val can actually feel his mind dividing against itself. He's so happy that he's *miserable*. But also: he's so *happy* that he's miserable. He hides the misery from Maya, but she gets glimpses of it when she finds him brooding after sex, when he visibly flinches as he tells her how he's never felt these feelings before, and when, one muggy afternoon, he shakes off her hand on the front steps of Hamilton Library.

"What the fuck?" she says.

"That's a Futures Studies professor," he says, pointing his chin toward the tall dude with the soul patch who is posting flyers for some protest or other on the bulletin board beneath the monkeypod tree.

"So?"

"So he already gives me a hard enough time about the Singularity without knowing that I'm in a relationship. It wouldn't help my case."

Dr. Payne is the youngest and least clueless member of the Futures Studies faculty. Harmon introduced them in the hall one day and they chatted for a few minutes. Payne was cool, at least by comparison with Harmon. Soul patch aside, he also knew a thing or two about the Singularity. Granted, he was skeptical of the "hard takeoff" or "FOOM" scenario (i.e. recursive, runaway self-improvement) and wary of AI's conceivable indifference to humanity as it pursued its own evolutionary ends (as if evolution had "ends"), but he was at least a techno-optimist of sorts. In particular, he advocated for arcological cities on the ocean and the exponential growth of spirulina, an algae, to keep pace with population growth.

Val has told Maya all about the Singularity, and she has listened nonjudgmentally. She takes a different stance toward it, however. "Whatever's going to happen is going to happen," she says. "Just be yourself and don't worry about it." There is wisdom in that, to be sure, but Val for one doesn't want to be blindsided. Their relationship is still young enough that they don't talk about the future much, but when they eventually do, the Singularity is going to be a huge stumbling block. He knows this.

"Shit," he says under his breath. "He saw us."

Dr. Payne approaches them. "Hello, Val. Out recharging your batteries?" They have a running joke—not very funny—about how Val is looking more and more like a cyborg by the day. Payne might be a bit more sensitive if Val told him about his fully implanted implants, but Val doesn't see any other reason why he should. He hasn't told Maya about them either.

"Actually," Val says, "I was just taking in some last-minute memories of human bodies before they become redundant."

Payne chuckles. "What a waste that would be," he says, turning his attention to Maya and extending a hand. "Doctor Payne," he says. "Not half as diabolical as I sound. Equally at home with Professor Pleasure."

Maya makes a face like *Who is this cornball?* but she shakes the hand anyway. "Maya Davis."

"Major?"

"Bio."

"Planning to be a doctor?"

"A pediatrician."

"Well then you two will have plenty to discuss, won't you? Here." He hands the couple a flyer.

"What's this?" Val asks.

"I'm organizing a rally against nuclear weapons. We'll have a booth at the sustainability fair. Come on by."

"Will do," Val says.

"A pleasure to meet you, Maya," says Payne, taking his leave.

Once he's out of earshot, Val snipes, "As if some rally in the middle of the Pacific is going to bring an end to the nuclear age."

Maya nods, but with pursed lips. "It's cool he's trying, though, yeah? Engaging with the real world instead of keeping his head in the clouds?"

"What's that supposed to mean?" Val asks.

"It's just that so many professors—"

"You think my head's in the clouds?" He can't believe it. After all he's taught her, she's still a skeptic, still an infidel.

She sighs. "Val, we're having a decent day so far. Can you maybe just take a couple of deep breaths and let this go before you get all worked up again?"

She's so smart she can read the future like this sometimes.

He does his best to hold back the avalanche of his thoughts: he takes the deep breaths, swallows what he can of his pride, forces a smile. "Gi melin," he says—Elvish for "I love you" (they haven't said it in English yet, but Elvish feels more sacred to them anyway).

"Gi melin," she replies, and she returns the smile too.

And then Val is compelled to remind her that the Singularity is fundamentally a *good* thing, that the posthumans of the future will be all-around better than the humans of the present. "Isn't that exciting?"

"Whatever," she says. "Let's go get some coffee. I'm tired."

So they go to Paradise Palms, the little cafeteria across from the library, and they drink coffee, which makes Val think about caffeine and its effects on the brain. Then he looks in Maya's eyes and thinks about love and its effects on the brain, and wonders if a drug is a drug is a drug.

Foom! Their love grows exponentially. The Singularity doesn't come, but there's a new iPhone. For some reason Val can't understand, Maya stays with him, and he wants her to, though her very existence continually erodes the core of who he thought he was. With the exception of The Rhetoric of Videogames (A+), his first-semester grades are mediocre. Embarrassingly enough, he got a B in Futures Studies and a B- in Computer Science. In theory, he is deeply interested in the latter; in practice he is distracted, troubled, confused. Maya keeps inviting him over to her house to meet her family, but he keeps resisting. It feels like some sort of symbolic point of no return, and he's not ready for that. He's not ready for anything anymore. He's not even ready for the Singularity and that's what he came to college for. At least he has Dr. Payne this semester instead of that Luddite Harmon.

Val's relationship with Maya is, as far as he can tell from literature and movies, utterly normal. To wit: They text each other variations on "I love you" about twenty times a day (though Val continues to balk at the Rubicon of that exact formulation).

They develop pet names for each other. He calls her his "Middle-earthworm." She calls him her "Valium."

Though they don't have any classes in common this semester—they may never again—they've taken to studying together most evenings down at Glazers Coffee, a ten-minute walk away, when they can find seats. Otherwise, it's UH's Sinclair Library.

Saturday nights Maya usually stays with Val in the dorms, where they go at it like orcs and then spoon until morning. And they spend literally every day of Christmas break together. Val's parents wanted him to come home for the holiday, but he declined. On Christmas Eve, she strokes his hair while his eyes water. He tells her how alone and unlovable he's felt his whole life. She tells him how it's in part that vulnerability and sensitivity that attract her to him. "I like fixing people," she says.

They go the movies at least once a week. They like to go to matinees at Dole Cannery because then they can go across the street after and splurge on comics at Other Realms. Val didn't get Maya into comics; she came to him that way. Their tastes run toward different genres, though. He still goes in for superhero stuff by and large; for obvious reasons, he has a natural affinity for mutants, aliens, and the technologically enhanced, whereas Maya tends to prefer sword-and-sorcery stuff and anything to do with animals or children. They complement each other, one might say, though the old Val would have said that he reads *toward* reality whereas Maya reads away from it.

She takes Val to a classy restaurant in Waikīkī for his birthday. They eat sushi and then walk along the beach beneath a Death-Star moon. Maya looks prettier to Val by the day. She lets her toenails grow too long, though, a good centimeter past the tips of her toes, like claws. He can't decide whether to tell her this or not.

They talk about taking a trip one of these weekends to Kaua'i where he's never been. He even floats the possibility of her coming home with him this summer to New York, where she's never been. Val wonders if his parents would like her. He also wonders if he cares.

Then one night in late January, having found no seats at Glazers, they are attempting to study together in the library. It isn't really working, so they declare a break and go outside. They take a stroll around the campus and end up lying under a svelte coconut tree in the darkling evening, searching out constellations. The only one Maya can point to is Orion, which Val finds kind of lame—her ignorance, that is, not the constellation. She doesn't even know about the nebula at the center of Orion's Belt. And she's a science major, albeit a different science. Val has always liked outer space. Even in light-polluted New York City, he spent many an evening of his childhood peering out his window through a telescope. Since he has begun seeing himself through Maya's eyes, however, he does wonder if it isn't a little sad or pitiful that he tends to prefer other worlds to this one, be they videogames, far-away planets, or The Future.

Maya puts her head on his chest and purrs, tickles his skinny thigh with a blade of grass. "Hey, do you know what today is?"

"Wednesday?"

"It's our four-month anniversary. It was four months ago today that you invited me over to watch *The Fellowship of the Ring*."

It annoys him, her noticing this, for some reason. "Okay, but that's sort of an arbitrary thing to celebrate, isn't it?"

"Not so arbitrary. It's a third of a year."

"I guess."

"What's wrong?" She's always asking him this lately. Actually, he's always asking it of himself too.

"I just hate to be so conventional about things," he says. "Can't we make an effort to be more, like, *organic*?"

"Making an effort to be organic sounds pretty inorganic to me," she says.

Touché.

She lifts her head from his chest and perches it on her arm instead. "And anyway, who's being inorganic? I just happened to notice that it's been four months since we started dating, so I expressed it. What could be more organic than that?"

"Are we 'dating'?" he asks. Somehow they've never exactly named it before, this thing they're doing, this relationship they're having. Indeed, Val has taken pains to avoid naming it, because names are not innocent, they're the vectors of expectations, and he knows he can't promise anything.

"I *think* we are," she says. "Would you prefer to call it something else?"

Of course they're dating. He's being an asshole. He knows this, but he can't seem to help it. His loyalties are divided. "I don't know," he says. "To tell you the truth, I'm feeling confused about pretty much everything lately."

"Did I do something?" she asks.

"I honestly don't know. In theory, I'm happy. I guess I'm just feeling . . . impinged upon or something."

"I'm *impinging* upon you?"

"It's just, I don't seem to know who I am anymore. Or what I want. Take this conversation, for example."

"What about it?"

"I guess I just never thought I'd be the sort of person who says things like this. It's all so . . . pre-posthuman."

She sighs. "Do you think we should take a break for a bit?"

He knows she's being sensible—he could benefit from some space probably, for soul-searching and whatnot—but that part of him that believed he would never have a girlfriend, and the rationalizing part that says he doesn't want one anyway because sexual reproduction is soon to be a thing of the past and yadda yadda, those parts of him find it hard to let her go, even for a bit. "I'm sorry," he says. "I love you, Maya. Of course I do, but . . . " He's getting all blubbery and disgusting. He is not supposed to be someone who ever says things like this. He hates himself and regrets being born.

"I love you, too," she says, acknowledging with a fleeting smile that this is the first time they're using these ritualized words in their proper order, "but if we're going to be in a real relationship eventually, I want us both to be a hundred percent. You're obviously not there yet. Which is *fine*. You shouldn't have to rush it. Anyway, we always knew we were going to have to deal with this sooner or later. You can't very well hold on to me and your Singularity."

"*Your* Singularity"—just what his mother had said. Maybe they're right; maybe it is just his Singularity after all.

"If we take a break," he asks, "are you going to see other people?"

"I doubt it."

"But you might?"

"I'm not interested in anyone else right now, if that's what you're asking. I can't say what will or won't happen, of course. Life is full of calculated risks."

"I can't stand the thought of losing you," he pleads.

"You'll never *lose* me," she says. "You're my friend, you've got my phone number, and I'm not going anywhere."

Val's face scrunches up against his will. She kisses him on the forehead and then stands up and goes somewhere he isn't. He doesn't say anything to stop her. This will haunt him for years.

He stays there under that tree for another hour at least, gazing up at the stars until he, too, loses sight of the constellations. Amid those myriad points of light, all he can see is darkness.

Caroline A. Garrett
MAGNITUDE

guessing. Getting good at it,
particularly in our homes
where we learn the crack and sway of joints . . . the house . . . our own . . . ?
the ride and rattle of these swells and shiver of earth.
Verifying . . . USGS online . . . yes! 5.3 . . . time, location, depth
colored balloons of data
gathering above the map
of our summit home
on Kīlauea
where *phantom quakes* overtake us without warning.
No definition needed. Everyone up here nods. *Phantom quakes.*
Was that one? Or did I just tilt . . . lose my balance for a moment?
We rock. And wonder.
Look at the cat. If wide-eyed . . . a quake. Still sleeping? Ah, it's *me.*
We blame these quakes for everything. Weariness. Confusion of mind.
    Can't recall the author . . . or why am I standing in this room . . .
if the printer doesn't work,
    if we seem to be losing water more rapidly from the pond,
        (never mind that it's summer heat, evaporating us)
    we suspect some quake-riven underwater crack we cannot see.
if TV reception spurts and stutters—or the cat throws up,
    it's the quakes, shaking things loose.

Often, it is not.   We catch and steady ourselves . . . again.

Bora Hah

A FREE LIFE

> *No man ever steps in the same river twice,*
> *for it is not the same river*
> *and he is not the same man.*
> —Heraclitus

Jun

Jun never understood his brother. The two looked different, to begin with, so much so that people hardly guessed them to be brothers: Jun had a square face and a medium height, whereas Chul had a pale, oval face and was already six feet tall by the time he turned sixteen. Their personalities were also different: Jun was a scholar, quiet and observant, versus Chul a fighter, outspoken and ambitious; and perhaps because of this, the two didn't get along very well.

It was a casual Tuesday afternoon. Jun was alone at home, a four-bedroom apartment in the heart of Pyongyang, watching *The Lion King*, a gift from his diplomat father. When the doorbell rang, he opened the front door. To his surprise, three men were staring at him with suspicious eyes.

"Are you Comrade Kim Chul?" asked one of the men.

Jun shook his head.

"He looks too young. He must be the younger brother," said another man. He was holding a photo of Chul taken at his high school graduation.

Before Jun could answer, the men pushed the door open and went into the house. First, they checked the kitchen and the living room, and later tried all four rooms, including two bathrooms and a small balcony. Then they began rummaging through the family's personal belongings, opening every drawer and closet. The house soon resembled a pigpen.

"Your brother, where is he?" the first man barked at Jun.

"I don't know." Jun recoiled, dropping his stare to the ground. But in truth, he knew. Two months ago, his older brother, who claimed himself to be a son of God, had crossed into China, following a missionary from South Korea. How Chul became a Christian Jun never knew. It must have happened while Chul was away in China to attend a university. His original plan was to obtain a degree, come back to the North, join the Worker's Party, and get married. Instead, Chul fell in love with God. The first night he came back from China, he called his brother to his room and showed him the Bible. At first, Jun didn't know it was a Bible because Chul had wrapped it with a newspaper that had the face of their Dear Leader, Kim Jong Il.

"I found life." Chul's eyes gleamed in delight. "I am free now."

The word *free* disturbed Jun. It reminded him of a South Korean propaganda flyer he found buried in the mountain several years ago. It was a photo of a naked girl seductively lying on the floor. Right below the photo was written: *Come to the Free World!* Having never seen a figure of a woman without clothes, Jun felt intimidated. He then quickly left the spot, leaving the flyer behind.

The second man emerged from the master bedroom, holding a bottle of Jun's father's whiskey in his hand. He sat on a dark cherry dining chair and pulled out a cigarette from his jacket pocket. Turning his face to the first man, he said, "Comrade, I think we lost him."

The first man ignored this. He looked at Jun squarely and said, "Did your brother leave you with anything? Like a book or anything to read?"

Again, Jun shook his head. In his mind, he recalled what Chul had warned him earlier: "If I don't return or you don't hear from me, do not try to find me. Discard all my belongings before the authorities come, and when they do, tell them that I ran away. Don't be sad even if I die; I will be in my Father's house." At the time, Jun responded with a cold contemptuous look. He thought his brother had gone crazy, spending stacks of U.S. dollar bills and fake travel passes to deliver the message of *Yesu Geuriseudo* to underground believers and fresh-off-the-boat defectors from China.

Finally, the men gave up.

"Don't ever think about telling people what you saw today," the third man said as he exited the house. "You don't want to know what happens if you do."

Jun nodded. Yet in the back of his mind, he had a bad feeling that the same thing would happen again in the near future; if Chul came back, he would continue his mission, including purposefully leaving pocket-sized Bibles in public restrooms. For this, he would get arrested, perhaps go to a prison camp. He would endure his time there, sometimes in sorrow, sometimes in pride, until his family bribed the camp guards to release him. That is, if only he came back home.

Hana

She had a dream that night. In her dream, she saw Chul. He was still eighteen, ambitious and beautiful. They were holding hands in a dark hallway. November, and it was raining outside. The electricity was cut again, but the two young lovers were rather pleased for that. "Your hands," Chul whispered, "they're too cold." Hana immediately blushed. She tried to release the grip of their folded hands, but Chul didn't let them go. So they walked like that, neither of them speaking much.

This relationship, Hana believed, made sense to her. Their parents had known each other since they were little, and although this love was a surprise for both, it also seemed natural, an easy and sure path: Hana would become an English teacher, Chul a proud soldier of North Korea.

Flashlights glared from a far distance, and the couple quietly parted. "See you later," said Chul. Before he disappeared, his long, delicate fingers drew the shape of an arc on Hana's left shoulder. It remained there like a tattoo of a butterfly.

Every fall the dream returned to her, and she woke with a broken heart. She did not know what made that ancient, childish, and fleeting nine-month relationship so strong. Many years had gone by, but it seemed as though their love never ended.

During those years, Chul went missing for an unknown reason and Hana got married to another man who used to be a monitor of her apartment complex during the widespread famine, the Arduous March, in the mid-1990s. Like her family, he was few of the privileged who did not have to worry about what to eat each day or take extra naps to quiet their stomachs because of hunger. Her husband liked her from the beginning. Hana felt it from the way he avoided her eyes and smiled at her like a child. She also understood that her husband mistook her pity for love, but she accepted this, as pity felt better than her longing for Chul. After marriage, she followed her husband to Japan, where his relatives had gone to live, for better lives.

From time to time, Hana wondered where Chul could be now. She hadn't seen him since their high school graduation. It was a difficult time then, their country suffered, and all colleges had shut down suddenly. Hana decided to wait, but Chul went away, to China. "I will miss you, every day," he said. But even years later, he did not come back. His family would not speak about this, and instead fled the country in the dead of night. But again, it was a difficult time: indifference and irrationality prevailed throughout the country.

Hana's pillow was damp with her sweat. It was still dark outside. She heard the slow breathing of someone lying next to her. She took a deep breath, prayed for a miracle, and opened her eyes: she saw a familiar face instead. She saw an old man who gave her a home and food. This was what she wanted, she realized at last. Hana closed her eyes once again, still hoping for hopeless dreams.

Bora Hah

Matthew

The morning traffic was awful since Matthew got into the cab. It was the beginning of a long Thanksgiving weekend and it seemed like everyone was going somewhere. Among many American holidays, Matthew hated Thanksgiving the most; it reminded him of home, and America was not his home. Long ago, when Matthew was young and passionate, he often left home, crossed many rivers until he knew how to read them in darkness and cold. It was much later that he understood what it meant to lose home, family, lover, even his own name. Yet it was too late by then. He had nothing to blame but himself, a young man blinded by youthful hopes.

"See the river over there?" The taxi driver with a strong southern accent pointed to his left, the Hudson River. "Last year a guy drove straight into that river."

Matthew quietly stared at the river. From the surface, the river seemed calm and clear. But Matthew knew better. Viscerally, he could feel the shock of cold water cutting his soft skin and a sudden change of current that would gulp him down like a hungry animal. He remembered the first time he had crossed the Tumen River. It was late at night, and a missionary who had been guiding Matthew presented a carton of Marlboro Red to a soldier guarding the post. The soldier with a square face casually accepted the gift and ordered them to take off their clothes. He watched them undressing and picked up Matthew's dark green corduroy jacket his mother had bought for him.

They had chosen the wrong night, however. The moon shone so brightly that it was nearly impossible not to miss them. "God is with us, God is faithful," the missionary repeated, more like a mantra than a prayer. Matthew was terrified, but secretly he felt good, thinking he was now joining the burden of the cross, that he was now one of them. When the two men reached the other side of the river, a Chinese pastor greeted them, took them to a safe shelter, and prayed all night. It was he who suggested Matthew abandon his Korean name, Chul. For safety, he said. Matthew was also told not to give his fingerprints to anyone; that way he could pose as a fresh refugee in many different countries.

"Funny thing is, no one, not even his wife knew why. He was just a forty-something plain old salesman, a husband and a father, and then out of the blue, boom! He drowned himself in a river. Man, what kind of life is that?" The chatty driver sounded almost excited.

Matthew's eyes began to twitch. It was a sign that a migraine was coming, that pain was about to begin. Matthew rolled his fists and counted numbers: *hana, dul, set* . . .

"Strange. You remind me of him, even though I don't really know his face, except for the small, blurry picture of him in the paper." The driver chuckled, but only silence was returned. When he looked back, he saw his quiet passenger staring intently at him, his face pale as a ghost.

William Hanson
HAWAIIAN HALL, BISHOP MUSEUM, HONOLULU

Since I can remember, this hall has been an enchanted place
Filled with images of temple gods and sorcery spirits
Still as fierce and unashamed as when first hewn
Born of experiences I cannot imagine

I enter and see rows of metal chairs, setting the stage for a performance
People gather, most of either European or Hawaiian ancestry
I, out of protective habit, secure a seat at the very back
The building's architectural grandeur before and above me

A group of Hawaiians approach
Three or four elderly women, touching, chatting, laughing
And a younger man, calm, silent, physically massive
Their driver, I assume, and likely also a son and a nephew
While the women settle in one of the rows in front of me
The man plants himself right next to me

I then do the unthinkable: I turn and look up at him
Beard, full and wild, hair, long and braided
Skin, smooth, the darkest shade of brown imaginable
Blue jeans, well-worn, a tent of a T-shirt, the color of dried blood
I look down: Feet and rubber slippers, the largest I have ever seen

All the while, he pays no notice to his curious, blond neighbor
He sits upright, hands resting on knees, gaze unwavering
His calm, physical presence radiates timelessness
It is as if I am now witnessing the last Hawaiian
Communing with the most powerful creations of his people

My mind races, but one thought is clear:
This moment will never return

William Hanson

DRAFT BOARD NUMBER 2, DOWNTOWN HONOLULU, ANNO 1971

Fear driven, we gather at this place of dread, island boys of tender age
Bowing to the will of a distant government waging yet another war in a distant place
We have been summoned to be registered, they say, but where will it end?
As wounded? As missing? As the decaying contents of a flag-draped coffin?
Or as just another young spirit broken by systematic humiliation?

Some pace to and fro, some sit bent forward
But we all struggle with ourselves, desperate to master nerves running wild
For we know, here at this threshold to earthly damnation
That we may soon be reduced to human chattel in uniform
To the expendable members of a dubious culture
A culture of advertising and entertainment at home
A culture of defoliation and carpet-bombing abroad

Then the realization: Here we stand as equals before an unknown fate
The lawyer's son from Kāhala, the construction worker's son from Nānākuli
The speaker of Standard English, the speaker of Pidgin
United, if only for a moment, in our fear of a paranoid empire's insanity

Weeks pass . . . I am spared! It is official
But the war continues, as does a familiar sight on Honolulu's streets:
The bumper sticker upon the off duty soldier's pickup truck shouting
AMERICA – LOVE IT OR LEAVE IT
I leave. I grow old abroad

WILLIAM HANSON

TEMPLE OF PUʻUKOHOLĀ

Coastal winds, dry and warm, buffet me
Forgotten the long approach, for I have arrived
My first thought, my only thought: So small I am, so very small!
I strain to see the sky's blue beyond the lava browns and grays that
    tower above
Great sloping walls made of countless round stones,
    the labor of thousands
Ominous the absence of the ancients at this powerful place

Then back to Camp Honokaia, our bus slowly climbing the dirt road
Leaving a trail of reddish-brown dust behind us
A shout! One of the boys has taken a stone from the temple!
The transgression makes us fear the coming night, and the nights to come
We all shout at him until he, panic-stricken,
Hurls it out of an open window

Jeffrey Hantover
GOETHE IN HONOKAʻA

[It] is said he [Goethe] could not tell a lark from a sparrow.
—Edward O. Wilson

The Chinese think a man unwise
who does not know the right names
who cannot love the world
without the names of things.

No one ever told him
the names of things
or maybe he didn't listen.
Nature was parks square and tended
flowers grew in neighbors' backyards
bloomed in the lapels of cheap sport coats.

Trees line the highway
they are just trees
flowers are flowers
red, yellow, pink
simple as a child's pop-up book.

The rain has stopped.
Petals from unnamed trees lie scattered
over gravel driveway and lawn
like bits of red crepe paper
to welcome home returning heroes.
He opens the door and steps outside
into the glowing pink light of dusk.

Mavis Hara

A FISH STORY

    Utaro urged the horse forward. He was sorry he had spent so much time talking with Pono. He had forgotten that in November, the light faded quickly here on the Windward side because the sun set far away in the ocean behind the mountains. The horse's hooves clopped softly up the new road that Johnny Wilson's company had built so that people could cross from Nuʻuanu, over the mountains, down to Kāneʻohe and back again. Now on the Kāneʻohe side, Utaro urged his horse on as the road inclined up toward the mountain ridge. He could feel the cool air settling over the horse and the wagon. The vegetation changed so that instead of walking beside shrubs and grasses, they passed beneath mango and banyan trees. Soon, he began to see feathery beds of palapalai fern. He looked back at his cargo in the wagon bed: rice from the Chinese farmers' cooperative mill, vegetables from Japanese farmers' stands along the roadside, and fish under burlap resting on salted blocks of ice he had bought this morning at the Pālama Ice House.
    The road angled upward and the cargo shifted back slightly in the wagon's wooden bed. Blood from the fish, mixed with the melted ice, ran along the side of the cargo box and dropped into the roadbed. Utaro was aware of the trail of small droplets he was leaving behind. The horse walked deliberately, straining against the weight of the wagon, now full of goods.
    Utaro had bought the fish from Pono, his old fishing friend. Pono and his family had fished for āholehole in the surf at the base of the Diamond Head lighthouse. Years ago in 1900, after Utaro's plantation contract had run out, he drifted to the Pālama section of Honolulu, where he found temporary shelter at a boarding house run by a Japanese woman from his home province of Kumamoto. He took the streetcar to see the sights of Honolulu and rode it until the end of the line in Waikīkī. He was drawn to the dusty excitement of the Kapiʻolani Park Racetrack, where he watched horses, owned by wealthy haole and Hawaiian gentlemen, running over an oval course. Utaro watched with sadness and frustration. Even though he had worked until his plantation contract had ended, he had been unable to save up the money he had dreamed of back in Japan. He was using his small savings to live on now; he was aware that he had no immediate prospects for a job. He could not spare money to wager on the horses. With unfulfilled dreams weighing heavily on his heart, he turned and walked away from the noise of the racetrack, and then wandered further along the seacoast. The ocean water, in beautiful shades of blue, sparkled as it lapped against the

shoreline with a sound like breathing. He stopped to watch a fisherman cast his net in a perfect circle into the waves.

Pono, black hair curling at the nape of his neck—his shoulders, back, and legs covered with a faint dusting of salt—was pulling carefully at the edge of a throw net, trying to keep the school of āholehole contained within the net's circle of knotted threads. Suddenly, the weight of the fish shifted to the edge of the net and the whole school of trapped silvery bodies seemed about to escape into the shallow water. Utaro, in his zori, cotton muslin pants, long-sleeved shirt and pāpale, waded into the water to secure the loose edge of the net and contain the fish. Pono, at first startled by another person's presence, was nevertheless grateful for the help and moved quickly to pull the circular net closed and throw the large bundle of fish onto the sand.

"Mahalo," Pono smiled at the small Japanese man who had come to his aid.

"No pilikia. Two falla hana hana mo betta," Utaro replied, using the words he had learned on the plantation in Kaua'i. A gust of cool wind, flowing out of Mānoa Valley and eddying around the foot of Diamond Head, swirled around the two men. Pono bent to the net and deftly picked out the still flapping silvery fish. Utaro watched as Pono sorted them carefully, throwing the large ones further up the sand and the smaller ones back into the gentle waves. Realizing that Pono needed to work quickly to disentangle the small fish so that they would have a chance to live and grow larger, Utaro again bent over the net to help Pono with this task. Pono smiled his thanks and soon the two men stood over a clean net and next to a silvery pile of fat āholehole.

Two small children who had been playing in the plants along the shoreline approached. An older girl, about twelve, also walked shyly behind them. Pono said something to the girl, who slipped back toward the brush line. She soon reappeared with three tī leaves and a piece of cloth. Pono wrapped three fine āholehole in the tī leaves and the cloth and handed them to Utaro.

"No, no . . ." Utaro protested, but Pono's smiles and repeated "Mahalo," convinced him to accept the gift. That night, back in Pālama, the delighted proprietress of his boarding house treated Utaro to a dinner of āholehole nitsuke. Several days later, he went back to Waikīkī to return the cotton cloth, which he had filled with sweet, red, green, and yellow fish-shaped candy. He spent the afternoon in the surf with Pono, fishing and then sorting the catch. It was the beginning of a long friendship. In the months that followed, Utaro learned some phrases in Hawaiian, the names of fish and seaweed, how to repair a linen fishnet, and found that the rhythmic breathing of the ocean could ease a man's mind and erase some of the longing in a man's soul for a homeland he would never see again. His life as a part-time fisherman could have gone on longer but it was the children, Pono's sisters and brothers, who made Utaro long for more. Playing with the children, Utaro dared to think that in this foreign place, he might be able to try to create a family of his own.

Utaro pulled his jacket closer around him. He could see the light green color of kukui nut trees high up on the mountain's flanks as the wagon clattered up the mountain road. He had rented the chestnut colored horse that he called Kuri and the wagon in Pālama that morning. He suppressed a shiver, hoping that the horse would not notice his anxiety. He tried not to think of the hundreds of skulls the road building crew was said to have found as they constructed the roadbed. Utaro thought instead of Mite, the mischievous Japanese woman he had met at the boarding house soon after he had begun his fisherman's life. Mite loved to play hanafuda cards. She could swear like a man. "Sonofa bitchi!" was often her comment as she threw down her cards after Utaro had won. They shared laughter, and after a time, secrets that they had carried with them to Hawai'i. Mite, anxious to escape a drunken father, had escaped on a sailing ship. The plantations needed workers and she jumped at the chance to leave Japan. Utaro promised his parents that he would return to Japan and marry a cousin that they had selected for him. He never returned and his parents were ashamed. Neither he nor Mite could go back to Japan. It seemed logical for the two of them to consider a new start in this Hawai'i as man and wife.

Pono too, had met a shy, beautiful girl at a family lū'au. Nani was a distant cousin and her brothers were also fishermen. They moored their small boat in Kāne'ohe Bay. One day, Utaro accompanied Pono as he rented a wagon in Pālama. Utaro envied Pono's ability to speak with hapa haole businessmen. Then, driving the horse and wagon to mercantile businesses on King Street, Utaro helped Pono bargain with merchants for a bolt of blue denim cloth and another bolt of cotton printed with colorful flowers.

Utaro accompanied Pono that morning as he drove the horse and wagon over the winding Pali road to Nani's house. It was the first time he had seen the Pali's sharp ridges. The mountains reminded him of a turtle's shell turned on its side. Once on the Kāne'ohe side, they drove down winding roads until they came to Nani's home on Kāne'ohe Bay.

"No! 'A'ole, no can oyogi. No can swim. Mahi'ai, farmer. No can swim." Utaro yelled as Nani's brothers tried to pull him into their fishing boat. Pono smiled and shook his head as he jumped into the boat with Nani's brothers. They were fishermen, but instead of shoreline fishing, they sailed their small boat into the bay and out into the sea to fish for large 'ahi. Utaro shook his head in puzzlement at Pono's courage. To sail away from the bright blue water along the shoreline and out into the deep blue-black ocean, out of sight of land was something that chilled Utaro's heart.

As he waited for Pono to return, Utaro walked the roads of the Kāneʻohe fishing village. He saw Japanese farmers selling daikon, lettuce, green onions, and carrots. Since they were far from the markets in Honolulu, the farmers sold the produce for very little money. Utaro calculated that even though he would have to rent a horse and wagon to make the trip, buying his products in Kāneʻohe and selling them in Pālama would be profitable.

After his marriage to Mite, Utaro made the trip over the mountain road and down the Kāneʻohe side once a week. Utaro brought Pono and his family medicine, needles, newspapers, and other sundries from Honolulu, and bought fresh ʻahi, mahimahi, ulua, and sometimes swordfish from their deepwater fishing trips. Ponoʻs wife, Nani, gave Utaro gardenia buds wrapped in tī leaves,

"For your wahine," she always said. Now on the mountain road, Kuri, the horse was slowing to a stop in spite of Utaroʻs repeated urging to go forward. He and Pono had spent too much time laughing at jokes.

"Nice, your hair and moustache, just like the old-time, King Kalākaua," Pono complimented him, "Kepanee no can grow that kind hair."

"Maybe the poi you teach me to eat," Utaro smiled proudly at him. Their words chased each other merrily as āholehole darting through waves. But they had talked too long and now it was getting dark. Utaro shook his head as he snapped the leather reins against the horseʻs neck to urge him on. Kuri snorted and shook his head. It was as if he could see something in the deepening shadows that shrouded the trail ahead. Utaro could see nothing. Utaro shook the reins again and shouted, "'Ike, i mua, hele aku, go!" in a collection of languages.

It did no good. In fact, Kuri, normally a gentle, good-natured horse, screamed and reared up on his hind legs, flailing at the air with his front hooves. Perhaps there were wild pigs coming down the trail to feed, and Kuri, fearing their curving tusks, was refusing to go on. Perhaps wild dogs, drawn by the scent of fish blood, were rustling in the bushes. Utaro ran over all the logical possibilities in his mind while he climbed down from the wagon to steady the horse. Yet he knew what was coming toward him defied logic and he tried to steel himself for the inevitable. The tiny hairs on the back of his neck rose as he felt something creeping forward through the dusk to challenge him. The cold that overtook him pressed against his body like so many clammy hands. Suddenly, he felt himself falling through waves of sadness. Thoughts swirled through his head. He remembered his first wife who had left his parents to go back to her own village after he had come to Hawaiʻi. He remembered his parents, old and frail, waiting in vain for him to return. He saw his own face, still and pale, lying motionless on a bed. He shuddered. He felt the cold press into him hungrily, trying to satisfy a longing, for the warmth of his blood, for the warmth of the horseʻs flesh. He felt himself surrounded by a craving that could never be satisfied, an emptiness that could never be filled.

"Namu Amida Butsu, Namu Amida Butsu," Utaro mumbled desperately toward the void. With all of his being, he wanted to turn back, to head the horse back down the trail as fast as he could go until they reached the lights of Pono's house by the shore. Yet Utaro knew he could not do such a thing. He thought of his house in Pālama, of his ten black-haired children, tumbling around the low dining room table like puppies. He wanted to submerge himself in the steaming hot water of his furo bath. He longed for the rich, sweet fragrance of hot rice bubbling in Mite's cooking pot, of okazu, of shoyu simmered fish and vegetables. He felt the empty money pouch around his stomach. He needed the coins that selling his load of fish and produce would bring so that he could feed his family. He needed the coins that the Pālama housewives would pay so that he could afford to keep one bag of white rice for his band of giggling toddlers. Though the cold pressed in against him, Utaro took off his jacket and moved slowly toward Kuri's head. He patted the horse's neck reassuringly, running the living warmth of his hand along the horse's tense muscles.

"Ii ko da, Kuri, good boy," he spoke softly as he wrapped his jacket around the horse's eyes. "Come, Kuri," he urged as he took the horse's reins in his hand and walked forward. Utaro forced himself to think about his children laughing as they took the steaming rice into their mouths, about his children as they unwrapped the sticky brown kūlolo made of coconut milk, brown sugar, and poi that Nani had wrapped in tī leaves for their dessert tonight. He walked forward, urging the frightened brown horse into the swirling mist. Then suddenly, inexplicably, Utaro felt the cold retreat, as though somehow he had been granted permission to pass. He felt the horse relax and breathe normally as it clopped forward under its warm hood. Utaro, Kuri and the wagon clattered forward into a gentle, ginger-scented rain. They passed the peak and Utaro could see the road begin to descend into the green valley of Nu'uanu. He slowly pulled his jacket off Kuri's muzzle, and petted him before climbing back into the seat on the wagon's bed. He drove forward with gratitude, following the last pink rays of the setting sun toward the warmth of a brown wooden house at the edge of Pālama town.

Gail N. Harada
AT KEAHUALAKA

We are Oʻahu women
used to city life
not rugged outdoorsy campers,
but hardy in other ways,
with our Kumu for three days on Kauaʻi,
without our cell phones and blow dryers,
not used to 5-minute showers,
navigating around bufo toads with flashlights
on the long walk between our cabins and the bathroom.
Stories are seeds, polyps, or planulae
waiting to metamorphize into polyps.
The last day, we hike up to the pā hula
Keahualaka.
This is where Pele saw
Lohiau striding up the mountain, strong, virile.
I remember this island was the honeymoon
destination of my parents' generation.
As I stand with my hula sisters next to the cliff,
waiting to enter,
the wind sounds like waves washing on the shore:
greens, blues, mountain, sky, ocean caught in the wind.
I feel my parents nearby watching me,
past dialysis, past strokes,
and suddenly a hollow weight,
an overwhelming void fills my chest
bringing unexpected tears that I push back,
and it's time to dance facing the ocean
cerulean, turquoise, azure blue,
feeling rough grass, small stones, ground under my feet.
When we are finished, one by one we place our lei
on the stone altar
and as each returns to her place,
I see eyes glistening.
In our circle, some share:
"I saw my tūtū's face."

GAIL N. HARADA

"I heard my mother's voice. She scolded me
again for marrying my husband."
Tears, laughter, tears.
Even the younger ones among us know loss and joy.
I am not a circle-talker. I do not say
"I felt my parents and they were happy."
In the ocean far below, a few dolphins appear.
Then there are many leaping in the waves,
diving in and out of the seafoam and bright water.

GAMAN TRILOGY

Gaman I: Otsu

In my father's favorite film classic,
The Samurai Trilogy,
the hero's true love waits for Musashi
to return from his quest
to perfect his art
She waits years
selling fans
by a Kyoto bridge
She will endure
rain, snow, anything,
track him through the lawless countryside
risk capture by murderous brigands
If she weeps when she sees him
is she failing to show gaman?
She weeps
tears like morning dew
her hair a glossy black river
down the back of her spring kimono
her feet which have traveled so far
tucked under
so demure
She weeps because her passion

Gail N. Harada

is pure
like a clear mountain stream
rushing over the rocks
She pursues him relentlessly,
arriving at temples or houses
just a day after he has already departed,
a fragile flower that never fades,
her eyes always gentle,
her cheeks the color of cherry blossoms
She sacrifices her health
falling ill
longing to see him again
She is an orphan,
a farmer's daughter
She does not know
she is his perfect woman
Hers is the face he carves on his Kwannon,
the face of compassion and womanly virtue
Her moment comes
as she faces his mortality
"Will you walk with me?" he asks
the night before his duel with Sasaki Kojiro,
the ultimate test of his swordsmanship
The question is not a simple invitation
She is overjoyed and struggles from her sickbed
to join him for a walk on the twilight shore
from which he will depart in the morning
She cannot restrain herself,
beseeches him tearfully
to abandon the katana
She just wants him
to be an ordinary man
instead of a swordsman obsessed with his art
"A samurai's wife would send him off with a smile," he says
and she straightens up and rises to the occasion
She sends him off without tears
With gaman
The musical score swells,
waves glint in the pre-dawn light,

as the boatman rows Miyamoto Musashi
toward Ganryu Island
as I am torn between frustration
and reluctant admiration
of Otsu on the receding shore.

Gaman II: Oshin

The Japanese soap opera addiction of the 80s
is back on KIKU-TV
25 years after refusing to watch
the interminable trials and tribulations of Oshin,
I understand
what my parents, aunties, uncles, and grandparents
saw in her story
She was born to an impoverished family in the Meiji period
had a hard life
was sent to work when she was just seven years old
endured the abuse of employers
suffered at the hands of the mother-in-law from hell
survived earthquakes and World War II
worked hard so her children could have a better life
started her life over and over
triumphed over all adversity
to arrive at a point in life in the early 1980s
when she finally enjoyed success
could reflect on her journey in life
from impoverished child worker
to mother of a successful supermarket owner
and could share her story with her favorite grandson
as they traveled to all the places she'd been
Oshin still lives on YouTube
She is a rosy-cheeked child who shows gaman,
enduring the abuse of cruel employers
without complaining even once
without getting angry even once
until she is wrongly accused of stealing
and runs away to go back home
wanting to see her mother

Gail N. Harada

She gets lost in a blizzard but is rescued by a stranger
who takes care of her until the snow melts
when he is killed for being an army deserter
She finally returns home to a tearful reunion with her mother
only to be beaten by her father and sent back
to work for another family
When she is older, her father tries to sell her
to work as a barmaid
so she runs away to Tokyo to learn a trade
as a hairdresser
falls in love with a good man
is happy for two minutes
loses everything in the Great Earthquake of 1923
is forced to move in with her husband's family
must endure the abuse of her evil mother-in-law
suffers a broken arm and can never be a hairdresser again
endures hard labor in the fields
and finally runs away to build a new life
Every happiness is fleeting
followed by another tribulation
which Oshin endures with gaman
with patience and dignity
never striking back
never giving up
bowing her head
accepting bad treatment
until some intolerable injustice
finally causes her to run away again
to try to rebuild her life once more
always working hard
triumphing in spite of hardships
showing gaman again and again
gaman gaman gaman
resilient like green bamboo
intrepid as plum blossoms in winter
unfailing perseverance
Oshin lives on
subtitled in Spanish
dubbed in Sinhala

translated on YouTube
speaking to people in 59 countries
inspiring admiration, aspirations.

Gaman III: Modern Woman Masako

In Natsuo Kirino's Japanese crime novel *Out*,
Yayoi, the pretty woman, may endure
unhappiness
in isolation
fighting with her no-good husband
but not complaining to others
for the sake of her family
with gaman
up to a point
but the effort takes its toll
if there is no relief
Pressure reaches critical mass
and one night she snaps
topples like a camellia blossom
like a decapitated head
instead of petal by petal
slipping off her own leather belt
strangling her wayward husband
The murderer wife feels no regret
but does not know what to do
It is her strong woman friend, Masako, who is the hero
who devises a plan,
calling on their two women friends to help
clean up the mess by chopping up the husband
putting pieces of him in 43 city-approved garbage bags
to be disposed of discreetly
in neighborhood garbage collection areas
before pick-up day, to obliterate him completely
erase him
But one friend, Kuniko, is untrustworthy and stupid
not following the plan
dumping her portion in trash cans at a public park
The darkest of secrets pulls everything apart

GAIL N. HARADA

sending Masako on a journey
into the lower depths
where gaman falls short
Survival depends on
cool intelligence
break from conventions
becoming tamahagane
"jewel steel."

JOSEPH HARDY
TINNITUS

our mother taught us neglect
as a hole in the air   an unpredictable
vacancy of mind

I have wanted to share it for years
as the taste of something awful
but it resists conveyance

like the sound of my sister's tinnitus
mine   a thin blade bowing the edge
of an unforgiving file
hers   I couldn't say—only
that as a child   sometimes it kept her from sleeping

perhaps that sound a freight train makes
steel wheels   re-polishing the rails on a slow curve
years ago   I lived above those tracks
bedroom window yards   from sixteen trains a day
and truly   like neglect   within a week unheard

except for long nights with flu or ache in bed
when the stuttering   laden cars at 2:05 a.m.
rolled south   squealing their long complaint
one hundred and sixty-four I counted once
going somewhere carrying something
out of mind any other time   and there

leaving me in need   wanting
all these disconnected years
a new way of speaking
the poetry a child expresses
stunned by a sharp and sudden pain
whose mouth opens
in the silent "O" we hear   we've all heard
before the shriek

Joseph Hardy

like my sister once
holding my mother's head against her own
and asking, *can't you hear it?*

Jennifer Hasegawa
ODE TO PEPEʻEKEO MILL CAMP

Grandma's house is held
together by a dozen rusty nails
and inhabited
by colonies of wild cane.

The front door
is covered in lichen,
growing in patterns
that type out essays
on forgetting.

The road to her house
crumbles at the edges
and is split down the center.

I scan the land
for a shred of aloha
fabric from grandma's rag mop
or a shard of the tin roof
that banged out bossa novas
in rain storms.

In the sting
of cane arrow
against heart,
I see her stepping
into the raging overgrowth,
her gray polyester dress
hiked above her wrinkled knees.

Moving farther into the breach,
deeper into the gulch of time,
where will she emerge?

Jennifer Hasegawa

TWO-MINUTE MEMOIR

When I was 18,
I sold expensive clothes
at the mall.

Tourists and sex workers
were the only ones
who could ever afford
to buy anything.

Out on Kūhiō Avenue on a Friday night,
Chantal shouted:
"*Hui!* Girlie! Like da dress? Looks good . . . right?"

And they were proud.
And they saw that it was pleasing to the eye
and that it was desired to make one wise.

She set me up
to babysit
for the owner of the club
she danced at.

Tony had a baby
and an ex-wife with no septum.

As I stepped off the bus
at his house at midnight,
he'd get into a Rolls Royce
and drive to the club.

I'd put the baby to sleep
reading from my geology
textbook: Mohorovičić discontinuity.

And the Lord God said,
Behold,
the man is become as one of us,
to know good and evil.

JENNIFER HASEGAWA

In the morning,
I'd heat the griddle
as the grill of his car
made its way through
the still-dark suburbs.

He'd pay me right
from a tight money clip
and eat a stack of hotcakes
like a sandwich.

*And so they ate it
and their eyes were opened.*

On his birthday night,
he put on his suit and python boots,
wandered around the house,
and passed out on his bed
with one leg hanging off the side.

*And they made themselves
garments of gold and lined them
with the manes of lions.*

Those mice and their scissors!

And the lambs
with their switchblades
have cut the roars
out of the beasts.

Wake to a wavering
tower of tongues.

Hold the heavy paw
of time—its slowing pulse

fooling you into thinking
the future is farther, kinder
than it is.

Ann Inoshita

FAMOLARE

Fo look taller my madda said,
"No can wear long tops or long skirts cuz going drag you down.
Gotta wear short jackets.
Wear high heel shoes. Famolare."

I no can wait until I was old enough fo dress like my madda
and wear da nice wedges wit waves engraved on da side.

Now no mo Famolare.
My madda said, "You no need Famolare. You tall already."

STICKERS AND HAPPY FACE STAMP

I asked my madda if I could bring stickers to school.
She said no cuz no good I bring stickers to school, but I brought da stickers
    anyway.
My madda was right. Everybody was saying stuff like, "Nice, your stickers! I like!"
By da end of da day, I only had a few stickers left. Lucky ting I neva bring my
    favorite stickers.

One odda time, I asked my madda if I could bring her happy face
    stamp to school.
She had one nice stamp dat she let us use at home.
She said I no can bring da stamp.
I neva listen. I brought da stamp to school.
Da whole class was so happy. Everybody was saying, "I like stamp!"
I was stamping everybody's hands. Den dey was saying, "I like try!"
Den odda kids was stamping happy faces on each odda.

My teacha took away da happy face stamp from somebody
and told da class dat she was going keep da stamp cuz not suppose to bring
    dis kine stuff.

I was sweating. Afta class, I told da teacha dat I brought da stamp.
I wanted da stamp back, but she said my parents had to pick it up from her.

Was all my fault. I not suppose to bring da stamp to class.
My madda and fadda came to my class and was talking to my teacha.
I shame not cuz my teacha was complaining about me.
It was how she was complaining. She was talking down to dem like
    dey stupid.

My skin felt hot, and I was sweating. Not my parents' fault I neva
    listen to dem.
I sat dea wishing it was ova.
I wish I neva bring da happy face stamp.
I wish I listened to my madda in da first place.

My parents neva say much.
Dey look at each odda and sigh
cuz no matter wat dey say
my teacha keep scolding dem.

Wen da conference was ova, I told my madda and fadda dat I sorry.
Dey knew I was sorry, and I not suppose to bring da stamp in
    da first place.
But da teacha not suppose to talk to us laidat.

Wat kine teacha dat?

Ann Inoshita

WAIPAHU RAIN

Nowdays, no rain too much in Waipahu, but befo time, we used to get
    plenny rain.
Wheneva we walk Cornet, we pass by canals wit small fishes inside.

Sometimes, rain so hard when we go elementary school.
Da frogs hop around da grass and get choke mushrooms growing everywhere.
Nobody eat da mushrooms cuz we know mushrooms get poison inside.

Even though get plenny rain, no need worry about flooding
cuz my jichan built one drainage system fo our house.
Wheneva rain, da water follows one path and goes down da driveway.

Wen raining and cold, my madda make corn chowder.
Sometime, she make chicken or turkey soup.
We all drink warm soup and talk about da rain.

Scott Kikkawa
Excerpt from RED DIRT

Harry Kurita's apartment on Kapiolani Boulevard wasn't a very large place. It was new and had the smell of a new place, of fresh paint and wall-to-wall carpet. Over the new apartment smell was the faint overlay of Black Cavendish, Harry's tobacco of choice. Sophisticated. Worldly. Just like the tomes on his shelves with the raised leather on the spines and gold leaf letters. The tiny parlor was crammed with them. What it wasn't crammed with was furniture—there wasn't enough room for it. An off-white loveseat, a walnut lectern with a large volume of Keats pretentiously opened to "Ode on a Grecian Urn," and a small coffee table piled with more old books and a decanter of scotch were the only things in the little room apart from the shelves stuffed to the gills with Romantic English Literature or criticisms on it.

There was no television. I met Harry Kurita in passing at a cocktail party hosted a year before by my sister Iris, a high school geometry teacher and advocate for political change. Harry was spouting some diatribe about the evils of television. He stood in the middle of my sister's parlor with a martini in his hand ranting about television being a bourgeois tool used to control the masses, or some such nonsense. He made this speech of his while I was trying to watch a previous day's ball game on my sister's television set. I asked him to hold it down, please—Mantle was at bat in the bottom of the ninth. Harry called me a "case in point" and shook his head with exaggerated sadness. Iris kicked me out of her house and wouldn't talk to me for a couple of weeks. It was nice to see that the exalted Harry Kurita practiced what he preached. Or maybe he just couldn't afford a television set like me and a lot of other people on a government salary.

Harry didn't need a television set to seduce the UH coeds he brought back for "study sessions." All he needed was his magnetic personality along with the loveseat and the books and the scotch. What he didn't need was competition from Ed Sullivan.

The little apartment was on the ground floor of a new three-story apartment building. The exterior was done up in brown moss rock and the building was dubbed *Kapiolani Suites* in modern white script on the wall facing the boulevard. The wall was flanked with ferns and ti leaves and a handful of black gas tiki torches skewed at stylish angles. All the new buildings were either "suites" or "arms" or "gardens" or "manors." I guess everyone wants to feel like their new address is swankier than their last, even though it's just as hot and miserable as the old place and a hell of a lot smaller. Only the new paint and carpet made it nicer.

Scott Kikkawa

The new place certainly wasn't more exclusive than the old place, either. In fact, it was probably much less so. Flashing my badge and a suggestion to the manager that he get an after-lunch drink with the dollar I slipped him got me access to Harry Kurita's little love nest. Try that with any daikon-cutting housewife in Kakaako and you're likely to end up posting bail for a trespassing charge.

The parlor didn't yield any interesting or relevant information. It was so sparse except for the books that there wasn't much of anything to look at. I moved to the bedroom. It's where Harry probably spent most of his time there, anyway. Even—and especially—during his "study sessions." The bedroom was stuffy and tiny, smaller than the parlor. The twin-sized bed in the middle of the room dominated the small space. There was a small nightstand with a small lamp and a maroon alarm clock with brass bells perched on it. There was a dresser against the wall at the foot of the bed and a closet door next to the dresser. I started my methodical search with the nightstand. It had an open space under a single drawer where Harry kept more old books. The books were all poetry collections—Keats, Shelley, Oscar Wilde, and W. B. Yeats—all stuff set aside for post-roll-in-the-hay recitations in the nude no doubt. The books had nothing in them except poems. I opened the nightstand drawer. Condoms. No big surprise there. Loose change. The poor girls needed bus fare home after the "study session" was over. Aspirin. Actual conversation with tittering coeds was probably less than fascinating for a big brain like Harry. And panties. Lacy, silky panties in assorted colors. Trophies. They were typical of someone with Harry Kurita's ego. He probably watched those girls in his lectures the way Uther Pendragon watched Igraine when he was a guest at Cornwall and probably plotted to bed them in pretty much the same fashion: in the guise of something he wasn't—a trusted academic who was solely interested in the intellectual "development" of young, impressionable women. Judging from the number of panties in his nightstand drawer his appetite was large. Half a pack of Choward's Violet mints to sweeten the breath rounded out all that was in the nightstand. All were indicators of nothing I didn't already suspect.

The bed itself was neatly made. Harry seemed like the kind of intense and obsessive individual who did this every morning. There was nothing under the bed or under the mattress. I moved to the foot of the bed and opened the closet door. Empty. There was nothing in there except for a winter coat twenty years out of style for the occasional mainland trip and a whole lot of wire and wooden hangers with nothing on them. The top shelf of the closet, which was usually the place for a suitcase, was also empty. No shoes on the closet floor. No neckties or belts on the hooks inside the door.

I shut the closet door and looked at the dresser. There was nothing on it but a fine film of dust. I opened all of the drawers. Empty, every single one.

There were only two more rooms to look at in the tiny apartment. The bathroom's soap tray still held a slightly used bar of soap and half a bottle of shampoo. The medicine cabinet was full of talcum powder and green and brown glass bottles of little pills from a University area pharmacy: sleeping pills, pills for back pain, vitamins, but nothing critical or life-or-death necessary. What wasn't in there was a toothbrush, cologne, razor, or shaving brush—stuff the well-groomed man on the lam can't do without. The basin and the tub were dry and looked like they had been for quite some time. The manager had told me that he hadn't seen Harry Kurita for about a month and that the rent would be due soon. He had gone over this a couple of weeks before with the Missing Persons guys, but they hadn't asked to see his apartment. Not yet, at least.

I went back out to the parlor and sat down on the loveseat. It looked fairly obvious that Harry Kurita had blown town. The Missing Persons guys would have checked the airlines and the passenger ships; I'd remember to ask about it later when I got back to the station. I started to perspire more profusely and the urge for a cigarette became overwhelming. I got up off the loveseat and walked to the opposite side the parlor to open the window. It took me all of three steps to get to there. When I put my hands on the frame, I looked down at the sill and saw splinters. I squatted just a little to get eye level with the sill and looked more closely. The catch was bent slightly and scraped underneath. I stood again and opened the window and examined the underside of the frame. Someone had taken a sharp-edged object and had undone the catch.

I pondered this while I lit up a Lucky Strike by the opened window. I took my hat off and let the slight breeze play through my limp, sweat-soaked hair while I smoked. If Harry Kurita killed Jiro Machida then fled the island, he took his time. The body was dismembered and burned and the charred remains were buried in a shallow grave in the middle of a Kunia cane field. He came back to his apartment and packed a suitcase with all of his clothes and some necessary toiletries then he disappeared. Why not? Who knows when anyone would have discovered Jiro's remains? Leaving the dog tags was sloppy, but he may not have known about them—there was evidence that there was probably clothing incinerated to hell with the flesh, and clothing would have hidden the dog tags. Only the bones remained, if you could call the brittle, barely solid state we found them in "remaining." And the dog tags. The tags were probably the only metal Jiro wore on his person. The skull was missing, probably to prevent dental identification. It was the work of a man who knew how to use his brain. Harry Kurita was a man who knew how to use his brain and he probably used it more discriminately than he used other parts of his body.

I discarded my cigarette butt by flinging it into the mulch under the ti plants and ferns outside the parlor window. Then, just for the hell of it, I turned to the kitchen and walked off the shag carpet onto the linoleum.

They invented the term kitchenette for the little space I was standing in. To call it a kitchen would be stroking its ego. There was a porcelain-coated iron basin under a tiny window hung with rough cotton curtains, no doubt sewn by Harry's doting mother. Standing in front of the basin, the icebox and the range were both within arm's reach in opposite directions. I pulled the chrome handle on the icebox door and peeked inside. The sour smell of old milk hit me in the face and there were other food items in varying stages of slow decay. The freezer was fuzzy with accumulated ice. Somewhere in there was a chicken and a box of peas. And one of those stick-in-the-oven dinners in compartmentalized foil trays. A bachelor's teishoku.

I shut the icebox door and jiggled the chrome handle to make sure it was sealed. Then I saw it. Next to the stove was a small wastebasket. It occurred to me that nobody had emptied the thing since Harry went on the lam. It was a veritable time capsule of the day he skipped out. I opened a small drawer next to the range, pulled out a pair of tongs and went fishing.

There was old tin foil with a crust of what was once brown gravy from the top of a frozen dinner. Under that, there was paper: mailers for some correspondence course on how to "increase your stamina" with some Charles Atlas look-alike in leopard briefs and oiled biceps, an old baking soda box, a paper bag from a liquor store, and a newspaper.

I pulled the newspaper out with the tongs and set it on the counter next to the range. It was a *Honolulu Advertiser* dated exactly one month before—probably a couple of days before both Jiro Machida and Harry Kurita were reported missing. I flipped through the pages, looking at every article and advertisement. I thought about Gid Hanohano and his habit of reading the newspaper every day cover to cover, missing no detail. Gid told me that it's something every good investigator should do. I tried to follow his example, taking in every column inch. The headline on the peace talks at Panmunjom and the weather report with its promise of miserable humidity brought back memories of the week I spent in hell working on the Miyasaki case. The paper was from that week. I thought of the heat and the kona winds. I thought of the friend I had to put down and the friend I almost lost. I thought of meeting and falling for Ellen. I thought of the poor girl we fished out of the harbor.

The harbor.

There it was, staring me in the face. Right on page three someone had circled the name of a ship under the vessel departures portion of the shipping announcements. The *Iwakuni Maru*, a Japanese flagged fishing boat, was scheduled to depart at Pier 32 at 11:00 a.m. on that date. I tore page three out of the paper and folded it and stuck it in my coat pocket. I threw the tongs back in the little drawer and I put my porkpie hat back on my head, snapping the brim down in front. I opened the front door, stepped outside, and closed the door behind me. I got another Lucky Strike out of the pack and lit it up. I stood in the cool green shade of the torch ginger leaves fronting Harry Kurita's apartment, enjoying the cigarette. Missing Persons would have talked to the airlines and to the big passenger ship lines that went regularly between Honolulu and the mainland or the Orient. They probably would not have talked to any of the tramp steamers and they definitely would not have talked to the crew of a Japanese fishing boat. If Harry Kurita hopped aboard a Japanese fishing boat, he might have gone far, far away indeed.

Waialua. Long drive. Hot. Red dirt. Biting insects.

Waialua was a little plantation town on the North Shore full of the sickly-sweet smell of cane being processed at its mill and blasted by the sun, a place on the edge of nowhere if Oahu was nowhere. I couldn't believe I was headed out to the cane fields again that day and this time to fields even farther away than Kunia. Jiro Machida's house was one in a row of rickety structures all covered with the same dark green paint meant to hide the red dirt but not doing a very good job of it. I had gone through three Lucky Strikes on the drive out from town. I lit up one more as I pulled up the driveway of white sand and crushed coral dumped and spread out over red dirt where the small lawn ended. There was a vehicle parked on the lawn, a nondescript gray-brown Ford about ten years old. I pulled parallel to the Ford on the sand drive and cut the engine.

The lanai was as Ellen had described it—hemmed in by metal screen rusted by the salt air of the nearby beach and sporting its own screen door at the top of the three rotten-looking plank stairs leading up to it. Inside the screens, I could make out a small whitewashed table and an old office chair. On the table was a black typewriter. I crossed the little lawn and put a foot on the first plank stair. The front door slammed and light, rapid steps thumped their way up to the lanai screen door, and the door was thrown open, narrowly missing the brim of my hat. I was face-to-face with a bald head in dark, round sunglasses and long black goatee. The rest of him was a spry, compact body wrapped up in the robes of a Buddhist monk. He smelled of Bay Rum aftershave.

"So sorry. Excuse, please," he said, blading his right hand vertically and holding it in front of his face in reverent greeting, bowing deeply.

"It's okay. Daijobu," I replied, bowing reflexively. The monk smiled with a mouthful of yellowed but sturdy-looking teeth at me, bowed again while passing me, and got into the Ford. He hit the starter, nodded goodbye, and then reversed off the lawn onto the road back toward the sugar mill and town. I shook my head. A homicide dick encounters all kinds of characters in the line of duty, but that monk was definitely one of the stranger-looking birds I had seen in broad daylight. I climbed the steps to the lanai. Off to the right side of the door was a getabako full of ritzy high heels. I knocked on the frame of the screen door.

"Did you forget something, Basho?" a high, slightly nasal voice called from the gloom of the interior of the little house. The voice had the sound of unintentional allure, of a trap set unwittingly by a child. It was the sound of a sleeping cobra, if a sleeping cobra made a sound.

"I sure did. I forgot to come at a better time. But I'm not Basho. Basho just made a beeline back toward town, like I should have. It's too hot to be in Waialua today."

"Some of us don't have a choice," said the voice, getting closer. Small steps padded toward the door until I could smell the warm spice of her body. A silhouette emerged from the darkness, graceful and curvy.

"Can I help you?" she asked through the screen. I could see black hair piled high and red lips through the screen and, I thought, the flutter of eyelashes downcast demurely.

"Mrs. Beverly Machida?" I asked. I pulled my badge from my pocket and showed it to her through the screen. "I'm Detective Sergeant Yoshikawa of the Honolulu Police Department. Could I trouble you for a word, Mrs. Machida?"

"You *could*," said the sleeping cobra, languidly with subtle heat. A small hand undid the iron hook that held the screen door closed. "Won't you come in, Detective?"

She was about five foot six if you didn't count the hair piled on her head. With the hair, she was almost as tall as I was and most unusually tall for a Japanese girl. She was built like a Radio City Rockette with skin bronzed by the sun, though not in the way Ka-san's was from years of hard labor in the cane fields; hers was the bronze of health and vanity, the tint of swimming and tennis. She had exceptionally large eyes and full, wet lips that glistened in the faint light of the sun through the lanai screens. She was wearing a simple white dress with the palest gold floral brocade that purposely drew attention to the dark, sensuous luster of her skin. She looked at me from under hooded lids, lazily and dreamily, as if she were looking through me at a pastoral Van Gogh full of gold and blue, something infinitely more interesting than my face.

"Thank you," I said. I removed my red-dirt dusted wingtips and followed her into the warm little parlor, shutting the screen door behind me. The room had a homey, rustic, island feel to it, furnished with a koa-framed sofa and koa-framed seats. The cushions were upholstered in white shantung silk and the coffee table held a large koa bowl filled with colored glass globe floats from Japanese fishnets. Across the sofa and the coffee table against the far wall was a television set and on the television set was a white porcelain vase full of freshly cut torch ginger, bird-of-paradise, and lobster-claw heliconia. It was the opposite of Harry Kurita's cramped little seduction library. It was a place where a woman was the predator.

"Won't you have a seat, Detective?"

"Thank you."

I sat down in one of the koa armchairs with my hat in my hands and my hands in my lap. Beverly Machida's manicured fingers pushed an ashtray on the coffee table toward me. I pulled my pack of Lucky Strikes out of my pocket and offered her one. She pulled one of the cigarettes out of the pack in a sensual, near-obscene manner like she was undressing it. I held the Zippo out for her and she grasped my hand while she lit up. Her hand was soft and warm and felt like something only felt in a bedroom. She let her fingers slide slowly off my hand when she was lit up and tossed her head back lazily while she slowly blew white smoke toward the ceiling. I lit up my own cigarette and stuck the Zippo back in my pocket. She regarded me from under dark, thick lashes.

"What brings you out to Waialua on this hot day, Detective?"

"News," I said. "Bad news."

"Jiro?"

I nodded. I was staring at the glass globes in the bowl on the table. I brought my eyes up to meet hers and found she was looking at nothing, staring right through me as if I weren't there at all. She suddenly had the dead, dull eyes of a reptile on a wet leaf with no spark of thought behind them. Or maybe her eyes were always like that and I failed to notice them when I first looked at her; there was a lot more about Beverly Machida to notice at first glance. I braced myself for the wail and the convulsions. They didn't come. Instead, she stood up calmly and walked over to a credenza near the television set. She bent down and opened a pair of doors and produced a tray with a crystal decanter full of scotch and a couple of tumblers. She padded back to the coffee table in small, mincing steps like a kimonoed geisha and set the tray down next to the koa bowl full of glass globes and removed the diamond-like stopper from the decanter. She looked up at me with a wide smile.

"Drink?"

"Why not?"

Her small hands lifted the heavy decanter with improbable ease and poured the dark amber liquid generously into the cut crystal tumblers. It was the most dumbfounding thing I had ever seen. In my short time in Homicide, I had broken the horrible news to newly made widows a number of times. I had witnessed the loud, terrible wail from the Portuguese matron who clenched her flour-covered fists and beat them on her huge apron. I had witnessed the quiet, intense stare of the Japanese housewife with watery eyes who was broken into a thousand pieces under the quiet façade of dignity. And everything else I had seen was something between the two: the young kanaka newlywed who repeated "Oh, my God" over and over again, the old Filipina plantation matriarch who crossed herself and bawled into her brown hands, the haole socialite who dug her fingernails into your forearm and asked, "Are you sure? There must be some mistake . . ."

Beverly Machida was something I had never seen before.

She coolly handed me the tumbler and stood close enough to my chair so I could feel her heat, watching me take my first sip of scotch. Her right hand rested on the dramatic curve of her hip and she reached out with her left hand to fix the lapel of my coat, all the while humming a Cole Porter tune with lascivious huskiness just under her breath. I stiffened unnaturally when her hand touched my clothing and my blood ran cold. This was the strangest manifest of shock I had ever seen.

She sat back down and took up the other tumbler, draining half of it in a single pull. She set it back down on the tray, looked up at me, and smiled some more. I thought I smiled back but I didn't really. I flinched. It only felt like I smiled.

"We found remains in a cane field in Kunia," I said, just to fill the air with something other than my discomfort.

"I already knew he was gone," she said, almost dreamily, still smiling and still looking right at me but not really at me, like she was looking at a spot in the air where my head was.

"How?"

"I felt it. And Basho told me so."

"The monk in the Ford?"

"Yes. He's my spiritual counselor."

"How did *he* know?"

"He said it was the way of things. That Jiro yearned to be one with the fabric of eternity, to add his own light to the lights of those who had already achieved that oneness. Basho said he was there in the tapestry of lights, shining more brightly than ever, even more so than he did here with us."

"He said that? Just now, before he left?" I took another sip of my scotch. It burned on the way down.

"Yes," she said, almost giggling.

"Lucky guess."

"In our lives, there is no guessing, Detective. There is only clarity in varying degrees."

"Sure."

I was beginning to feel like a drunken peasant watching a medieval passion play, admiring the pretty colors and the pretty noises paid for by his hard-earned coin but completely missing the point. Beverly Machida sat there staring in my direction with a vacant smile on her tanned face. She raised her tumbler to her lips and drained the rest of her drink. I did the same.

"Another drink, Detective?"

"By all means."

She poured another drink for both of us, just as stiff as the last. I watched her raise her tumbler to her lips with both hands and nearly empty it. I didn't touch mine. I looked at her trying to determine if her queer behavior was some off-the-deep-end reaction to the news that her husband was dead.

"I'm a Homicide Detective, Mrs. Machida," I said, trying to elicit a more normal reaction from the strange young widow.

"Beverly."

"Pardon me?"

"Call me Beverly. Mrs. Machida is my mother-in-law."

"I'm a Homicide Detective . . . Beverly."

"It sounds like an interesting job." She continued to smile and poured herself another drink. At this, I lost it.

"Interesting job? I'm not trying to small talk you into a date, *Beverly*. I'm trying to tell you your husband was the victim of foul play. Murder. Murder most foul. Someone hacked his body to bits and burned it in a cane field. Does that mean anything to you?"

She set her tumbler down on the coffee table and her smile became a spoonful sweeter. "It doesn't matter how he got there, Detective," she said, now looking just a little medicated as well as inscrutable. "He's one with all existence, the way he always wanted to be."

"Stop. No more mystic proclamations or introspective talk of the fabric of existence or any other assorted Buddhist mumbo-jumbo. I'm trying to tell you that someone killed Jiro Machida and cut him up and incinerated his pieces in the middle of a Kunia cane field. Jiro Machida. Your husband. Would you do me a big favor and play along just a little bit? If you don't want to cry, you can sit there and look astonished. Or angry. Or even catatonic. Just don't be serene. I might get hysterical if you give me more serene."

"You're tense," she said, smiling like a jade carving. "Would you like a massage?" I shot up out of the koa chair and nearly sent my tumbler of scotch hurtling to the floor.

"I need to use your bathroom," I said.

"It's in the back, behind the kitchen." Beverly Machida continued to sit and smile and drink like we were at some hotel lounge trying to put up the show of getting to know each other before angling for a kiss goodnight. It was more than I could wrap my brain around. Her strange behavior actually made my head hurt. I made my way through the cozy little parlor into a clean plantation kitchen with new Formica on the counters and new linoleum on the floors. The bathroom was a little annex attached to the rear of the main house, like it was in most plantation houses of the era in which it was built. I exited the back of the kitchen through a windowed door and descended two steps to reach the bath annex. A whitewashed board with hinges and a handle served as the door. I pulled it open and yanked a chain dangling in front of my face to rouse the naked light bulb.

The floor of the bath annex was a bare poured concrete slab, which replaced the original pine boards. There was a drain in the middle of the floor, a deep wooden furo and a commode and basin on wall opposite the furo. Mounted on the wall above the basin was a medicine cabinet with a mirror door. I walked over to the basin and twisted the "C" knob for cold tap water. I splashed my face with it and looked in the mirror at a haggard, irritated face. It was the face I imagined on Arthur after he had been betrayed by Lancelot and Guinevere, lined by grief and haunted by his burden of rule. At the moment, though, my grief and burden were being caused by my inability to read a strange young widow's bizarre reaction to her husband's murder. It made for a dramatic picture all the same. I dried my face and hands off on a fluffy white towel on a hook next to the medicine cabinet then I opened the cabinet.

It was full of man's stuff: shaving brush, razor, after-shave lotion—Bay Rum. Basho's scent. Was the strange little "spiritual advisor" spending the night? Neither of them was even supposed to know Jiro was dead until I told her that afternoon. Then again, if what Ellen said about Beverly and Harry Kurita was true, Beverly wouldn't have much of a problem carrying on with the monk right under Jiro's self-righteous nose. All of the girly stuff was probably in the bedroom at some dressing table, and there probably was a dressing table in the bedroom. Mrs. Machida was pretty continental for a girl who lived in a Waialua plantation village house. There was aspirin, too. Lots of it. The way she sucked the scotch up, she probably needed it.

I looked down. The floor was wet near the furo. Someone just had a bath. Either Beverly took one just before coming to the door or Basho did before getting in his jaunty Ford and hightailing it out of Waialua. The whole place still had the smell of soap and a little Bay Rum. Basho. It didn't surprise me at all. Beverly may have offered *me* a bath if she thought it would make me less "tense." Maybe I was overreacting. Maybe she was just really eccentric and this was her way of dealing with terrible news. Maybe I should just get the hell out of Waialua and pick up some flowers to take to Ellen's and just forget about the whole damn thing. What the hell. I tried. Sometimes breaking the bad news to the new widow wasn't all the drama it was supposed to be. With Beverly Machida it wasn't even close. I'd spent enough time on the fringes of the island up to my knees in red dirt and misery. Time to call it a day and clock out.

I got my head together and exited the bath annex. The sun was now dipping toward Kauai and shining directly in my eyes. I took a quick look at the little yard and garden in the back, fenced in by a makeshift barrier of bamboo stakes and chicken wire, no doubt meant to keep the chickens at the Filipino's house next door from wandering into Beverly's little cucumber patch and pecking away at the long green fruit near the ground. I climbed the two steps to the kitchen door and went back into the house.

I crossed through the kitchen and my socked feet nearly tripped on something on the parlor floor. It was a white dress with gold brocade flowers. I looked up and saw Beverly Machida sprawled on the sofa with her hair down and her eyes closed and the same empty smile gracing her dark face. She was wearing nothing but her brassiere and a slip, both starkly white against her tan skin. She held her tumbler of scotch high on her bare midriff just below the breathtaking swell of her lace-sheathed bosom.

"I'm sorry," she said vacantly but with a seductive undertone. "It's hot."

"Just like I said."

I was already headed toward the door. This bizarre display was too much. Eccentric or not, no grieving widow ever shed her clothes for me as a reaction to the terrible news I gave her.

"Would you like to join me?" she asked, eyes still closed.

"Thanks, but I've got to run."

I took a calling card out of my coat pocket and dropped it on the coffee table next to the scotch decanter. "Sorry about your husband. Call if you have any questions." I put my hat back on my head, snapped the brim down in front and opened the screen door. As I got back into my wingtips, a husky giggle came from the sofa.

"Don't go," she said. She hadn't budged.

"I have to."

"Please stay and lie down with me, Harry."

Harry. Maybe it was the shock. More likely it was the scotch. I tied my shoes quickly and started for the lanai screen door. For no reason at all, I looked at Jiro's typewriter and walked over to it. It was clean and well maintained and there was an old towel draped over the back of the chair, probably used to cover up the typewriter when not in use to protect it from dust and the salt air of the North Shore. I opened the top, yanked the ribbon spool out and stuck it in my pocket. I listened to the sound of nothing floating through the screen door one last time. I got off the lanai and into my car and drove as fast as I could out of Waialua.

Maya Kikuchi

PACIFIC

if you put your ear to mine, you can hear the ocean.
my father told me it was a myth, my mother called it truth.
a crashing tide contained, the sound spilling over, or
just the effect of a resonant space re-sounding the atmosphere.

my father told me it was a myth. my mother called it truth
that truth is how you take it. my father took her to be
just the effect of a resonant space re-sounding the atmosphere.
i see two shells colliding to sand, hear my sister sifting.

that truth is how you take it. my father took her to be
his image. the ocean is no mirror so he took us to the lake.
i see two shells colliding to sand here, my sister sifting
through piles of fish, but i'm stuck taking out the hooks in

his image. the ocean is no mirror. so he took us to the lake
where i learned patience, the lack of our voices,
through piles of fish. but i'm stuck taking out the hooks in
my eyes, burning with salt from my mother and the sea

where i learned patience. the lack of our voices
a crashing tide contained, the sound spilling over, or
my eyes burning with salt from my mother and the sea.
if you put your ear to mine, you can hear the ocean.

Brenda Kwon
REFUGE

Some sanctuaries have holes in their roofs so large
that they swallow the sky.
You stand under cover
beneath only what is solid,
ignore the jagged and splintered edge in your periphery
that frames large wish-swallowing skies.
Long before your forgetting began,
you commanded details like soldiers
kept in formation
in battles and wars against the unknown.
Not knowing was a luxury only for those
whose fathers weren't
hunted by the Imperial Police,
whose dogs weren't shot
to keep the hiding hidden,
whose treasures didn't contain
shrapnel having just missed soft flesh.
For you,
vigilance was safety;
information, survival.
Even after the wars had run their course,
you clung to the knowing that had served you so well.
You asked the impersonal—
we supplied you with facts:
flight itineraries, what we ate for lunch,
when we'd last serviced our cars,
if we'd gotten new pets.
To us, it was tedious, conversational minutiae;
for you,
the affirmation that we were alive.
Now, there is usually only one question,
pinpointing the day's most pressing need,
like the time our mom stayed too long at the doctor's,
and you called and asked,
"Where is your mom?"

Brenda Kwon

I quickly learned the rhythm of your memory:
the ping of the phone,
the flash of your name,
then
Incoming Call,
Decline or *Accept.*
Each time you dialed, I took your call,
replied as if I'd never before.
Each time I heard your relief anew
carrying you forward, knowing you'd be back.
Together, we built and rebuilt your safety,
replaying assurance like a favorite song.

We keep our dance to small, tight circles
beneath solid shelter
just adjacent to storms.

Kapena M. Landgraf
MAKA

He's only been here for seven months, but in the conversation of place and culture, *how different is that from a decade, a year, a lifetime?* I thought.

"I'm just curious to know more about the culture . . . its ins and outs," the physics instructor finished. I give the guy credit; there's sincerity in his voice, an almost child-like demeanor to his wide smile and nuanced nod of thanks.

I sit back and wait . . . listen.

Local people . . .

Local culture . . .

Aloha spirit . . .

Mainland people and local people . . .

And while they all speak, I slowly slip my hands into the warmth of my pockets. These workshops are always held in the coldest rooms.

Then, someone says it, blurts it out like a game show answer just before the buzzer.

"I'm not Hawaiian, but I feel like . . . ." I lose interest.

Someone beside me clears their throat. I glance over at her and make eye contact, intentionally. She smiles, folds her arms and swings her legs back and forth beneath the chair.

Someone else talks about Hawaiians and "host culture." He's young and says he IS Hawaiian. I nod at his points.

After he speaks, the conversation goes back to "local," "multiculturalism," and the "melting pot" metaphor.

When the workshop is over, people congregate at the main entrance to continue the discourse. They block the doorway with a circle of "wells . . ." and "I thinks . . . ."

I walk around the desks and leave out the back. The young guy who spoke about host culture is sitting on a step, soaking in the warmth of the afternoon Hilo sun, swiping his thumb across a large phone with a shattered screen. The woman who sat behind me is pulling away in her Chrysler minivan. I take my sunglasses from my head and wipe fingerprints from the lenses. My thin polyester shirt can't collect the oils and the effort turns the fingerprints into smears and smudges. On the drive home, I try to ignore the distortions.

Lanning C. Lee
FALSE WILIWILI

Talk about chomping at the bit. I was entering my final semester as a senior at the University of Hawai'i at Mānoa, so eager to get out and head for the graduate program in English at the University of Wisconsin. I'd heard from everyone and his mother that it would be colder than hell come winter in Madison, but I didn't care. I was tired of Honolulu, sick particularly thinking about my ex. I wanted out. But . . . .

Anna was a second semester freshman. Born and raised on the Big Island of Hawai'i, she'd graduated from Hilo High. She said she was a Viking through and through. I mentioned how much I loved Hilo, how my family had camped there often.

She said, "My heart, you know, it'll always be there in Hilo. I've never visited a place that I thought was better."

We were in ECON 130, for me, the last core curriculum class. The first day we sat side by side in the front row. This was a 12:30 class, post-lunch for lots of folks, pre-lunch for me, given my back-to-back-to-back classes. We were in Bilger 151, the big Chemistry auditorium.

Dr. Miller steamed into class, puffing and a little bit red in the face. He donned the neck mic with a bit of difficulty and, leaning against the large desk in front, greeted us, announcing right off—Remember, this was the mid-70s. Times were different—"Hello all. I have to warn you folks down in the first three rows or so, that I always enjoy a liquid lunch at Pizza Hut, so you may want to bring umbrellas or wear raincoats since I sometimes spit when I get passionate about the subject matter."

Anna and I looked at each other and grimaced.

A guy just behind me said, "You're kidding, right?"

"No," Dr. Miller said. "Truly, I am not."

The guy and most of us in the saliva zone groaned. The folks up in back were cracking up.

After going over the syllabus, spitless so far, and telling us that we'd really enjoy the textbook because he wrote it himself, so we all had to buy it because he lived off the royalties rather than his teaching salary, which was so low, he said, "I leave you with this final thought. By the time this semester is over, if you learn nothing else, you will understand exactly what I mean when I tell you there is absolutely no such thing as a free lunch. You may not know what that means at this moment, but you will by the end, and, be prepared, I give you this huge hint that you'll have to explain what it does mean on the final exam. Remember: There is no such thing as a free lunch."

He released us, and as Anna and I headed for the exit, I said, "I don't know what he means by there being no such thing as a free lunch, so while I'm still this ignorant, if you didn't eat yet, can I buy you lunch, which would mean that it'd be free for you, although, I guess, it really wouldn't be."

Anna crinkled up her nose, then laughed. "Well, I ate just before class, but you could buy me a free cup of coffee."

I could tell she was hapa—half-Caucasian and, by her last name, half-Japanese.

Because it's not so obvious with me, I told her that I was hapa—half-Caucasian, half-Korean. "My last name's a Korean Lee," I said, "and I'm Norwegian. A Viking just like you."

"I'm hapa too," she said and explained her mix. What I'd known already at first glance, she confirmed. The combination in her was pretty stunning.

We both grabbed coffee, me a sandwich too, at the cafeteria. Sitting outside, I asked her about growing up, what school had been like, what got her to UH-Mānoa.

She wanted to know about the English major because that was one she was looking at. She talked about winning the English Scholar Award in her senior class, and how much she loved reading and writing.

Then she asked, "What are you going to do after this semester, after you graduate?"

I hesitated, gave her a long, "Ahhh . . . ."

Did I want to tell this woman that I was up and leaving Hawai'i? I was definitely attracted to her. Would this kill any chances with her? I had no idea whether she was attracted to me.

Bottom line: Should I lie to her right off the bat?

I was raised a good Lutheran, so there are three things I know for sure. One, if it looks like bread and wine, then that's all it is, bread and wine; two, you cannot buy your way into heaven; and three, lying is very, very bad. I speak from experience, guiltily so, when I say that it is not good if you lie during a conversation that may lead to a relationship with someone who revs your engine.

"Ahhh, I'm headed for Madison, Wisconsin, for a graduate program in English."

This admission made me feel that any romantic relationship possibility was automatically out of the question. For a second. Hope springs eternal. Hey. I'd heard of long-distance relationships working. I tell you, I'm famous for making all kinds of plans when some woman knocks me out, having no idea of whether romance is even a possibility. I'm always way out ahead of myself.

Anna was very impressed by this. The Hilo girl said, "You do know it's going to be cold in the winter over there."

"Yes." I smiled. "Yes, I think I've heard that."

We had a great, long talk. The kind of talk that makes you think you're not being an ass, or boring, or are spitting on the listener. Her mom was a teacher at Hilo Union Elementary School, and her dad worked in a facility up at Pōhakuloa where they were breeding Hawaiian nēnē birds, our local geese that are also our state bird. I hadn't known that the nēnē were an endangered species, and that there was an intensive effort to increase the population.

"Oh yes, it's not good right now. There are fewer than one thousand all together on Maui and Hawai'i combined."

Her mom was a Hilo native, born and bred, and her dad was from Japan. They'd met at UH-Mānoa—she an education major, he majoring in zoology. It was actually her mom who got the full-time job offer back in Hilo, so they moved, and her dad had found his way to the Nēnē Project while lecturing at UH-Hilo.

"I go to Japan every summer to stay with my grandparents."

Funny, how I jumped to the thought that I wouldn't see her that summer because she'd be in Japan. Like I was even going to be around myself. I'd planned to leave for the mainland the week after graduation. The pre-falling-in-love thought process is a strange thing.

"Are you fluent in Japanese?"

"Yes, I am. I placed out of the language requirement here. I'm still wondering about majoring in Japanese, though."

"Wow. English and Japanese. Are you looking at other majors besides those?"

"I like to draw, and I really enjoy history."

She was taking a life drawing course and the second of two semesters of world history required for core.

"Do you work?"

She had a 20-hour-a-week student job. "I'm with an office on campus called the KOKUA Program. They help all students with disabilities. And not just here at Mānoa, but also at the community colleges. I've even audiotaped a geography textbook for a blind UH-Hilo student."

Apparently the other campuses, while they did have some services for students with disabilities, did not have the resources to provide all that was needed, so UH-Mānoa helped out.

"Right now I'm recording textbooks for a History major with low vision. It's great. I'm reading books on Japanese and Indian history. I'm good with the Japanese, but my pronunciation of Indian terms and phrases is pretty much a best-guessing prayer. We do have to spell foreign words and phrases when we tape, though, so that makes me feel kind of better about probably totally destroying the vocabulary.

"The other part of my job is taking notes for students who can't take their own. This semester I'm taking notes for a Japanese history course."

"Wow, you must be a great notetaker."

"No, not so much so, really. But the kind of note-taking I do, what's called visual note-taking, means I only have to write down, and then tape-record after class, the things that are written on the board or are on slides and overhead projections. The student is responsible for all the verbal information in the class."

"That's great. Sounds like the kind of job where you get a lot of personal satisfaction from what you're doing."

"Yes," she said, "there's definitely that, but I have a younger brother who's developmentally disabled, so I grew up helping, you know?"

I liked this woman more and more. It was actually getting late by the time we broke up the meeting.

"I have to go back to the dorm to eat and then study," she said.

We stood up. "Which dorm you in?"

"I'm in Johnson Hall. A bit of an armpit, but it's okay. I have a great roommate."

I was headed in the opposite direction. "See you in class on Thursday?" I asked.

She said yes, then smiled one of the most amazing smiles I've ever seen at that critical moment right before I know I'm absolutely in love.

Thursday couldn't come around fast enough. When I arrived at Bilger, I noticed that the first two rows were empty, except for the seats next to the very edges of the room. Dr. Miller had shown a tendency to pace the full stage area, but that stage didn't run the entire length of the hall. The edges, apparently, were considered probably spit-free zones.

I scanned the first few occupied rows, but I didn't see Anna. Then I scanned, very carefully, every row all the way to the top. No Anna.

I decided I would make myself obvious to her by sitting in the second-to-last seat in the first row on the makai, or ocean, side of the auditorium. This would leave the last seat by the door open for her.

Class time arrived. I kept looking up into the back. Nothing.

After a few minutes, Dr. Miller came puffing into class. He dropped the copy of his published liquid-meal-ticket on the front desk.

"My apologies for being late," he spluttered. "I'm still figuring out how long it takes me to get here from Pizza Hut. Hopefully next time I'll be right on the dot."

He surveyed the room. "Hah! I see you've taken my advice about hiding out in the hinterlands." He focused on me. "Yet there exists one brave soul so hungry for knowledge of macroeconomics, that he is willing to risk being showered by my words."

The class laughed.

I sort of did too, but my mind was very much occupied. Where was she? God, I thought, what if she's dropped the class?

I cursed inwardly.

Or what if she was ill?

Whatever doctorly, or motherly, or nursing tendencies I had, they kicked in instantly. I would go to her bedside in Johnson Hall, read her textbooks to her, type her papers as she dictated them, her voice weak yet discernible. But how would I handle her drawing assignments? That would take some thought.

The door to my left opened. My heart stopped. It was just some guy. He looked at the available seats, then sat next to me in the one I'd left open for Anna.

"Thanks in advance for being my shield, man," he said.

He didn't sound like he was joking.

Dr. Miller, apparently super-hydrated that day, spat and spittled onward. I half-absorbed what he said. Class ended. I sat there, dazed and exhausted from all the near heartbreaking stress I was feeling.

Anna did not come to the next class either. I kidded myself about her being too sick still to come back. I tried extra hard to suppress any thought of her having dropped the class. I attempted listening to the lecture, but Dr. Miller's mouth moved like that of a silent movie actor.

No Anna the class after that. Irrationally, I started to hate Econ then. Why had I registered for this class? There were other social science classes that would have fulfilled the core requirement. God, I wanted to be on the frickin' mainland already.

I'd given up trying to follow our tipsy teacher, sat doodling all the way through. Every once in a while I would catch a word or two, but everything was fractured and out of context, so nothing really made any sense.

Then, toward the end of class, it hit me. Damn. Was I brilliant or what? I knew she lived in Johnson Hall. Why didn't I just go over there right now and see what was up?

I didn't think of myself as a stalker at the time, but I can see now that my behavior came close. I walked right over to the reception desk at Johnson Hall and asked the student on duty if Anna was still living there.

"I'm sorry, but we don't give out that kind of information."

I look at him, puzzled. "Do you know who she is?"

"I'm sorry, we can't tell you whether we are familiar with a particular student."

Man, this guy was a tough case. "Then you can't tell me if you've seen her recently, right?"

He gave me the kind of look I would eventually use when I dealt with annoying customers at the Madison record store where I worked a few years later.

"Nothing about her at all, right?"

He continued his brah-I-have-had-it-with-you stare. No reply was forthcoming. I suppose if I'd been in his position, I might have been about ready to call Campus Security, but when you're very probably in love, well, it's hard to see lots of things clearly.

I wheeled around, unsure about my next move, pushed through the door and stepped down onto the walkway. I took a few totally confused and dazed steps toward the Dole Street sidewalk, and all of a sudden a car pulled up and out stepped Anna.

She carried a small suitcase and hadn't noticed me yet. I wasn't sure what to say, or if I should say anything.

Anna looked equally in kind of a brain fog, but as she walked toward me recognition dawned. "Lanning?"

"Ah, yes, it's, ah, me. Hey, you. How're you doing?"

Anna burst into tears. This confused me further. I mean, I knew from experience I can have this kind of effect on women, but I didn't think I'd done anything to get Anna crying. Not yet.

She just stood there sobbing. Now, if we'd been a longtime couple, I might have thrown my arms around her or some such romantic-scenario-type thing, but I didn't know what might be appropriate behavior given that I'd only actually met her once so far on that first day of class.

I decided the best thing to do would be to relieve her of the suitcase, so I, very gently, slipped it out of her hand.

Anna put both hands to her face. "I'm so sorry," she said, her sobbing subsiding. "I'm . . . ."

Reaching in her pocket, she produced a humongous wad of tissue that looked well used. She blew her nose and wiped her eyes. This settled her a little.

I still had the overpowering urge to just grab her and hug her. But, I mean, we really didn't know each other very much at all.

She returned the wad to her pocket. "I'm so sorry about that," she said.

"Hey, ah, no problem. You okay?"

Brilliant question. Really. Obviously she was not okay.

"What are you doing here?" she asked.

I put down her suitcase, trying to come up with some kind of innocuous, non-incriminating answer. "I was, well, I . . . ."

I had a strong feeling that saying "I was worried about you," even though I had been plenty worried about her, would still be a little too familiar, so I settled for, "I didn't see you in class."

Now if this was an answer to her question, I'm not exactly sure, but it was all I could think of that wasn't too chummy and also didn't make it seem like I was hunting her down. Which of course I was.

Big relief. She seemed satisfied with my statement.

"I went back home. My brother. He's sick, really sick. I had to go. They thought he might die."

My eyes widened with shock and sympathy, but I said nothing. She walked past me and sat down on the step. I went over and sat beside her. Not too close.

"I'm sorry to hear that," I said. "Is he better?"

She shook her head. "No, he's much worse. He was hospitalized in Hilo, but his respiratory system, for some reason they can't figure out, it's failing. Not working the way it should be. We just flew him to Honolulu this morning. He's in Kapiʻolani Hospital."

Kapiʻolani is the main women and children's hospital. I'd been born there.

"Your folks came with you?"

"Yes, both. My dad is who just dropped me off."

She reached in her pocket and pulled out the wad again, holding it to her eyes. Her shoulders heaved up and down a few times. I wanted so badly to put my arm around her shoulders.

She stood slowly and picked up her bag. "I have to go in. I haven't been sleeping. I need to sleep."

I nodded, even though she wouldn't have seen that. "Okay," I said. "Hey, if you need any kind of help, please call me."

I tore a sheet of paper out of my composition book and wrote down my number. Me, giving a girl my number. Stop the presses. This was a first. I'm usually too shy to even ask for theirs.

"Thanks, Lanning. I'll see you."

I hoped so badly that this would be true, and I could hardly wait for it to happen. I went to the door and let her in.

Two days later, I sat in the second row of Bilger Hall, again one seat from the end. My heart pounded harder and harder as class time approached. I watched folks piling in the door, wondering if Anna was feeling well enough to make it to class.

And then she came down from the back and sat next to me. All was right with my world.

Lanning C. Lee

Ever the brilliant conversationalist, I managed, "Hey." If there'd been any more adrenaline running through my system, I think I'd have had a heart attack. I imagined her giving me CPR. I'd of course come to during the mouth-to-mouth.

She smiled. That best freaking smile ever.

"Hi," she said. "Thanks for the other day."

Not quite sure exactly what I'd done, I said, "Oh, yes, sure. No problem. How's your brother?"

"He's better. Stable. Thanks. It looks like he'll probably be okay."

"Good," I said, "that's good. I'm glad."

She smiled again.

Dr. Miller plowed through the door. I checked my watch. He was early by a minute and bright red.

"I'm here," he announced loudly. The class burst into applause.

"Thank you, thank you," he said. "I actually had some solid food for lunch, along with my beverages. And do you know why?"

Some guy yelled out: "Because it was free!"

Everyone laughed. Even Anna. I felt very relaxed all of a sudden.

Dr. Miller, laughing too, pointed up toward the voice. "Young man," he said, "you're not going to do very well on the final exam."

There was more laughter.

He looked around the room. "A colleague did in fact treat me to a sandwich. But even so, there is no such thing as a free lunch. There are always costs involved. Always. We've talked about a few, and we're going to talk about more of them. Costs, people. Everything costs."

He launched into his sermon of the day on something I'd never heard of before, even though he called it a brief review of last time's information. Then he referred to something we'd apparently studied last week.

As the lecture progressed, I realized two very important things. First, this was the first time I was actually listening to him since day one of class, and second, I understood very, very little about macroeconomics. The first exam was coming up fast, and the only thing I knew well was that the free lunch issue would not need to be addressed until the final exam.

Everything that bubbled out of his mouth was a mystery to me. Dr. Miller seemed to be speaking in tongues. I saw, too, that my half-assed reading of his Rosetta tome was paying the exact measly dividends I deserved for being so cursory and distracted.

What the hell was I going to do about the first midterm?

That night I tried to read the Economics text with the same intensity I read the material for my English courses. Maybe fifteen minutes into the attempt, I found my mind wandering, kept reading the same page over and over again. I was looking at a graph example of aggregate demand and aggregate supply. The point was to show the equilibrium price level and real gross domestic product.

What. The. Hell.

If I understood anything about this stuff, reading and rereading the definitions of the terms, the glossary bleeding highlighter ink, it was that I really should have picked a different course to fulfill this social science requirement.

But then, of course, I thought about how I wouldn't have met this woman. Anna. Hmmm. I wondered if she might understand the material.

Next class, Dr. Miller had us practice answering sample questions that might be on the exam. It was a pretty big class, but he'd point to someone, saying, "You there in the blue aloha shirt, what is the next move I need to make in labeling this graph on the x and y axes," or "You with the green blouse, give me a concise definition of a nominal interest rate."

I cringed each time he looked in my direction. Anna would sometimes actually raise her hand to answer a question. This, I tell you, looked very promising.

When class was over, I suggested coffee again, and again she agreed. While we sat there, I voiced my concern over my lack of knowledge about macroeconomics, how the math and graphing hit on my math phobia and basically froze my soul.

"I can help you," she said. It was like magic. "You want to get together and study for the exam?"

"Wow, that would be great, Anna. How about this Saturday? Do you have any time?"

"Yes, the afternoon would be best. I like to go see my brother in the morning."

We agreed that I'd pick her up at Johnson Hall at 1:00, then we'd head up to my place to study. This was all falling together like the proverbial fairy tale coming true.

When we got to my house, we settled down at the coffee table in the living room, and Anna began to perform some kind of miraculous brain surgery, packing the mysteries of macroeconomics into my skull for me.

The two of us went at it for four hours or so. "You're really on top of this stuff, huh?"

"Well, I took AP Econ in high school, so this is mostly a review for me. Of course I kept up with the reading while I was back home."

Of course she did. "You're kind of a natural teacher. Your mom being a teacher and your dad a former teacher, it's gotta be in your genes."

Anna laughed. "That may be true."

She changed the subject. Looking out the screen door to my lanai, she said, "Looks like you must have a pretty big yard out there."

"I do," I said, "and it's a lotta work. Wanna see it?"

"Oh yes, please."

We walked outside.

"Oh my God," she said. "That is the biggest false wiliwili tree I've ever seen."

It was true. I'd seen some around town, but none that could match the height of this one. It was by far the centerpiece of the yard.

"So you know this tree?" I asked.

"Oh yes," she said. "I love to collect the red seeds. I boil them for a little bit, then when they're soft, I sew them into bracelets. My aunt has a pretty good-sized tree, but nothing like this."

"You can boil and eat those seeds too," I said. "And folks from the Polynesian Cultural Center come here when the pods fall and collect the seeds to sell as bracelets they make out there."

Right then Anna walked up to the tree, put her arms around it, and hugged it. Tight. The expression on her face was one of great happiness.

Finally she let go and stepped back.

"Man, you can really feel the mana in that tree. It is powerful. Oh, Lanning, I love this tree."

I couldn't get over her enthusiasm for my false wiliwili. All the way back she talked about it, asked if she too could come collect the red seeds, described types of bracelets she'd made.

When I dropped her off at Johnson Hall, I thanked her for straightening me out with the Econ. She thanked me for introducing her to my tree. Said she wanted to see it again soon so she could absorb more good energy from it.

Back home, I popped a beer and sat out on my lanai, staring at my false wiliwili tree, picturing Anna hugging it. This all really was coming together like a happily-ever-after ending.

The following Tuesday was our last day to review before the exam. I waited. Class started. I wondered where Anna might be. Probably running late. Dr. Miller again called on people. At one point, he pointed at me, and I was able to correctly label a production possibilities curve.

At the end of class, I contemplated going over to Johnson Hall again, but then I thought about the great guy at the front desk and how he might call Campus Security on me if it started to look like I was harassing him or Anna.

The morning of the exam, I half-heartedly reviewed the notes I'd made with Anna's help. When exam time came, I watched the empty seat remain that way as the test papers were passed out.

Dr. Miller gave us the signal to go. I had about seventy minutes to dump everything Anna had taught me. Even though I had my mind on why she might not be there, I could feel that I was doing things correctly on the exam. In fact, it seemed easier than I'd imagined, and I actually finished with ten or so minutes to spare.

Even if we finished early, we'd been asked to stay seated until time was called so as not to disturb the folks who were still working on the exam. That ten minutes crawled by like an eternity. I should have been feeling good about doing well on the exam. All I felt like doing was cry. What had happened?

A couple nights later, I was sitting in the bathtub soaking, a damp washcloth covering my face, thinking about Anna. The phone rang. I stepped out and went into the next room.

"Hello?"

"Lanning, this is Anna."

I stopped breathing. I could hear her sniffling. "Anna, I . . . . Are you all right? You missed the exam."

How stupid. She certainly knew she'd missed it. Brilliant to point it out to her.

"Yes, I had to come home. My brother, he, he passed away. We have the funeral next week."

My synapses nearly stopped firing along with my heart, but I managed "Oh geez Anna, I'm so sorry to hear that. So sorry."

She blew her nose. "Thanks, Lanning. I wanted to tell you that I'm withdrawing from school for this semester. I'm even thinking I might be at UH-Hilo next year. My folks are wrecked. I might need to be here."

I felt so sorry about her brother dying, but at the same time I wanted to curse. Curse myself, my life, my lost chance. At that instant, I felt the life had been sucked right out of me.

All I could muster was "Oh, I'm so sorry to hear that."

"Anyway," she said, "I wanted you to know."

"You take care," I said. "Thanks very much for calling. Please give my best to your parents."

"Thanks, Lanning. You take care too."

The click of the phone, it killed me. Killed me.

Now the damn days were really dragging. Econ was an unbearable scene. I'd scored an A on the exam, but there was one more midterm and then the final. It would be a struggle to the finish line. Dr. Miller's words were more and more like gibberish. Ask me nowadays why no lunch is free, and I'll tell you, "Who the hell cares?"

The rest of my classes went cold on me. Even my English courses seemed pointless. I barely pulled out the papers I needed to write, and I kept wondering if I had the energy to head off to Wisconsin and dig into the MA program.

Lanning C. Lee

A couple days after graduation, as I was packing to leave, there was a knock on the door. I opened it and the mailman stood there holding a large envelope.

"Couldn't fit this in your box," he said, handing it to me.

"Thanks."

I closed the door and stared at the envelope. Please do not bend. There was no return address. I tore it open.

It was an ink drawing of my false wiliwili tree. Huge. Stunning. Beautiful.

And standing beside the massive trunk was a little me.

There was a brief note: Lanning, stay warm in Wisconsin. With great love and aloha, Anna.

I carried the drawing with me out onto the lanai, stood there looking from the tree to the drawing to the tree, back and forth, back and forth.

Finally, I placed it on a chair, then went down into the yard and stood in front of the tree itself.

I looked straight up, trying to see the very high top. The enormous tree seemed to bend over me, almost as though it were curving down to touch me. I felt as though my spine could crack from bending so far back.

I closed my eyes, took a deep breath, and wrapped my arms around the gigantic trunk. I hugged it hard, hard and tight, hugged it as if I would never let it go.

Lenny Levine

AUTOCORRECT

Greg Blake's troubles began as he was sitting on his buddy Roy's couch to watch the Giants-Eagles game. On the sixty-inch TV, the teams were lining up for the kickoff as Greg glanced over at Roy in his recliner and the ice chest next to him. "Toss me a brewski, bro, will ya?" he meant to say.

What he said was: "Toss me a brewery, brow, will yacht?"

"Huh?" Roy said, not taking his eyes from the screen.

Greg blinked in confusion.

Roy looked over at him. "No, really, man. I didn't get that."

"I wanted a beer," Greg said carefully.

"Well, hell, that ain't a problem." Roy reached down and plucked a bottle of Coors from the cooler. "Here ya go." He flipped it over to Greg, who nearly dropped it.

On the screen, the Giants kickoff returner was breaking a tackle. He made a quick move to his left and busted it up the sideline.

"Yeah! Yeah!" Roy cried out.

What the hell just happened? Greg thought. *Did I have a stroke or something?*

"Nice return!" Roy enthused, as the runner was forced out at the Eagles' forty. "Now, maybe we can get some offense going."

He must have been distracted, that's all. He still felt okay, as far as he could tell. He flexed his fingers and toes. Nothing seemed to be paralyzed or anything. Slowly, he began to relax and watch the game again, as Eli Manning stood over center, surveying the defense.

"Awright, Eli, let's get 'em!" he intended to say.

His actual words were: "Ore rights, Eli, let's get them!"

Roy glanced over at him. "What was that?"

"I don't know," Greg said nervously.

"Well, that makes two of us. Whoa, baby!"

On the screen, Eli launched one downfield in the direction of Odell Beckham. It fell just beyond Beckham's diving attempt to pull it in.

"Fuck!" Roy shouted. "The offensive line never gives him enough time!"

Again, Greg checked himself. It still didn't seem like anything physical was wrong. He didn't feel dizzy or anything. But this stuff with the words . . . .

He realized he was still holding the bottle of Coors in his lap. He unscrewed the cap and took a long, satisfying swig. That first, icy-cold swallow. Nothing like it.

"You want some of these?" Without moving his eyes off the screen, Roy was extending a bag of Lay's potato chips at him. Greg had a sudden flash of wit.

"Sure, 'Lay' 'em on me," he tried to say, but instead, said: "Sure, laymen on me."

He couldn't believe this was happening.

"Shit," he said. It came out: "Shift."

"That's not a shift. That's a balanced formation. Hey, do you want these or not?" Roy was still holding out the bag of chips.

Greg silently took it from him.

"Third and eight," said Roy. "C'mon, Eli!"

Manning dropped back to pass, but the Eagles ran a safety blitz and nailed him for a sack.

"Ooh!" Roy moaned. "Now we're not even in field-goal range. What's the matter with these guys?"

The phone hummed in Greg's pocket and he slid it out. It was a text from Susan.

His first instinct was to ignore it. They'd had a pretty big fight before he left her place this morning. He was hoping the game would take his mind off it.

But he was curious. Maybe she wanted to apologize; that would be nice. He opened it.

The message said: *Is it happening?*

Well . . . that didn't sound like an apology. Was it supposed to be sarcasm about the game?

What are you talking about? he typed.

On the TV, the Giants were punting.

On Greg's phone, it said: *You should be asking yourself that question.*

The only question Greg was asking himself, as far as she was concerned, was why were they still together?

As human beings they were polar opposites. She'd graduated cum laude from Princeton and was an English professor at the university. He was a mechanic who'd been lucky to get out of high school.

She told him she loved his earthy, man-of-the-people quality. He told her he was in awe of her intelligence.

They each pretended it wasn't a load of crap. What kept them together was the amazing, ever-changing, glorious, sometimes athletically challenging, beyond-incredible sex.

But it came with fights, like the one they'd had this morning. They were having coffee at her kitchen table, and he'd used the wrong word for something. She'd corrected him in her snarky way, and this time, it happened to annoy him.

"What the fuck difference does it make?" he'd snapped at her. "You knew what I meant by it. Get off my ass."

She'd chuckled, which also got on his nerves. "You hate it when I correct you because you love being ignorant."

To which he'd replied, "Yeah, like you love being a smug, stuck-up, smart-ass bitch."

She'd slammed her coffee mug down on the table and stomped out of the kitchen.

"You want some weed?" Roy gasped, holding his breath and extending an oversized joint toward him. The game had gone to commercial after the Giants' punt bounced into the end zone for a touchback.

Greg shook his head, thinking maybe he'd better not right now.

"Something wrong with you, man?" Roy asked, tendrils of smoke rising from his nostrils. "You've been real quiet, and when you do talk, it's all crazy shit. What's the deal?"

He knew he had to speak.

"I dunno," he mumbled, but only got as far as "I donut" and stopped.

"Fuck!" he said. It came out: "Fudge!"

Now Roy was really staring at him. "You want a fudge donut?"

Greg glanced about the room for something to write on. He pantomimed the action of writing, looking desperately at Roy.

"Okay," Roy said, extricating himself from the recliner. "Don't get your balls in an uproar."

It took several drawers before he found a pad and pencil, which he gave to Greg. "You're acting very strange, dude, you know that?"

The game had resumed with the Eagles taking over on their own twenty. Roy sat down in the recliner and flipped it back. "C'mon!" he exhorted the Giants' defense. "Stuff them!"

Greg hesitated, his pencil above the pad. What if writing didn't help? What if the words still came out funny?

Then he had another thought that was much more disturbing. One he should've had right away if he hadn't been so discombobulated.

Susan had texted, *Is it happening?*

She knew!

She knew what was happening to him. Because somehow, some way, she'd done this to him.

How could that be?

Carson Wentz, the Eagles quarterback, threw a quick pass into the flat that was tipped at the line. It floated into the hands of a Giants linebacker who took it, unopposed, into the end zone.

Roy exploded out of the chair. "Yes! Yes! Yes!" he shouted, doing a little dance in the middle of the room.

To Greg it was all far away. He tried to remember this morning, after she'd stalked out of the kitchen.

He'd sat there awhile, finishing his coffee and feeling pretty good about himself. It was one of the rare times he'd gotten the last word in, and he was savoring the moment. After the coffee, he planned to head home for a shower and a quick change of clothes. Then it was off to Roy's for the big game.

He hadn't been at all concerned that the fight would affect their relationship. Sometimes, in fact, the fights made sex even better. No, he thought, everything was probably fine.

Then she came back into the kitchen, carrying her laptop.

"Hey, asshole," she said, so he knew this wasn't over. She set the computer down in front of him. "Since you're so good at fixing things, why don't you fix this? It just popped up on my screen and I can't get rid of it."

He knew something about computers, since cars relied on them these days, but he was no expert. He thought he should make that clear to her in case he couldn't find the problem, but decided not to.

He looked at the screen, which showed a myriad of swirling letters. It resembled a bowl of alphabet soup being vigorously stirred. The display was dizzying to watch, but he couldn't take his eyes off it. The letters roiled and churned, half forming then disappearing as others took their place.

Hitting the escape key accomplished nothing, the same with delete. He pressed the on-off button to no avail. The letters kept spinning, faster and faster.

And then they stopped. The screen went blank for a moment, then returned to Susan's home screen.

He looked at it, deciding if he should take credit, and figured, why not?

"Here you go." He turned the laptop so that it faced her. "No problemo."

"You are such a phony," she said. "I tried the same things you did and they didn't do anything."

"Maybe you didn't try hard enough," he said with a shrug.

"You have no idea why that screen changed back, do you?"

"No," he said, getting up from the table. "And I don't care."

Her look of disgust made him pause.

"No, of course you don't," she said. "It's just another of the billions of things you don't care about, or are even curious about. All your brain is good for is watching football with your idiot friend."

She picked up the coffee mugs and took them to the sink, where she stood with her back to him.

"Get out of here. I can't stand looking at you right now. And I hope whatever team you're rooting for gets their asses kicked."

Back in the present, Roy was finishing his victory dance as the touchdown was replayed from different angles. He gave Greg another odd look.

"You sure you're okay, bro?"

It was those letters on the screen. He must have been hypnotized.

He had to talk to her right now, none of this texting bullshit. He got up from the couch.

"I'm sorry, man, I've Gouda make a call," he blurted out, realizing what he'd said and not caring. He pulled his phone from his pocket as he headed for the door. "I just need to go outside to do it, but I'm gonorrhea be right back."

He didn't look to see Roy's reaction. He stepped out the door and onto the lawn, where he tapped Susan's name on his phone.

It seemed to ring forever, and then she picked up.

"Well, hello there!" she sang out. "Are you enjoying your game?"

"What the fork did you do to me?"

She burst out laughing, and he nearly lost it.

"Stop laughing!" he said. "Stop laughing at me, you miserable country!"

She laughed even harder, and then toned it down. "Relax, honey, relax," she said. "Go with it. The app only lasts for a little while."

"The app?" He'd almost said "apple." "Where is it? In my phone?"

"No, it's in your left temporal lobe."

He couldn't believe he'd heard her right.

"My what?!"

"Don't worry, its effectiveness will fade. They're still working on duration."

His mouth hung open.

"There's a computer program planted inside me?" he stammered.

"In a manner of speaking. These friends of mine in biological cyber research figured out how to do it, something connected with eye recognition. Anyway, they're coordinating on a project with the English department. We're developing a sort of autocorrect program for the human brain. And I thought, since you hate being corrected by people, you might try it out."

"Try it out," he repeated.

"Yes, and I can see it's working. How do you like it?"

If she were right in front of him, he might have strangled her.

"You miserable bit!" he growled. "How the frock do you think I like it? It sacks!"

"Now you'll notice," she said, "that you're using an extra feature we've added to help bring civility to public discourse. It goes beyond what standard autocorrect programs offer. You'd eventually learn to avoid using words like that on your own, but as I've said, this particular app is temporary."

"Temporary," he groaned. "Well, it's also torture! How long is this bull shot Ghana last?"

"Hard to say, maybe an hour, no more than two. Relax, honey, relax. Try not to use words like 'gonna.' That would help."

"Thanks for the tip."

He shut off the phone and stood staring for a moment. Then he went back into the house.

Roy was still ensconced in his chair, but the game was now tied 7-7.

"They ran back our kickoff, dude," Roy complained. "We can't catch a fucking break!"

Greg sat down on the couch, picked up the bottle of Coors, and took a long, deep swallow.

"Lemming tell you something, brow," he said. "It could be the greatest sex in the history of the world, but it aim worth sheet."

Virginia Loo
WOMEN'S WORK

Debbie, the office manager,
tells me they built the Taj Mahal
without real mortar,
only marble blocks
and large vats of dahl
to stick it together.
Trust me, she said, *it's true*.

That was just before Debbie begins
instructing me
in how to tie a sari.
First, once around the waist
and tuck.
Leave it, she commands me.
Gather up the other end,
fix the length of the pallu
behind you.

Later, I learn
the pallu displays
your sensibility as a woman,
how gracefully it trails you
pleated or loose,
how close to the ground.
But the first time,
Debbie does it for me,
looks me up
and down,
judges where to pin it
at the shoulder.

This is the secret, she says,
your control panel—
the fixed point at the shoulder

Virginia Loo

starts the diagonal line
across your breast,
wraps around,
leaving open the window
to your lower back,
left side, then belly,
curving path
to your power,
the falling pleats
an ancient symbol of fertility.

Secure the sari at your left hip
a small tuck,
a place holder. *This,*
she said, opening
the wide circle of fabric
between us,
is how you know
what you have to work with.

How many widths of palm
can you get
out of the remaining length?
She pleats my skirt
between her pointer and thumb,
until her hand was flat
against me, pulls out
the waist of my petticoat,
so we can both see my feet,
then flips the folds,
thick like the ticket book
of a traffic cop,
tucking the whole thing
under my wide-eyed navel.
She has me walk
In front of her.
Do you feel secure?
The tops of your shoes
should fan open the pleats

Virginia Loo

as you step,
just a bit,
the way a peacock teases,
deciding
is it worth opening its tail?

This strange trust placed,
in workplace women
starts by
standing in front of Debbie,
in only a petticoat
and a midriff baring top,
learning something so basic
as how to get dressed,
to attend a meeting.

And the next time?
Can I trust
in the large pin
I fix at my own shoulder,
Is it enough
to have knowledge
of my power, how I control
all else simply folded,
one tuck that
keeps it all
from coming undone.

Virginia Loo

THE ARGUMENT

The Setting:

They call this *Jagganath Confronts a Monk*.
a study in contrasts,
I—with my dark face, wide eyes, crazy hair,
You—wearing the classic look of a Chinese scholar—
eyes half closed, calm like a cloud-colored tunic
over loose pants and sandals,
even your toe hairs lay neatly,
combed so they point toward Nirvana.

This dispute has been reincarnated
again and again over the centuries.
With some irony, you have managed
the situation
with the placid bureaucracy
of colonial India,
imposing a promised time and place
for the Resolution that suits
some unexplained protocol.
Meanwhile, I spin
with the endless energy
of the modern CCP* machine.
If my wheels could touch the ground,
my shovel feel the earth,
I would push forward,
eager to construct
what ego makes inevitable.

The Analysis:

This is a classic conflict, but
what exactly is being argued here?

Outside Observer, look more closely.
Notice the large snake lying between the two.
Is it dangerous or desirable?

Does it offer fatal venom or an elixir to raise the dead?
Where did it come from, how did it get there?

>(No one would suspect
>it was released from beneath the monk's robes.)

Jagganath shouts,
>This is not a debate on the qualities of the snake.
>The argument is about whether it can be let go
>before it is forgiven,
>Or must it be forgiven first, to let it go.

The monk demurs,
>The argument is purely academic,
>the snake already being dead.

*Chinese Communist Party

PAVARTI PICKS HER BATTLES

Rani is the regular maid
but she won't do toilets due to caste,
she is touchable, not scheduled or backward,
which leaves Parvati to clean up her own shit
on Saturdays while her kids
are at exam school studying maths.

While at Thunderbird in Phoenix
she started the weekly practice
of cleaning her own bowls.
Never told her mother when she called home.
Never called herself "Indian" while in Arizona.
It confused the locals—used to Apache, Hopi,
Navajo, not Hindu.
They, clueless as to what it meant to be a Tamil Brahmin.

Virginia Loo

The closest she got to knowing looks
was when she talked of Gandhi—
everyone could conjure up Ben Kingsley's face
and know exactly where she was coming from.
Americans never got close
to saying her name the way it was intended.
In class, the prof called her Poverty
So, second year, she started calling herself Pavs,
with a flat Midwestern "ah," the ring of "alacrity."

When she cleans on Saturday, always alone,
Her mind wanders a bit from the porcelain,
just some loud thinking addressed to herself,
Which is a greater affront to one's sense of self:
to clean your own toilet
Or somebody else's?
What would Rani say, as someone
closer to the frontline of daily indignity.
It depends, she might say, if you care more
what people imagine when you say your name
or what they call you when they see you.

WHAT GOES AROUND

The nuns are giving birth
to the babies of the monks.
The alms are being used
for child support.
There are vinaya available
to codify the schedule
of the chanting,
kitchen duties,
the sleeping places
and visitation
of the babes.

This means these
happenings were common
enough,
expected even.

How is the pregnant nun advised
to continue on the
Eightfold Path?
She is well versed in Right View:
Actions have consequences;
as for Right Speech,
she knows to hold her tongue
in the Great Hall
when passing the guy who knocked her up.
But how to rededicate herself to
Right Conduct, Resolve,
Livelihood, Effort,
Mindfulness, Meditation?
When the wheel in her mind spins
it makes her slightly nauseated.

Leading by example,
the monk continues
to circumambulate the butter lamps,
drone past the prayer wheels,
his path
    uninterrupted.

Darrell H. Y. Lum
COMFORT CHICKEN

Long time ago. We used to have pets dat we love and feed and take care dem. We save da bes piece of leftovah meat fo dem. We fogive dem even wen dey go shi-shi or numbah two wrong time, wrong place. We jes tell, "Das okay, bebe . . . ." Dey depend on you.

And den get Seeing Eye dog fo blind people. Dey depend on da dog. Errybody know, no stop and try pet da dog 'cause da dog stay WORKING. Make sense.

But nowadays, get all kine PETS inside da supermarket, riding da cart or walking around in da store looking at tings. Some get da red vest fo make like dey one service animal. But dey not WORKING like one Seeing Eye dog. Maybe da owner should be da one wearing da red vest 'cause dey one "service human" navigating da store fo da dog. Maybe da service human going stop in da pet food aisle and ask da dog fo choose. And da service human so proud when you stop and tell, "Cute your dog, wit da hair ribbons." Yeah, da dog stay WORKING their humans. Da sign outside says, "Service Animals Only" but might as well say, "Whatevahs, 'cause we no-like-make-a-scene animals only" when somebody tell dey need their "comfort animal" inside da store.

So nowadays people no leave da dog at home for watch da house. Guard dog: bark, bark, bark at da mailman or da burglars or da stray cats. Now you gotta bring um wit you inside da market 'cause you so lonely you no can buy eggs witout your comfort animal. Maybe you need somebody to talk to, but you no even talk to da funny kine neighbor down da street even when you see him waiting fo da bus outside wit da 25-pound bag rice. You know where he live.

Last time I went Gina's BBQ, one lady walk in wit her Foodland bag and one big purse. She get one chicken inside her purse, da rooster head popping out, looking like he stay looking fo feed. Maybe he smell my barbeque chicken plate.

What da hell? You no can leave your chicken at home when you go out buy lunch? Or go market to buy eggs? Maybe you bringing him to Gina's fo tell him if he no win da next fight he going end up ovah here wit his cousins. You probably get one cute comfort chicken vest in dat bag too, just in case somebody stop you. Da ting look so GOOD on um, especially when he puff up his chest and crow, "I da BIGGEST COCK in dis house." All 'cause you get one disability dat require da assistance of one chicken fo make sure you no go ballistic in da store.

Brah, I might need one comfort animal fo make sure I no choke your fucken chicken in Gina's or da store. I might bus your eggs.

A‘ALA LYMAN

DEATH

There is nothing pretty I can say about death
About the way it unfolds you
Carves into all your nooks and crannies
Scrapes you away from yourself
And everyone else
The way it finds all your hiding places
And the many forms of you crouching
In them
And how you cycle through yourself reenacting yourself
Fighting yourself
With yourself
And if death is kind
Or if you are kind to yourself
You get to decide that enough is enough
And you cease resisting while
It turns you inside out and
Empties you of yourself

FEAR

I spent the first three weeks
Studying the long-term outcome of bilateral brain bleeds
Browsed the web for Handi-Vans
And wheelchairs like I saw the mothers pushing in the hallway,
Their children looking like they'd been frozen and then left out in the sun.
I wanted to stare at this my likely
Future.
And it wasn't politeness that turned my face away but the terror of
Carting around my broken burden weighing down my shoulders
Fattening out my middle
Sucking out the color
In my hair.

A'ala Lyman

I spent nights researching how to negotiate the conversations of a DNR
The ethics of pulling the feeding tube when comfort care is started
The statistics and the prospects of it taking days
And sometimes weeks
For your child
To finally give up
On you.

GRIEF

It's the weight of it, like the lead they give you to cover your body
when receiving an X-ray
It spreads out from the abdomen
Into the chest
It feels like how you're afraid emptiness feels.
It bypasses all the ways we distract ourselves from ourselves.
It confronts you,
And there's a rushing inward,
You'll find a place in the center
In your being
That isn't yours
And maybe never was
And because it's not yours
There is no way to touch it.
So you circle around and around this emptiness,
Causing a whirlpool
That threatens to drag you into it,
To turn you inside out,
And after awhile,
You let it.

Marion Lyman-Mersereau
LEI CONVERSATION

"Manuahi" is a word I remember hearing for the first time when I was quite young and I went to Maunakea Street to buy lei with my dad. Dad bought several lei and when given a few extra—he was told by the lei seller, "For you, manuahi." Walking back to the car, I asked dad why he got extra lei and what did "manuahi" mean. My dad explained that "manuahi" means "free" or "gratis" and that the lei seller was being generous.

I was reminded of this since I heard a conversation on the radio this morning about lei sellers as I was, coincidentally, stringing a lei using kou blossoms—the bright orange pua that look like wrinkled, bombucha ʻilima. I'd learned recently it's one of the few native flower lei. The blossom comes from a tall tree so that you can only gather the flowers that have fallen to the ground—this requires a lot of bending and squatting—a great morning workout. Throughout the conversation on the radio I kept listening to the recorded stories from lei sellers back in the day but I didn't hear the word "manuahi" mentioned but maybe it was—I tuned in late. I tried to call in, I had so much to share, but my call didn't get through . . . .

I also wanted to share about the place where I used to pick white ginger buds for lei. When we opened each bud they looked like butterflies and we would string them with stamens lined up and overlapping so they resembled a feather lei. Our old ginger patch is now a parking lot where Paradise Park used to be, making me think of what happened to paradise in the tune "Big Yellow Taxi" by Joni Mitchell.

And how before canoe regattas my crew would get together after we picked grocery bags full of plumeria and we'd make so many lei for our fellow Hui Nalu Canoe Club paddlers. And one year we gathered kaunaʻoa from the University Ave. off ramp where the burnished gold parasitic plant, Lānaʻi's "flower," crawls over the dry grass. We entwined the kaunaʻoa with rope tī leaf lei and together they were stunning and perfect since gold is one of our canoe club's colors. Nowadays after you finish a race you're lucky if you get a lei made from one strand of yarn with a candy bar tied to it—still a gesture of kindness and congratulations, I suppose, but sans the beauty and fragrance.

And how there is a war in lower Mānoa between three vines occurring on a chain link fence my neighbor erected around his vacant lot—my pakalana and stephanotis and the invasive banana poka are vying for supremacy and I want to make sure the banana poka doesn't win and the stephanotis and pakalana learn to live together peaceably.

And how it's a joy to string or wili flowers into a lei—to work with nature in a way that allows us to wear Her. I've never had the patience to make feather lei or weave lau hala and I so admire those who do. I enjoy how quickly a lei, unless it's an intricate wili creation, can be quickly strung and yet give so much joy—especially when there's no reason for the lei other than there were flowers so a lei was made and given.

And how I know there's a school where I used to pick puakenikeni on a daily basis and make several lei to give teachers but now, since I don't go there very often anymore and nobody else seems to be picking the flowers, there are hardly any to pick. When I pick the few blooms there I have to make sure I don't cut the stems too short or there will only be enough for a lei poʻo.

Some plants, I've learned, will keep re-creating flowers as long as they are picked, which, I think, makes the plant feel that it's appreciated. I feel a silent, gracious nod from the flowering bushes or trees after I finish picking when I say mahalo for their kahiau—a single Hawaiian word which takes six English words to define it: lavish generosity without expectation of return.

FOR A GOOD WHILE

after I wake
my eyes well up with tears
which makes me wonder
if there lies a deep-seated grief
that fills
some psychological dam
during the night
then spills over
in the morning
or maybe
they are tears of joy
just to see another morning
witness my breath
hear birds' melodies
feel the great press
of gravity that gives
my body solidity

MARION LYMAN-MERSEREAU

or could it be
joy and grief combined
without my awareness
or possibly—simply
my vision
needs a good wash
from whatever fearful nightmares
or fanciful dreams
visited me when I wandered
where I was not fully there

JUST CLOUDS

Sept. 13, 2001

On any other day
the perfect puffy cloud
just behind the mango tree
backlit by this morning's bright sun
highlighting its soft white, curved edges
would bring to mind
cherub cheeks, risen dough,
cotton candy, chubby, dimpled babies' butts
Rubenesque women's breasts
but today the round cloud
framed by blue and green
only makes me think
of the billows of smoke
that first burst from the building
soon after impact
that wrapped ethereal arms around
the proud structure
then concealed its total collapse
like the Houdini vanishing act
where the sheet is pulled up
over the magician and in moments

Marion Lyman-Mersereau

when the cloth is dropped
he's gone—
yet in that act
the magician instantly reappears
elsewhere in the theater
in this act there is no reappearance
there is no magic

I long for clouds
to just be clouds
not shaped like huge mushrooms,
not full of pollutants,
not smoky bundles of dust
vaporized steel
concrete
marble
wall board
bone

Jennifer Santos Madriaga
OBSCURING

In between birth and death
are the spaces too many to count
and remember, but some survive
the abyss.
Like the time I saw the sun's delicate corona,
gray and green, tendrils so fine
that no photograph can capture it.
The moon's shadow
cooled the afternoon by 20 degrees,
and the insects hummed in
the most surreal twilight I will ever know
during an early August afternoon
in Greenville, South Carolina.
Beside me stood a man
who could never love me,
but he placed his arm around me
as I shed tears at the sight
of a fully blocked sun.
He could not love me, and yet
he was here, locked with the unforgettable.
I looked over to my son,
who loved us both, his face
bathed in streetlight and eclipse
shadow, and I hoped he
would only remember the purity
of the moment, not the fighting
beforehand or the trip home after
(where we struggled through backroads
traffic so terrible that some cars pulled over
in surrender to wait it out.)
That man could never love me
but he knew enough to be tender,
to walk over to kiss my son
on the forehead. Some moments
are so quiet. Those are the ones
that break me wide open
with the strength of their staying.

Jennifer Santos Madriaga

BANISHED/VANISHED

The body contains memory
that the conscious mind has forgotten.
In my dreams my mouth
speaks Ilocano fluently,
and I can sing the highest
notes on pitch.
And my body is pliable
and able to climb high places
without fear.

I am haunted by the shadows
of large mango trees
in passing. I can still remember
the juice that overflowed
upon peeling their fruit,
my mouth and hands always
grateful and sticky.
The emerald world was full
of noise and talking in
my native dialect.
People I loved were still alive,
laughing and smoking
brown cigarettes, and
the air hazy with burning
and a pending rain.

All these things are buried now
and belong to an amnesiac earth.
Certain moments I feel
the full weight of their disappearance.
Like when it is quiet at night,
and I realize returning is only illusion.

Marcia Zina Mager
EPITAPH

Write me a poem.
Use the words you were born with,
the words you grew up with,
the words you speak every day of your life.

Don't bring me a rose
from a garden you did not grow.
Better the thick green stalk
of a weed grown wild and unbidden
behind the steps of your back porch.
Better a handful of parched grass
plucked fitfully from your own lawn.

Write me a poem
and let me hear your voice.
Unsmooth, raucous,
irritating as the sound of a rusty tricycle
trundling by.

Let me see your face.
Scarred and uncared for,
unwashed and unshaven,
tender and sad.

Write me a poem
and deliver it to my mossy grave
with a ragged bunch of flowers
planted and picked by your hand
and read me your words.

I will listen.

And beneath the earth
and upon the winds
and across the seas

MARCIA ZINA MAGER

I will sound my applause
in the song of the tiny sparrow
as she flies forever home.

ENTRANCE

Finally
I understand the lotus
the Chinese masters sing about.

Our lives, like petals,
push up and open,
grand and fruitful,
bounty in bright yellow.

We *think* our lives prepare us
for something so much greater . . .
a hidden blossom, a secret berry,
teasing like a streak of sapphire
before the rising of the sun.

But like the lotus
we prepare for nothing.
The Chinese masters giggle,
they understand the joke.

We open, finished.
We open, fruitful.
Forever opening,
reaching toward an entrance never there.

Carrie Frances Martin
HĀMĀKUA COAST

The moon ascends
a great white ship out of the Pacific
    mesmerizing and powerful
        rousing the sea

alone in the opaque beauty

on the eastern flank of Mauna Kea
a darkening night, the wind and rain come
like soldiers marching up the verdant headlands
shaking and pounding the windows

        howling across the deep ravines
to scrawl incantations on my door

    a sublime concerto
        torrents of water quench the porous land
        rush down
        the narrow promontory
            to Onomea Bay

In velvet silence, outside these clamorous hours,
where the sleeping dwell
    your voice, whispers
        intimately of home
of some puzzle, some intricate piece, misplaced

until waking I remember. . .
I left long ago . . .

Ages I wait
tethered in the blur
between dream and waking
    for the tempest to still

CARRIE FRANCES MARTIN

with the first thin ray
of grey dawn,
a slender touch upon the broad horizon
I rise
at once translucent

then a slip of hand, a rose bowl shatters,
scattering glass shards over porcelain tile
an upheaval of memories, fragmented.
Carefully I sweep the slivers into a neat pile
on bare knees,
looking closely for that one missed sliver . . .

so no one will cut their feet

. . . the feet of people I do not know
who do not know me,

of the woman I was
that once my hair hung long
dark as rich coffee
knowing not the nuances,
        the hundred bouquets I arranged
          of such wild jubilation

            . . . that once . . .
              I was your bride

Rick McKenzie
1967

In 1967, I was thirteen.
The news came from San Francisco.
It went all around the world:
This is the Summer of Love.
In my all-white suburb
Just one half-hour from Detroit,
I really did agree with it.
What was there not to like
About the Summer of Love?
Some girls I knew from junior high
Stopped wearing their brassieres.
I was totally in favor
But I did not tell a soul.
Pop songs were very optimistic,
But there was what was Vietnam.
It seemed like no one thought about it.
The radio kept singing about love.
I thought I knew what I knew, but I didn't.
Then, in July the Motor City burnt.
The riot was the summer of hate.
All that love went upside down,
And I started to suspect
That love was rich kids smoking dope,
And rage and power were the real deal.
I was thirteen and confounded.
That fall, I actually fell in love.
Of course, next to nothing ever happened.
I wonder where you are now, Carol.
So much we didn't know, so much we really did.
It's ridiculous how old we are today.

Tyler Miranda

THE WRETCH OF MAKAKILO: ON FAMILY

You know, why bother you bring da kids
wen all I get to see is ugly faces?
Look, da younger one over there,
no even come give his elder one kiss hello,
too busy wit' his lousy phone.
Why one small boy need dat kine?
Who him talking to?
And what fo' him get dat salty face?
I his grandparent.
What more important dan family? Hah?
And your older one on da couch,
look her, rolling her eyeball.
Her tink I dunno what dat mean?
I know dey no like come here.
What fo', you bring dem?
So I see their ugly faces?
You know, da damn younger generation,
dey no can come see their grandparent 'cause dey like,
out of da kindness of their heart,
den no need! Damn selfish.
And dem born from my own damn kid.
I get less and less years left, you know?
Why I like spend 'em looking at their ugly faces?
Wen dey sit my couch, ugly faces.
Dey change my TV station, ugly faces.
Drink my Canada Dry, eat my mango, mess up my mahjong tile:
ugly, ugly, more ugly faces!
What fo' you come, hah? My own damn kid.
How many time you wen' look your wristwatch already?
Only been fifteen minute!
You come four hours late.
I wen' call you six-thirty dis morning,
and look now,

TYLER MIRANDA

almost lunch time, half da day over.
Why, you had more important place fo' be,
dan wit' me, your *family*?
You tink you wen' spend 'nuff time?
Den just go already.
I no like see only ugly faces.
I like people be happy fo' come see me,
not fo' come make me feel how *inconvenient* me
'cause you damn kids no can even act happy fo' be here.
My own flesh and blood,
and all I rate is your ugly faces.

THE WRETCH OF MAKAKILO: ON DIVERSITY

You know, these younger generation,
dem get too many choice nowadays.
Only make more complicate dat.
What fo' get hundred TV station?
These kids just like me,
only watch da same one.
But dem tink dem so better.
My granddaughter,
da middle one,
her tell get MTV *Real World*,
her no like watch *Kung Fu* wit' me.
But ass my favorite, I tell,
David Carradine good actor, you know.
But you know what her say to me,
her own flesh and blood,
her . . . elder?
Her tell, "You so *racist*, Grams.
He not even Chinese."
I come so angry,
I tell, "So? Why I no can like him?
So what him white?

Tyler Miranda

Him da good guy."
Her roll her eye at me like I dunno all dat *her* know,
so me, I turn off da damn TV
and throw da remote control in da trash can.
These damn younger generation get all kine new idea,
tink dem so smart
'cause dem buggahs get da kine internets, ah?
And da small phone dem always play wit',
and da uku-billion TV station.
But dem no even know how fo' treat their own grandparent!
So damn disrespectful!
Dem lose all da cultures and traditions.
Get so much damn kids nowadays *make* themselves . . . homo, ah?
Or make da kine *yakuza* tattoo all over,
or make *chi-chi*-kine earring.
'Cause too many choice dem nowadays.
So many free time on their hand.
What happen to these younger generation?
Us old timers neva had dis kine problem.
No more TV back den, ass why.
Us buggahs all get along in da camp,
da *pakes*,
da Buddhaheads,
da *yobos*,
da *parés*.
Nobody tell, You *racist*.
Somebody call you one Buddhahead,
why come mad fo'?
You one Buddhahead!
No big deal.
Ass 'cause us had da kine respect fo' da elders.
Us neva thought us was better dan our own grandparent.
Us know how important
fo' carry on da cultures and traditions.
Who these damn younger generation going learn dat from?
Hah? Da TV?
Bullshit dat!
Eh, at least David Carradine remember his elder,
and pray,

Tyler Miranda

and show da respect.
Him just like me,
treat ev'rybody da same.

FLIP DA BIRD

Sticking middle finga wen' save my sista's life.
We all know not suppose to flip da bird,
neva know who you going offend.
Better fo' just let ev'ryting be.
But wen one jackass disco-moke
in one beat-up Buick Skylark
wen' cut her off 'Ewa-bound on H-1,
my sista made sure he seen her middle finga
in his rearview mirror.
But dat's wen it happen:
her finga came stuck.
Was so sore,
she knew someting was wrong,
she said she no could even use her hand fo' drive.
All da way to da hospital,
she tinking how we was always scolded for be careful,
no make ugly faces,
bumbye going stay dat way.
She thought was funny:
all da years sticking middle finga
despite what we was taught
finally wen' catch up wit' her.

So wen she told me
da doctor found one cancer tumor on her knuckle
and good ting dey got 'em remove early,
I thought,
How da fuck dat work?
Sticking middle finga neva catch up wit' her,
da buggah finally wen' *pay off*.

Tyler Miranda

Not suppose to flip da bird.
But my sista going be A-OK
because she wen' stick middle finga?
Seem like my *taran taran* Portagee sista got 'em right after all.
Maybe time fo' all of us change 'em around too:
Big fucking deal if you aiming at one *haole* or one *sole*?
Better fo' not worry—
flip dat bird.
Be free, let 'em fly
'cause your life might depend on it.

Tamara Leiokanoe Moan
KAʻENA

We walk crabwise over rocks
and rounded lumps of coral,
sun flashing its last heat.
The water glints bright and dark
in alternating bands to the horizon.
My hasty feet catch
at the edge of tide pools
rippling with wave splatter.
Our line of field-tripping writers
disperses, contracts, our stories
shared in new combinations
as cliff shoulders loom above us,
greened by winter rain.
At the rock where souls
make their leap
I place our lei,
ropes of maile,
tī and kukuna-o-ka-lā,
leaving their entwined stems
to wither and disintegrate.

Out on the point where seas collide
we unpack dinners
and chitchat until a seal
snorts and we all turn
to search for his sleek dark head
among the rocks.
An apricot sky peeks
from beneath a suspended anvil
of dense gray cloud.

In deepening dusk
we reassemble,

Tamara Leiokanoe Moan

turn back.
We are not alone.
Wheeling albatross
and shearwater gulls
shadow us,
scores of them filling the air
with movement.
Awe slows our feet
as darkness gathers.

Velvety humid blackness
accompanies us now
as unsteady feet follow
our tiny man-made lights.
We own fewer words
on this return journey,
minds still overflowing
with wings, with flight,
with the leaping of souls.

Dawn Morais

SHENANDOAH
for Zubin, July 20, 2000

Best seat in the house:
Long grass loops around my chair
Swift water laps my back
But I do not care
Except delightedly.
Will I be carried back?
Or is this just the flow,
The shimmer of a dream
Purposeful?

Like you, my son. Fast,
Hard to pin down,
A steady rush of energy
Contained yet chafing past
Restraining banks. Pure light,
Restless, robust, bright.

Liquid silver laces over
Tree-green water running deep.
See it skate sand and stone,
Smooth shape and hone
The ground below.

Fish leap out of the steady hum
Into the light that streams down
From ridges that run
With the river in endless
Possibility.
A million suns
Have warmed the thick boughs
That stretch across big water,
Reaching far and out,
Design and destiny.

Dawn Morais

The artist I will never be
Commits these moments
To memory. I see
Your strong arms swing
Your bat in mad ecstasy
Yelling, "Pops! Catch!"

Knee-deep in the water
Pops holds up his prize sun
Fish, baited and brought
Up, only to be let go
Into the current. Swift,
Unceasing, seeking bigger
Waters, a braver show.

Sitting in this mighty
River, my shen*
Lifts in doa*, and I'm
As eager as my son.

I feel the current.
And I let go.

* Shen: (Chinese) spirit, part of the psyche
* Doa: (Malay) prayer

Susan Miho Nunes
THE WALKING LADY

The first time Harry Crooks saw the woman on the highway was about six months after he moved to Maui. He was whacking back the wild ginger in the front yard when his dog Mickey started barking, and Harry looked up just in time to see the woman shambling by the mailbox at the end of the driveway, heading toward the Sacred Pools. She was bent almost double beneath a lumpy green backpack, and her hair looked like it hadn't encountered a comb in a while, but her legs were long and tanned, and Harry wondered if maybe she lived in the vicinity.

He whistled for Mickey, who was still barking up a storm by the mailbox, and returned to the ginger. For the rest of the day as he mowed and raked and put things in piles, he found himself thinking about her, and later the thought of those legs eased the ache in his hip that began shortly after dinner and Harry owed to the yard work. He hadn't considered a woman that way in a while, not since breaking up with Louise. In fact, that night was the first night since moving to Hāna that Harry hadn't lain awake worrying about his circumstances and whether he'd done the right thing, settling in the boondocks just short of his eightieth birthday.

Harry Crooks' move to Maui took all his beach friends by surprise. Sure, Hāna was gorgeous, but Jeezus Christ, Harry's no spring chicken, and what's he going to do there all by himself?

When you thought about it, though, you couldn't see Harry Crooks spending the rest of his life in a Honolulu walkup too close to the freeway, or in a retirement home that wouldn't allow dogs. Twelve miles out of Hāna the rents were still affordable, and you could almost forget how isolated it was, fifty miles of winding coast road, the kind of road where every so often a car drives off the side and into the sea.

The next day Harry woke up refreshed. He treated his hip with aspirin for a few days and, when that didn't work, decided to drive into Hāna and buy a bottle of ibuprofen at the general store.

"You okay, Harry?" Gloria, the cashier, asked when he limped to the register with his shopping basket.

"Just a twinge in the old hip," he said, watching the register as she rang up his purchases.

"It happens," she said and recalled how her grandmother had been complaining of the same thing. "Sometimes a cane helps," she added.

The thought of a cane gave him the willies. The village of Hāna was full of eccentrics, and Harry had worked hard at being one, not just another lonely old man. He'd grown a beard, tied his fine white hair in a ponytail. He wore khaki shorts or lava-lavas, often went shirtless, showing off his hairy chest. Someone told him he resembled Ernest Hemingway in his Cuba days, which Harry took as a compliment.

Harry counted his change twice, put the receipt in the pocket of his shorts, and winked at the cashier as he hefted the two bags of groceries. "See you Saturday," he said.

His mood lifted as he steered his pickup truck past Hāmoa and watched the clouds retreat up the mountain. He'd chosen rightly to live on the dry side of Hāna, which was very different from the north side where it rained every day. Here cattle grazed behind driftwood fences. The land rose in gentle foothills toward Haleakalā, and the sea was never far away.

The twelve miles went quickly, and by the time Harry turned into his front yard it was with a sense of pride in what he'd accomplished. The setting was Edenic, the rent only three hundred fifty a month. The little house still needed work, but he'd managed to fix the leaks in the roof, repair the water catchment tank, and coax some cooperation out of the primitive plumbing. Of course, he'd had to haul in his own gasoline to run the generator, and lugging those ten-gallon cans was hard on his back, but all in all he was pleased with the way he'd settled in.

For Harry Crooks, experience was still inexhaustible. His life had been a series of choices—his two ex-wives, Mavis and Keiko, and Louise, and of course Peter, Peter, most of all—but he still felt he was damned lucky he could still make them, and hadn't they all led somewhere worthwhile? He ignored the twinge in his hip and climbed out of the truck with his groceries.

In spite of the ibuprofen, the twinges grew into an ache that refused to go away, and a few days later, with the cashier's words in mind, Harry decided to do something about it.

After finishing his morning chores, he drove with Mickey down to Manu George, his nearest neighbor. "Hey, you got a piece of lumber I can buy?" he asked the wizened, sawdust-covered woodcarver. "Maybe six feet long, a little thicker than a broom handle?" He held his hand at head level.

Manu George considered the request over the head of his half-carved statue. "What for?" he asked.

"Thought I'd make me a walking stick."

"Walking stick, huh." Manu George scratched his head, thought a moment. "You mean like them hikers use?"

"Yeah, maybe wide enough at the top to carve." The idea, shaped in words, pleased Harry. Maybe he'd also burn his name into the shaft. Harry M. Crooks.

"Let's see what I can do," Manu said.

While Manu rummaged through some remnants piled against the main house, Harry sank into the raggedy car seat Manu kept for visitors. Manu George was about seventy, Harry guessed, and had lived in Hāna all his life. He'd been a ranch hand in his youth. Now he carved tikis and salad bowls for the tourist trade, sold them in the general store. Everyone knew Manu George and Manu George knew everyone.

"Ever meet a haole woman living around here?" Harry asked. "Tall, long legs, not bad looking?"

"Who, Grace White?" Manu George asked.

"No, younger." Grace White, a retired schoolteacher, had to be at least eighty.

"Can't say. Did you say six feet?"

"She's not that tall," Harry said before realizing Manu George was talking about some 2×2s he'd pulled from a crawl space under the house. "Six feet will do fine." He stood up slowly as Manu emerged dragging a length of lumber.

"I knew it was here somewhere," Manu said. He pointed to the wider end. "It was supposed to be a canoe paddle, but I busted the tip about two years back. It's koa and no termites. Should polish up good."

Harry hefted the piece. It was a bit weathered, but with no splinters, and just about the right length and thickness. With a little sanding and shaping it should turn out fine. He could carve the wider end, add a rubber grip. He leaned on it to test the strength. Yes, it would do fine.

"Thanks, Manu," he said. "How much I owe you?"

Manu George waved him away.

Harry spent several intense, happy days sanding and polishing. He had some good hand tools, and he loved the feel of things unfinished and in need of doing. As he worked, he glanced from time to time toward the highway, filled with expectation, not unlike the feeling he got waiting for his pension check to arrive, only better. When the woman didn't appear, he thought back on Louise, his longtime companion, and what went wrong.

What happened was, shortly before Harry's seventieth birthday, in one of his sudden moves, Harry splurged on a two-week vacation to Hawai'i. He'd been living in Bowling Green, Kentucky, for more than twenty years, where he'd settled after leaving Japan, and longed for something a little more exotic. Arriving in Honolulu, he'd tried to contact Art and Louise Rutherford, old friends from New Jersey who'd retired in the islands, and instead discovered

Louise newly widowed and eager for some male companionship. Within a week he'd moved in with her with Mickey, a little mixed breed mutt he'd found wandering the beach.

Life was good. In the late afternoons, he'd make himself a Bombay Martini and Louise a Long Island iced tea, and they'd sit on the deck and watch the sunsets and tell themselves how lucky they were. Their sex life was satisfying, Louise an eager pupil, he a still virile teacher. They'd discussed marriage, of course, but their financial situations argued against it. Besides, as Harry reminded Louise, living in sin kept them young.

Thanks to this shared arrangement, Harry was able to live within his means, with enough left over to indulge himself. One of his great pleasures was inviting people home for dinner, a pleasure second only to that of cooking the meal. Louise didn't seem to mind the parade of people. "Just promise me, Harry, no strangers in my house while I'm away," she'd say before leaving for New Jersey every Christmas to visit her daughter.

The young couple he invited over New Year's Eve he'd met on the beach the previous weekend, and liked, and the invitation was out of Harry's mouth before he realized what he'd done. They all drank too much of the champagne Harry provided (along with dinner) and so it seemed reasonable after the fireworks to invite them to sleep over and avoid the drunks on the road. How could Harry have predicted that one of his guests would fall out of the bunk bed in the guestroom and injure his back? Or that he'd hire an attorney and sue the living daylights out of Louise? How could Harry have known that Louise would opt to forsake the house, and their good life, rather than fight the bastards in court?

"I'm tired," she'd said of the lawsuit that consumed their lives for the better part of a year. She seemed almost relieved when Harry said he'd not be moving to New Jersey with her.

The night Harry finished the stick, he stood with it in front of the mirror. Overall, he was happy with the effect. His legs had gotten a little thin, he noticed, but with his long hair, beard, and the red lava-lava arranged around his hips, he resembled a handsome if somewhat worn character out of *Tales of the South Pacific*. He looked forward to the next day's drive into town for chit-chat and supplies.

Harry started off after breakfast. As he passed the pools on a flat stretch of road about a mile from Wailua, he caught sight of the woman plodding toward him, her head bent low beneath the hump of her backpack. He slowed but resisted the urge to stop. It was enough to know that he'd been right, that the woman did live in the vicinity and that he'd see her again and there'd be time to act in a more neighborly way. He watched her in the rearview mirror until she disappeared around the bend. She was not unattractive, but there was something else, he thought as he rounded Wailua Cove, something harder to define. What Harry saw was a quality both aimless and purposeful, as if on the one hand she were determined to reach her destination but on the other was in no hurry to arrive.

Of course, this wasn't unusual in Hāna. The locals took their time; only the tourists tailgated and then sped past, honking, as if the pools might disappear if they didn't arrive on time. Harry wondered where she was heading. Not too far, he hoped.

In the weeks that followed, lugging the gas cans proved increasingly difficult, and Harry was forced to conserve on his electricity use. He packed away his sander and drill. He made difficult choices, like between reading at night and listening to his stereo. He still drove into town, enjoyed flirting with Gloria at the general store and showing off his stick. The nights were long, though, and he took to lying in bed and listening to music by the light of the kerosene lamp.

That old lamp had a way of carrying Harry back fifty years all the way to Hiroshima, where he'd worked after the war, which reminded him of Keiko and the closet-sized apartment they shared above a shop that sold pots and pans fashioned out of scrap metal. Harry made enough in those days to send his wife, Mavis, something every month and to keep Keiko-san (as he called her) in the kimonos he liked her to wear. He and Keiko were happy, and their feelings for each other assuaged Harry's guilt for abandoning Mavis and Peter in New Jersey.

In the light of the old kerosene lamp, Harry Crooks would wonder about the turns life took and how those choices had led him to wondering when he'd see the woman on the highway.

One Saturday afternoon, about a mile from the general store where Harry had bought his supplies, there she was. This time they were traveling in the same direction. Harry slowed.

The woman's hands were clasped behind her back beneath the heavy body of the pack, the way women carried children in Japan. Maybe she'd been shopping, he thought. Did she really intend walking the entire twelve miles to Kīpahulu, where he assumed she lived? Harry waved as he passed her and then stopped some ways ahead to wait.

"Can I give you a lift?" he asked when the woman drew abreast of the truck. She was clad in a low-cut halter top that covered her midriff, and a pair of faded denim shorts, cut high and unraveling at the crotch. She glanced up and down the road, and then over her shoulder at the driftwood fence and pasture beyond.

"You walked by my place recently," he said, hoping his smile was reassuring. "I live this side of Kīpahulu. The house with the red water tank and the torch ginger in front."

She eyed him from the safety of the road's shoulder, like a stray cat ready to run. "Sorry," Harry said, thinking maybe he'd better move on, "I didn't mean to frighten you."

Right then Mickey jumped on his lap and stuck his head out the window and yipped a couple times. Harry rubbed the dog's soft, pointy ears.

"Mickey's saying that load you're carrying looks awful heavy," he said. "And we'd enjoy your company."

Mickey barked again, and the woman started toward the truck. Leaning across the front seat, Harry threw open the passenger door. When she bent to climb in, Harry glanced at the swing of her breasts.

That's when he saw the scar. It was bright pink and began about two inches above the V of her halter top and disappeared in her cleavage. Shaken, he looked away. Mickey yipped and wagged and the woman wedged her backpack beneath the dashboard and climbed in.

She declined to buckle the seatbelt and kept her hand on the armrest near the door handle, as if to enable a quick getaway. Only after Mickey licked her face and laid his head in her lap did she relax.

"Nice dog," she said hoarsely, still staring straight ahead.

Harry was remembering where he'd seen scars like that. Raised above the skin, as if something alive had been burrowing underneath.

"I'm Harry," he said.

She let go of the armrest to stroke Mickey's ears.

Harry drove slowly, trying to make conversation, sneaking a few looks in the long and frequent pauses. Her breasts were surprisingly full and deep for someone so thin. He could smell her sweat, her hair, the canvas of her backpack. He was aware of Mickey's head buried in her lap, just above the line of her shorts.

She didn't say much as the road dipped and curved through shady gulches, past waterfalls and tumbling cliffs trailed by white ribbons of surf. They'd passed Puʻuiki before he asked where she was heading.

"Just drop me anywhere," she said and continued to stare out the window.

"You live around Kīpahulu?" he asked and mentioned again seeing her near there.

She shook her head. "Just walking." When he asked where she lived, she said, "Around."

By the time they passed the pools Harry was facing the fact he'd picked up a homeless woman. There were deep lines etched into her face, some from squinting into the sun, others from somewhere else. Her body was youthful, her belly flat as a young girl's, but her nails were ragged and torn and black with dirt.

When they got to his house and she was still with him, he asked whether she wanted a cheese sandwich.

"Okay," she said.

"Soon as I take care of these cans," he said, reaching for his stick.

He felt her watching him as he unloaded the gasoline cans and hobbled up the steps with the first one. The generator was in a shed next to the outdoor shower. When he started back for the second can, he realized she'd followed him with it. "No, please," he protested and tried to take it from her.

She pushed past him and set it next to the other in the shed and then followed him back to the truck. "What happened to your leg?" she asked.

"It's my hip. Some kind of strain."

Together they lugged the last can by the handles to the shed and then carried in the groceries. She asked if she could use the bathroom, and he showed her where the toilet and shower were outside. While she was there, he made her a sandwich of jack cheese, mayonnaise and iceberg lettuce, and when she joined him she'd thrown a loose T-shirt over her halter top and combed her hair. She ate hungrily, sitting across from him at the dinette.

"Another?" he offered, and she ate that, too, wiping her mouth afterwards with the back of her hand.

When she finished, he made her a cup of coffee, and she looked around the room for the first time. Her gaze took in the big bed in the corner with its red-and-white Tahitian-print spread, the bookshelves, the stereo, his two rattan chairs, the seascapes on the walls, and the framed photograph of Louise on the bureau.

"That your wife?" she asked.

"A close friend," he said.

"She kick off or something?"

"What makes you think that?" he asked, a little startled at the question.

"Figured someone like you wouldn't be here by himself."

That's when the story sort of poured out of him, Louise and the lawsuit and how he'd let her go and ended up on Maui, living with his dog in a one-room shack.

"You got any kids?" she asked.

"Hey, I don't even know your name," he said.

She met his gaze with pale green eyes as lifeless as broken glass. A moment later the blankness was replaced by a look of wariness and cunning that gave Harry a chill. She said, "A girl can't be too careful, the nasty things a man can do."

Harry stood up so quickly he knocked over his chair. "Look, Miss," he said, wagging his finger at her, "if I wanted to hurt you, I wouldn't have wasted a damn cheese sandwich!"

She drew back, hugged herself, and began rocking back and forth.

"You're making me nervous," Harry said.

"Well, shit," she blurted. "You try running from them, see how you feel."

"Running from who?"

She rolled her eyes, as if he were the child. "Indians! Mexicans! Don't you know?"

"What, in Hāna?"

"Wanting to cut me up." She rocked back and forth, talking to herself.

Harry hastily gathered the dishes and limped to the sink. Her rocking was becoming more agitated, and he worried she'd rock herself clean out of the chair. He sat down again. "All I wanted was to give you a ride. I needed company." He waited a beat or two. "How about some Oreos?"

The rocking slowed, the arms unloosed themselves, and it was as if a storm had passed. They sat there in silence while she finished her coffee and ate a dozen cookies, splitting each and licking the filling off, like Peter used to. Then she said, "Thanks for lunch. Time to move on." She gathered her backpack, and spent a minute or two petting Mickey.

"I'm Maureen," she said before starting out the door.

He stood at the end of the gravel driveway watching her figure get smaller. She never turned once, not even to wave, just walked slowly and deliberately along, heading—where?—nowhere, he supposed, just forward.

Later, lying in bed listening to the rain, it occurred to him that even with Mickey, the house felt empty. "Maureen," he said to himself and liked the way it sounded. He found himself repeating it at odd moments in the days ahead.

When Harry mentioned Maureen at the general store, Gloria looked shocked. "You hanging with the mental lady, Harry?"

"Just gave her a lift," he said.

"A lift," she snorted. "You know what she does? Walks around the island, around and around. Always the same direction." She made circles with one hand as she stuffed groceries into the bag with the other. "Kahului, Wailua, Hāna," she said, naming the coastal towns, "all the way past Lapehu Point, down Mākena way and then Kīhei and back to Kahului and all around again."

"How long has she been doing this?" Harry was astonished and impressed at the mileage Maureen covered.

Gloria thought a moment. "Three or four years. I heard she used to live in the park in Kīhei before she started walking. She has money, comes in here, buys food." She shook her head. "Watch out, Harry."

Harry left the store feeling muddled and depressed. Was this what he'd been reduced to, hanging out with a crazy woman? He thought about what had set her off the day he'd fed her lunch and wondered if the scar explained her craziness. The scar was a sign of a wound, and he knew trauma could drive a person crazy. He'd seen them in Japan. And he'd been half crazy himself when he'd gotten that accusing phone call about Peter. "Your Army 45, Harry," his brother-in-law had said. Dwelling on pain made it worse. Maybe that's why Maureen had to keep moving. He remembered how gentle she'd had been with Mickey, and how the dog had liked her from the start. He thought about the Oreos. He knew he wanted to see her again.

A few weeks later, a storm blew in from the sea. It rained for several days, so hard that Harry couldn't drive into Hāna for gasoline and relied for light on his kerosene lamps. His hip was especially bad one day. He scrambled eggs on the gas stove for dinner, drank a cold beer, read late into the night. The rain beat so hard on the roof that he didn't hear the knock until Mickey started barking at the door. He opened it, and there was Maureen, blue-lipped and soaking wet.

He threw a towel over her shoulders, but she just stood there dripping onto the linoleum. And so he dried her off and helped her undress.

She was as docile as a child, placing a hand on his shoulder as she stepped into the pajama bottoms he held out for her and then letting him lead her to the couch. He opened a can of soup, but by the time it was hot she'd fallen asleep. He covered her with a blanket and sat for a long time watching her, unable to shake the image of what he'd seen as he peeled off her clothes.

The scar ran down the top of her right breast and down her sternum, emerging beneath the sag of her left breast and zigzagging across her navel to her right hip bone. She had no belly button; whoever sewed her up hadn't attempted to reconstruct it. Her left breast was covered with smaller, radial scars.

She stayed for two weeks that time. Harry had a water heater that had to be hand-adjusted when someone took a shower. Maureen never did learn how to do that, and so while she bathed, Harry would adjust the heater and wait. He never touched her. Doing so would trespass some unspoken boundary between them.

Maureen must have noticed his interest in the scars—how could she not? It became almost a game between them, his desire to know how she'd gotten them, her desire to not say.

He learned not to ask questions. Asking about her family, for instance, sent her into a tantrum. Eventually, though, he learned that she was from New

Mexico, that her mother still lived near Silver City. When he'd ask about her father, she'd say, "Don't care, don't want to know," and start with the Mexicans and Indians again. But most of the time she was companionable, and Harry forgot how crazy she was.

Maureen left as suddenly as she appeared, just packed up on a Wednesday and walked away. But then a month later, she turned up again and stayed three weeks.

Then one time toward the end of the year, she knocked on his door in the dead of night with her arms and hands covered with cuts. She said she'd slipped off the road and fallen against a barbed wire fence.

"You can't go on like this, Maureen!" Harry shouted. Maureen began to wail. Harry lowered his voice. "I don't know what happened and I won't ask, okay? Look at me." She snuffled a bit and finally looked at him. Harry said, "Would you like me to give you a back rub?"

He started with her shoulders, and, avoiding the cuts on her arms, worked his way down her back and her legs, all the way down to her callused feet, which were as hard and dry as old leather.

When she turned over, Harry took a deep breath.

The scar had a texture completely different from the rest of her skin. In some places, it seemed to be contained by the boundaries of the original wound. But in others, like across her belly, a dense network of tissue overwhelmed the original wound. In the bombing of Nagasaki, some people more than a half mile from the center developed keloid scars like these that continued to grow for years. Harry touched the scar with a finger and began tracing its path. The pain in his hip seemed to ease.

Over the next few months, Maureen's stays with Harry grew longer. His budget hadn't allowed for two, and so he had to make more adjustments. His computer went, then his portable wine cellar and the wines he'd saved for his dotage, sold bottle by bottle to the manager at the local resort. He gave up the martinis he used to enjoy at sunset, then his cigars. He tried not to look too far ahead.

Maureen called Mickey her little fox. By then Harry had accepted her ravings as quirky aspects of her nature. The Indians and Mexicans had mutated into various and sundry men with names like Broken Arrow and Luiz. One of her stories was that she had a husband, Ramon, young, handsome Ramon, who was madly in love with her and would kill to be with her. Harry didn't like it when she talked about Ramon. "If he loved you so much, why isn't he here taking care of you?" Harry would say. And then they'd argue and she'd walk out. A few hours later, maybe a day, she'd be back on his doorstep.

Harry liked to think that living with him gave Maureen a sense of place and the first permanent address she had in years. He felt he was doing her the favor.

One day, carrying a can of gasoline up the steps, Harry felt a stabbing pain in his groin. The can and walking stick went tumbling, and he fell to the ground and vomited. "I'm dying," he thought as the pain came and went in waves. It took all his courage to stand up before Maureen found him.

She helped him to bed and made him lie there with a hot water bottle. The next day they drove into the clinic in Hāna. After a two-hour wait, the doctor gave him pain pills and referred him to a specialist in Kahului.

"Can you drive?" Harry asked Maureen.

The ride along the coast the next day was a hair-raiser. Maureen gripped the steering wheel in both hands and hunched so close to it that Mickey couldn't put his head in her lap. A line of cars trailed behind and the ones who were lucky enough to pass honked and the drivers yelled and Maureen yelled back and Mickey barked and barked. But every pothole and bump felt like a stake driven into Harry's hip. His groans made Maureen even crazier, and soon she was in the grip of one of her Mexican and Indian tirades, and Harry was in too much pain to stop her.

It was even worse when they got to Kahului. The traffic terrified Maureen, and twice she stopped the truck in the middle of the road and walked away, only to come back waving her arms and tearing her hair. "This place makes me crazy!" she screamed at him. "Don't make me do this again, Harry, please not again." He was drenched in sweat and exhausted by the time they found the clinic.

"Hate these places," she said, handing him his stick and refusing to accompany him inside.

After the examination, Dr. Kawamoto, a young, round-faced woman with a businesslike manner, explained that Harry would have to come back for more tests. "You should plan to stay in town at least a week," she said, "unless you can find someone to drive you every day." She made an appointment for Harry at the radiologist's for the next morning.

"You okay?" Maureen asked as she helped him into the truck.

"Fine," he lied.

"They sure took their time."

"They need to do more tests."

He had her drive around Kahului while he looked for a cheap motel because he didn't want to attempt the coast road in the dark. If her ranting wasn't enough, and if the fifty dollars he had to plunk down wasn't enough, including an extra twenty for the dog, he had to spend a half hour persuading Maureen it was safe to enter the room.

"Don't like this place," Maureen said when he locked the door.

"Please don't leave," he begged her. "Who's going to walk Mickey? And we can both use a hot shower."

Two days later they drove back to Hāna. Harry packed a small suitcase, rested a day, and they repeated the long, teeth-gritting drive back to Kahului. This time, though, the pills helped and halfway there he took over the wheel. Maureen settled down and seemed calmer, though she sulked when he left her in the clinic parking lot.

They spent a week in Kahului, then two, filled with more tests and appointments and even a one-night stay at the hospital, during which Maureen slept in the truck with the dog. Manu George came to visit him at the hospital while Harry waited for the results. "You want me to take care of Mickey?" he offered, but Harry told him it would only upset Maureen.

"Don't say nothing to her, okay?" he told Manu.

Manu shook his head. "You sure you're going to be all right, Harry?"

"I'm fine," Harry said.

Manu George paused at the door. "Maybe I'll make you a cane."

Alone in the hospital bed with his thoughts, Harry wasn't sure what was worse, the fear of what was wrong with him, or the fear of the decision he'd have to make once he knew.

The news from Dr. Kawamoto wasn't good. "I don't know how you stood on it for so long," she told Harry. Treatments would require regular stays in town. He'd be sick.

"Can't they give me this stuff in Hāna?" Harry asked.

Dr. Kawamoto shook her head. "Maybe you should consider moving into Kahului, once we get you on a protocol," she told him. And she thought he should use a walker, they were free through Medicare.

"I need to think," Harry told her. "Can I give you a call in the next few days?"

"Okay," she said reluctantly, "but if you wait, Harry, the pain will get worse." She offered to put him in touch with social services. They would find him a place to live, at least for the initial treatments.

"You mean a nursing home?" Harry said.

"More like a convalescent home," Dr. Kawamoto replied. "You'll get good care."

"Will they take dogs?" Harry asked.

"Probably not."

Well, Harry thought, if they wouldn't take a dog they sure wouldn't accommodate a crazy lady. "I'll let you know," he told Dr. Kawamoto. "Can I sit here and rest a while?"

He found Maureen and Mickey walking circles around the parking lot. "It's about time!" she called out as he hobbled toward the truck.

"We're going home, honey."

"Thank God. I hate this place."

"Me, too, Maureen. Me, too."

The ride to Hāna in the afternoon took almost four hours, and this time Harry was grateful for it. He watched the sky change, remembered all the sunsets, the colors on the slopes of Diamond Head, Louise and her Long Island ice teas, the frosty glass streaked where her warm fingers had held it, the taste of good gin. There were no sunsets in Hāna, for the coast faced east, and the sun sank like a stone behind Haleakalā. He hadn't missed them, he realized. Not with the sunrises he could still experience every day. He thought about Mavis and Keiko, and Peter especially, but they now seemed part of a past so distant it was all but lost. Even Mavis's words at Peter's gravesite had lost their sting. Harry let himself remember them in all their fury, just to be sure. *You might as well have pulled the trigger, you son of a bitch.*

Harry Crooks had always looked ahead, moved on, and if one thing was certain, he would not end his journey in a hospital room. He fingered the small bag that held the prescription pills. There were more where those came from, he thought, and if things got really bad, well, he'd face that, too.

It was dusk by the time they reached Kīpahulu. The strange thing was (he might have thought as Maureen inched the truck into the driveway and he heard the satisfying crunch of gravel) the sicker he'd gotten the less crazy she seemed. Maybe the demons that drove Maureen on her endless circling of the island had been appeased, and wasn't that a good thing?

"We're home," she said and Harry agreed.

What he wanted that night, more than anything, was to run his finger down that scar, follow its path into the hollow of her breasts, and down the flat plain of her belly, until the sharp rise of her hip bone reminded him of a truth he'd been avoiding for too long, that this was truly as far as it went, that there simply wasn't more.

Claire Oasa
NAJUMA

We knew the rain would come but didn't expect such a strong wind. We watched the old banyan tree sway and twist. We knew it would swing towards us and we stood to the side of the cage. A large gust of wind suddenly pushed a large branch and with a crackling snap, it splintered from its hollowed trunk. It came crashing down on the wire fence folding it over like savannah grass. We flew up and above the crushed cage. People came running with long handled nets but we flew over their heads.

Over the stone walls, I flew into a large open plain. I looked behind me and mate was not there. I heard her call. I turned back but could not see her, she was still inside the stone wall. I hovered over the banyan trees but did not return to the cage. I flew towards the mountain at the edge of the plain. I landed amongst the dry and leafless trees. I surveyed the area for food and water. It could have been a home for us.

But I was only one.

Joe

There is usually leftover food from the Saturday morning farmer's market. We are discreet and polite and the vendors know us. They give us the leftover greens in plastic bags. I don't like single-use plastic but we can't wash and rinse reusables easily. The bakers give us scones but we can't eat a lot of sugar so I scrape off the frosting. Sometimes I find unfinished containers of plate lunch in the trash cans, but avoid food that's been sitting in the heat. Mayonnaise salads, half-eaten sushi and sashimi can be iffy. We've gotten sick before.

Kai and I have been together for a while, I don't know exactly how long. She is a good partner, always trying to keep things clean and neat. The tent belongs to her, the sleeping bag is mine, we share food. I don't know where she's from and I don't talk about my family but the past isn't very relevant when you are just trying to find a place to sleep. We tried staying at the shelter several times when there were sick men wandering the streets. Don't get me wrong, the shelter people are helpful but the rules are difficult. The dinners tend to be good when served by certain churches and the toilets are clean. But the park toilets are also decent and showers are free. So, we try to live on our own. Recently Kai has been slowing down; we both have. Some time ago, she said her chest hurt and saw a doctor but eventually gave up on getting refills on her medication. I can tell when she is in pain. I try to help her but she is resigned to be this way.

Kai's tent is small and camouflages well. We try to be hidden and out of the way. We used to camp in Ala Moana Park but it was a hassle to move out every night. The men in ʻAʻala Park are scary and the canal is crowded. We moved to Diamond Head but the summer is hot and dry and we can't be too close to the shady base where the houses are. The residents get upset when they see us; there are some really expensive ones at the bottom of Diamond Head. Even the owners of older houses were paranoid that we might become squatters. We had to move higher up, close to the bunkers. We moved several times to avoid hikers and the park rangers who sweep the area daily. We finally settled on a spot midway on the Koko Head side, within a patch of thorny kiawe bushes. Not ideal but no one will bother us there.

One night we heard a loud scuffle outside our tent. We thought it was a wild pig or mongoose. It sounded like a large, heavy animal so we turned on our flashlights and shone the light on the inside, hoping to scare it away. The sound stopped and we went back to sleep. The next morning, we looked around the tent. We didn't find any tracks so we didn't move. A few evenings later, we heard the same shuffling sound and went outside with our flashlights. We heard a flutter and then nothing. Early the next morning, we woke up to a large screeching sound. We went outside and saw a very large black bird with a long black bill and bright red throat. His eyes were surrounded by red. The bird stared at us, screeched again, and then flew away. I looked at Kai and didn't know what to think. I had never seen a bird like that before. I wondered if I was seeing things. I sniffed the air; it smelled moist. That afternoon, it started to rain.

It rained hard and we were not prepared. We bundled and wrapped our sleeping bag and tent in a plastic trash bag. We then hiked up to the other side of Diamond Head to find shelter. We passed only a few hikers and made our way to the tunnel at the foot of the first set of stairs. We were thankful we made it there because it rained all day. It rained the second day; there no hikers but we had to hide from the park rangers at the end of the day. When it finally stopped raining, we stayed another day because we knew the path back to our tent would be muddy and slippery. I did not want to slip and fall as I knew it could all go bad after that. We found some half-eaten granola bars and sports drinks in the tunnel. I softened the granola bars in water and diluted the sports drinks which had too much sugar. Kai didn't complain but I could tell the hike and cold was hard on her.

"Do you want to go to the shelter for a while?" I asked. She shook her head.

"No, I don't want to go there. I just want to lie down in my tent."

"Okay," I said. "Let's go back and we can go slowly." She nodded. Her sweat pants were soaked from the day before and she shivered even if it was a warm

Claire Oasa

day. We made it to the site by late afternoon. I set up the tent and aired out the sleeping bags. Kai burrowed inside and stayed still for a long while.

"I'll get some food and be back soon." I could see her head shake in the sleeping bag.

I made my way to the park entrance and in the garbage cans, found some half-filled water bottles and a plastic container with leftover fried chicken and rice balls. I also found two soft bananas wrapped in newspapers. I took all of these back to the tent. I got Kai to sit up and we ate together. Kai just wanted to bundle back up in the sleeping bag.

I threw out the chicken bones and banana peels and watched over Kai who now had a fever and kept shivering. The next morning, I smoothed out the old newspaper and read an article:

> Large Hornbills escape Honolulu Zoo after storm. Two African Ground Hornbills escaped when a tree branch fell on their cage. One was captured and the other remains at large. There has been one sighting in the Diamond Head area. If you see this bird (picture included) please do not try to apprehend but call 911.
>
> His name is Najuma.

So, the bird we saw was real. I laughed at the description that made the bird sound like a fugitive. When I read the article to Kai, she smiled. There was a second article about the African Hornbill and I read it silently. It was interesting but Kai started to cough and bend over. She spit up phlegm and blood. She didn't look afraid and reminded me: "I don't want to go to the shelter. I want to stay here."

I looked to see how to make her a little more comfortable. I wondered if I could somehow find another sleeping bag or even a small mattress. I thought I saw a small mattress in one of the remote bunkers where kids hid out. The next day, the ground was still muddy but I made the trek up again.

On my way, I heard the familiar screech. I looked up and saw the Hornbill standing on a large kiawe branch, watching me. He was big and the branch bowed under his weight. He moved his head side to side as if wanting to show me his red throat. I didn't move and said slowly,

"Hey Najuma, how are you doing? Finding enough food?"

He just looked at me and didn't waver. I chewed on the last leftover chicken I brought with me and threw the bones over his head. He flew off in the direction of the bones.

I made my way to the bunker and saw the mattress. It was too bulky, sagging in spots, and stained. I found a small wool blanket under the mattress so I folded it to bring back with me. I had the newspaper article still, took it out of my pocket, carefully unfolded and read it again:

> The Southern Ground Hornbill is found in northern Namibia and Angola to northern South Africa. They require a savannah habitat with large trees for nesting and dense but short grass for foraging. They feed on reptiles, frogs, snails, insects and mammals up to the size of hares. The Southern Ground Hornbill is well-known for its association with rain, drought, lightning, and general weather forecasts. It is believed by some that early morning calls are a sign of rain.
>
> The Hornbill has also been associated with the ability to alter human perceptions. Through traditional rituals, the bird can be utilized to improve or change a human's ability to alter reality, create illusions and expand awareness. In certain cultures, it has been found that the Southern Ground Hornbill is associated with death and unluckiness. The Ndebele believe an elderly person will die if a Southern Ground Hornbill comes near the home.

From then on, I threw leftover meat as far away from our tent as possible. I am not superstitious by nature but that bird had me thinking. I saw the Hornbill almost every other day, especially when I threw out food. I had to forage harder to feed the three of us. Kai grew weaker and ate less while the Hornbill seemed to eat more of her share. Kai hid her pain but it was easy to see she was getting weaker. Her bones began to stick out and her arms looked so frail, I was afraid to pick her up. She had a hard time breathing, especially at night. I finally said, "Kai, I need to bring you to a doctor." She shook her head and said "no" as loud as she could. At night, she started to talk in her sleep. She called out names that I didn't know; her body shook in conversations I didn't understand. I wrote down the names in case, well in case, I needed to contact someone.

I started to throw food closer to our tent. The Hornbill came regularly. I saw him one day, picking up the remnants of a spam musubi. He looked up and shook his head, his red throat flapping.

"Najuma, are you doing ok? Do you miss the zoo?" I wondered if that was a stupid question and tried again.

"Do you miss your mate?" I thought of Kai.

"Do you remember where you came from?"

He shook his head again and flew away, his large body rising above the kiawe bushes.

It was Saturday so I hiked down to the Farmers' Market. It was late morning and crowded. There were Japanese tourists, locals with armfuls of anthuriums for graves, young families eating scones and musubi. I looked into the trashcans and found half-eaten roasted corn and plate lunch with rice omelet. I wandered to the produce stands; one of the vendors recognized me and gave me a bag of bruised papayas. They were soft; Kai would like these. I sat on a curb and scraped the corn kernels from the cob and chewed gingerly. It was sweet and reminded me of another place, a place where sweet corn was plentiful in the summer. I watched the families around me and saw an older couple, both white-haired, sitting on the curb, sharing a plate of noodles. I got up, looked into the trash cans one more time for meat for the Hornbill and started to hike back to Kai.

She had a difficult night. Early the next morning I placed the meat leftovers at the entrance of the tent. I needed him to come close. I went back into the tent and held Kai. I heard him land, his wings brushing the sides of the tent. I heard him pick up the pieces of spam, linger a bit, and then fly away. Kai lay there with her eyes closed but breathing hard. I hoped for more from the Hornbill.

Kai died the next morning. I brushed her white hair; it was matted and dirty but I tried to make it look neat. I took a wet rag and wiped her forehead and cheeks. A sticky liquid dribbled out of her mouth and when I turned her on her side, a steady stream poured out so I carried her out of the tent. I put her in my sleeping bag and zipped her up. I decided to bury her but the ground was hard and dry and I was too tired to dig much.

The Hornbill came by that afternoon, looking for food. He hopped close to Kai in the sleeping bag and stood waiting, expectant.

I sat on the ground next to Kai and closed my eyes. I saw Kai, younger. I was with her, young as well. We were both clean and neat, sharing a plate of noodles. I opened my eyes and the Hornbill was still there, watching.

"Najuma, I need rain." He stepped closer, his large beak approaching Kai's body.

"No, Kai is gone. I need rain."

He shook his body and unfolded his broad wings. He flew up into the sky, his white wingtips brushing the kiawe branches. He emitted one long screech.

That night, it started to drizzle.

Claire Oasa

WILD PIGS AT NIGHT

They are bolder this year,
venturing forth from
their mountain burrows
into our valley,
hunting for avocados,
liliko'i,
fallen guava

leaving
an uneasy bed
flattened heliconia
splintered roots

I have heard
foraging in the dark:
heavy grunts breaking
the quiet, moist Nuʻuanu night.
I have felt them
below my window,
their hard bristled
bodies bruising their way
through the tangled
vines and ferns
draping the sloping ʻauwai.

They have caused quite a stir
among our neighbors
with their manicured lawns,
well trained dogs,
precisely set alarms.

I wait for them at night,
remove the traps
set among the ferns.
They will return again
when the guava trees are heavy
with fruit,

Claire Oasa

waiting to be
shaken
and plundered.

WALK ALWAYS

They eat quickly
sticky rice ladled from a
worn brown dimpled bowl,
smeared with condiments:
pickled plum, chilies,
fermented beans.

They sip weak tea
from thick mugs lettered with
World's Greatest Grandmother.

Hand in hand
they walk always
Booth Road, Lau Poo
Pauoa Valley
bus stop.

Worshipped by her creations:
ribbon leis
knitted beer can hats
bunka shishu tigers,
fishscale patchwork.

She reigns in her green house
plucking slugs with chopsticks,
dropping them carefully
into empty kim chee jars.
She is the savior of her subjects:
dendrobium, cattleya,
ginger.

CLAIRE OASA

When we return to pay homage,
she waves us off with a laugh
and treats us to
pig's feet saimin.
We ignore the cockroaches
roaming freely among the silverware.

Derek N. Otsuji
A PAIR OF WHITE TERNS

Sunday morning. Two fairy terns are playing tag
in the sky—white winged bodies
in a bright field.
That blue freedom. Clear summer air.
A frolic and tumble down shafts of sunlit space,
bodies free
in themselves yet yielding themselves
to that spirited whirl and chase above the spire
of a stone church,

in the New England style,
but adapted to our weather, and with a wide green lawn
sprinkled with

a few bottle palms, monkey pods,
a royal poinciana in exuberant bloom. I resume
my walk
down Punahou, thoughts wrapped
in the business of the day, the noise and swirl
of early traffic

beginning to stir when I feel above
my shoulder, the one to the traffic now turned,
a hovering. I look—

and there are the white terns!
—come down from the fields of the brilliant day
to query,

with whirring intensity, my being here
this Sunday morning hour on the casual sidewalk.
I look into

the face of the one closer to me.
The small bird face, snowy, innocent of expression.
He is looking at me—

Derek N. Otsuji

and I feel every sense of my body
arrested by the attention of the bird, its pull of cool
otherness drawing up

from secret wellsprings
of being a sharp clarity of answering intention
and seeing
in response to his wordless question.
And some quality of mind that had gone missing
in me, lost

in the swim of thoughts and noises and signs,
returns. I am at once more alive in the animal body
and more human,
imbued with holy curiosity
that is my regard for the bird as he regards me
so that we become,

in the day's strengthening light,
actual to each other, like two pedestrians at the moment
of passing

who exchange a flash
of recognition, that lights each face with momentary joy,
and love's

greeting embrace before each melts
back into the anonymity of the street. A kind of salutation
from the air

to which I have no language
to reply, except to acknowledge (with a bow), my fellows
of the skies,

with rights and privileges like mine, here
in our city by the glittering harbor mirrored by the hard
glittering air.

Kathy J. Phillips
BY LANTERN LIGHT
for Leialoha Apo Perkins, 1930–2018

To brush your dragon on paper,
first you must learn
to wrestle its three-dimensional self
onto a two-dimensional stretch
but still give the illusion
of three.

But then, to drape your dragon
on a lantern, 16 inches by 20,
you must learn
to forget your dimensional tricks
designed for two,
and imagine what this flat dragon
on paper with bamboo backing
will look like in the round,
when really curving 3D again.

To live your life,
first you must learn
to embrace your friend,
totally,
with all her
brilliance and energy and quips:
a wen of impatience under the eye,
a wit you relish, and letters
where even the envelopes
sprout scales of last-minute poems,
translations from the Hawaiian
of street names, and effusive thanks
to the letter carrier.

But then, when your friend
fades,

along with the
gorgeous, emptying thunderclouds
of her boisterous talk
and bountiful poems,
into some other dimension
entirely,
can you still hear her laughter,
feel her thinning cheek
pressed against yours,
and see her dragon flounce
still coming round
from the other side of the lantern?

Anthony Russo

KID ROSS

Kid Ross was a boxer. They say he was pretty good . . . could have been a contender for the light heavyweight crown. Kid Ross loved to drink beer with his friends at McGinnis's Bar on Second Street. He liked the idea of being looked up to as the neighborhood hero. Swaggering into the bar with his duffle bag and a small white Band-Aid over his left eye he would be greeted by his young friends as well as the old, snag toothed gents sitting at the corner table with their wine. Usually if he won a prelim bout on Tuesday night he would set up the house— "Beer for the house, Josie, and wine for the old timers."

He was my big brother, the oldest of us all. I was the youngest. We all lived together with my mom and pop in a large brownstone in South Trenton. I can still remember the long musty hallway leading to a steep flight of dark stairs. On the right, a lighted doorway led to the parlor. Against the wall, a giant sofa sat trimmed with lace dollies. The smells from the kitchen were a strange blend of garlic, olive oil, and coal tar.

Pop usually sat in the kitchen next to the wood-burning stove sipping his wine. His name was Salvatore. The Kid always called him "Big Sal" or "Sally." Pop was big—probably the strongest man I ever knew. He had a large handlebar moustache, carefully waxed, which dominated his square jug-like jaw. His two dark eyes punctuated his face. Pop didn't like boxing. He thought it was stupid for two grown men to try to hurt one another for no good reason. Pop wasn't a sportsman at all . . . thought it was just as funny to see men chasing a little white ball around a field. "What for you do such stupid thing?" he would ask when the Kid came home with his face messed up.

Mom never said anything. She would just cross herself and look up to heaven. "It's not bad, Pop. Don't worry huh?"

"You stupid . . . I canna believe a grown man . . . stupido!"

"Look, Pop, what else can I do? Millions out of work . . . I bring home some money."

"You can work with me."

"Hauling shit around all day? I'd starve first. I make more in one fight than you make in two months."

"Yeah, but I'm no bigga shot—I don't waste my money drinking beer . . . bigga shot!"

"Ahhh," the Kid dismissed the remark with a wave of his hand. "For Christ sakes, Big Sal, this is 1933 America not nineteenth-century Italy. Have you seen the bread lines lately? Thank God I can bring some money home."

ANTHONY RUSSO

"I no like to see you hurt."

The Kid hung his head a little and wiped his nose with the back of his hand. These little bursts of affection always embarrassed him. "Eh, Big Sal, I got something for you."

"Eh?"

"Look . . . just came in from Sloane's Drugstore." The Kid took a hickory pipe from his pocket. "Got some tobacco, too, down at the cigar factory . . . got a girlfriend who works there."

"Oh . . . thatsa nice, Joseph. You're a good boy . . . but sometimes stupido." When Pop called him "Joseph" the Kid's face softened. There was lots of love between them. I mean, Pop loved us all but the Kid was the first-born. Once I sneaked a look at Pop's gold pocket watch. Inside on the lid he kept a picture of Mom with the Kid as a baby in her arms. I remember staring at it for a long time. Are all mothers really that beautiful when they're young?

The Kid was my hero. I followed him around everywhere—did errands for him, accepting his attention gratefully. He always slipped me two bits whenever he had a few bucks in his pocket.

"Mickey, do me a favor, huh. Go down to the back door of McGinnis's Bar and give him this envelope."

The Kid played the numbers every week for a buck. He never hit but one day he hit for two hundred. That night he dressed up in his new suit, straw hat, and spats. He came downstairs and slipped Mom a hundred. "Madonna mia! Where did you get all this money, Joseph?"

"Robbed a bank, Ma," he smiled, his gold tooth sparkling.

"You been fighting again, eh?" Pop spit the words out through a cloud of pipe smoke.

"No, Big Sal, I hit the numbers."

"Yeah, yeah."

"I did!"

Looking down at his soft ankle high boots Pop changed his tone.

"Eh, Joseph. My boss he say he got a place for you maybe part time."

"No, Sal . . . no sewers for me."

"Okay, okay, bigga shot. Go get your head knock off."

The Kid smiled, patted Pop on the back, kissed Mom and was off.

"A big date," he said. The Italian-American sportsman club was having their annual Democratic Party rally. The Kid didn't care about politics but was flattered at being used to gather votes for the political bosses of the ward.

The Kid fought a lot after that. He hardly trained. His face was a mess—too much booze and too much leather. I begged him to take me to the Arena to see

Anthony Russo

him fight. He knew Pop wouldn't go for it. He suggested to Pop once that I could make five or ten bucks emptying corner pails and cleaning up. "No! Never! You a grown man . . . you want kill yourself go ahead. Michael no get bad idea from you!"

"For Christ sake, Pop, he can make a few bucks for school!"

"He no need . . . I will give him the money. Father Cabrini say no worry. I no want talk no more."

The Kid looked worse and worse every Tuesday night after his preliminary bouts. He came home for dinner, his face a mask of ugly cuts with swollen eyes. We were all nervous because of Pop. He didn't talk to the Kid anymore. The Kid would try to speak to him but Pop would just hold up his hand and shake his head. He was in a bad temper. We all walked on eggs when Pop was upset.

He yelled at Mom for nothing.

"You call this pasta . . . itsa like glue." He slammed his fist down on the table and stormed out to the porch to smoke his pipe.

He smoked his old pipe. I never did see him smoke his new hickory. The Kid began to stay away from dinner, especially Tuesday nights. He came in late most of the time—usually after Pop went to bed. Drunk most of the time . . . sometimes he would just sleep in his clothes. He came to depend on me more and more. I fixed hot towels for his face . . . gave Mom his clothes to be washed, starched, and ironed.

"It's not going so good, huh, Joseph?"

"Ah—just been gettin' some bad deals lately, Mick. I'm still as good as ever. Won my last fight didn't I?"

After that fight with Slovinski, the Kid had both eyes almost swollen shut. Slovinski was a bum . . . the Kid should have laid him out in two rounds. Manny, the Kid's trainer was disgusted.

Manny brought the Kid home that night after the fight.

"I'm not gonna let you fight no more, Kid. I don't want to see ya murdered. If ya don't train and stay off da booze, I'm gettin' me another boy."

"You son of a bitch, Manny! You're gettin' your percentage. It's my face not yours. You set up the fights. I'll worry about winning them!"

"You'll never get a chance at the title . . . you looked like shit. Promoters saw what that Polack did to you . . . a bum . . . you should have kicked his ass . . . . He almost whipped you!"

"He didn't, did he? I just had a bad night. Now get the hell out of here . . . leave me alone God damn it! Just leave me alone."

Manny shook his head, shrugged and left. I helped fix the Kid's eyes with ice packs.

I passed McGinnis's Bar one day on my way home from school and saw a brand new poster plastered on the wall.

Ten rounds Kid Ross vs. John Henry Jones. God! John Henry Jones. He was that tall mean black guy we all was hearing about . . . knocked out Terry Sullivan, the ex-champ not long ago. Man! The Kid fightin' John Henry. Wait till the guys at school hear that!

The Kid was in good spirits. He trained a lot more but still didn't give up the drinking at McGinnis's. His face was clean and dinner time was a little better. "Pop—Mom, I'm gonna quit fighting."

Pop looked up startled. "What you say?"

"I said after my fight with Jones . . . if I don't win I'm gonna quit."

"Always one more, eh . . . always one more!"

"Look, Pop this is a big one. I could get a shot at the title . . . then we'd be rich. No more sewers for you, Pop . . . no more hauling shit for sixteen hours a day."

"I do alright . . . I do honest work . . . support my family."

"Okay, okay, but I could help set us up. We could buy a store . . . sell groceries or something. Eh, Pop?"

Pop liked that. His eyes softened and gazed pass Joseph—faraway. "Yeah, would be nice . . . we see, we see. Just no fight no more." The night before the fight the Kid dressed up. He said he was just going out to dinner with some friends . . . said he'd be home early.

"You gotta get some rest, Kid. Tomorrow's a big day."

"Right, Mickey, and I'm gonna beat ole John Henry's ass—don't you worry."

"John Henry is mean, ain't he?"

"Don't say that, Mickey. He's a good man but I'm better." With a smile and a wave he sauntered out the door.

Pop didn't go to work the next day. We all stayed home worrying about the Kid. It wasn't until eleven o'clock that morning that some friends helped the Kid in. He was drunk . . . almost out on his feet. Mom started to cry. Pop and I helped the Kid up the stairs and put him to bed.

"Michael!" Pop was mad. "You gonna sit here in this chair by the bed. If Joseph moves you tell me . . . if he moves! You understand?"

"Yes, Pop."

"He's no gonna fight tonight . . . I kill him first. And you . . . you listen to me, Michael. You watch him, understand?"

"Yes, Pop." I was scared. Pop seldom got mad but when he did . . . . He licked me once when he caught me smokin' behind the wash shed. I'll never forget that.

The Kid lay curled on his side . . . like a little kid suddenly in a king-sized bed surrounded by brass rails. The sun moved off the tan window shade and the room became less bright. The Kid rolled his head and opened his eyes.

Anthony Russo

"Wha...? Wha, time's it? He Mick... wha...?"

"Hi Kid. How do ya feel?"

"Oh God... shitty. What time's it?"

"It's almost 4:30."

"Jesus Christ! I gotta fight John Henry at eight. Holy Sweet Jesus! Get me some coffee, Mick... Oh God."

I went down to get him some coffee. I told Pop the Kid was awake. Pop slowly climbed the stairs. When I got there with the coffee Pop's face was distorted with anger.

"You listen to me you drunken bum... you no goin' anyplace. Ifa you come out that door I break you in half, capisce? Eh, understand, big man?"

The Kid groaned and lay back on the bed.

"Michael, you stay here. Ifa he move, you call me."

"Yes, Pop." I sat in the large rocker, my eyes riveted on the bed. The Kid's face was smooth and soft in the dim light. He snored loudly and every now and then would rub his stubble of a beard with his sausage fingers.

At six o'clock, the Kid opened his eyes. "Mickey, what time is it?"

"Six. You alright, Joseph?"

"Yeah, boy, I'm fine... just a little tired." He looked up at me from the edge of the bed, grabbed my head, and kissed me on both cheeks. He hugged me and if I didn't know better I could have sworn I felt a warm tear on my neck. "How would you like to go to the fights?"

"Wow! Oh gee... do ya think I can? Oh no, no... Pop will kill me. No... I can't." I started to cry. I was torn between the Arena and the heaviness of Pop's hand.

No—I was scared.

"Look, Mickey I got a plan."

I sobbed and shook my head at the Kid. He ignored it.

"We can go out this window. The drainpipe down to the fence... I did it when I was your age. It's easy."

"No... please," I was almost hysterical now.

"Mickey, we could be over the fence and to the Arena and Pop won't know."

"He'll find out... he'll find out. He'll come up later and find us gone. I can't ... I can't."

"Stop crying, Mick—listen. By the time Pop finds out I'll have whipped John Henry. I'll have a shot at the champ... money for our own store. Pop'll like that won't he?"

"Yes, but...."

"But nothin'. You want to see Pop hauling shit around all his life, huh? Do you?"

"No."

"Okay then you gotta help me. Get my duffle bag out of the closet. Don't make a sound. I'll let you sit at ringside with Manny."

That did it . . . courage. The fights. We made it down and over the fence without a sound.

The South Trenton Sports Arena was fantastic. There must have been a million people there that night. My heart pounded. The noise of the crowd swept me away with excitement. Through the smoke, I could see people pouring into the balcony. Manny was rubbing down the Kid who just came in to loud cheers. John Henry hadn't come in yet. When he did, the crowd went wild. My mouth dropped open. I stared at the huge black hulk as he walked down the aisle to the ring.

Big . . . black . . . my god he was black as night. He was lean and hard. He walked right past me. He looked at Manny and smiled. "You boys ready?" His face was full of white teeth. My heart pounded. I looked at the Kid. This was the first time I had seen him in the ring. His thick neck and massive shoulders were covered with hair. The referee brought them together in the center of the ring. God . . . John Henry was big. My heart was pounding through my rib cage.

The first three rounds John Henry and the Kid traded good ones. The Kid crouched low, all tucked in like a huge turtle. John Henry stood up right and lashed out with long arms at the bobbing hulk.

"Stay low, Kid! Stay away from him . . . . Counter to the guts, Kid . . . in the breadbasket with the right." Manny's neck was bulging and red. He chewed on an unlit cigar.

At the end of the third round, the Kid was breathing hard. He sat heavy on his stool and greedily took his mouthful of water.

"Stay away from him, Kid. He's got the reach. Gotta get him in the stomach . . . don't try to slug it out. Hit him in the guts, tie him up, and move away."

The Kid nodded.

The bell rang for the 4th round. A right hand reached out so quickly none of us saw it. The Kid's head was distorted and his mouthpiece flew out of his mouth and landed at my feet. The Kid was on his stomach—blood pouring from his nose. His lower lip was ripped open, almost hanging from his jaw.

"Stay down for eight, Kid!" Manny's cries were lost in the roar of the crowd.

I was ten feet from him. I'll never forget that . . . I'll never forget the pain and ugliness of that moment. I wasn't excited anymore—I was sick. I wanted to run for Pop.

The Kid got up and round after round got hit with everything John Henry had. The Kid's eyes were swollen. He moved around the ring, flat-footed, dazed almost like a zombie, lashing out with a heavy left hand, and grabbing John Henry in a clinch. The crowd didn't like that.

"Come on . . . fight!" They screamed for more blood.

"Kill him! Kill the Kid . . . . Murder the bum!" The smoke hung heavy over the arena. Each dull thud of John Henry's gloves on the Kid's body was cheered by the crowd.

A little old lady behind me was screaming, making no sense at all with half a hot dog in her mouth and mustard on her chin. I started to cry . . . I wanted to throw up. Why did I come? Oh god, Pop . . . why did I come?

It was the middle of the eighth round—we heard Pop shouting, running down the aisle. "Thatsa my boy . . . stop the fight . . . stop!"

Manny tried to stop him as he climbed the ring ropes. One swipe of the hand sent Manny into the seats of the first row.

Pop was like a maniac. He pushed two other trainers away. He ran into the ring, picked up the referee, and threw him into the corner. John Henry was already out of the ring. He was surrounded by his trainers and some police.

Pop grabbed the Kid, spun him around, and dragged him through the ropes. Manny threw in the towel . . . he signaled the police to stay away. It was over anyway. Pop, Manny, and me—we dragged the Kid to the dressing room.

Pop was crying . . . he looked at the Kid's face and cried out in anger, "Beasts!"

We got the Kid dressed and took a cab home. Pop didn't say anything . . . nobody said anything.

"Get him fixed up . . . now!" Mom gasped and went shrieking to the medicine chest in response to Pop's order. I was scared . . . I don't think I've ever been so scared.

"I'm okay, Pop. I'm okay," the Kid could hardly speak through his swollen lips.

"Shut up!"

"I'm sorry, Pop . . . I'm sorry."

"Shut up, Joseph."

"I need a cup of coffee."

"John Henry, he beat you up good, eh?"

"Oh . . . Pop, don't . . . ."

"Shut up!"

It took Mom a half hour to patch the Kid up.

"You got him fix up good, Momma?"

"Yes."

Pop looked at the Kid who was hunched over a chair hands between his legs looking up dazed and confused. Before anyone could have seen it, Pop punched the Kid square in the face knocking him over the chair and onto the floor.

I ran upstairs to my room. It was an hour before I heard those footsteps on the stairs . . . slow and deliberate.

Mia Sara
VOCABULARY

I'm beginning
to lose them,
the words
for everything
I've been.
Some of them
I want to forget.
It's time to stop
spinning myself into
projectile daydreams,
slippers and gowns,
sun-soaked
heritage leather
hustles, too many
throw pillows.
My biology
isn't fooling anyone:
aging white female,
looking for
a soft landing,
afraid to admit
I might be irrelevant.
I tell myself
to tell it like it is.
I tell myself
to be generous
with my loss.
I tell myself,
what's left of me, raw
inarticulate organ,
is enough.

Stuart Jay Silverman
THE CHANNEL AT MĀʻALAEA
Painting by Pam Andelin

Pale teal trailing across the sky at Kahoʻolawe,
a wispy buffer for the hard blue that hangs
just under the upper slat of this koa wood frame.

The island hangs in the middle distance,
a mound of shell-shocked ash,
island of dead goats, kiawe prickly with heat.

Foregrounded, a tangle of boats
gathers the eye working a crisscross of spars
that sway over teak decks from side to side.

On either side, the water speaks its piece,
garrulous if silent on the canvas screen
which holds in its wavery ancient cry.

A towheaded boy leans back in the cockpit
of one boat pressing a bulkhead. In the buff,
he reads in the comfort of his shaded skin.

The water gapes alongside, sloshes around
the uprights of a dinghy hoist which specifies
the center and holds the eye to middle ground.

Paler than Prussian blue, yet darker than the sky,
the Pacific slops against the weathered wood
as though it were lipping a Fabergé cup.

The boy will not move, though the unseen sun
hunkers down all afternoon outside the frame
before making its way to the dawning night.

It has left a ghost skirmishing in the oils
by which this simulacrum prods a world to be
acquiring the finish inadmissible in life.

Stuart Jay Silverman

CROSSING THE CALDERA
Halemaʻumaʻu

petal-of-ash walls
rock scree cutting shoe leather
tufa leaking smoke

a sulfur plume peters out
halfway to the lowest cloud

stone heats the trapped sole
the trail back up still far off
cut from mountain rock

lava seethes the fragile crust,
a heart swollen with fluid

the trail back crackles
weeds poke from the rocky wall
spiraling its way

up toward the edge edged by sky
cinders speck the parking lot

nightfall enlarges
roots snagging unwary feet
trying to hurry

next day the floor collapses
a lake of magma bubbles

blisters the base rock
a runnel of green turns ash
kiawe shrivels

eaten by the heat, faces
high up flush in a light rain

STUART JAY SILVERMAN

shirt backs dampening
tourists lean looking into
the hazy canyon

a backpack, unnoticed, tips
and is gone in a moment

bouncing against
the caldera walls until
a few puffs of smoke

rise where something soundlessly
touched invisible bottom

John E. Simonds
THE LOOKING GLASS

To have the scope but lack the vision
could be the curse of our heavenly reading.
A mountaintop's sacred to some,
cold and remote to many,
a volcano barnacled
by stations of science,
our ultimate high-rise
island of growth—
higher and colder than Howard Hughes
and the sprouting toenails
of his Kakaʻako skyline—
to deep, dark air,
the perfect place
for eyeing space,
because it's there.

The upside down flags
may affront the eyes
but symbolize
the kapakahi way
we prioritize.
We don't need a clear-day-forever view
to see our own planet
as one sand grain
on the universal beach.
But it's the one we live on,
and our level of care
has been lost in the glare
blinding our floating rock
and the lives hanging on
in our flying gridlock
of survival mode,
of outer air (to breathe)
and inner space (to live),

JOHN E. SIMONDS

of marking time and losing direction
in the search for intelligent life.

Why not turn the lens around,
focus the power of its mirrors here?
People in tents on sidewalks,
shopping cart chauffeurs in parks,
others caught in street motorcades,
of life-or-death crosswalks,
racing buses to juggle their jobs,
late sitters and hours to pick up
kids from schools short of air
in spaces too close to the sun.

NASA's aims for moon and Mars,
our astro-gazers seeking fortunes in space,
or fellow descendants of ocean voyage—
we're all about celestial navigation—
linked in our own discoveries,
not faulting the stars,
but ourselves,
if we've lost our way
and cannot answer
who we are
or where we're going.

Cathy Song
THE SHORT SWEET FLIGHT

Flame of the root that spawned me
in the red-dirt town of my beginning,
after the heat of the plains
shimmered up the slopes and shriveled the ponds
into slipper-swallowing mud cakes,
I broke through with the coming of the rains.
The deluge splattered sloppy raindrops
on our tin roof, festooned our yard with toads.
At night my mother could hear the blighted bodies
sucking sustenance out of the spongy ground.
I burst through the bath-warm waters of her belly
to receive the butterfly kisses she planted,
pollinating skin as honey-colored as the passion flowers
strung like lanterns among the towering eucalyptus.

Sun-speared ocean that surrounded me
in the swimming hole of my baptism,
I floated, buoyed by the cautionary
voice of my father—wave-torn, weary—
slowly receding as limbs lengthened,
gathering distance, pulled away from shore.
Wilting for the boy who prowled proud and nocturnal,
I waited, defiantly homeless.
Into the sallow yolk of morning,
I crawled out of the beach naupaka
unable to hide the mumbling shame,
the fumblings thrown in a fit of sand
like a bonfire carelessly doused.
Before I could be forgiven, I had to listen.
The harangue about ingratitude
sunk its rust-driven nail.

Ferns that sprang from the heart of the trunk
closed behind us, fronds you parted with tender certainty.
Accepting as our own the flaws we saw in each other,

you wooed me to live peacefully in the rain light
among old trees, fur-draped,
like a council of elders under pelts of moss.
We came to claim the right to be happy.
We sought the kindness of their blessings,
the wind carrying the names of our children
who waited to come out of hiding.
Gathering wood, hauling water,
we called for the smallest one
before returning to feed the fire,
the constant tending of so much green.

Blue dome before dawn that widened
into an aperture of silence pressed cold with stars,
the poems, in the half-light of waking,
glimmered at the mind's edge
and retreated, sleep-slurred, unsung.
The morning grew louder.
The nudge to rise and repeat the day's migrations
from bed to stove to market piled the hours
into laundry, wet clothes waiting to be hung.
Feathering the leaves the birds made
music of their short sweet flight.

Clouds of incense that link the passing
of one light to another
involve a reconfiguration of the elements,
petals heaped like snow, the ashes,
a thread of solace for us who remain stranded
like travelers at a station
in queue for our own departure—
for the light that flamed and flowered,
resisted and settled,
a wish for the last thought moment
to be as seamless as the wind's dispersal,
carrying the sound of the stream to the sea.

CATHY SONG

THE TREE OF LIFE

Blessings upon the boy who despite himself
climbed the tree of life.
Discouraged by what he perceived as the ease of others—
those who scrambled quicker, higher—
he fell.
The worm of doubt entered the heartwood,
splintered his vision into a prism of glass shards.
Thoughts twisted into twigs,
kindling for the story he kept trying to light,
spelling with the alphabet of fear
all the ways he was not good enough.
The story grew, unmanageable, lit by a single
feeble bloom of sulfur.
He fell into fissures hidden by air-spun moss.
He fell into groundlessness.

Those who loved him shouted,
calling him back.
He could see them peering over the rim,
arms waving frantically.
He could see their mouths moving,
exhorting him to help himself.
He watched as the rope they flung
hung cursive like lace, and collapse.
They receded, dim figures trapped
in a paperweight of falling snow.
He sought sleep as a refuge
but sleep, pierced by whispering tongues,
refused to come.

The mother sat outside the door and wept,
and when she was done
she began to repair that which had been left
untended, that which had become undone,
beginning with the smallest tasks,
a missing button, a frayed pocket.

She pulled the invisible thread of grief
into finished seams as if by such stitching
she could in her vigil return the boy to his skin.
The father sat and waited with the patience of stones,
and when he was done
he began to dig waist-deep into night.
Shoveling veils of dirt, he shifted earth,
carried water, bringing into shimmering
form what had been rubble.
By morning a pond appeared—
cloud-flecked, wind-rippled—
its surface returning to stillness,
undisturbed.

Rain pearled on a leaf
like a tear on the boy's eyelid.
Silence seeped in with the persistence of water
dripping through rock,
dislodging the boy from the cramped
letters of his name.
Bowing under the weight,
the leaf tipped, spilling pools,
and gently lifted empty.

Eric Stinton

THE WEIGHT OF DEPARTURE

I decided to swim in the storm.

After living in landlocked Seoul for four years, I refused to allow a measly tropical storm—the meteorological category right under "hurricane"—to ruin my weeklong vacation back home in Hawaiʻi. Storm categories are determined by average sustained wind speed, and while tropical storms aren't strong enough to peel roofs off houses, they are strong enough to be given names. This one was algorithmically assigned "Olivia." Officially, storms are named to clarify communication between scientists and everyone else, but the act of naming clarifies other things, too. Wind isn't perceptible, despite being phenomenologically obvious. Names become boundaries by which we see shape. Naming helps to make sense of powers unseen yet undeniably felt, forces that, until their inexorable exit, are in a state of perpetual arrival.

My mom makes a daily decision to either be exhausted or in pain. Most days she chooses exhaustion.

"Your mother has the gift of discernment." My dad tells me this on the ride home from the airport. After nine years working at the Bible college, she was pushed into retirement six months early against her will. She saw it coming but couldn't stop it. In Christianity, discernment is considered a "spiritual gift" that allows someone to determine whether a spiritual force originates from God, evil, or from within the human soul.

Rheumatoid arthritis is a forked- and silver-tongued devil that tricks the immune system—whose sole purpose is to discern pathogens from its own healthy tissues—into attacking joints as it would a virus. Cartilage slowly erodes. Bones scrape against each other like tectonic plates. Joints loosen and deform. Damage can't be reversed. There is no cure. It just comes and comes and comes, forever. "Forever" being the length of a human life; any other kind of forever is abstract theory, pure speculation.

My mother, whose daily reality has always been dedicated to matters of the spirit, now spends her waking life fighting phantoms.

I jogged briskly into the water and dove in. Thousands of miles away from their open-ocean genesis, storm swells reached their ultimate revelation and rolled into mounding waves. Sand from the ocean floor stirred into colloidal suspension, the strength of the swells churning up the tiny particles before they got a chance to fall back to the floor. The water was warm.

The sky scrolled above me. Clouds hurried in the wind, a reminder that they are real objects and not just texture. The setting sun splashed gold and pink streaks across dark gray rain clouds. Bloated puffs in the distance dragged sheets of rain behind them like the tentacles of a Portuguese man-o-war.

Life swirled around me. I bobbed and splashed in the chaos.

Flotsam bumped into me and moved along with aimless insouciance. The waves crashing on shore retreated back to the ocean's expanse while sets continued to roll in. I was caught between.

"Grandma didn't always have wrinkles." My mom says this to my five-year-old niece, who is fascinated by the elastic pleasures of aging skin.

"Grandma used to be beautiful."

"I like the wrinkles," my niece says.

When I was a little older than my niece is now, my mom loved reading the Left Behind novels, about life on Earth after all the True Believers have been taken to heaven. She would wistfully think aloud about how it would feel to meet Jesus in the air and transcend the physical realm. Almost conspiratorially, she would voice her belief—half-hunch, half-longing—that Jesus would return in her lifetime. I didn't understand then that her hope to experience the rapture was also a hope not to experience something else.

She still resides Elsewhere, albeit in a more secular and concrete version; she talks of moving to British Columbia or California, of travelling to Europe. The adventurousness of her youth took a 30-year detour when she became a mother of four boys. Now she's trying to make up for lost time.

"I want to see all the places I've always wanted to, before . . ." She trails off and heads to her room to lie down.

The waves were mid-sized, but too crumbly and disorganized to body surf for more than a few seconds. I caught one and was driven head-and-shoulder-first into the shore. I emerged scraped and lightheaded and deliriously happy. Baptism through abrasion.

I let the current suck me feet-first into the waves. When they started to crash, I tucked my knees into my chest and flipped underwater. Sand and saltwater rushed through my nostrils.

But mostly I just was, there in the water. The only difference between me and everything else getting pushed along by the storm was that I had the ability to choose: to ride the wave, to make its unstoppable force my own.

The sun began to vanish, but the noise of the storm persisted.

Eric Stinton

"I have one request for you before you leave," my mom says to me. She holds out a small cardboard box as I pack my suitcase to go back for my fifth year in Korea. I never intended to stay away so long, but that's how life seems to happen; moving on means leaving behind, and we're perpetually between those phenomena.

Inside the box is a small vial for me to fill up with saliva and send to a lab to find out the precise percentages of my ancestry. My mom has obsessed over this sort of thing for the last few years—our genetic heritage, our ancestors' role in the American Revolution, when and how they migrated across Europe and the U.S. I'm not exactly sure why. Maybe it's simple curiosity, maybe it's a longing to be a part of something bigger, to feel the existential balm of being in the middle of a larger narrative that continues on after our own individual stories have finished.

I gladly spit in the tube and sealed it for shipment, though I don't particularly care about the results. Words like "Scottish," "Welsh," "Irish," and "Jewish" don't mean much to me, since none of those are mine in any identifiable way outside of my saliva. They represent where I've been about as much as my name represents who I am. After all, the purpose of naming something—"Olivia" for a storm, "agnostic" or "Christian" for a person, "methotrexate" for a daily routine—is to delimit the vast, objectify the ineffable, confront the terrifying. You don't always have to see something directly to know it's there, to feel its obvious presence.

My mom and I chat about our ancestry and my plans to move back home. The next time I see her I'll be back for good, though she made it clear in her distinctly passive way that she would prefer me to settle somewhere other than Hawaiʻi. Two of my three brothers live on the mainland, so if I were to join them, there would be ample reason for my parents to sell the house and move somewhere she'd rather be. Instead, I'm tipping the scales in the opposite direction. All of this seems important in the moment, snug in the assumption that there will be a next time I see her.

She's tired again. She exhales heavily and retreats back to her room, leaving me in the dumb silence of words unspoken, both of us tethered to the same stifling weight of departure.

Outside the water, the warmth of the day had begun its Sisyphean retreat. Sheets of cold rain fell upon me under the darkening sky. Soon I would have to trudge through the whitewash back to the shore, resisting the ocean and its coquetries, those whispers piercing through the static roar coaxing me to come back, just for a little longer. Waiting for me on the shore was the dim illumination of the path back to the car, back to my mom, back to everything I left behind and everything I came back for. The weightlessness of the ocean would be replaced by the familiar tug of the world.

But not yet. I was still free in the water. The ocean's patient gravity allowed me to move in any direction, or to be motionless, momentarily disconnected from everything—my life back in Korea, my plans to move home, that nagging nameless feeling that had loomed like a dark storm cloud ever since I got back and noticed how much and how quickly my mom was slowing down. I was unanchored.

The wind skipped across the surface and chilled whatever skin was exposed. I huddled into the warmth of the water, clinging to its amniotic comfort. The water eddied around me. The sky crawled forward in perpetual arrival. The expanses above and around and within stretched out infinitely in all directions. I floated in absolute freedom, in the shallow and narrow border between everything that man made and everything that made man, buoyant with potential. If only for the moment.

Shelley Stocksdale
Six Ways of Catching Fish in China

Let me tell you about the six ways
of catching fish in China.
The most time-tested play
is to cast away
stick, line, sinker, and float.

Throwing big, wide, rope net
into waiting water
and fleeing fish
is common in the countryside.

A bamboo basket,
one small opening opposite
large opening—
moved through seaweed murk
by the fisherman,
allows him to trap
helpless, swimming creatures.

Train scope to outer spaceman
angler, stalking the lagoon bank—
bearing wooden box
holding batteries on his back;
the electric prod he waves
in water zaps alien
flat, finned aquamarine animals.

Fisher transforms hunter
who raises gun
above pond's shore,
shoots gunpowder into lakes—
rolling funeral wakes
for fish forsaken.

On a hot day if water is warm enough,
fish can be grabbed up by hand.

Coralyn Sunico
KUMON

My hands hide, flickering, under the desk,
Trying to add 12 and 9,
Waving like her flashcards,
She interrupts,

"Why do you count with your fingers?"

Her cracked pink polish reflected
The pink of her pencil case, like the pink
Tint in her lips, tilted, as
The pink matched the smirk of her face.

Her hair curls like the bows of Christmas presents,
Always showered with rewards
After passing a level.

Distracted by her new sparkly sandals
That shone like the countless golden stars
Next to her name.

I hated it there. Every Tuesday at Fern,
I thought it wasn't fair.

My mom asked,
"Why can't you write nice like her?
Why aren't you smart like her?
Why can't you be more like, her?"
I asked myself, too;

My eyes are too brown, mom;
They don't sparkle sky blue,

My hair is too black.
Like the stains on my hand-me-down shirt,
My skin too tan,

Coralyn Sunico

Mudded by the shame of my genes.
I thought I wasn't fair.

I hated Kumon,
I was still on addition while
She did division,
I sat next to her but I was always behind.

Samantha Tetangco
RICE STREET HAIBUN

    On the drive to the university, my grandmother keeps pointing to the geese, the open land, the dormitories, the trees, asking, who owns that house? Who owns that bird? She's nearing one hundred and her mind is reduced to a repetition of questions about mango trees and chickens, about ownership. But even she understands the injustice of it all while my mother packs her bag. When I help her with her shoes. When we tell her she must go. When she wants to know why we can't just leave her in her house alone. Why she can never return home.

    Somewhere in Bawang
    her mango tree bears new fruit
    we will never taste.

Samantha Tetangco

PORTRAIT OF A FILIPINA ON HER 37TH BIRTHDAY

The morning is full of teapots   the promise
of board games
          and willow trees bursting with
 gray hairs.   Farouk says,
We are all on the far edge of the age group now.
I want nothing more
than to be in the large warm mug
 of my own body.
To spend the day in a pair of Adirondack chairs
near a yard aching with roses.

In the afternoon,   we replant the ficus
that's been brewing
in the same small pot for the better part of a decade
and I think,   isn't it better this way?
to be here with this birthday cake
of spreading roots,
our hands cupping dirt
and you—there, still—

watching me with those color-changing eyes.

Delaina Thomas
DAY BEFORE OBON
Rinzai Zen Mission, 2010

I.

Mrs. Tamanaha is 90
the age my grandmother didn't want to reach
leaving her body two weeks before that birthday

when I explain that she reminds me *of my Baban*
she lets me take her photo
her chin and nose are more pointy
but the gentleness in her eyes
twinges through me reminiscent

her dark blue cotton blouse with a rolled collar
has scatters of tiny yellow flowers
her white hair in a bubble style curls
softly frizzy from decades of perms

hands lain over each other in her lap
she looks into the lens
after I click she asks in a chirpy voice *who you?*
the question I've asked myself most of my life
should not startle me
given the spontaneity of our culture

an inner voice responds *I am That*
Thou art That all This is That

I wouldn't try that on her
or say I'm a granddaughter
who stopped climbing the steep temple steps
once her Baban was gone

Delaina Thomas

and that now on this different island
I am reminded of those Obon nights
when the monstrous gong resounded
at McCully Shingon Mission
sending a shudder through me
as Baban bowed and lit sticks of senko
in remembrance of family members I'd never met
the woodsy smoke coiling into the night

we'd sit side by side on zabuton
in a sea of old people
the life-size golden Buddha
surrounded by chrysanthemums
mochi and tangerines
the priest's voice droning in somber waves of verses
Baban nodding slightly in my direction
when I fidgeted

II.

I answer Mrs. Tamanaha
I live Maui 20 years
Honolulu I from
my Mother Uchinanchu
it's hard to tell if that appeases her
her placid expression doesn't change

in this elderly congregation
of less than a hundred members
most of whose children and grandchildren
live in Honolulu or on the Mainland
why would she not wonder why
a new face should pop up

though for several years I have brought
my husband and daughter to watch
the bulgy-eyed shiisaa
leap and tumble to the grass
his yellow and pink raffia fur whirling and glistening

his massive jaws widening as he lunges
at the heels of a boy who lures him with a gong
in the ceremonial scaring away of evil spirits

while in the semi-darkness
finding myself among so many people
descended from the homeland
I search faces that must resemble some of my ancestors'
these strangers wrapped in indigo yukata and purple obi
their dance a slow procession
to centuries-old rhythms of the sanshin
and the beat of Eisa drums

III.

sitting in the lawnchair next to Mrs. Tamanaha
Mrs. Tengan also 90
tilts her head at me
she holds a can of Coke in one hand
and a Chinese pretzel in the other
she peers out from under puffy eyelids
Honolulu? she rubs in
yuh I reply *I stay Ha'ikū side now*
knowing at some point enough information
might ease the disdain
neighbor-island old-timers often feel
for those from O'ahu

I can take your picture too? I ask
her lips soften into a smirk
she adjusts the shoulders of the black knitted vest
she wears over a striped blouse
in the August humidity
two hundred yards from Pā'ia shoreline
where we have gathered to make pink nantu
and Chinese pretzels
to sell at the only Bon dance in the State
featuring exclusively Ryukyuan music
I pause for a moment

hoping her darkly penciled eyebrows
that have remained raised
creasing her forehead since I got here
might lower
they do not
I refrain from the urge to brush back the lock
of coarse straight pixie-cut hair
seawind has blown shaggily over her earlobe

she offers the lens a piercing look
I smile and pat her on the shoulder
for who indeed am I
to rehearse for only a month
and dance tomorrow night in a borrowed yukata
while my daughter and her Maori father
jump and twirl as they beat Eisa drums
all of us joining in the shout *ha-iya-*
iya-sasa

IV.

the trays of nantu have been laid out to set overnight
the pretzels are packaged and labeled
the woks of oil cooled and emptied

I tell the ladies *I go home now*
I see you tomorrow
Mrs. Tamanaha gazing
at the pink paper lanterns bobbing from white ropes
turns her focus vaguely towards me
and raises a hand to wave

Mrs. Tengan shakes her head
and says in a gravelly voice
we used to dance before every time
but now we onee watch
onee slow can walk
too much dainja

Ken Tokuno

PIANISSIMO FINALE

Marissa saw the woman still seated after even the orchestra had left the stage. She must have fallen asleep and needed to be roused. "Ma'am, you need to wake up and leave so we can clean up," said Marissa, touching her on the shoulder. The woman appeared to be very haggard but she seemed so much at peace. The expression on her face was one Marissa had only seen before on a painting of the Madonna. The woman remained motionless. Marissa had a terrible thought. Could it be? She would need to get Ms. Hasegawa to come over and look.

Ms. Hasegawa was heading in the direction of the main seating anyway when she saw Marissa hurrying toward her. "Ms. Hasegawa, I think we might have a dead woman in row 8."

"Is she one of our regulars?" said Ms. Hasegawa.

"I don't recognize her, but she might be. She's pretty well dressed for a matinee crowd." Following her usher's footsteps, Ms. Hasegawa went up to the seat in the middle of the concert hall and felt for a pulse.

"Elise, time for your piano lesson." This is what Elise heard every Wednesday after school, although her mother knew that her daughter would never miss a lesson because she enjoyed it too much. She would rather practice her piano than go to school, play with her friends, or even have a chocolate sundae, which was her favorite dessert. Ms. Chung, her piano teacher, was very nice and had been teaching her from the very beginning when Elise was only six. Elise already showed signs of becoming a virtuoso from that age. Ms. Chung soon encouraged her to play some very difficult pieces, such as Chopin études and Liszt sonatas. Elise, as Ms. Chung liked to tell everyone, played with joy and gusto. At the same time, she commented on Elise's weight, suggesting that five fat fingers made for poorer piano playing. Elise did like to eat, but was just pleasantly plump. She ate too many chocolate sundaes.

"Elise," said her father, Frank. "Do you know where we got your name?"

"Yes, Daddy," said Elise for the thousandth time, "from Beethoven's bagatelle, 'Für Elise.'"

"And who is your favorite composer?"

"Chopin," said Elise, which was her reply just to tease her father because she knew how much he liked Beethoven, especially his symphonies. The family went to the Honolulu Symphony concerts as often as they could afford to go, but never

Ken Tokuno

missed any performance of a Beethoven composition. Elise had come to like Ludwig van Beethoven as much as her father did. She imagined herself on the stage, gown flowing, hair flowing, fingers flowing to see how it would be one day to be the virtuoso pianist for a Beethoven concerto. She could definitely picture herself playing his "First Piano Concerto in C major." What made it even more fun was that they would go to Zippy's after the concert and she would feast on hamburgers and her usual chocolate sundae. Often, she and her father would hum several bars of a piece they'd just heard and laugh at the bemused faces of other customers.

Frank loved to sing and he had a decent voice. He said that his voice was his instrument. Since it was part of his original equipment, he frequently joked that it cost him nothing, unlike Elise's piano, which was a Steinway upright. Once in a while, he would ask Elise to play a popular tune and he would sing along. Elise loved those moments best. She would try to sing, but would get embarrassed and her voice would strangle and only squeaks would come out, so she gave up singing by the time she was nine despite encouragement from her father: "We could sing duets, Elise."

Elise was digging through the trashcans in Admiral Thomas Square where she spent nights in her tent. It was August 2018 and she had forgotten how long she had been homeless, how long she had been hungry. She had forgotten when she had lost her parents or where they were buried. She had forgotten if she had any friends beyond the familiar faces she saw poking out of the tents in the Square or along Victoria Street. She had forgotten how long she had had this bad pain in her chest, not that she could ever afford to see a doctor about it. She did not think that she had forgotten how to play the piano, or how much she loved its sound, or how long it had been since she had heard truly good music.

Digging through the trash, she had found a flier for the symphony. The Honolulu Symphony! One of the many reasons she had placed herself in the squalor of Admiral Thomas Square was that it was right across from Blaisdell Concert Hall. Some nights she would sneak near the entrance to try to hear a few strains of a sonata or a prelude, but security always chased her away. But wait, this flier said something about a concert that only cost $5.00. How could that be? It was even on her birthday, September 19. Was this a sign that it was destiny for her? It was some kind of preview for the Symphony's season. What would they be playing? How could she scrape together the money? As it was, the few dollars she was able to beg paid for what little food she could get that wasn't out of a trash bin.

In the eighth grade, Elise had won the Honolulu Junior Piano competition given to the best young pianist in the city. In her first years of high school, she was

KEN TOKUNO

getting ovations at piano recitals and being asked to play at parties. Just like after a concert, her parents would treat her to hamburgers and a chocolate sundae after a good recital. And she had a lot of good recitals, but was getting to be shaped like a cello. Still, her fingers could move as well as ever. The music teacher at McKinley was all but certain that she would earn a scholarship at a mainland university or conservatory and become an internationally renowned concert pianist.

Around the end of her sophomore year, things changed. She lost focus on her piano and even stopped eating very much. Concerned when she had lost a lot of weight, her father took her to a psychologist who specialized in adolescent mental health, Dr. Bernadette Kramer. No, she did not have an eating disorder. It was most likely, said Dr. Kramer, that Elise was suffering from what was a mild bipolar condition. She recommended cognitive behavior therapy, which was her expertise so she would treat Elise and ask her psychiatrist associate, Dr. Navarro, to prescribe a light antidepressant medication, Tofranil. Insurance would cover the costs.

It was not unusual for Elise to be at the edge of some summer festival they would hold at Thomas Square and she would see little girls walk by enjoying a chocolate sundae. This always threw her into one of her depthless depressions as it made her think of her father and how he would make her feel so special. What was it that he had told her about her name? If somehow she could get to that symphony presentation, perhaps she would feel as good as she did in those days.

So far, this summer had been no different with all the festivals, especially after they renovated Thomas Square. Elise hoped that this summer would be different. This summer would end with her attending a concert. How much had she saved so far? She rummaged around in her Longs shopping cart to see if she could find a single dollar or a quarter or two. She found only three nickels and two pennies. Well, she was not beyond doing what some of her friends did: dig in trash cans, garbage bags, and even recycle bins to find aluminum cans she could turn in for their deposits. A problem was that most of those were the territory of J. M. or Icarus, two of the more ferocious guys who hung around the Square. She didn't dare get them mad at her. She could resort to begging for money, something she had done before but only when she was starving. "Who am I kiddin'?" she thought to herself. Even if she could find the money, how could she go in the Hall wearing these rags, smelling like she did? The sheer impossibility of her dream brought on that ineffable sadness that no one can describe, only experience.

She had all but given up on attending the concert when she saw her one friend Hazel. "Hi Elise," said Hazel as cheerfully as ever. Like most women on the street, Hazel frequently hooked up with a homeless man. They did it for both comfort and protection. Hazel called out, "What you lookin' at there?"

"It's a flier from our neighbors over yonder," said Elise. "You know how I love music? I'd love to go to this real cheap concert, but I have nothing to wear, even if I had the money to get a ticket."

"Aww, don't give up, honey. I can loan you my special dress, the one I was able to swipe from the Goodwill store down the block. Y'know the red one?"

Even though most of the others would resort to that if they were desperate enough, Elise found Hazel's capacity for theft distasteful. Hazel sometimes convinced her to shoplift groceries. She would tell Elise that the worst thing that could happen was she could get caught and thus be able to get a meal and shower in jail. Now Hazel was offering something that was more risky than stealing a ham sandwich.

"You'd do that for me?" said Elise.

"Sure," said Hazel. "We can even lift a nice handbag for ya."

In the middle of her junior year, Elise's father was killed in a car accident on his way back from his work at Pearl Harbor. His life insurance had allowed them to cover a large share of their mortgage, so Elise and her mother were able to stay in the house, but they needed to skimp on some things. The survivor benefits covered the basics: food, utilities, toiletries. They also covered Elise's college tuition, but little else. Elise's mother, Doris, had always worked but at a low-level clerical position, so it was just enough for them to get by.

Elise missed her father more than she could have missed anyone else in her life. Frank had been the main reason she loved the piano so much. She did not need the sundaes to play well. Just seeing her father's smile was reward enough for her. She knew that he had always wanted to play an instrument but never got the chance to learn, so it was kind of like she was playing for both of them. Now, between her grief and her depression, she barely touched her piano. Doris urged her to play by telling her how much Frank would have wanted to hear her. She loved her mother, of course, but found no reason to play the piano for her, especially as Doris, always the strict parent, got even more strict after Frank was killed.

"Elise," Doris said, "I don't want you dating any boys until you finish high school."

"That's okay, Mum." said Elise, "I'm not that interested in any boys anyway. This was a half lie. She had had a crush on Brad, a senior, for the past two years. She and her best friend, Eliza, had the same crush as well as probably half the girls in the school. Brad was cute. With her father gone, Elise really had no interest in anyone except Eliza. The two of them had laughed at the similarity of their names when they first met as sophomores, but they found that they had a lot in common. Eliza played the clarinet and, for that reason, preferred Mozart to Beethoven, but their shared love of classical music was in real contrast to all the other girls who had crushes on the Beatles, the Rolling Stones, or some other long-haired British rock band. Eliza was the one she now sought comfort from over losing her father. Eliza was sympathetic to her friend, but was not helpful. All she seemed to want to do was to offer tissue to Elise when she was crying. Gradually, Elise saw her less and less, so by the time they graduated from high school, they were just two girls who used to be best friends. Neither one was especially distraught over it, but Eliza had found some new friends whereas Elise was still struggling with her depression and grief.

Doris was aggrieved over Frank's death but did not share that grief with her only child. Their relationship was mostly pragmatic. Still, it broke her heart when she had to tell her daughter: "Elise, I'm sorry that we can't afford your medications any more now that your father is dead and we lost his insurance. We won't be able to see Dr. Kramer anymore either. I hope you can stay in school and finish at least your Associate Degree at Kapiʻolani Community College."

"I'll try, Mum," was all Elise could reply.

Sleeping, Elise would dream of being at the piano again, playing Chopin, Tchaikovsky, or Beethoven. Sometimes, increasingly rarely, she would have a lucid moment when she could remember the last time she had played well. It was the night before she and her mother had had to move out of their house. Challenging herself to see if she could still remember it, she had played one of the more dreary Chopin nocturnes, the B-flat minor larghetto. Sad as it was, it had somehow comforted her that she would somehow turn out fine. When she recalled that feeling, she would laugh bitterly. Bitter laughter was the only laughter she could muster these days.

The thought of being in the concert hall now gave her hope. During the day, she was able to slowly gather together the recyclables she needed. It was September 2. She resorted to begging for money for food, but bought very little food with it. She had to have enough for that concert ticket. Or was it really going to be worth the effort? She should try to find out what they would be performing.

One of the security guards, Kiana, had been not so mean to her, so one night she walked over to the area of the concert hall and asked her if she knew what the symphony would be playing.

"Hah?" came the rough reply, "You goin' try get in den? No can. And no try leesten at da door. I like you, Elise, but I got one job fo' do."

"No, no, Kiana, I want to see if I can get enough money to get a ticket, but I want to know what they will play."

"Dey gonna preview the season, kay? Bumbye I get you da season schedule. Try come nex' week."

Kiana had been as good as her word to Elise, getting her a full schedule of the Honolulu Symphony season, featuring Verdi, Rimsky-Korsakov, Brahms, and Beethoven. Not any Beethoven but the fabulous Fifth Symphony, Elise's favorite, especially the grand final movement with its sweep of strings and a melody that seemed to take the soul to heaven. She now had renewed energy to get into that performance. The nearness of the event made Elise's youthful feelings of ecstasy for her music come flowing back into her. She almost felt healthy, almost pain free.

The community college was great at first. Elise should have had a lot of friends there since it was right behind McKinley, their old high school, but they seemed to be avoiding her. Her favorite class was piano, but she was not doing as well as she had expected. Elise was trying to continue the level of piano playing as she once had, but her fingers did not seem to work anymore. She thought too much of her father every time her fingers touched the keys. As much as she enjoyed the piano, she had to drop out due to her personal feeling that she was not doing very well. The instructor expressed his surprise, "But you're my best student, Elise." She felt uninterested in her other classes where her mind often drifted. Nothing, it seemed, could make her happy any more. Before she finished one semester, she had to drop out of all her classes.

At the age of 20, Elise thought her life was over. She had found work in the neighborhood at Foodland, but it was so boring and she felt down all the time. The piano sat mostly unused in the living room. When her mother got an aggressive breast cancer, they had to sell the house to cover her medical bills and rented a small studio in upper Makiki. The piano, which they had to leave behind, was no longer close at hand, even if she wanted to play it. When her mother died, a normal life was no longer within reach, for Elise had no other family in Hawai'i. Her depression caused her to lose even the menial work she was doing at Foodland. She had to live on the street, but never far from her childhood home in Makiki. She never wondered what happened to her friends, only the piano.

Her first days outside of her house were dazed ones. She kept thinking that someone she knew would take her in. No one ever did. She was too proud to ask Ms. Chung or any of her former schoolteachers. Ms. Chung would be her first choice, but she had not seen her since 1965 when she stopped taking lessons. She had no idea where to find food, feminine hygiene products, or a shower. She tried to avoid any of her old classmates and neighbors and, apparently, they were just fine with that, feigning to not recognize her or simply ignoring her.

Elise had an old tent she would sleep in. An old homeless man named Gus had offered it to her if she didn't mind that his friend had died in it. She had little choice but it afforded her minimal shelter and no protection from the homeless men or druggies who tried to take advantage of her. She could use it to sleep in after two years of trying to find doorways or carports where she could avoid passersby, dogs, or owners who would chase her away. Gus was nice and he introduced her to some women in Makiki who were also homeless. One of them was Hazel. They showed her how to hang out in the back of restaurants to get food, how to panhandle, and how to make makeshift sanitary napkins out of the paper towels they had in restrooms. She did not get to know any of the other women at all, but she and Hazel began to form a bond.

Once when Elise and her father were walking home from a piano recital at the nearby Makiki Christian Church, they saw a very skinny, dirty woman pushing a Longs shopping cart. Frank said, "Don't stare at her like that, Elise. That poor lady is probably homeless."

"You mean she has no house to live in, Daddy?" said Elise.

"Yes. She has to live out here. That shopping cart carries everything she owns."

Elise saw that the cart contained a lot of plastic bags, ragged old clothes, a bunch of cans and a naked Barbie doll. The lady rounded a corner and was out of their sight. "What happened to her family? What does she do for food? What happens to her when there's a storm?" said Elise.

"Those are all good questions, Elise, but I just don't know. I'm just guessing but she might have a mental illness. Did you see that old doll she had?"

"Can we help her?

"Elise, sweetheart, you are one compassionate child," said her father, "but if we tried to help all of the homeless people in Honolulu, we'd be homeless ourselves."

Elise shuddered at the idea of being homeless like that poor woman.

Elise started to have sex with men she knew and trusted as much as a homeless woman can trust anyone. Some of them beat her, but they always protected her from strangers and a few were even affectionate. There was certainly no love involved on Elise's part. She could hardly remember any of the men, who would stay with her for a few weeks or months. Wasn't one of them named Brad? Her tendency to cry a lot, for no or very small reasons, made most men want to leave her after not a very long time; then she would try to find another one. Her constant worry was pregnancy, but here fate gave her one gift for she never got pregnant. Had that happened, she would have had to abandon any child at the police station, which was only about a block away from Thomas Square. As she aged, Elise got more confused, filthy, and depressed, thus she had nothing to attract any of the men.

Elise seldom went far from the Square. If she did it was those few times when she wandered to the neighborhood where she grew up on the Diamond Head side of Pensacola Street. She would stand in front of her old house and think about those days when her only concern was earning a chocolate sundae. By the time she was 30 she stopped doing this because of the way her depression deepened to near suicidal levels for many days after.

It seemed like she had known Hazel all of her life now, but that was impossible, of course. In fact, she vaguely recalled that she had been a denizen of Thomas Square well before Hazel was there. They got along really well from the very beginning. It was a true act of friendship that Hazel was willing to help her out, for the homeless rarely do anything for anyone that does not somehow benefit them.

As September 19 neared, Hazel, whose red dress not only stunk but had gotten torn in a fight with another meth addict, told Elise that she did not think that dress would be good to wear to the concert. Instead, she asked Elise to help her steal another dress from the Goodwill store down the street on Beretania. All Elise had to do was cause a distraction in the store by pretending to have a fit in an aisle far from the women's section. That was easy since Elise had seen so many of the psychotics have fits. She and Hazel went into the store and separated. As soon as Hazel saw everyone running toward Elise, she not only found her a nice blue dress in her size, but a small violet handbag that matched it. They both almost looked like new. Her shoes, well, she hoped no one would notice her dirty sneakers with both big toes visible. The concert would be in two days. Elise could hardly wait.

Kiana told her that the tickets to the event would not be sold in advance and that seating was not reserved but open. The concert was a matinee that began at 3:00. If Elise got there early, she would be able to sit near the front and in the center where the sound was the best. With her parents, they could never afford those choice seats, but almost every time they went there, her father would point down from the balcony and say to Elise, "See there, about eight rows back and right in the middle? That's the best place to sit to hear the orchestra." So, on the day of the concert, Elise planned to get in line at 2:30 even though it would be hard for her to stand for half an hour before the doors opened, then she would rush to those choice seats in front.

Elise took great care of her dress and purse, hardly leaving her tent except to use the restroom. She only needed the purse to make her look like she had possessions. There was nothing in it. The pain in her chest was really intense plus she felt like she was starving. To save enough for the concert, she had not eaten for a week.

The day of the concert was warm and bright. Elise woke up with the first light, which was something she never did. She spent the morning reading the program over and over, counting her money and guarding her dress. She tried not to think about her pain and hunger. At noon, she got dressed slowly and with some effort and went to show herself to Hazel. Hazel said, "You look gorgeous, Elise. One more thing, dearie, rub this lip balm under your pits. Y'know, you kinda stink."

After she thanked Hazel for all she had done, Elise made her way painfully toward the concert hall, the place she had looked on for all these years with such longing that only music could express it. Crossing King Street, she subtly raised her arms and smelled herself to see if she was offensive, but her sense of smell had been dulled by so many years of diving in dumpsters. She would have to judge by the sneers on people's faces. She saw none.

Shaking with excitement as she made her way to the box office, clutching her three one-dollar bills, five quarters, six dimes, and three nickels. Steadying herself, she said to the cashier, "One please." Looking at the door she noticed a few people lining up, but it was still early. She made her way to the lawn and sat as far away from anyone as she could. She was surprised by how many of them were dressed—jeans, shorts, very casual. She would look over-dressed, but that was just fine. People were buying meals from the food vendors scattered around the building and the aroma was only making her pain worse. She wanted to get inside. Listen.

People were starting to line up. It was not quite 2:30, but Elise, struggling to stand, made her way to the entrance and stood behind some young couples staring into their phones. No one spoke to her and she felt that maybe they were starting to smell her. At this point, she didn't care. When the doors opened, she rushed in as fast as she could. She was feeling a joy she had not felt in so long that she was literally dancing her way to the seats.

Music was the thread that wove throughout her childhood, binding her to her father and her father to her. Her mother liked to listen to her play and even to Frank when he sang. Those were the moments Elise was very joyful. It seemed to her that the sorrow over the loss of her father was proportional to that joy.

"Listen," said Ms. Chung. "Can you hear the difference between these chords?" Here she played a C major chord then an A minor chord. "Do they make you feel differently when you hear them?"

"Yes," said Elise. "The first one sounds joyful. The second one makes me feel a little sad."

"Very good, Elise. The second one was A minor and composers use it and other minor keys to create feelings of sorrow and longing in us. Remember that these chords bring out those different feelings and when you listen to good music, try to see if you can tell if they are major or minor keys."

When Elise's father died, she felt that all of the songs they played at his funeral were in minor keys.

Finally inside the concert hall, Elise had made her way to the center of the seats, since it was open seating. Stomach rumbling, she sat next to a local couple who were in the very center. This seat was fine. She did not want to sit too close to the couple and she hoped no one would sit next to her either. She was so hungry. Her chest complained bitterly to her over the pain. The Verdi Overture that began the concert was in a major key. Then the music started and she forgot about the pain. She no longer felt hungry at all. She only felt the waves of sound rushing into her being, raising the memory of her father telling her about Beethoven's "Für Elise," tickling her even as she tried to play the piano and hugging her.

The orchestra sounded like they were inspired. They followed the Overture with a dazzling excerpt from Rimsky-Korsakov's *Scheherazade*, then a movement from a Brahms symphony with which Elise was not familiar. Or had she forgotten it along with so many other things? Well, tonight was not a night for regrets. Was that her father she heard humming along to the music? As the concert drew to a close, her heart rose in her chest as they began the final movement of Beethoven's Fifth Symphony. Elise felt herself lifted out of her seat with the rapture she felt. Nothing on this earth could feel better.

Julie Ushio
CROSS WORDS

When Edith was admitted to Prairie Haven Nursing Home, her daughter Kim flew from Hawai'i to Nebraska to stay for a month. Edith had fallen and broken her hip while stepping down from a footstool in her living room after watering her plants. Her feeble cry for help was heard by the mailman the next morning. After a stay of four days in the hospital, she was moved to Prairie Haven for rehab and physical therapy.

"I have no choice," Edith told Kim, her voice dull and faint over the phone. "But it's temporary, till I get better."

When Kim got the call about her mother, she planned to go back for a week, but it was difficult to assess how serious her mother's condition was, how long her recovery might take. Kim talked to her husband Bert and said she was thinking about staying a month.

"You're flying from Hawai'i to Nebraska, spend a month with your mother, when your brother lives a state away?" Bert asked.

"Steve travels for his job. And he's coaching the twins' soccer team." Kim's younger brother Steve lived in Kansas City, a manager for the Burlington Railroad. He'd married late, a father of twins at forty. He hadn't been back to visit their mother since their father's funeral three years before.

"Still making excuses for him."

Kim bit her lip to keep in her retort. She didn't want their conversation to escalate into a full-blown argument. She was already going back twice a year to deal with her mom's finances and knew there'd be even more travel in the years ahead. Eventually, she'd have to deal with the house. A month with her mom in the nursing home would give her a chance to start cleaning. And Kim had time. She wasn't teaching summer school this year. Bert was busy with a big project at work. Their two kids were settled into their own lives on the Mainland.

Bert softened after not getting the expected stinging rebuke from Kim.

"Go. Your mom will enjoy having you there."

Kim knew Bert didn't understand her relationship with her family, so different from his. How she could live so far away and yet feel so close. How protective she was of a brother she rarely saw. Every Sunday, Kim and Bert went to his parents' house in Mānoa for dinner. They'd stay into the evening, visiting with aunties, uncles, and cousins. Sometimes Bert played his guitar, the Mānoa breeze rustling leaves on the mango tree that canopied the backyard. Stars peeked through. The constellations unchanged from the night thirty years ago when they first met at a beach barbeque.

Julie Ushio

After the kids left for college, Kim sometimes begged out of Sunday dinner, saying she had a pile of papers to grade. Bert knew Kim just wanted to be alone. His family had learned over the years to give her space, attributing her slight eccentricities to being a kotonk, a mainland Japanese, and from Nebraska too. Who even knew there were Japanese living there?

The evening after Kim flew into Nebraska, she went up to the nursing home. Her mother looked so small and helpless, dressed in a thin cotton hospital gown, her grey hair straight and uncombed, purple bruises on her arms and hands from the IVs in the hospital. Her mother's eyes were closed, but hearing footsteps, she opened them and smiled a wan smile of recognition.

"When did you get in? How are the kids?"

"Fine, fine." Kim leaned over and gave her mother a kiss on her cheek.

"How tall is Jason?"

It was the same sequence of questions her mother always asked, whether they talked on the phone or in person. Several years ago when her mother repeatedly asked how tall Jason and Merilee were, Kim realized how much her mother's memory had deteriorated. How she'd developed little conversational ditties for different situations. If Kim was with her mother and they ran into someone who paused to say hello, her mother would smile and say, "Well, hello. How nice to see you again." After the person walked away, Kim would ask her mother who the person was. Her mother would say, "I don't know now, but I used to know them."

"Jason's almost six feet," Kim answered her mother. "Tall for a Japanese."

"*He is?*" Kim's mother raised her eyebrows in wonder. "And Merilee?"

"Five-six."

"*She is?*"

Kim didn't say that Jason and Merilee were adults, had stopped growing years ago. Even though Jason and Merilee had visited Edith last summer, in Edith's mind, they were still the smiling children in photos taped to her refrigerator door.

A nurse came in to take her mom's vitals. Another arrived to give her pills for the night. Kim kissed her mom goodnight and left.

The following morning Kim met with Lorna, the Prairie Haven care coordinator, and toured the facility. She followed Lorna's bouffant highlighted hair through the three wings of the nursing home: green wing for temps, where patients like her mom stayed as long as Medicare paid for their physical therapy; yellow wing for permanent residents; red wing, behind secured doors, for memory

JULIE USHIO

patients. Kim read the names on the doorplates as she walked down the hallways, familiar names from her childhood. After Kim's dad passed, her mother had lamented the absence of her friends. Edith knew some had passed away, but others she never saw anymore. Now Kim knew where they'd gone—they were all at Prairie Haven.

Every morning, Kim went up to visit her mother, returning again in the evening for another visit. She brought up her mother's CD player, books, and crossword puzzle magazines. During the day, her mother was out of her room at physical therapy. Afternoons and evenings, she was often sleeping. When she was awake, Edith complained of pain in her hip, often confused at where she was and why she was there.

"Where am I?"

"In a nursing home, Prairie Haven."

"I am?"

When Edith tried to rise out of her chair, a chair alarm under her rear end sent out loud electronic beeps.

"What is that noisy thing?" Edith asked.

"A chair alarm," Kim said. "You can't get out of your chair because you fell and broke your hip."

"I did?"

"Yes." No matter how many times Kim answered her questions, Edith never remembered and ten minutes later, asked the same questions all over again.

Sometimes in the evening, Kim sat by her mother as she slept, listening to her measured breathing, wondering if she would ever walk again, if this was going to be the triggering event that would lead to her decline, the slow downhill slide towards death.

Kim was surprised at how little energy she had at the end of that first week. It was all she could do to go up and see her mother; sort through the piles of mail, bills, and Medicare statements; meet with the staff and doctors about her mom's condition. There was no time to deal with the house and little time for herself.

After ten days, Edith's pain was under control. The doctor took her off the heavy pain meds, which lessened her confusion. Kim brought in a framed photograph of her father and placed it on her mother's nightstand next to her bed. The following afternoon when Kim visited, her father's picture was lying face down on the nightstand. When Kim went to place it upright, her mother stopped her.

"Leave it alone," she snapped. "I don't want to see his face right now."

Julie Ushio

Kim put the picture back down, surprised at her mother's tone. Her mother was doing a crossword puzzle clipped to a plastic clipboard. Edith paused, her pencil in midair. She didn't look up as she spoke.

"We were married almost sixty years. Sixty years! In all that time, he *never* once told me he loved me. I sat next him when he was dying, held his hand, told him how much I loved him, saying it over and over. *I love you, I love you,* like it would pull him back. Did he say anything? Open one eye just a little? *No.* Just silence. And then he up and died when I left the room to go to the bathroom.

"After he died, I went through his desk, his files. You know how he saved everything, filed everything away so neatly. He saved every little note that some stranger sent him, programs from the church, obituaries of everyone who died for the past twenty years, but he didn't save one, NOT ONE, of the cards I gave him. Every Valentine's Day, every Christmas, every birthday for fifty-nine years, I gave him a card. Always a Hallmark, not those cheap ones from the Dollar Store. I always signed them, *Love your wife, Edith.* Did he save *one* of them? *Not one.* There wasn't a card of mine in the piles he saved, from you and Steve, his army buddies, friends from church."

Kim did not know what to say.

Her mother, anger spent, silently resumed her crossword puzzle, attacking the page with a vengeance.

Later that evening, when Kim came back, her father's photo was standing upright on the nightstand next to her mother's bed. Her mother looked at Kim but did not say anything. Kim wondered if her mother had been crying because her mom's eyes were moist, her nose red like it got when she cried. The nurse came and gave her mom her nightly meds and turned off the overhead light while Kim stood beside the bed.

Her mother took her pills and eased back on to the pillow. She turned her head to look at the photo of Kim's dad.

"We were so happy," Edith said softly. "I miss him so much."

The house was not the same house that Kim and Steve had grown up in, but a small brick Tudor eight blocks north of their old home in a newer part of town, across the street from the park. Her parents had bought the house after Kim and Steve graduated from college. Kim's children called it "Grandma's house" and loved coming to visit each summer. They played in the yard, rode bicycles in the street, and walked to the swimming pool, experiences they didn't have in urban Honolulu where they were driven to soccer games and play dates.

"It's better than Disneyland," Merilee used to say. "Grandma's house has bunnies and squirrels in the backyard."

JULIE USHIO

Over the past ten years, Kim started to notice that her parents' once tidy, organized home was accumulating clutter. Like a slow growing fungus, every time Kim returned, the detritus grew and morphed. Piles of newspapers in the kitchen next to the door, stacks of magazines on top of the bookcase, knitting caddies with skeins of yarn and half-finished afghans next to the recliner. Her mother's closet overflowed with bags and boxes stacked so high that the door would not close. In the bathroom, cans of scouring powder, toilet bowl cleaner, and foaming bubble scum remover lined the tile floor beside the bathtub. In the kitchen, the white speckled laminate countertop was barely visible through assorted jars of jelly, peanut butter, honey, a ceramic chopstick holder, stacks of napkins from fast food restaurants, a toothpick dispenser in the shape of a hula dancer.

Wandering around the house, Kim felt like a ghost, living in the shadow of her parents. Sometimes she was an anthropologist, recreating lives from fragments left behind: piles of old letters, a thick envelope stuffed with newspaper clippings from the war, yellowed old photographs of people dressed in kimono. There were other surprises too, nests of pills tucked in kitchen towels, an open package of lemon cream sandwich cookies shoved under the recliner.

One evening, Kim walked the three blocks from her parents' house up to Prairie Haven. After she said goodnight to her mom she continued walking south to the old neighborhood. A train whistle blew, low and mournful through the darkness, the same lullaby she heard years ago as a child. She paused in front of the house she grew up in and looked up at her old bedroom window. Nothing had changed she thought. It was as if she could step back in time, walk into her old house, and go up to her bedroom, her parents asleep down the hall, Steve in the room next to hers.

Late one morning Kim arrived at the nursing home shortly before lunch. The residents were gathered in their wheelchairs in the open area by the main nurses' station, waiting for lunch. Her mother was sitting in her wheelchair towards the back of the group and as Kim walked through, she thought the group seemed a little livelier than usual. Her mother was wearing the peach-colored sweatshirt with the appliqué flowers on the front, her favorite top reserved for special occasions.

Lorna, the care coordinator, pushed up an elderly lady in a wheelchair and parked her next to Edith.

"New guy in town," Lorna said to Kim. "Causing quite a stir among the ladies."

"I noticed," Kim said.

"Chet Simpson. His son Skip brought him in yesterday evening. Fell out of the back of his pickup truck and broke his pelvic bone. He can't stay alone at the ranch anymore. Not to mention his dementia is pretty bad."

Julie Ushio

"Simpson of the Simpson Ranch?" Kim asked. The ranch was one of the largest cattle ranches in the Sandhills, sixty miles west of town. Kim had gone to school with Skip. Skip, like his dad, was tall, good looking, his Stetson hat pulled down low over his tanned face. Sandhill cowboys, belted and booted, were a dying breed, more at ease with cattle than people. Unless you got a little booze in them.

"Yeah," Lorna said. "His wife died a couple years ago but the old man kept the ranch going. Until this happened. He might have to go into the Memory Wing later, but right now there aren't any beds."

Lunch was being served and the line of wheelchairs started to move. Some residents pushed themselves along, while others were wheeled by aides. Edith waited quietly, waiting for Kim to finish talking with Lorna.

"Seems like Chet has taken a fancy to your mom." Lorna winked at Kim. "Remembers her from when your folks ran the steak house. But he calls her Edie."

"Not interested," Edith sniffed, as Kim began to push her mom's wheelchair. "Been there, done that."

Later that evening, Kim called Bert. He'd just returned from Sunday dinner at his mom's.

"Everyone sends their love," Bert said.

Kim updated Bert on her mom's condition but not much had changed since she'd talked to him three days ago.

"How's work?" she asked.

"It's coming along," Bert said. "Heard anything from the kids?"

"No," Kim said, "but I'll call them this weekend."

After she hung up the phone, Kim realized that like her mother, she and Bert had developed their own conversational ditties. Abbreviated, scripted interchanges. How had they evolved to these parceled out, edited conversations?

"You teachers are all bossy," Bert often complained. "Stand there. Hold this. Don't do that. You order me around like I was one of your students."

Kim's dad had been like that. Always ordering Kim and Steve around. He thought raising kids was like being in the army. Fighting in the war had taught him discipline, how to make a bed, shine a shoe, fold his socks. A platoon, a group of unwieldy cadets, a family, needed to work together. It just needed someone to tell everyone what to do.

Kim's mom was soft spoken, but her words often carried an underlying message. When Kim called home from college, her mom's "Why, hello!" always put Kim on defense. Her mom's lilting greeting ended in a question mark, implying that it'd been ages since Kim had called.

"Steel hand in a velvet glove," Steve used to say of their mom.

JULIE USHIO

Throughout her childhood, Kim had lived with the tension between her dad's abrupt demands and her mother's simple but emotionally veiled one-liners. She'd almost forgotten how bad it was. In their later years, both parents had softened, their differences melting away. Maybe that would be the way it would be with she and Bert. As they grew older, they wouldn't remember what they were so upset about.

The night before she was to leave, Kim went up to see her mom to tell her goodbye. Not that her mother would remember. Her mother already knew that Kim was leaving, or had possibly already left, but her mother knew that Kim would return. Kim had put a note on her mother's bulletin board of her next visit in December.

When Kim came into her mother's room, the lights were dimmed and her mother was sleeping. Kim sat in a chair by her mother's bed holding her hand. The hall outside the room was empty except for the nurse at the far end, dispensing night medications one room at a time. Kim heard the squeak of a wheelchair coming down the hall, growing closer, until it stopped outside her mother's door. A man's voice, called out, quietly.

"Good night, Edie. I love you."

Amy Uyematsu
LITTLE TOKYO HAIKU, 2019

I want to go back—
      this hip, touristy J-town
           would make Grandpa cry

While we were in camp
      the streets jumped to Bronzeville jazz—
           and then we returned

Just twenty-five bucks,
      a train ticket, camp to home—
           Mom cannot forget

San Kwo Low is gone—
      so is the best almond duck
           I ever tasted

It's chinameshi—
      Chinese food made J-A style,
           affordable too

Sidewalks filled with foodies,
      sansei with hapa grandkids
           and all these homeless

Skateboards and pink hair,
      more common in J-town than
           Issei descendants

Old as my Grandpa
      I keep looking for faces
           resembling my own

Amy Uyematsu

DAZZLING

Like my mother, who at 93 still turns heads
with her snow-white hair and flair for design.
Over her black and white geometric print shirt
she wears a chain of chunky black beads,
on her feet the latest style in sneakers.

She's always had women friends
who don't get jealous. They know her
good looks come with a generous heart
and more than a few smarts. Naturally
men admire her from near and far.

Dad used to tell us how proud he was
walking down the street with her,
even the white guys in our racist town stared.
I wasn't so sure I liked him describing
Mom like some kind of trophy.

Now as my own hair grays, I'm thankful
watching everyone stop to admire
when my mother enters a room.
Sure, beauty is only skin deep but
no eyes can resist such abiding bloom.

J. Fumiko Wong
THE PASSAGE

This is how I know what month it is.

September: faces, hopeful and refreshed, come to my counter. They look in their daily planners and sign up for their college conferences.

October: pimples have multiplied on those faces. They know they have to be nice to me and make small talk. I let them into the counselor's office. After their thirty minutes of statistics and reality, most of them shuffle away, eyes downcast.

November: the crew cuts have grown shaggy; the girls' eyebrows have sprouted outside once perfect arcs. They come to me with letter of recommendation forms. I send them away if they do not have the top portions filled out; I send them away if there are no stamps.

December: the faces have no smiles. Each one believes his or her life hangs in precarious balance, hinging on *Evaluate a significant experience* or the inane: *You have just completed your 300-page autobiography. Please submit page 217.* They show up to make more appointments with the counselor. Everyone needs their fifteen minutes to cry in her closed room.

January: older faces, those of the parents, just as downtrodden as their children's. They approach hesitantly and ask in a whisper for tips on financial aid. I tell them if you own a house in Hawai'i, you are considered a millionaire and are sunk.

February and March: faces—fewer white than brown—diligently come by, picking up the latest scholarship information. The girls' eyebrows are plucked. The boys' chins are more carefully shaved. Ditching school is not happening, but they know they don't have to get perfect test scores plus extra credit this second semester.

April: the cruelest month. These seniors I do not recognize. Exuberant smiling aliens barge into my office and hug me without asking. Minutes later, girls with red eyes and disheveled hair run to the counselor. They only got into Cornell, not Princeton. Or *how do I get off the waitlist for Stanford?* I overhear.

J. Fumiko Wong

May: some stragglers come in. I give them one of my black ballpoint pens. I watch them fill out the front-and-back University of Hawaiʻi application. I open my drawer and fish out my secret stash of stamps.

Lois-Ann Yamanaka
CAT HATER, CAT LOVER
for WTL because

Big Betty says that people are born either dog lovers or cat lovers.

I am a cat hater. Ever since I can remember, "I no can stand their slit eyes, Betty. And the way they make *ppprrrrr, ppprrrrr*. And the claws, you can stand the claws? Bugga give me chicken skin. And when they rub against my leg I like climb the walls. And no let one black cat cross your path or your mother going break her back."

Mama.

"Sorry. You no mo' madda," she said.

One too many obake neko movie at the Mamo Theater with Papa Toe and Granny Goose. I really went only to share the buttered popcorn, Carnation chocolate malteds, Red Whips, and dried red octopus legs with Big Betty and Timboy. I would laugh when Timboy screamed as the innocent rice farm girl turned into a back-arching, hissing obake neko with satanic eyes and spit strings. But I was screaming too. Inside.

Afterwards, Timboy would get back at me.

"What am I?" he'd ask, lying face down on the living room floor upstairs.

I'd shrug my shoulders. "Dead toad on the road?"

"No, flat cat."

"What am I?" He'd stick his arms and one leg out.

I'd try to ignore him.

"Rigor mortis cat."

We all learned the meaning of rigor mortis from Papa Toe's best friend, the taxidermist across the street from the theater, Harry Yagyuu. Heads by Harry. Papa Toe at one time was an animal collector. If our pets died, they became home decoration.

I didn't hate all cats. Last year we were riding our bikes home from Sunday School when we heard a mewling from the empty lot up the street. We found a gray kitten whose paws had been slashed and whose whiskers had been cut off so she could not find her way home. Big Betty named her Hoppy for obvious reasons.

She was so little that when we brought her home, she bonded with Big Betty's brothers' hunting dogs and ended up behaving in doggie ways. She ran with the pack. We never really considered her a cat. And Big Betty and me never really bonded with her. She could be house decoration, for heaven's sake. Mounted on the wall next to Big Betty's brother's mouflon or billy goat that he shot up Mauna Kea.

But along came Michi-san. And Mama called Father at midnight. *Mama.* I heard them on the phone. I cried. I wanted to hear her voice too. The Japanese believe that black cats who come to you can cure your sadness if you take them in and place them on your belly to sleep. They will absorb your tears. I see it all in slow motion, that little black ball running toward me. She was being terrorized by Big Betty's Puerto-Rican-wannabe brother's pit bull. The little black cat who ran across the street straight for me. Listen to the violins playing, the wind goes through my hair as I hold out my arms to a *cat?*

Halt the obake neko film. Rewind the Kurosawa.

She's so tiny. She has to be only four weeks old. We'll have to keep her. They'll gas her at the so-called *Humane* Society. I'll give her to Big Betty. No, not another Hoppy doggie wannabe. The guilt, oh, the guilt. And the Japanese thing about black cats coming toward you.

"Fate," Papa Toe says."It's fate, paht-nah, I tell you. We keep neko-chan."

I vow to overcome my lifelong fear of cats and bring her in. Papa, Timboy, and me go to Hilo Pet Center and buy all the kitty stuff: special milk for kittens that comes in a box, kitty kibble, litter, and a litter box. Cats don't need much care not like dogs.

At first, my autistic big brother Dominic won't have it. This tiny little eight-ounce ball of black fur playing with *his* toys. What is this *thing?* It can't be a dog. They live outside at Big Betty's house and weigh 125 pounds. When Michi-san goes for his Happy Meal, that's it—Domi picks her up and tosses her away. For weeks, I see a black kitten flying through the air from the corner of my eyes. And if you were wondering, it's true. Cats always land on their feet.

The first few nights, Michi-san is so tiny, barely weaned, she decides to sleep with me on my futon upstairs. I think she thinks that my warm body is her mother so she claws against my pajamas and *ppprrrrs* like she wants to drink milk. Yikes, those razor sharp claws and sinister purring. *Obake neko.*

Later, I ask our vet if we can declaw her. "If you let me cut off the tips of all your fingers," Dr. Richardson tells me, "I will gladly declaw your cat." I have grown fond of my fingertips, thank you very much.

The cat stays. The cat is quirky. It is the first thing that I like about her. The way Michi-san decides to bond with Domi. The way she nudges the screen door open to follow him outside to play with his river rocks. The way she stretches herself in the warm sunlight in the upstairs living room on Sunday mornings. The way she stays clean all by herself. The way she turns her head from side to side when she looks at me. I swear there's someone I know inside that cat.

Mama.

The way she absorbs all my sadness.

We love buying her kitty treats on sale at KTA and catnip toys and fish guts from Suisan. She wears a fluorescent pink collar with a little bell. She squeezes under the gate and is the first to greet us when we get home. She waits at the edge of the tub when I take a shower. She comes running when I call her name—most of the time.

Yet she is not in need of all my love and attention. Like a dog. Or like Domi. Michi-san is graceful, peaceful, calm, weird, serene like a Buddhist priest. But this is how Michi-san changed my life:

Dominic gets stuck on things. Now he likes noses. All noses. My nose. Our father's nose. Timboy's nose. Aunty Narcissus's nose. The home decorations's noses. And now Michi-san's nose. He loves to press the spongy tips of all noses with his fingers or his lips. Or rub his nose against your nose. It makes him giggle. What amazes me is how this cat lets him kiss her with his lips saying, "Nose, nose." The cat closes her eyes and lets Dominic kiss his spongy wet nose. Then he rubs his nose against Michi-san's nose. All the while giggling, "Good night, cat."

And that is simply that:

I became a cat lover.

BAMBOO SHOOTS
Selections from our online writing contest

Doreen E. Beyer
MEMORIES OF HOME

My memory of home sweeps
like the trade winds past clotheslines
—billowing frayed bedsheets,
jiggling pinned cotton underwear,
knee-high socks and plastic Ziploc
bags turned inside out—
flowing through jalousie windows,
pausing at rice cake and fruit offerings
to deceased Buddhist elders,
chasing fat flies from soft tofu,
green onions and thin beef slices
near the sink
where takeout spoons and cups dry.

My memory of home hears Ohta-san
replay "Song for Anna" on a music CD,
a small dog yipping at passing motorists,
brown hands belt-sanding a canoe,
sticky half-naked bodies talking
story—backs to the breeze—
cold beer in their hands.

Doreen E. Beyer

NEWELL'S SHEARWATER

You are—
the dark speck flapping in the eye
of the sun,
the passing cloud over the ocean's face,
white underbelly concealing talons,
wingtips shearing ocean tides.

You navigate the currents,
a partner to an ancient choreography
of a spinning globe, wind, sun,
and moon. Where you dived for squid,
fishermen found yellowfin tuna.

Once a year you return to land
where your clumsy feet cannot walk,
to nesting burrows that hold your
single egg.

On a cool, cloud-filled night,
your fledgling will favor
the false flight path of white halogen
lining a football stadium
over the distant celestial guides
to the sea.

Doreen E. Beyer

WHISPER

At the edge of consciousness,
a rhythmic sound
like breath
of leaves being swept,
of leaves sweeping
the window, the wall,
the rooftop—
distinct from the floating thunder
of Lunalilo Freeway,
consistent in its persistence,
persistent in its anonymity.
Dream state descending,
the ascent of awareness,
In the shroud covered stillness
I hear her—whispers of a ghost
that came with the house—
on the other side of my dream.

Lanning C. Lee
MIDWEST ALOHA

Four fresh-faced white Wisconsin farm lads
maybe raised on this morning's milk and cheese and home churned butter
rocket their beat-up red sedan through the city of Madison

Perhaps looking for action different from daily farm chores
they slow down to visit me on the side of the highway
one, maybe 18, rolling down the passenger side window

"Remember Pearl Harbor," he shouts, smiling at the greeting
then all four explode in red-faced laughter, speed off
leaving me not quite realizing my first encounter with racism

From my home on Oʻahu, I can see Pearl Harbor
picture bombs bursting, the flames, the screaming
all of that horrible, deadly disaster that led us to world war

I can see U.S. internment camps, Nazi concentration camps
my father fighting in the European theater
Hiroshima and Nagasaki, the extermination of Jews

All this leaves me wondering, their hatred not yet registering
how did these young white boys even know where I lived
or think that I'd ever forget the place I come from

Vanessa Lee-Miller
KĀLOA PAU:
NOTES FROM A FISHERMAN'S DIARY

Pre-dawn beasts clutter the sky . . .

Kāloa Pau

Cold morning.
Fisherman shuffles
to the calendar on the wall,
squinting at the tiny print.

Oh, Kāloa Pau moon,
fishing supposed to be "excellent."
We'll see about dat. . . .
He shuffles away, shaking his head.

Cold morning,
"double jacket" kine cold.
Fisherman steps out to gaze at the sky.
Pre-dawn beasts clutter
the black velvet canvas.
Big Bear, Little Bear snarl at hissing dragon.
Snake slithers by.

Darrell H. Y. Lum

BOY AND UNCLE: VALENTINE'S DAY

—So what you going get for your girlfriend? Valentine Day l'dat?
—I no mo girlfriend, Uncle.
—No mo? Bettah get one before you get too old like me.
—You had girlfriend? Or was always Aunty?
—Girlfriends, boy. Girlfriends. I was one Romeo and all da Juliets went call fo me: "Romeo, Romeo where fo you stay?"
—Not!
—Yeah. I no kid you. You gotta know how.
—How you got your first girlfriend?
—My first one? Wanda Hu. Da guys all used to tease her, sing da "Book of Love" song to her, "Well, I Wan-da, Wan-da, Hu, who wrote da book of love . . ." Me too, I used to sing wit dem cause I donno how ack in front of one cute girl, so instead we ack stupid.
—Das funny, Uncle!
—Jes no ack stupid, boy. I saw her cry little bit one time when we was being stupid. So I went give her my hankerchief.
—Went work?
—Of course. When she gimme back my hankerchief, all wash and ironed, I told her she can borrow anytime she like. As long as I nevah use um first. Made her laugh.

SILENCE

Our house, we neva talk. Daddy come home and only tell about work. Not even one long story but one short, Morse code kine story. Like we supposed to know. "Boss said . . . errybody said yeah, yeah." Same old, same old. He ansa his own question. "Whachugoingdo?"

Mama only tell what she need, "Rice running out." "Gotta go buy hoo-jook." Daddy tink erryting "A-Okay" cause my big bruddah Russo no say nutting except sometimes tell "yeah" or "no," when he gotta say something. Me, I learn how fo keep my head down and side-eye errybody who not talking. We all stay eating. And Mama putting stuff in our bowl. We eat.

AFTERWORD: A BAMBOO RIDGE PRESS LEGACY

WING TEK LUM
PRESERVING *BAMBOO RIDGE*

On February 13, 2020, at Kapi'olani Community College, Bamboo Ridge Press celebrated the launch of its digital collection in the University of Hawai'i System Repository (found at <dspace.lib.hawaii.edu>). One of the speakers, Wing Tek Lum, delivered the following remarks.

I serve as warehouse manager of Bamboo Ridge Press. I somehow also became de facto archivist of the hard copy publications. Around 1989, founding editors Eric Chock and Darrell Lum dropped off what they had saved of the earliest issues to put in my basement for safekeeping. We had discussed setting up an archive ideally with ten copies of each publication, to save these writings for posterity (or perhaps for Stephen Sumida, Jr. to wade through when he embarks on a new annotated bibliography of local literature a generation from now). However, for a few of the very earliest titles, e.g., issue #1 and some of the unnumbered issues, we could only find 4 or 5 copies to archive.

After we established this hard copy repository, we decided as a matter of policy to remove ten copies from the first printing of each publication for the archives. Moreover, if a title is popular enough to go through more printings, we wanted to save another five copies of each reprint as well.

By my count, the press has published 107 books to date. Plus eleven cassette tapes, four compact discs, twenty different T-shirts, one cap, and three tote bags. The last three accessories are not necessarily included in the archives.

With respect to the books, there may be some confusion. From 1978 to 1985, Bamboo Ridge not only published numbered issues, but also six unnumbered ones as well. The first of course was Eric's chapbook *Ten Thousand Wishes*, which came out during the Talk Story Conference in June 1978. One hundred and fifty copies were printed.

But during those heady initial years the press also released some additional unnumbered titles, e.g., the *Talk Story Big Island Anthology*, Clara Jelsma's short stories entitled *Teapot Tales*, and the most well known, *Poets Behind Barbed Wire*, a collection of tanka by four local poets who were interned during World War II.

In December 1978, Eric and Darrell took the ambitious step to publish numbered issues as a periodical that lovers of local literature could collectively support with subscriptions. Bamboo Ridge was not going to be just a publisher of occasional books—which has the implication that the press had the freedom to publish but also cease to publish whenever it wanted to. To me, becoming a periodical was their commitment to a disciplined future, a formal promise that there was more to come. Issue #1 was an anthology of 16 authors. There are no specific records of the print run, but on the copyright page for issue #5 it does say that that issue had 500 copies printed. So maybe the founders were already optimistic enough to print the same quantity for their earliest numbered issues.

The earliest *Bamboo Ridge* issues were slim, around 60+ pages, printed in black ink on white paper, except for the single-colored cover, and stapled along the spine. They were 5.5" x 8.5" in size, except for issue #2 which was for some reason double the size. Later, in 1987, with my first book (issue #34/35), the size was enlarged to 6" x 9". Also, starting in 1980, with issue #8 (Darrell's first collection, *Sun*), more and more of the books were perfect bound instead.

To me, one of the most interesting of the earliest issues is issue #17 because of its colorful cover. That was not because of the printing though. I still remember going to Darrell's home one night and his instructing us to physically glue onto the front cover these labels he purchased from Honolulu Broom Factory.

Bamboo Ridge was initially billed as a quarterly publication, meaning that a subscriber was promised four issues for an annual subscription. However, by 1986, coming up with so many issues a year became more of a challenge, and many of our publications turned into double issues, especially our single author collections. So from 1986 to 1995, an annual subscriber might actually receive three books: a regular issue, then a volume of poetry by a single author billed as a double issue, and then another regular issue. Then in 1996, we simplified our publication schedule even more; starting with issue #69, we decided to go back to numbering our issues with a single number but providing an annual subscriber with only two books.

So again, while our latest publication, Scott Kikkawa's *Kona Winds*, is issue #116, it actually is only the 107th publication of *Bamboo Ridge*.

Of these 107 titles, 47 are what we consider our regular issues, an anthology of the best poetry and prose (and sometimes dramatic pieces) being written at that time. For instance, our most recent regular issue #115 contains 57 pieces by 35 writers. These regular issues typically feature a single artist, both for the outside cover and for interior artwork. (Starting with issue #44 we consciously tried to showcase the elder statesmen within our local visual artist community; but more recently the interest among our present editors has been with up-and-coming artists.)

Another 39 books are single-author collections of poetry or prose, or like Scott Kikkawa's, a novel. Juliet Kono, of course, is our favorite, as we have published two volumes of her poetry, a collection of short stories, and her novel

Anshū. Our *Kauaʻi Tales* series, the retelling of legends of Kauaʻi by Frederick B. Wichman with illustrations by Christine Fayé, also consists of four titles; in fact these latter books have been our best sellers, having sold over time over 40,000 copies in the aggregate.

Lastly, there are 21 titles which are anthologies on a single theme, e.g., #12 *Small Kid Time Hawaii* (a collection of poems written by elementary school students), #42/43 *Paké* (our bicentennial celebration of the arrival of Chinese to Hawaiʻi), #76 *Intersecting Circles* (which featured writing by hapa women), and #83 *He Leo Hou* (a collection of plays by four Native Hawaiian writers).

A few years ago our webmaster crunched the numbers in our author database, and counted over 1,000 unique authors. This to me is a major testament to Eric and Darrell's vision and perseverance. Over the now 41 years that we have been publishing local literature, Bamboo Ridge Press has indeed tried to live up to its mission statement: to foster the appreciation, understanding, and creation of literary, visual, and performing arts by, for, or about Hawaiʻi's people. And now through the partnership with the Hawaiʻi Council for the Humanities and Kapiʻolani Community College, we are making these works more readily available in this new digital repository. To date, we have converted into digital files 23 titles out of our 107 hard copy books, so we are well on our way. You will be able to download gratis out-of-print issues, which will appear as permissions from authors are gathered. Check out Bamboo Ridge Press publications in the UH System Repository at <dspace.lib.hawaii.edu>.

CONTRIBUTORS

Dana Anderson is a retired English professor who owned a bookstore on Martha's Vineyard and moved home to Hawai'i where her family has had roots since 1849. She lives in Nu'uanu Valley and occasionally teaches poetry in the Osher Lifelong Learning Institute at the University of Hawai'i.

Doreen E. Beyer is a school nurse with a passion for poetry. She lives in the island of Sacramento with her husband and two dogs. Her most recent works have appeared in the *Song of San Joaquin*, *Tule Review*, and *Pacific Review*.

Sally-Jo Keala-o-Ānuenue Bowman grew up in Kailua, O'ahu, and boarded at Kamehameha School for Girls, where she graduated in 1958. Her favorite rendition of "Namings" is a recording she made with a cellist and pianist playing "Hawai'i Aloha" and "Aloha 'Oe." She holds two degrees in journalism, taught writing at the University of Oregon, and, as a freelancer, wrote for regional and national magazines about Hawaiian culture. Many of those articles, profiles, and essays were collected in *The Heart of Being Hawaiian*. She now lives in Springfield, Oregon, with her husband, David Walp.

Carol Catanzariti writes poetry, fiction, and nonfiction. Her work has appeared in *Evergreen Magazine*, *The Lyric*, *Colorado Woman*, *Hawai'i Review*, *HAPA*, *HONOLULU Magazine*, *Honolulu Poetry on the Bus*. She co-authored a poetry chapbook, *Seeking an Answer* (Finishing Line Press). *Hawai'i Pacific Review* chose her "Age Old Understanding" as one of the best poems of the decade (2000–2010). She co-edited *Sunset Inn: Tales of the North Shore*, an anthology by Hawai'i writers; won first place in the National League of American Pen Women Lorin Tarr Gill poetry competition and in *The Honolulu Advertiser* children's short story contest. Her poems were the editors' choice for best poetry in Issue 108 of *Bamboo Ridge*. "I write because words can be architects of a better life."

Jacey Choy was born and raised in Honolulu. While she now returns to the islands as much as she can, she does spend many days and nights on the mainland longing for Hawai'i. She is deeply grateful for her family and to Hawai'i for shaping who she is, which is often reflected in her writing. Jacey has some advanced degrees, has taught a bunch of years, and has a few publications under her pāpale. She has admired Bamboo Ridge Press for a long time and feels honored to be published here.

Brian Chun-Ming was born and raised on Oʻahu, graduated from the University of Oregon, served in the Marine Corps, and spends his free time writing, working on his motorcycle, body surfing, or playing music.

Legislative Aide by day, sweary mom by night, **April Melia Coloretti** began writing poetry while at Punahou School. After finishing the Master of Professional Writing Program at the University of Southern California, April returned home. She has published poetry in *Sheila-Na-Gig* and *Hawaiʻi Pacific Review*. She has collaborated with other poets and professional photographer David Foster to produce *Image and Word* at the Doris Duke Theater. She lives in Hawaiʻi with her husband, sons, and their dog.

Earl Cooper lived ten years in Japan in an *obake* (haunted) house outside Kyoto; spent ESL teaching breaks exploring Japan and backpacking China and SE Asia; taught language and computer skills in the Immigrants & Refugees Program at Edmonds Community College in Washington for another ten years (most fulfilling job ever). Published a collection of offbeat travel stories in 2018, *No Compass Needed: Travel Tales from Asia and the Pacific*, and now writing short fiction for keiki and YA.

Sue Cowing lives and writes in Honolulu, on the shores of Maunalua Bay.

Brian Cronwall is a retired English faculty member from Kauaʻi Community College. His poems have been published in numerous journals and anthologies in the United States, Australia, Japan, France, the United Kingdom, and Ireland, including recent publications in *Bamboo Ridge*, *Chiron Review*, *Hawaiʻi Pacific Review*, *Ekphrasis*, *Pinyon*, *Colere*, *The Santa Fe Literary Review*, *Grasslimb*, *The Carolina Quarterly*, *The Briar Cliff Review*, *Wild Violet*, *Avocet Review*, *Poetry Ireland Review*, *Common Ground Review*.

Diane DeCillis' first poetry collection, *Strings Attached* (Wayne State University Press) has been honored as a Michigan Notable Book for 2015, won the 2015 Next Generation Indie Book Award, and was a Forward Indie Fab Book Award finalist. Her poems have been nominated for three Pushcart Prizes and Best American Poetry. DeCillis' stories, poetry, and essays have recently appeared in *CALYX*, *Columbia Review*, *Minnesota Review*, *Nimrod International Journal*, *Connecticut Review*, and *Antioch Review*. Her new collection *When the Heart Needs a Stunt Double* is forthcoming from Wayne State University Press in 2021.

Kathleen DeSaye is an emerging author of fantasy and adventure. Earlier this year, she published her debut novel, *Best Wishes from Hell*, the first of a series. An artist from a young age, she hand draws illustrations to create vivid visual flare to accompany her writing. She lives in the great city of New York, is an avid reader and gaming enthusiast.

Elena Savaiinaea Farden is a nonprofit executive director by day and wannabe graphic facilitator by night, who lives for indigenous fashion and poetry, but mostly lives in Makiki with her husband and daughter. Her moon musings are inspired by *kilo mahina* (observations of Hawaiian moon phases) and intentionality in connecting with our environmental intelligence. This is Elena's second poem published in *Bamboo Ridge*.

Tom Gammarino is the author of the novels *King of the Worlds: The Lost Years of Dylan Green* (2016) and *Big in Japan: A Hungry Ghost Story* (2009), and the novella *Jellyfish Dreams* (2012). Shorter works have appeared in *American Short Fiction*, *The Writer*, *Entropy*, *The New York Review of Science Fiction*, *The New York Tyrant*, and *Hawai'i Review*, and he received the 2013 Elliot Cades Award for Literature. He teaches literature and writing at Punahou School.

Caroline A. Garrett: I spent the 70s, together with Eric Chock, coordinating Hawai'i's Poets in the Schools program. At that time, there were about ten poets working statewide to encourage students to explore their own best uses of language. Now, half a century later, having retired to the Volcano rainforest two decades ago, I still occasionally volunteer at Volcano's Charter School, inviting Mrs. Hatch's 5th grade class to write. We all wrote about Kīlauea's largest eruption in a century.

Bora Hah is a bilingual writer who writes fiction and nonfiction about the two Koreas in today's world. She has received the Kim Yong Literature Prize for her short story, "Koreatown," and her interview has appeared in the *JoongAng Ilbo*. Currently an MA candidate in English with Creative Writing concentration at the University of Hawai'i at Mānoa, she divides her time between Seoul and Honolulu. This is her first publication written in English.

William Hanson: I was born and raised in east Honolulu, graduating from Kalani High School in 1971 and the University of Hawai'i at Mānoa in 1980. I have since become a professional sculptor working in Europe. My medium is wood, a natural choice given my early exposure to the powerful sacred images of the ancient Hawaiians at Honolulu's Bishop Museum. My formative years in the islands, especially my experiences during the Vietnam War and the rise of the Hawaiian sovereignty movement, have kindled my passion for issues surrounding cultural identity, nationalism, and colonialism. My website: www.hanson-art.com.

Jeffrey Hantover is a writer living in New York. He is the author of the novel, *The Jewel Trader of Pegu*. His poems were first published in *Bamboo Ridge* many years ago. He is forever grateful to Cathy Song for her advice and encouragement.

Mavis Hara lives in Honolulu. "My grandfather came to Hawai'i from Japan in the late 1880s. He was a peddler in Pālama. This is a story his sons told about him at family gatherings in the 1980s."

Gail N. Harada loves cats and dogs. She is a Pushcart Prize winner and author of *Beyond Green Tea and Grapefruit* (Bamboo Ridge Press).

Joseph Hardy is one of a handful of writers that live in Nashville, Tennessee, that does not play a musical instrument, although a friend once asked him to bring his harmonica on a camping trip so they could throw it in the fire. His wife says he cannot leave a room without finding out something about everyone in it and telling her their stories later. His first book of poetry, *The Only Light Coming In*, is being published later this year by Bambaz Press.

Jennifer Hasegawa is a Pushcart Prize-nominated poet who has sold funeral insurance door to door. She was born and raised in Hilo, Hawai'i and lives in San Francisco. The manuscript for her first book of poetry, *La Chica's Field Guide to Banzai Living*, won the Joseph Henry Jackson Literary Award. Her work has appeared in *The Adroit Journal*, *Tule Review*, and *Vallum* and is forthcoming in *Bennington Review* and *jubilat*.

Ann Inoshita was born and raised on O'ahu. She has a book of poems, *Mānoa Stream* (Kahuaomānoa Press), and co-authored *No Choice but to Follow* and *What We Must Remember*, linked poetry (*renshi*) books (Bamboo Ridge Press). Her short play, *Wea I Stay: A Play in Hawai'i*, was included in *The Statehood Project* performed by Kumu Kahua Theatre and published by Fat Ulu Productions. Her creative works have been anthologized widely in local, national, and international journals. Her poem "TV" (written in Hawai'i Creole English, Pidgin) was published in *Reel Verse: Poems About the Movies* (Penguin Random House). She teaches at Leeward Community College.

Nora Okja Keller lives with her family in Honolulu. She sometimes dreams of Marie, who visits to tell her she sees all now, with a "Buddhist Eye."

Scott Kikkawa is nostalgic for a Honolulu that existed before he was born, when detectives wore suits and drove enormous cars. However, he is not too keen that those same detectives smoked two packs of cigarettes a day and beat their suspects with impunity, so he's glad he only writes about it and doesn't have to live it. His debut novel from Bamboo Ridge Press, *Kona Winds*, is about that Honolulu where good people did bad things and a man with a badge had to sort it all out.

Maya Kikuchi is a graduating senior from Swarthmore College, where she studied Asian American literature, Japanese poetry translation, and creative writing (both doing and teaching). She is from Kailua and enjoys mountains.

Brenda Kwon is a writer, yoga teacher, animal lover, and English professor who is often mistaken for someone who was born and raised in California. While she is fluent in Hawai'i Creole English, she will not speak it on demand unless there is beer around. She is grateful to everyone at Bamboo Ridge Press and their ability to see the local girl inside.

Kapena M. Landgraf: I grew up in Pepe'ekeo and Pāpa'ikou, later moving to Wainaku, Pana'ewa, and finally settling in Kaūmana, where my parents live to this day. I moved to Honolulu in 2006 to pursue creative writing at the University of Hawai'i at Mānoa. I lectured there for several years after completing my studies. In 2018, I returned to Hilo to teach English at Hawai'i Community College. I'm grateful to be back in my community, teaching, learning, and writing among the sound of the Hilo rain. My work is a navigation of self; a personal journey in (re)discovering ancestry, place, and (hi)story.

Lanning C. Lee was born and raised in Honolulu, earned his BA and PhD from UHM, and his MA from the University of Wisconsin, Madison, all in English Literature. Part of the first class of PhD candidates in English at UHM in 1987, he authored the first dissertation of creative writing. His poetry books, *866 Love Haiku* and *155 Shakespearean Love Sonnets*, are available on Amazon. He recently submitted a memoir and the first two in a series of Honolulu-based crime novels to literary agents and completed the first draft of 155 Hawaiʻi sonnets. Lanning tries to write one draft every day. He's challenged himself to do this since 2013, posting on Facebook, and, since April 2019, on his daily author's blog at LanningLee.com. His goal is to keep generating a draft a day until he shuffles off.

Vanessa Lee-Miller, poet, playwright and freelance journalist, was born and raised in Hilo, Hawaiʻi, where she still keeps one lūʻau foot firmly planted on her ʻohana's kuleana. The other lūʻau foot often travels, performing Hawaiian in verse or drama in venues ranging from working class pubs to the British Library and Pembroke College, Oxford. Often identified as a Hawaiian language activist, she describes her decades-long struggle to keep ōlelo Hawaiʻi alive as essential to preserving our culture: "The ōlelo is the place where its soul thrives."

Lenny Levine attended Brooklyn College, graduating in 1962 with a BA in Speech and Theater. He then forgot about all of that and became a folk singer, then a folk-rock singer and songwriter, and finally a studio singer and composer of many successful jingles, including McDonald's, Lipton Tea, and Jeep. He has composed songs and sung backup for Billy Joel, Neil Diamond, Peggy Lee, Diana Ross, Barry Manilow, the Pointer Sisters, Carly Simon, and others. His short stories have been widely published in literary magazines and journals, and he received a 2011 Pushcart Prize nomination for short fiction.

Virginia Loo grew up in central Oʻahu and is a writer of poetry, embellished memoir, compelling holiday cards, and gripping statistical reports. These poems come from a series called "Foreign Bodies," exploring old cul-de-sacs of memory from a time living in India. She is also completing a memoir about making a baby via non-traditional methods.

Darrell H. Y. Lum: Being a former editor doesn't get you in the "fast lane." You still gotta write, submit, and wait. All part of the process. And sometimes you get the thrill of being selected for publication! Thank you editors and BR gang. Try write online on the new Bamboo Shoots! Chance um!

Wing Tek Lum is a Honolulu businessman and poet. Bamboo Ridge Press has published his two collections of poetry, *Expounding the Doubtful Points* (1987) and *The Nanjing Massacre: Poems* (2012).

Aʻala Lyman was born and raised on Oʻahu, Hawaiʻi. She attended Kamehameha Schools and graduated from Whitman College with a BA in Fine

Arts. She has two children and spends her days tending to them, and her nights writing poems.

Marion Lyman-Mersereau: I'm honored to be included in the pages of this *Bamboo Ridge* issue with words to honor Joe Tsujimoto, one of my writing mentors and dear colleague, who had a book and many poems and stories published by Bamboo Ridge Press. Joe was a great friend, a master teacher, and my favorite curmudgeon.

Jennifer Santos Madriaga resides in Durham, North Carolina, and is a native of Honolulu. Her fiction and poetry have appeared or is forthcoming in *North American Review*, *Bamboo Ridge*, *Hawai'i Review*, *The Bellevue Literary Review*, *Crab Creek Review*, and others. She has completed several residencies at the Vermont Studio Center, Byrdcliffe Arts Colony, and the Virginia Center for Creative Arts, including the international location at the Moulin á Nef studios in Auvillar, France. She is a recipient of the Durham Arts Council/NC Arts Council Ella Fountain Pratt Emerging Artists Grant in Literature.

Marcia Zina Mager is an international author of 12 books translated into 10 languages. Her European best-sellers, *Believing in Faeries: A Manual for Grownups* and *The Hidden Kingdom: Discovering the Divine Presence in Nature* were both inspired by the Hawaiian Islands. She's also an award-winning poet, performance artist, and playwright. She co-wrote the hit two-woman musical, *Money Talks: But What the Hell is it Saying*, which has been performed all over Hawai'i. In addition, she works as The Write Coach <www.321write.com> helping men and women birth the book they've always wanted to write.

Carrie Frances Martin: Originally from the Philadelphia area, I am a published poet, teacher, and traveler currently living on a small macadamia nut farm along the Hamakua Coast. Much of my life has been defined and shaped by land, water, and journey. The most memorable periods of my life are bound with specific regions of country and continent entwined with the human story, dynamic and deep-rooted traditions, territorial struggles, resilience, and diverse artistic expression. My poetry emanates from deep emotion, an outpouring of love and loss.

Rick McKenzie lives in Florida where he enjoys snorkeling, canoeing, camping, and hiking. He taught pre-school, then worked as a park ranger. He treasures visits with granddaughter Sophie in Montreal and is trying to learn French. His work has appeared in several literary magazines, *Yale Review*, *Mantis*, *The Round*, *Wisconsin Review*, and *Talking River*. He is especially proud of the readings he gave at the American Museum of Natural History in New York.

Hard to believe, but **Tyler Miranda** is, in fact, Portagee. Despite his apparent ability to speak and write complete sentences without the use of Crayolas, 23andMe confirms it: he's MEGA-Portagee. He would like to thank Rap Reiplinger, *Pidgin to da Max*, and the linguiça for helping him become the prolific writer he hopes to be some day.

Tamara Leiokanoe Moan is an artist and writer living in Kailua on Oʻahu. She teaches art at the Honolulu Museum of Art School and also works as an editor and massage therapist. She assists annually with the Mokulēʻia Writers Retreat. Her poem "Kaʻena" is the result of a retreat field trip in 2018.

Dawn Morais: I began writing "Shenandoah" in July 2000. I watched from the shallows, as my son, Zubin, out in deeper water, fished with his sister, Sheela Jane, under the guidance of my husband, John Webster. Seeing this poem published is a gift. Other poems and prose have found their way into *The Red Wheelbarrow* (St. Andrew's University), *Fugue* (University of Idaho), *The Merton Seasonal* (Bellarmine University, KY), the *Baltimore Sun*, *Civil Beat*, and the *Honolulu Star-Advertiser*. Daughter of Victor and Gladys Morais. Grandmother of Ara Victor Menon. Community advocate. Adjunct instructor, University of Hawaiʻi. Blogs at **www.dawnmorais.com**

Susan Miho Nunes is the author of *A Small Obligation and Other Stories of Hilo* and several children's books. Her short stories have appeared in *The Best of Bamboo Ridge* and Graywolf's *Stories of the American Mosaic*. "The Walking Lady" is from an unpublished collection of short stories, *Paradise Cafe . . . and other old men*. Born in Hilo, raised in Honolulu, she now lives in Berkeley, California.

Claire Oasa was born and raised in Honolulu. She attended the University Laboratory School, obtained degrees in engineering, and recently retired from working in the oil and gas industry. She published her first poem in 1984 and is grateful to *Bamboo Ridge* for including her work again after a "brief" 36-year hiatus.

Derek N. Otsuji teaches writing at Honolulu Community College. In 2019, he received a Tennessee Williams Scholarship from the Sewanee Writers' Conference, where he studied with the poets Robert Hass and Marilyn Nelson. You can find his poems in *The Threepenny Review*, *Pleiades*, *Rattle*, *Tahoma Literary Review*, and *Poetry Daily*.

Christy Passion is a critical care nurse and award-winning poet, author of *Still Out of Place*, and co-author of *No Choice but to Follow* and *What We Must Remember*. Her work will appear in *When the Light of the World Was Subdued, Our Songs Came Through: A Norton Anthology of Native Nations Poetry*, edited by Joy Harjo, the 23rd Poet Laureate of the United States.

Kathy J. Phillips: While a professor of English at the University of Hawai'i, I published five books with established presses (my "respectables"); after I retired, I published six books with CreateSpace (my "rogues"). *The Moon in the Water: Reflections on an Aging Parent* (Vanderbilt UP 2008), a creative nonfiction, was selected by *Library Journal* for inclusion in its "Best Books of 2008." The poem printed here for Hawai'i writer Leialoha Perkins is from a collection-in-progress, *Postcards from Hawai'i to Hokusai*. The poem here refers to Hokusai's round lantern called "Dragon and Tiger."

Michael Puleloa, PhD, was born on Majuro in the Marshall Islands and raised on Moloka'i and O'ahu in Hawai'i. He has taught composition at Kapi'olani Community College and the University of Hawai'i at Mānoa. He is currently an English teacher at Kamehameha Schools, Kapālama, where he is also the advisor for Ho'okumu, the school's award-winning student literary journal. His most recent publications appear in *Huihui: Rhetorics and Aesthetics of the Pacific*, *Hawai'i Review 79*, *Home(is)lands: New Art and Writing from Guåhan and Hawai'i*, and *Black Marks on the White Page*.

Anthony "Tony" Russo: Undergraduate education at U.S. Naval Academy, Marine Corps officer during Vietnam War. Studied Nuclear Engineering (MS) at University of Wisconsin, was employed at Gulf Atomic Labs in San Diego. PhD in Oceanography from Florida Institute of Technology. Retired professor of ocean science in University of Hawai'i System (36 years). Adjunct professor of Mathematics at Chaminade University after retirement. Hobbies: Writing, ink art, Shoto Kan karate black belt.

Mia Sara was born and raised in New York City. At fifteen she began a career as an actress, her credits include: *Legend, Ferris Bueller's Day Off, Time Cop, Queenie, A Stranger Among Us, Jack and the Beanstalk: The Real Story*, and many others. Her writing has appeared or is forthcoming in *Whistling Shade, Pudding Magazine, Bluestem, Mudlark, Chapparal, The Cossack Review, Edison Literary Review, Superstition Review, poemmemoirstory, The Southampton Review, The Write Room, Smartish Pace, PANK*, and *Cultural Weekly*. Her chapbook, *Still Life With Gorilla*, was published by Dusie Press in 2014. She lives in Los Angeles with her husband and children. She misses New York every single day. For more: miasara.nyc

Cavan Reed Scanlan was born and raised on the island of Oʻahu. His mother is from Westwood, Massachusetts, and his father is from Nuʻuʻuli, Tutuila, Samoa, and his work is often inspired by such intersections of life. He lives in Pālolo Valley with his wife and two sons, and teaches high school English at Kamehameha-Kapālama. He prefers paperbacks to hardcovers, offshore winds to onshore winds, and live instruments to backing tracks. He enjoys the words "spatula" and "bubble" and looks forward to the day when people no longer selfishly crowd the baggage claim carousel.

An East Coast expatriate retired from college/university teaching, **Stuart Jay Silverman** divides his domestic life between Hot Springs, Arkansas, and Chicago, Illinois. Over 600 of his poems appear in 100+ journals/anthologies in the United States and abroad. His *The Complete Lost Poems: A Selection* was published by Hawk Publishing Group. His second book of poetry, *Report from the Sea of Moisture*, was published in May 2020 by Atmosphere Press. He thinks of poems as creating possible experience, whether actual or imagined, whether realistic or fantastic, not primarily as vehicles of self-expression.

John E. Simonds, retired Honolulu daily newspaper editor, has lived with family in Hawaiʻi since 1975; previously wrote for newspapers from Washington, D.C., and elsewhere. A Bowdoin graduate, former East Coast and Midwest resident; writing poetry since the 1970s and author of two collections, *Waves from a Time-Zoned Brain* (AuthorHouse 2009) and *Footnotes to the Sun* (iUniverse 2015).

Cathy Song is the author of five books of poetry. *All the Love in the World*, a collection of short stories, was recently released by Bamboo Ridge Press.

Eric Stinton is a writer from Kailua, O'ahu, where he lives with his wife and wiener dog. He is a columnist for Sherdog, and his fiction, nonfiction, and journalism have appeared in *Bamboo Ridge*, *The Classical*, *GEN*, *Harvard Review Online*, *Honolulu Civil Beat*, *Ka Wai Ola*, *KHON2 News*, *Longreads*, *Talking Writing*, *The Under Review*, and *Vice Sports*, among others.

Shelley Stocksdale has taught writing and English courses at Chinese colleges and universities for many years in The People's Republic of China, as well as library media in Colombia and the U.S. Her poetry has appeared in *The Marjorie Kinnan Rawlings Journal of Florida Literature*, *The Penwood Review*, *Time of Singing*, and *Orange Peel*.

Coralyn Sunico is an English teacher at Farrington High School, her alma mater. Her writing is inspired by her memories of growing up with a single Filipino mother in Kalihi and the struggles that came with it. In her classroom, her students explore their own struggles to discover their voices, identities, and beliefs to create and claim their own stories of successes and challenges.

Samantha Tetangco is a Filipino-American writer and teacher. Her short stories, creative nonfiction, and poetry have appeared or are forthcoming in dozens of literary magazines including *The Sun*, *Zone 3*, *Gargoyle*, *Phoebe*, *Gertrude*, and others. She has an MFA from the University of New Mexico and is the Associate Director of Writing at the University of California Merced.

Delaina Thomas: Thanks to Maui Ryukyu Culture Group, Ukwanshin Kabudan, and Reverend Yamaguchi of Pa'ia Rinzai Zen Mission, for unforgettable Obon nights.

Ken Tokuno: After being recognized as a poet, I am very glad to have this story accepted by *Bamboo Ridge*, since it is my first piece of fiction to be published. It is based on an actual event in which my wife and I were at the concert mentioned in the story and I saw an elderly woman seated, alone, close to us. I want to give special thanks to Craig Howes for his voluminous and invaluable feedback on an earlier draft of this story.

Julie Ushio lives in Honolulu. This is her second appearance in *Bamboo Ridge*. The first chapter of her novel in progress, *Persimmons*, won first prize for novel at the 2019 Mendocino Coast Writers Conference and will appear in their 2020 *Noyo River Review*.

Amy Uyematsu is a sansei poet and teacher from Los Angeles. She taught public high school math for 32 years. Highlights of her retirement include her grandsons Tyler and Mason as well as teaching a writing workshop at Little Tokyo's Far East Lounge.

J. Fumiko Wong is a proud University of Hawai'i graduate.

Lois-Ann Yamanaka continues to write several YA novels. Second wind? Maybe. Power to the people who create in such uncertain times.

GOYA BE HAPPY!
bitter days ahead

CANEHAULROAD, HAWAI'I
© 2020 GKAGIMOTO